Banner's Bonus

CAROLE ANN LEE

LOVE SPELL NEW YORK CITY

*This book is dedicated to
Rod, my own Noble Rogue, the
man who taught Nick Banner everything he knows.
My husband.   My hero.   My life.*

LOVE SPELL®

May 1995

Published by

Dorchester Publishing Co., Inc.
276 Fifth Avenue
New York, NY 10001

Printed in the United States of America.

With special thanks to:

Science fiction novelist extraordinaire William C. Dietz, whose gift of riveting detail and intriguing hero Sam McCade sparked my desire to write Nick Banner's story. Thanks, Bill, for the inspiration, the advice, and encouragement over the years.

Linda Clarke, who believed from the start that I could do it; Sandra Millet, who never gave up on me even when I thought I'd never get it straight (oh, and Sandy, thanks for you-know-what); Pink Widdows, who understood Nick long before I did; Maggie Grover for her unceasing patience and to-die-for quotes, and Vicki Adolf whose contagious enthusiasm and sound advice kept me going to the end.

Last, but far from least, I wish to thank Alicia Condon for giving this kid a chance, and to Sharon Morey, the sweet voice on the other end of the phone and a joy to work with.

Banner's Bonus

Chapter One

Earth Date: 2105

Port Ireland, Terra Four
70 A.C. (After Colonization)

"I don't give a damn what game or whose bed you have to drag him out of, *just get Banner!* You hear me?"

Standing behind his massive desk, bracing his weight on the knuckles of firmly planted fists, Jonathan Loring's voice boomed out into the main hallway of LorTech Equipment's Central Control.

In his late forties, Loring was handsome. His dark hair, dusted with gray at the temples, lent him added distinction. Though generally good-natured and quick to find humor, now a frown creased his brow.

"According to his itinerary," Loring continued with less volume, "he should have arrived in port sometime this afternoon."

Dan Garrett's shoulders slumped at the thought. "He's

9

here all right, Mr. Loring, but it's been over two hours since I last saw him. He'd just finished unloading a large shipment and said something about heading up to the Starcruiser. Sir, I'll never find him in that place—providing he's still there.''

"Listen, Garrett . . ." Loring's tone had turned unpleasant again.

"I'll find him," Garrett quickly interjected.

The Starcruiser was noisy and crowded. The atmosphere was a mixture of simulated alien music, loud voices, laughter, and a heavy blanket of smoke. A wide variety of people mingled together. Some were off long-haul freighters, eagerly celebrating the end of an eight-month run. Then there were the miners—"diggers," as they were called—just in from the asteroids and anxious to set their fantasies into motion, most of which had been months in the making. Still others, like Nick Banner, were there merely to celebrate the payout of a six-week cargo run.

Like most cargo pilots, Banner was sole operator of his ship, simply because most cargo ships were not large enough to necessitate a crew. Nevertheless, many pilots would make it a practice to take a woman aboard on what was loosely dubbed an "Agreement." In essence, she needed a lift to his destination, and in exchange offered her companionship with all its connotations. Although not every woman was that type, *that type* could always be found hanging around the ports of entry. Terra Four's port taverns, as well as the love-starved crewmen who frequented them, were no different now than they were on Earth a little over two centuries ago when the schooners and clippers would sail in from the seas.

But Banner wasn't interested in that kind of arrangement. Six weeks in deep space can be very long and lonely, but it can also be a big mistake when stuck with someone you don't happen to get along with. Banner had never known a time when he wasn't surrounded by women vying for his consideration. He'd never once paid for a woman's attentions, and taking one along with him on his runs didn't happen to be his idea of a good time.

Nick Banner had been barely twenty-one when he'd fallen hopelessly in love with Linnae, the most beautiful girl he'd ever known. He'd turned his back on all the others, even walked away from the gaming tables and asked her to marry him. He was so head over heels in love with her that when the ugly rumors began he closed his mind to them.

"She's a whore, Nick! Dammit man, open your eyes; she's using you. Why can't you see that?"

More than once Nick's fist had split his older brother's lip for those very words. Even his friend, Zeke, had tried to dissuade him, to no avail. Stubborn and hardheaded as they come, Nick Banner had defended Linnae's honor right down to the bitter end, when he'd shown up unannounced one evening. As the door opened, Nick simply stood watching in mute shock while a man scrambled about for his clothing. Drunk and giggling, Linnae tried to coax Banner to join in the fun, but he turned and ran. And in many ways he was still running.

Banner left home shortly after that incident. Setting out for a small, untamed world called Echo, he spent the better part of two years burying his heartache, anger, and frustration in hard labor and life-threatening assignments.

If nothing else, those years had taught him the meaning of being tough and living hard. He'd also made good credits for his endeavors, and when he'd returned to civilization it was with a determination to live again.

The first thing he had done was place a hefty down payment on a small cargo ship, already christened the *Victorious*. Not long after that he had formed a partnership with a drinking companion. It was a business venture that entailed using his ship to make short runs for a local courier.

The partnership eventually had failed due to conflicts of interest between Nick and his partner, Quint Kendyl. Look-

11

ing for bigger and better brought Banner to Terra Four
where, operating under the name of Banner Enterprises, he
picked up a variety of freight and mail runs within the
sector.

By now he was over Linnae, though the scar of her be-
trayal ran deep. Vowing no woman would ever own his
heart again, women became nothing more than playthings
to him, entertaining diversions to be used and then discarded.

Nick Banner had been branded a hard case back then.
Come payday he could usually be found bucking roulette
at one of the local port dives, where he drank everyone
under the table, fought half the security with his bare
fists, and generally wound up passed out in some woman's bed.

But that was *then*. Recognizing his ingrained honesty and
reputation as a hard worker, a man named Sam Sheldon
took Banner under his wing and in time introduced him to
Jonathan Loring.

Dan Garrett entered the doors of the dimly lit Starcruiser.
To his left, a fight had broken out in the corner, and two
men seated at a nearby table were taking bets on the winner.
To Garrett's right a group of inebriated coworkers were
starting the next game of Bounty.

"Hey, Garrett, come on over. You wanna get in on this?
We've got room for one more." James Cleary had a stupid
grin plastered on his face and eyes at half mast. Four others
in the same condition were poured into their chairs around
the game table, full mugs of ale within reach. One of them
absently shuffled a deck of cards while the others had already positioned their pawns on the holograph game board.

"Not tonight, Cleary. I'm looking for Banner. You seen
'im around?"

"Yeah, not more than thirty minutes ago," Cleary answered.

Just then one of the other men spoke up. "Ee's 'ere . . .

somewhere ... lucky devil had two blondes a'hangin' on 'im.'' The man grinned, then added, ''Both of 'em clinging to 'im like *Shateries.''* With that, the men at the table burst into a round of raucous laughter. It seemed that the *Shateri* was always the brunt of someone's joke. The small fur-bearing animal, found along the southern coastline of Terra Four's main continent, was not only known for its luxurious fur but was also notorious for its enthusiasm for procreation.

Garrett couldn't help but grin; their laughter was contagious. ''Thanks, fellas. If you happen to see him again, tell him I'm looking for him.''

Dan Garrett continued making his way through the crowd, his eyes intently sifting a murky sea of smoke and faces. Finally he climbed a set of wide stairs that led to a mezzanine from which he could survey the entire main floor. The mezzanine was an extension of the bar, a balcony furnished with tables and chairs that completely ringed the room.

Garrett found an empty table near the balustrade, claimed it, and methodically began scanning the entire main level from his perch. Behind him several drunk and boisterous crewmen were engaged in singing a bawdy song. All around, people were drinking and laughing, either burying their fears and troubles or celebrating their luck.

Banner, who rarely had either fears or troubles to bury, was drinking to his luck when Garrett's eyes finally locked onto his. Seated at a game table on the opposite side of the room, true to form, Nick Banner was casually sprawled in his chair, all six foot four of him. And from the smug grin tugging at the corners of his mouth and the stack of game chips at his elbow, there was little doubt who was ahead.

There was an unconscious grace about Nick Banner. He always seemed to turn women's heads. In all honesty, Dan Garrett was mildly envious of Banner's candid magnetism and innate sexuality. Though it was a trait he yearned to possess himself, he had resigned himself long ago to the fact that he simply didn't have it and never would, for that matter.

Even the faded, scarred leathers Banner wore would have looked offensive on anyone else. But with his dark hair, mysterious blue eyes, swarthy features, and hard, lean body, the well-worn attire lent a primitively appealing air of danger.

Reaching for his mug of ale, Nick Banner laid the winning cards on the table. "Gentlemen, I believe this completes the game and it looks like I win." He grinned and added, "again."

Grumbling, the four men at the table watched as he raked in his winnings.

Banner liked winning. He liked winning at anything. However, cleaning up on a table of drunken comrades wasn't much of a challenge, not to mention the fact that it grated against his sense of fair play.

A radiant brunette now stood at his back, both hands draped possessively over his shoulders, as though she might lose him to another should she dare to let go. Suddenly leaning down, she whispered something in his ear that brought forth a crooked grin as he downed his last swallow of brew.

"Fellas, what can I say? I hate to win and run, but worse yet, I hate keepin' a lady waitin'. Here," he said, tossing a large handful of coins back onto the table, "the drinks are on me." With that, the men at the table burst into a round of boisterous cheers, and Nick Banner rose to escort his luscious companion to the nearest exit.

He no sooner began guiding her with a well-placed hand at the small of her back when someone called, "Hey, Nick, wait up!"

Banner turned to see Dan Garrett elbowing his way through the crowd to catch up with him.

"Garrett, what's up?"

"Loring wants to see you."

"Fine. Tell him I'll drop by in the morning," Nick said, again pivoting toward the exit.

"Banner, he means to see you. Now."

Groaning inwardly, Banner stopped short, turning to face Garrett with exasperation. "And it *can't* wait till tomorrow. Right?"

It was clear, just from the look on Garrett's face, that he was painfully aware of his bad timing. "Sorry, Nick, but I don't think so. I wish I could tell you what it's all about, but I'd wager it's important."

With a heavy sigh of regret, Banner turned to the girl. Tightening his hold on her, he drew her near. "Gina, honey . . ." he began, capturing her chin in a possessive yet gentle hold. Banner nuzzled his face into her dark locks and whispered something that brought an instant flush to her cheeks. Whatever he'd said was then thoroughly punctuated with a lusty kiss.

Turning back to Garrett, he growled, "Let's get outta here 'fore I change my mind."

A land craft waited outside the Starcruiser for the 30-minute ride from Port Ireland to the headquarters of LorTech Equipment. The sleek, low-slung vehicle was a small two-seater model. Her shiny black exterior said she was new; the logo on her doors said she belonged to LorTech.

"Well, I see Jonathan finally broke down and replaced a few of those tired vehicles. How long have you had this?" Banner asked, running an appreciative eye over the smart new rig.

"About three months now," Garrett answered, fishing a remote from his pocket and entering a code. In response, both doors disengaged, slid silently backward, and disappeared into the rear quarter panel on each side.

Emitting a low whistle, Banner climbed in and continued his appraisal from the inside. The complex dash was a mini cockpit, loaded with options ranging from a host of digital readouts to a small rear display monitor.

"Nice," he drawled approvingly as the control console snapped to life the instant Garrett's weight settled into the driver's seat.

Owned and operated by Jonathan Loring, LorTech Equipment was a fast-growing research equipment company, booming right now with their recent contract to supply research equipment and supplies to Echo, a small and relatively unexplored rim world.

Traffic was heavy at first, but it thinned progressively the farther they traveled from the city. Soon the landcraft picked up speed and the landscape began whisking by in a blur. Banner patted his pockets, found a cigar, and lit it. Both men remained silent, each deep in his own thoughts.

The environment was particularly dreary, consisting mainly of processing plants and warehouses. Then the scenery gradually changed. The buildings became taller and seemed to stretch farther apart. Some had tanks attached to them. Others had pipes that ran from one building to the next. Eerie puffs of vapor rose from their stacks, illuminated by the surrounding floodlights.

Terra Four was a Class E planet located within the Sector Five System. Its distance from Earth measured in time was roughly six weeks. Before Stellardrive, it had taken several years to reach the Sector Five System.

First discovered around the turn of the century by an unmanned probe during Earth's so-called "Race for Space" era, Terra Four was the fourth of five planets that were named for their likeness to Earth. Colonization didn't occur, however, until almost 35 years later.

The first settlement formed was a tiny mining colony, Port France, nestled high in the Rampart Mountain Range, Terra Four's northernmost mountains. Eventually more colonists came; more settlements sprouted up, and with them various forms of livelihood developed. Ultimately, through economic evolution many small mining towns became thriving cities. Port Ireland became the largest and most advanced city on Terra Four.

Pulling up to LorTech's outside gates, Garrett flashed the required credentials to the security guard and they were waved through.

As Banner palmed the security lock at the main entrance to the massive complex, a hidden scanner began cross-checking his palmprint and retinal and voice patterns with his stated identity. "Come on . . . *come on."* he muttered, releasing an impatient sigh as they waited. As if prompted by his impatience, a tiny green light snapped to life on a panel mounted on the wall before him and the lock on the door clicked open. Banner wasted no time barging through, and Garrett followed at his heels, trying to keep up with Nick's ground-devouring stride.

Taking the steps three at a time, Banner hastily made his way up a flight of stairs and down a long carpeted hallway until they finally came to a door with JONATHAN T. LORING, PRESIDENT, inscribed on it. Without so much as an announcement of his arrival, Nick hit the pressure plate and led the way in as the door slid open.

"Ah, Nick! Thank God, he found you."

"Yeah, and as usual your timing's impeccable, Loring." His tone left no doubt of his annoyance.

"Have a seat," Loring said, indicating one of the two imported leather chairs in front of his desk. Then he turned to Garrett, thanking and perfunctorily dismissing him.

Banner sank into the comfortable chair. "So, what's goin' on?" he asked, planting a hand on the booted ankle resting across the opposite thigh.

Suddenly becoming strangely quiet, Jonathan lifted an envelope off his desk and wordlessly submitted it.

Reaching out to take it, Banner held eye contact with his friend, assessing the undisputable mixture of terror and anger in the man's eyes. Then, without a word, he withdrew the note from the envelope and began reading.

Mr. Loring,
I overheard part of a conversation that could cost my

*life as well as that of my family. For that reason, I
choose not to reveal myself at this time, but I want
you to know that Tressa's life may be in danger. I
wish I had heard more, but I strongly suspect* The
Leader.

Without comment, Banner casually withdrew a slender
brown cigar, lit it, and blew a lazy stream of smoke toward
the ceiling, where it was instantly ushered into the nearest
vent. "I seem to be missing a few lines here, Jon," he said
calmly. "Maybe you'd better take this from the top. And
who the devil's the Leader?"

Staring at Banner with blank eyes, Loring began.
"That's just it; I'm not sure. There're several possibilities.
Rumor has it there are at least two megacorps that want
total possession of Echo."

Holding eye contact with Loring, Banner took a slow
drag from his cigar, sending a stream of smoke toward the
floor. "Just exactly who are these *supposed* corporations?"

Loring hesitated. "Hell, it's a rumor, Nick. Your guess
is as good as mine.

"Then guess, dammit!"

A long moment of silence passed before Loring reluctantly offered a name. "Frontier Enterprises could be one."

"And?"

"These are just guesses, Nick. There's no way of—"

"*And?*" Banner persisted.

"Possibly . . . Chase Explorations."

Banner examined his cigar intently, deep in thought as
he watched the smoke curl off the tip. "Chase Explorations," he mused. "Aren't they based off Paragon? What
the devil are they doing clear out here, messin' around with
a small rim world like Echo?"

"Howard Chase has become greedy over the years,"
Loring explained, dragging his hand through his thick hair.
"Chase Explorations has grown, but at the expense of oth-
ers."

"You figure they're the Leader?"

Loring shrugged. "It's possible. They've managed to stomp down anyone in their way. It's known they want control of Echo, and LorTech is one of the few left in their path who casts a bigger shadow."

"Making you their target now. Right?" Not waiting for an answer, Banner lifted the note for emphasis. "Does *she* know about this?"

"No. And that's the way it stays ... at least until I can get her out of here. Knowing Tressa, she'd refuse to leave."

Reading the note over again, Banner stuck the cigar between his teeth, wincing against the smoke inadvertently trailing up into his eyes. "So ... I take it you have a plan."

Jonathan dragged in a deep breath, letting it out slowly. "Nick, I want you to take Tressa off-planet for me," he said directly. "Surely you know of some place where she would be safe until we find out what the hell this is all about."

Lifting one eyebrow, Banner casually drawled, "It's a bit outta my line, wouldn't you say, Jon? I'm not a bodyguard. Sounds to me like you need a hired gun, not some randy cargo pilot traipsing all over the galaxy trying to find a safe place to stash—"

"And since when didn't you fit that bill, Banner?" Loring interrupted, slamming his fist down on the desk. "Dammit, Nick, you're a hell of a lot more than just a cargo pilot, and we both know it.

"I'm not asking you to assassinate anyone," Loring said. "All I'm asking is that you get Tressie out of here until we can get to the bottom of this." Loring's voiced eased off, betraying the depth of his feelings. "If I thought there was anyone else ..." He left the sentence hanging.

Banner calmly leaned forward, depositing a lump of ash into the ashtray on Loring's desk. "You know how I feel about taking a female with me into space," he said softly. "It's askin' for nothing but trouble, Jon. Besides,

I still have two deliveries to make. I can't just take off like that.''

"I can understand your position. Go ahead and make those deliveries. I don't see where that will be a problem. I just want her out of here.''

Nick blew a long, slow stream of smoke toward his lap. Doubting the wisdom of the plan entirely, he proceeded to caution Loring again. "Yeah, well, that takes care of the deliveries part, doesn't it, but what about the trouble?''

Before he could explain, Jonathan interrupted—once again missing Banner's point. "Tressa's intelligent, Nick, and catches on quickly. You could always give her something to do if she gets underfoot.''

In total disbelief, Banner tensed, shifting uncomfortably in his chair. Glancing away, he smiled in polite restraint. "Underfoot is not exactly what I meant,'' he said, returning his attention to Loring. "We're talking about a chunk of time here, Jon. Possibly as long as three weeks during which your enticing daughter would be alone in my company on board the cramped quarters of the *Victorious*. You sayin' you don't see a problem with that?'' There was no hint of humor hidden in the bluntness of Banner's words.

"Hell, you know my reputation, Loring,'' he continued. "Most fathers would call me out if I so much as got near their daughters, let alone take them into space with me. I'm flattered at your confidence, but let's get serious.''

"I've never been more serious in my . . .''

"You know what you're askin'?'' Banner interrupted.

A frown creased Loring's brow and his gaze darkened as he slowly rose and moved from behind his desk. There was no misreading the grim look on his face as he came around and settled hip-shot against the desk's front corner, directly before Nick.

"Make no mistake,'' he began slowly, his tone laden with warning. "I know full well what I'm asking of you. Just as you do.''

Slowly, Loring's grave expression eased. "Besides, you seem to forget, I've always seen more in you than you see in yourself. If I didn't, believe me, I'd never entrust Tressie into your care for even so much as a single minute." A faint grin stole across Loring's face.

For a silent moment Banner stared at the smoke trailing up from his cigar. "Your belief in my abilities, Jon, humbles me." His tone was close to a sneer.

Jonathan laughed. "Besides the fact that it's *my daughter* you'd be taking on board, Tressa's all but engaged."

Banner's eyes lifted to meet Loring's. "Is that right? Anyone I know?"

"Not likely. He's new around here. Name's Sinclair. Anyway"—returning to the matter at hand, Loring chose his words carefully—"if you decide to do this, I'm not saying it would be easy, and granted it would put a considerable strain on your powers of self-control, but . . ."

Banner broke in with a snort. "That's *one* way of putting it," he drawled sourly.

Disregarding the sarcasm, Loring began again. "I'll be up-front with you, Nick; Tressa's been known to be headstrong at times. So right from the start you'd need to let her know who's boss in no uncertain terms. I guarantee that once you have that firmly established, she would settle right in for you."

"And those rumors you've probably heard aren't true," Loring added. "Tressa hasn't inherited her mother's ability."

Banner shot Loring a puzzled look but said nothing. Regarding him coolly, he sent out another stream of smoke, this one spiraling to the floor. It had been six years since he'd first walked through the doors of LorTech Equipment. Tressa had been just fourteen at the time. Looking back, he remembered her as a giggly teenager. With her away at school most of the time, their initial introduction had never progressed much past a nodding acquaintance. It had only been in the past six months that he remembered seeing more of her around the complex. She'd definitely grown up. And her personality had changed from giggly to politely aloof.

He'd heard about her desire to make a career at LorTech, and whether her aloof indifference was due to shyness, conceit, or professionalism was hard to tell. At any rate, he'd never lost much sleep over it; she was Loring's daughter, and as far as he saw it, that made her off limits.

Now all of a sudden here he was, doomed to baby-sit this spoiled, liberated woman/child for the next two to three weeks. Worse yet, he'd be expected to still be on speaking terms with her by the time they arrived at their destination—wherever the hell that was.

"Well?" Jonathan asked with an edge of desperation.

Doubt, spiced with irritation, coursed through Banner. "Let me see if I understand this correctly," he began. "You're askin' me to take a pampered, selfish, headstrong female into space, within the limited confines of the *Victorious*, for as long as it takes to find a safe place to stash her. Am I correct?" he asked, risking a strain on Loring's goodwill at his brazen description of Tressa. But at that point Banner was beginning to feel desperate. He wanted out, almost at any cost.

"Pampered? Headstrong? Yes, but not selfish, Nick. Not selfish. Why, if Tressie thought someone needed them, she wouldn't hesitate to give the very clothes off her back."

That brought Nick's head up with a jerk. With one eyebrow raised, his eyes flew from studying the note in his hand to Loring's face.

Obviously not catching the double implication, nor Banner shaking his head in faint reproof, Jonathan continued. "And besides, it might not hurt for you to stay off-planet for a while. If that electroblade had gone much deeper . . ." Jonathan left the sentence hanging.

There was a long moment of thought-filled silence before Banner's deep voice calmly broke the tension. "Selfish or not," he said with low-voiced composure, "it's *keeping* the damn clothes on her back that is precisely what concerns me. And as for that attempt on my life, I'll deal with it in my own way. I'm not hiding, Jon, if that's what you're suggesting.''

Banner's entire left side still ached fiercely, a pain that up until then he'd been tuning out successfully. For a brief moment he reflected on the night he'd been attacked. What little he remembered clearly stood out in his mind. He'd just finished loading a shipment into the hold. Turning to key in the security, he'd suddenly detected movement in the shadows and a glint off something metallic. Banner vaguely remembered whirling to ward off the attack, but too late to evade the thrust. The next thing he knew, a gut-wrenching pain began in his lower back and ripped up his side as he went down.

In that clouded moment he glimpsed and vaguely recognized the face of one man: Quint Kendyl, his ex-partner.

For a while the pain kept him semiconscious as he lay facedown on the scarred surface of the landing zone. Although he'd been able to distinguish little more than the grating edge of voices and the words they said, there was no doubt about the distinctive boots of the man who stood directly before him. ''Kendyl'' was the last thought that registered as Banner slipped into unconsciousness.

''Are you listening to what I'm saying?''

Suddenly brought back to the present, Banner leaned forward, depositing another lump of ash into the ashtray. ''I hear ya,'' he mumbled, shoving the cigar between his teeth.

He leaned back and unconsciously studied Loring, wishing like hell he could come up with some alternative. Although questioning his own sanity, he had to admit that Loring's plan made sense.

Finally, directing a stream of smoke to the ceiling, his tone hesitant, he asked, ''So when do we leave?''

''You'll do it, then?''

''Under the circumstances I'd say I don't have a helluva

lot of choice. I'll take her to Acacia. It's a three-week voyage from here. Hopefully that will buy you a little time. Delta will enjoy the company, and after I see Tressa safe I'll do what I can to help.''

Silence passed as Banner contemplated the plan. ''I'm going to be up-front with you, Jon,'' he said, calmly raising his eyes to meet Loring's. ''No matter how careful we are, there's no guarantee that Acacia's going to be a safe haven. It's not common knowledge I'm from Acacia, but if someone gets to nosing around, it's on the security records. You have no way of knowing how big this operation is, or who's watching whom.''

''I'm aware of that, Nick.''

Jonathan suddenly relaxed. ''Look, I know this won't be easy. But you won't regret it! I assure you there will be a bonus in it for you. You have my word on that. I'll double your high-risk credits on this one.''

Banner just grinned and shook his head in disbelief. ''I'm not in this for the bonus, Jonathan. Anyway, even if I were, you couldn't afford a bonus big enough to entice me into this for any length of time.

''And as far as regret is concerned,'' he continued grimly, ''I felt that the minute I heard Garrett's voice.''

At the memory of Garrett's intrusion Banner took a long drag from his cigar, directing another lazy stream of smoke toward the ceiling. Once again he fought down the mental image of Gina, the stunning brunette he'd reluctantly left behind at the Starcruiser.

Ignoring Banner's ongoing flow of cynicism, Jonathan continued, ''Now, I figure if you come back to the place with me, we could work out the details of a plan on the way. Then we'd just bring Tressie back with us. Besides, I *know* Mary's going to want to meet you. Hell, she'll probably want to speak privately with you.''

Banner groaned out loud. ''Oh, that ought to be *real* interesting. I just got into port, Jon. I'm not only beat, I'm half-crocked. Mary ought to be impressed, don't you agree?''

Still questioning his own sanity, Banner rubbed the back of his neck and tried to sort through his feelings. Having hit port three hours ago from a five-week run, he'd spent the first ninety minutes overseeing as well as assisting in the unloading of cargo off his ship. He was tired, and the way he figured it he should be getting drunk, getting laid, and counting his winnings—in roughly that order.

Though past experience had taught Loring that Nick Banner was a man of his word, the moment of silence prompted him to actually look at Banner for the first time since he'd entered his office. Unshaven; worn leathers; swept-back hair curling down over his collar. He grimly admitted that Banner looked every bit the rogue of his colorful, not to mention questionable, reputation. Jonathan was certain Mary would never let Tressa leave with him. In fact, he was tempted to question the wisdom of the plan himself.

Banner's eyebrow arched knowingly. "Second thoughts, Jon?"

"I haven't got time for second thoughts!" Loring growled. The laughter in Nick's eyes and his reckless grin were maddening. "I'll go on back and square things away at home. You, on the other hand, have exactly two hours to make yourself presentable. We'll meet you back at the *Victorious* at that time.

"Oh, and, Nick . . . any other, uh, of your needs, had best be taken care of here in port, if I make myself clear."

Banner's maddening grin simply got broader.

"In only two hours, Jon?" He released a low breathy whistle, shaking his head in mock astonishment. "I'm going to leave one unhappy lady."

Swinging his feet down, Banner stood, took a final drag from his cigar, crushed it in the ashtray, and headed for the door. "But on the other hand," he added smugly, "I've been known to be ready for lift-off in less than ten minutes.''

Nick's eyes twinkled with pure deviltry as he left Loring staring after him with what could only be described as a blank look on his face.

Chapter Two

Banner found Garrett waiting for him as he stepped out of the complex. Sprawling into the front seat of the landcraft, he instructed Garrett to drop him off at the space port.

He couldn't believe he'd actually agreed to such lunacy. Totally insane was more like it, he thought as they sped toward Port Ireland. A muscle twitched in his left cheek at the prospect of almost three weeks confined in the cramped quarters of the *Victorious* with Loring's daughter.

The last time he'd had a woman on board it had been at *his* invitation, and even then it had turned into a total disaster. He never did find out exactly what happened, but he figured it must have been something he'd said.

The lights of the port facility gradually came into view, and Banner was pulled from his thoughts as the landcraft hissed to a halt before the front entrance of the space terminal.

Climbing out, he reached for a cigar, bent his head, and lit up. Releasing a stream of smoke into the cool night air, Banner gazed out over the landing field. At last his eyes came to rest on his pride and joy, his sleek cargo ship, *Victorious*, as she sat patiently awaiting the completion of routine space port servicing.

A maze of high-octane fuel, fresh water, and liquid waste pipes snaked their way across the durasteel decking and rose up into the belly of the ship. Each pipe, as it serviced the *Victorious*, had its own tiny pulsing light system traveling its length. From a distance they appeared like blazing arrows chasing one another in a merry race across the landing zone.

Once again he asked himself just what the devil he was doing. Loring's daughter of all people. It was crazy and gut instinct told him that sure as gravity, he'd regret it before they even cleared the atmosphere. Hell, one hour ago he was sitting up at the Starcruiser enjoying himself and thinking he had his evening all planned out.

Withdrawing a small comp remote, he tapped into the *Victorious's* primary onboard computer, releasing the security on the main entry port. Making his way across the landing zone, the familiar stench of exhaust, the fumes of raw fuel, and the high-pitched whine of a nearby ship assailed his senses.

Once on board, Banner spent the first of his two hours making himself, as well as the inside of his ship, presentable for a woman's presence. The ship alone was a major undertaking.

Showered and freshly shaven, he dressed in a comfortable, snowy white crew shirt and his usual snug-fitting black trousers. His sable, collar-length hair was swept back neatly, the ends curling over his collar. Though worn long by the standards of some, it was getting a little too long even for him, and he'd fully planned on doing something about it while in port.

The next hour was spent plotting the coordinates for the voyage that lay ahead and running a diagnostic check on the ship.

* * *

Mary Loring stared at Jonathan in shocked disbelief. At forty-six her beauty was exquisite, almost fragile. "I can't believe I'm hearing this, Jonathan." In spite of her reserve, there was a tinge of exasperation in her voice. "Why Tressa? Surely there are others who can handle the clearance on that equipment. And who, again, is this man who is taking her?"

"One question at a time, Mary," Jonathan said calmly, masking the flood of emotion that was threatening to over take them. As much as he hated it, there just wasn't enough time for two stories: the truth to Mary, his concocted version to Tressa.

And if Mary was to know the truth, Tressa would take one glance at Mary's face and the entire plan would be blown.

Firmly reminding himself that at this very moment there was a ship waiting in port to take Tressa to safety, Jonathan Loring once again bolstered himself for the task ahead.

"First question," he began. "Yes, unfortunately, Tressa *is* the only one besides myself. And the name of the man she will be traveling with is Captain Nick Banner." He'd thrown in the title with the intention of reinforcing a mental image of honor and respectability. "And, yes, before you ask, I trust him."

A look of anguish crossed Mary's face. "She'll be *alone* with this man?"

"Yes," he replied, knowing his air of nonchalance was totally out of character in this instance. He was opening himself wide for criticism . . . and for Mary's special *gift.*

"Why, Jon? I can't believe what I'm hearing."

"Tressie's responsible, Mary. Besides, there's nothing hard about this. It's just a matter of signing a few—"

"You're avoiding the real issue here, Jon. You're sending our daughter off *alone,* galavanting about for God knows how many days with some strange man."

Jonathan groaned inwardly, hating the truth—hating the lie and hating the front of nonchalance he had to keep up.

More than women's intuition, more than just reading body language, Mary was right a hundred percent of the time when it came to understanding his emotions. She didn't just know them; she *felt* them the instant he did.

He'd learned long ago the art of masking his vulnerable side when it became necessary to protect her. Usually he hid behind a bright, cheerful facade. Sometimes he even hid behind anger. And if he concentrated real hard, either worked.

"You *can't* be serious about this!" she admonished him once again.

"Hey . . ." He laughed lightheartedly. "You act as if I'm sending her off with an Airian mountain wolf!"

Swallowing hard, Mary looked away. "What kind of a man is he? How old?" she asked softly, without looking at him.

"I *know* him, Mary. He's a good man." His tone grew serious. "One of very few to whom I can give a responsibility and *know* it will be done right." Again he rallied his sense of humor and added with a silly smirk, "As for his age, I'd say he's about ninety, bald, walks with a cane, and has—"

"Jonathan."

Still grinning, he shrugged his shoulders, "I don't know. He's about thirty I suppose, maybe a little older." Jonathan paused, fighting for self-control in the face of her intense scrutiny.

Tough it out, Loring. You've got to do this.

He knew what she was doing—looking for a weak spot in that jovial exterior he was working so hard to keep up. Yet as much as it repulsed him, the lie was worth his daughter's life.

"If he's so honorable," Mary added pointedly, "why isn't *he* able to effect that special security clearance?"

"Simply because it takes a principal of the firm to release it," he lied. Offering her a tender smile, he continued.

"You see, this shipment isn't just a usual security pickup, it's—"

"And Tressa is one of the principals, is she?" Mary asked sardonically.

Jonathan hesitated. This was getting worse by the minute. "No," he replied at last, "but she's being groomed for a position down the road . . . if she wants it."

He held himself still under her scrutiny. Praying she couldn't break through the mask he had erected.

Some called her ability a gift, the ability to *experience* another's emotions. Creohens called it a curse. A spouse called it an intrusion. Whatever; Jonathan was especially thankful at this moment that the *gift,* if you could call it that, didn't also include mind reading.

"Jonathan . . ." she began, her eyes piercing the distance between them. "What is it you're not telling me?"

He crossed the room, coming to a halt before her. "Mary," he said, reaching for her hand and kissing her open palm, "you know me better than that, darling. Besides, *when* have I ever been able to keep anything from you?"

Oh, how he longed to unload the burden he carried. He would tell her the truth, but only after Tressa was safely off-planet. Like it or not, Nick Banner was the only man he trusted this side of the Milky Way to take his daughter to a safe haven. He had nothing to worry about; she'd tested negative for her mother's ability.

"I might be only half Creohen, Jon, but I *know* what I'm feeling inside. And these are *your* butterflies in the pit of my stomach. Not mine!"

He winced. He hadn't been completely successful with his plan to block her insight. Damn.

This wasn't the first time he'd rued the day Terra Three had been colonized, opening the lid on Pandora's Box with its damned Creoh mines. Mary's father had been just one of many young miners affected by the raw mineral. By the time they discovered the irreversible brain-altering side effects of Creoh, the damage had been done. And by the time they were discovering that the disorder was almost always passed on to the offspring, Mary had been conceived. Leaving Jonathan, after twenty-five years of marriage, still scrambling to keep at least some things secret from his wife's powerful ability to sense his deepest emotions.

Tressa knew something was amiss the minute she entered the room. Despite her mother's serene countenance, the air was thick with tension. "You wanted to see me?" she asked, her eyes falling upon her father.

"Yes. Tressie, please come in. Have a seat, honey." Jonathan motioned to a nearby couch.

Tressa sat down. With wide-eyed curiosity she glanced first at her mother and then back to her father. "Is something wrong?"

"No, no, dear," Jonathan replied casually. "I just need your help with an important errand; that's all." Tressa's face lifted slightly as Jonathan went on. "There's a crucial piece of equipment that needs to be picked up and delivered to Echo. I need you to accompany one of our pilots to Shaiel and sign for the clearance on the shipment."

"Shaiel?" Tressa's mouth dropped. "That's a five-day flight from here."

"Yes, it is," Jonathan admitted. "I'd go myself if I didn't have to be here for that board meeting coming up. I'd hoped that with your security status you'd go in my place."

It seemed strange—the whole idea of her being the only one qualified to go. Nevertheless, Tressa's devotion to her father was stronger than any sense of doubt she had begun to perceive. Pushing the threads of disbelief to the back of her mind, she focused on the excitement of an off-planet flight.

"All right," she agreed hesitantly.

"Good. Now I want you to go and quickly pack a couple of travel cases. We don't have much time, honey."

"Pack? You mean I'm to leave now?" she asked in disbelief.

Jonathan quickly stepped forward, tenderly wrapping his arm around her shoulders. "Tressie, honey, listen to me: As we speak there's a ship waiting in port for us. Yes," he confirmed softly, "it's critical that you leave tonight to make schedule."

For a long moment there was silence as Tressa studied her father intensely. Then at last she nodded in compliance.

Nick was just in the process of tapping information into the ship's NAVCOMP when a soft chime announced the arrival of company. Engaging the surveillance camera, he saw Jonathan and his daughter approaching. "Smart female," he mumbled, noticing that she had only two travel packs.

Although he couldn't quite make out her facial expression, just from the set of her shoulders and the staccato sound of her walk, she didn't appear any happier about this than he did. "Real smooth, Loring. Real smooth," he muttered.

Folding his arms across his chest, Banner leaned back in the command seat and continued to observe the advancing couple on the ship's monitor. Suddenly Tressa stopped mid-pace about a hundred feet from the ship. "Now what?" Banner leaned forward, watching intently as he reached for his mug of steaming Tengo tea.

"How could you?" Tressa stamped her foot on the decking for emphasis. "I can't believe you would do this to me. You conveniently never mentioned the *Victorious* because you *knew* what I'd say, didn't you?"

"Tressa, I'm sorry," Jonathan offered lamely. "Despite all the things you've heard, Captain Banner is one of the most honorable men I know."

"Oh right!" she said, rolling her eyes.

"Believe me, sweets, I'd never send you off with him if I didn't believe that with all my heart."

Tressa turned and faced him squarely. "I'm sure you believe that," she said softly, meaningfully. "And maybe you know something I don't, but honorable doesn't exactly coincide with what I keep hearing." With that, Tressa whirled around and continued her high-geared trek toward the awaiting *Victorious*.

"Wait a minute, Tressie." Jonathan picked up his pace.

"I feel like I've just been thrown into the den of an imperial snapper," she muttered, not waiting for him to catch up.

Wincing at her words, Jonathan moved quickly, spinning her around to face him. "And just what is it you keep hearing? Huh? Are they firsthand stories, Tressa, or dreamed-up rumors?"

Jonathan studied her intently. "You think I'm old, don't you? Too old to pay attention to the rumors about the *notorious* Nick Banner? Too old to notice the way young girls throw themselves at him down there in Shipping, and maybe even too old to understand?"

Tressa lowered her eyes. "I never said that."

"Of course you didn't," he said softly, "but it's what you meant. Let me tell you what I do understand, Tressie," Jonathan continued with fatherly gentleness. "Judging from what I see, and given the fact that none of those eager young ladies in Shipping have yet to personally boast of her social experiences with Nick Banner, I'd venture to say it's more wishful thinking and a whole lot of fantasizing than anything.

"Don't get me wrong, honey: I'm not dismissing or defending his reputation, but neither am I blind or deaf to what really goes on. I'd say there's a lot more rumor than there is truth in the things you've been hearing."

He didn't need to say more. It was true; not one of those stories she'd heard was at first hand. And, to the best of Tressa's knowledge, none of LorTech's girls had ever socialized with the illustrious Nick Banner, despite their seductive enticements.

Defiance returning, Tressa lifted her chin a notch. "Yeah, well, those rumors had to have started somewhere. He's just too smart to try anything right under your nose." With that she turned and once again resumed her march toward the ship.

With a frown and a heavy sigh, Banner headed for the main entry port. At a touch the inner hatch cycled open, and he palmed the outer lock, meeting Jonathan and Tressa as they made their way up the ramp. A set of recessed lights in the ceiling of the entry snapped to life as the two boarders stepped over the threshold.

Mahogany highlights in Tressa's rich brown hair danced as she unconsciously lingered beneath one of the twin beams of light. Despite Jonathan's presence, Nick was finding it hard to drag his eyes from her. She was even more beautiful than he'd remembered, and he'd be willing to bet that there was a heart-stopping body beneath that liquid-soft jumpsuit she wore.

It took every ounce of determination Banner had to suppress his amusement as Tressa gazed about the cabin, surveying the compact and painfully limited living quarters.

"Nick, you remember my daughter, Tressa." Jonathan said, breaking the tension.

Tressa offered her hand. "Hello."

"Yes," he said, reaching for her hand, "of course I remember. Welcome aboard the *Victorious*, Tressa."

Banner turned to Loring. "For now, Jon, just stash her things under my bunk."

With a nod, Jonathan turned and headed toward the berths, just astern of the main entry.

"Uh . . . Nick, you want to come back here a moment?" Loring asked, his eyes riveted on a crate in the far rear corner of the cabin. Excusing himself from Tressa, Nick made his wasy back.

"Yes? What is it, Jon?" Loring left no doubt but that he was concerned about something.

35

"I'd say that's an extensive inventory of ale you have stashed back there," he began in a low voice. "I know it's . . . it's none of my business, but under the circumstances, just what are your intentions?"

Nick simply grinned. "You're right, Jon. It *is* none of your business. But under the circumstances . . . that crate of ale you're referring to was loaded up two weeks ago, just before I left Echo. And before you even ask . . . No, I don't intend to kill it off by the time we reach Acacia."

Still lingering just inside the main hatch, Tressa continued her visual inspection of the surrounding area. Eventually her eyes came to rest on her father and Banner, engaged in conversation near the rear of the cabin. Although she could only make out part of what was being said, from the look on her father's face it was clearly something unpleasant.

Trying not to stare, she quietly watched as Nick politely responded in a voice too low for her to understand. Occasionally he would nod his head, and Tressa could only imagine what sort of idiotic stipulations were being laid down.

Banner had positioned himself against the bulkhead. Folding his arms across his chest, he'd braced his shoulder against the partition in a negligent stance. Unable to resist the impulse, Tressa discreetly raked his form. Starting at his booted feet, she worked her way up his long, muscular legs, past his broad chest, and finally came to rest on his ruggedly handsome face. He simmered with sensuality and, with his dark hair and luminous blue eyes, was handsome enough to take a woman's breath away.

Tressa recalled how he'd done just that about six years ago. She had been fourteen at the time, and Nick Banner was by far the most gorgeous man she'd ever set eyes on. When the rumors began Tressa was not immune. She'd probably heard each story at least half a dozen times. In her innocence, Nick's fast lifestyle and seductive manner made the stories almost romantic.

Often she would give in to her secret fantasy and imagine Nick's hard arms wrapped around her, his lips tenderly caressing hers, and his sensually low voice murmuring words of undying love in her ear. Reality was, with her having been away at school so much, Nick Banner most likely didn't even know who she was, let alone remember their initial introduction six years ago.

"Tressie, I'm going to leave now." Jonathan's voice broke into her thoughts as both men came forward and farewells were exchanged. Within minutes Tressa was seated in the passenger seat located to the left behind the pilot's seat, her heart pounding in anticipation of an off-planet flight and a mixture of conflicting emotions racing through her mind.

Turning her eyes toward Nick, Tressa found his very presence both disturbing and exciting as she discreetly watched him go through the process of sealing the ship.

At last she averted her gaze toward the window. *Careful that you don't go dropping at his feet in worship like all the others.*

Tressa had no sooner formulated her plan of immunity when Banner swung around, regarding her with an intensity that made her insides flutter. Suddenly he leaned forward and pulled a safety harness across her lap, fastening it in place.

"You ever been off planet before, Tressa?" The velvet timbre of his deep voice calmly broke the silence.

"Only once," she answered, masking her anxiety behind a facade of enthusiasm. "Actually, I was nine at the time." She laughed nervously, then quickly added, "However, I've flown many times to neighboring ports here on Terra Four."

"Uh-huh." Banner nodded politely, but Tressa caught the look of stifled amusement. His eyes practically twinkled with suppressed mischief. "Well, this will be just a little different than port-hopping," he said. "I'll explain what to

37

expect as we go along. In the meantime," he said and grinned, "relax."

"I am relaxed," she insisted.

Languid laughter filled his tone. "No, you're not," he said, turning his attention to the control panel, all business as he ran through the pre-liftoff procedures.

Tressa felt hot words of denial catch in her throat, but she swallowed them. Judging from his expression alone, she'd already succeeded in entertaining him.

With a hard swallow she turned her attention toward the viewport to her left. A tiny pulsing strobe light caught her eye as it marked the very tip of the port wing. Suddenly four high-intensity landing beams snapped to life, instantly bathing the surface of the landing zone—or L.Z., as it was termed by pilots—in bright light.

It was dark outside, and Tressa pressed closer to the window, blocking out the reflection of the ship's interior. Cupping her face with her hands, she peered out at the surrounding space port. The docking bays were occupied with everything ranging from large freighters to small mail boats. Several docks, in particular, were a bustle of activity.

Tressa was jerked from her thoughts when a subtle vibration became the low rumble of ignition. She turned just as Banner flipped an overhead switch. In response, a bank of tiny green lights came alive on the console, and when he tapped a final button the low rumble slowly began building into a muffled, high-pitched whine.

Banner opened the com-link. "This is the *Victorious*, Delta Beta, six-niner-four, requesting clearance for liftoff."

A terrifying wave of apprehension swept over Tressa. Swallowing the instant lump in her throat, she turned toward the viewport, searching out the terminal in a desperate attempt to glimpse her father just one last time.

Chapter Three

"That's an affirmative, *Victorious*," a monotone voice responded. "You are cleared for vertical lift to five thousand feet."

The controller had no sooner given clearance than the whine of the ship's thrusters began escalating. Inside the cabin the sound was muffled, but outside the high-pitched whine rose first to an ear-piercing scream and then a deafening roar as the *Victorious* lifted.

Pinned to her seat, Tressa watched with renewed fascination as the lights of Port Ireland became smaller and smaller, gradually disappearing into the distant horizon as Nick set the course for Port Canda.

"I've got a couple of stops to make first; then we'll put into space," he said without taking his eyes off the console.

Tressa's gaze shifted back to Banner, only to be lost in a perusal that wandered over every virile inch of his profile, from the smooth line of his freshly shaven jaw to glossy black hair that lay shaggily over his collar to the way his shirt clung to the corded muscles of his strong back. Slowly

Tressa's gaze traveled southward, visiting a flat-planed stomach and hip, settling at last, and lingering much too long, on a hard muscled thigh.

A curious tightening in the pit of her stomach drew her from her reverie. With a dry swallow Tressa looked away, silently denying the surge of excitement charging through her veins.

You're practically engaged, Tressa! How can you even look at this arrogant brute, especially when Sinclair represents everything this man isn't and probably never will be?

It was true. Everyone knew Nick Banner was a maverick, an insolent nonconformist who cared less what people thought of him. How could such exquisitely wicked feelings be stirring to life? Feelings she'd buried long ago?

Settling in, Nick swiftly finished entering the coordinates into the NAVCOMP. His swarthy features were softly illuminated by the orange glow of the console, and Tressa found herself drawn to him in spite of herself. Swallowing hard and clenching her hands in her lap, Tressa straightened her back, firmly reminding herself that she was no longer a lovestruck teenager.

Finishing a final procedure, Banner turned to face her. The knot in the pit of her stomach tightened in response. There it was: that easy smile that had captivated her the first day she had ever set eyes on him.

"You can get up now and inspect your new home if you wish." Tressa didn't miss the hint of mockery in his voice as she unfastened the harness and rose from her seat.

The ship was efficiently compact. The main entry port through which she'd first entered was located on the starboard side toward the bow of the ship. From there forward was an open cockpit.

Next came the sleeping quarters, located just aft of the main entry port. It consisted of two bunks, a stationary lower bunk and an upper one that had yet to be unlatched and let down from the bulkhead. The berths were boxed in by two floor-to-ceiling partitions, one at the head and one at the foot.

Dogging her steps, Banner drew her attention to the lavatory. Though tiny, the "head," as he crudely referred to it, seemed complete. Tressa was glad to note it even included a shower, a triangular-shaped unit situated in one corner.

"Small but functional," he said in a tone that was anything but apologetic. The brute was standing directly behind her, far too close for propriety, too. Crossing the cabin to the port side of the ship, Tressa came to the entry of a small galley.

"Cozy, isn't it?" Banner drawled, once again failing miserably to rein in his sense of humor, which most of the time bordered on downright sarcasm. As they stepped into the galley, interior lighting that responded to life illuminated the room. "Have a seat, Tressa," he said, motioning toward the small lounge.

Remembering Jonathan's advice about laying down ground rules, Nick turned for the kitchenette along the aft wall as Tressa took a seat. "You want something hot to drink?" he asked, reaching for a couple of mugs.

"Thank you."

Nick opened a container and began spooning green crystals into the two mugs. "Ever heard of Tenga Tea?"

"Tenga Tea?" She frowned. "No, I don't think so."

Banner nodded. "It's made from the crystallized sap of a small bush on Shobano."

"I don't think I've heard of Shobano either."

Nick grinned. "Probably not. A friend in the importing business gave me a supply of this stuff." He positioned one of the mugs beneath a small spigot and began filling it with steaming water.

Returning to her side, he handed her one of the mugs. Tressa inhaled the flavorful aroma. "It smells good," she said, gazing curiously at the steaming green liquid.

Banner just grinned. "Don't speak too soon, Sunshine."

He took a seat beside her, then lifted his mug for emphasis. "Someone said this stuff's supposed to be better for you than Terran coffee," he said.

A moment of silence passed and then, with a heavy sigh, Nick began. "Tressa, we need to take a minute here and go over some things."

"All right." She looked up at him expectantly.

Nick adjusted his position. "First of all," he began hesitantly, "despite the fact that I work for your father, the name Loring pulls no weight on board the *Victorious*. You're strictly a passenger, and it's that simple."

Tressa's jaw dropped.

Ignoring her bewilderment, Banner pressed on. "As long as you remember that, then everything should go smoothly. Oh, and one other thing. If you've got a complaint, unless it's life threatening, I don't want to hear about it. The *Victorious* is set up to haul cargo, not passengers."

Swallowing hard, Tressa lifted her chin and boldly met his gaze with an arrogance all her own. "For your information, this ship isn't that much smaller than the dorm I lived in at school."

Nick raked his hand through his dark hair. The amusement he'd barely suppressed earlier had vanished. "You may find this to be just a little different than . . . a girl's dorm, Sunshine. We're talking about two and a half weeks of living with each other, and unless we get a few things straight and a few rules understood between us . . . *cozy* just might not adequately describe it by the time we reach our destination." His tone had taken on a definite leer.

"I understand."

"Do you?" he countered, not missing her revealing flush. "With the exception of the lav, my dear." He continued, "seclusion around here will be virtually nonexistent." He paused long enough to light up a slender cigar, expelling a slow stream of smoke high over her head.

The crimson flush had now begun working its way down

her throat. And there was no doubt that she was beginning to grasp the gravity of his message.

"Go on." she said softly. "I believe you're about to make a point?"

At the moment she was a model example of poised dignity, sitting there with both hands clasping her mug, head held high. Just from her expression alone, he knew he'd provoked her, and for some strange reason he had an unexplainable desire to crack the fragile shell of composure that surrounded her.

One corner of his mouth lifted, forming a mischievous grin. "All right," he began slowly, as though accepting a challenge. "Since I rarely take passengers on board, I'm not particularly in the habit of being, uh, shall we say, modest? The *point* is, given the lack of privacy in general around here, combined with my lack of modesty, I'd say we have a potential problem."

Nick leaned back, stretching his long legs out before him. Grasping his cigar between his thumb and fingers, he took a slow draw. The crowning touch of arrogance came, however, when he had the audacity to blow three irritating smoke rings into the air while awaiting the impact of his words.

An eternity of silence passed before he calmly added, "The only way you and I are going to coexist for the next three weeks is if we set down a few rules and stick to them." Leaning forward, he flicked a lump of ash in the general direction of a nearby ashtray. It missed, sending an avalanche of ashes cascading to the deck.

Setting down her mug, Tressa lifted her chin to speak, flashing him a glare of such disgust, he nearly doubled over trying to stifle his laughter.

"It's obvious you haven't the vaguest notion of what the word *decent*, means Capt. Banner."

Humor twinkled in Banner's intense blue eyes. "You're probably right," he responded with an annoying air of condescension, "but I'll tell you what: I'll make you a deal. I'll try my damndest to *act* decent," he grinned, "just for you. But you must promise to do the same, and that includes, darlin', making sure I'm not subjected to your, uh . . . intimate belongings drip-drying off every hook in the lav."

He paused long enough to draw from his cigar, then calmly added, "Under those conditions, Irish, I make no guarantees on the decency of my behavior."

Tressa was silent for a long moment. For an instant Nick thought he'd actually struck her speechless.

Finally she rose to her feet, her face flushed. "You are really, *really* rude!"

"Yeah, I know. I've been accused of that at times."

"Furthermore, you're uncivilized and despicable."

He grinned. "That bad, huh?"

Tressa glared at him. "Every crude thing I've ever heard about you is absolutely true, isn't it?"

His eyebrows rose. "I wouldn't go so far as to say *everything.*"

"I'm not even going to waste my breath commenting on the conditions of your so-called deal," she continued. "And furthermore, I'm not so naive that I would ever consider your conduct *guaranteed,* as you so loosely put it, under *any* conditions. Regardless of what you may think, I'm not simpleminded."

Stifling his amusement, Nick remained in his sprawled position. "I never said you were." He punctuated his smooth composure by expelling another stream of smoke toward the vent. "Like I said . . . we've got three weeks ahead of us, and the only way we're going to manage is if you understand the rules around here."

"Your arrogance amazes me!" Tressa shot back, looking away in disgust. "*You* are the one who needs to understand the rules, Nick Banner. I can assure you, I understood them long before I ever boarded this . . . this bucket of rivets."

Banner arched an eyebrow in response to her insulting

slur against the *Victorious*. But the slight quiver in her voice brought an easy smile to the corners of his mouth. Thoroughly enjoying her discomposure, he found her sense of propriety refreshing and more than just a little intriguing. He wondered if she had any idea of just how enticing she looked right now standing before him with her hands planted on her hips in challenge. His eyes roamed boldly over her in appreciation.

Either too naive to notice his look, or too angry, Tressa continued. "Believe me, I can think of a thousand other places I'd rather be right now than on board this ship with a rake like you. To be perfectly honest, I want to stay here only marginally more than I want to die trying to escape at the moment.

"I was all but forced into running this so-called errand," she continued, "and the only reason I agreed is because my father has never before asked anything of me. You, on the other hand, surely could have come up with a thousand reasons for declining, but apparently you decided to hire out your *noble* services. Am I right, *Captain?*"

"Go on." Nick folded his arms across his chest and fought to keep the smirk off his face. This was even better than he'd anticipated.

Tressa's mouth thinned. "May I suggest, as unpleasant as it may be, that we make the best of it. And rest assured I have no intentions of interfering with your captainly duties in any way whatsoever. Nor..." she paused, as if hesitant, then proceeded. "Nor will you *ever* find any of my personal belongings hanging about the lav or anywhere else for that matter."

Banner grinned, completely unrepentant. "Terrific. Everything should be just wonderful then, shouldn't it?" He took a slow draw on his cigar. "I just don't want any misunderstanding between us," he added with low-voiced composure.

"Oh, there won't be. I assure you your message was received loud and clear, Capt. Banner... *sir.*"

Thoroughly pleased with himself, Banner's eyes danced with laughter. A *rake* ... he thought. Where the devil did she dredge up that name? His half-frown merged into a grin as he began focusing on the deep dimple right in the middle of her stubborn little cheek. Funny he'd never noticed it before.

He was the image of cocksure arrogance, and Tressa had an overwhelming urge to kick him in the shins. Fortunately, good sense won out, and she squelched the impulse as she turned to exit the galley.

How could her father actually expect her to travel anywhere with this brute? This ... this swamprat posing as a ship's captain? How could he have subjected her to this?

Tressa quickly headed for her place in the cockpit. How would she be able to manage for ten solid days with the likes of him? "*Swamprat*," she muttered. "Arrogant, chauvinistic, overbred, bubble-brained jerk," she continued. It was perfectly clear he didn't want her on board and that he had every intention of making her life miserable for the duration of the trip.

Decent. There was little doubt but that they each had their own definition of *that* word. "Bossy brute; you probably snore too ..." Tressa's thoughts turned to the sleeping arrangements. Glancing toward the bunks, the shock of discovery hit her full force—there were no privacy curtains!

By the time Banner finally strolled up front, Tressa was sitting stiffly in the passenger's seat, staring out the viewport at absolutely nothing but blackness. Actually, with the cabin lights fully lit, what she saw was the mirrored image of the cockpit, and in the reflection Tressa watched as Nick took the pilot's seat. No words were exchanged between them, least of all the apology that she was sure he owed her. Rising from her seat, Tressa marched back toward the galley.

"Don't stay back there too long," he tossed over his shoulder. "We'll be hitting dirt in about twenty minutes."

Cord Wheeler rounded the corner and headed away from his office. Another day was coming to an end. Starting down the duracrete walkway, he had the unmistakable feeling that he was being followed. Whipping around, he scanned the open street with a glance. No one looked particularly suspicious. But then, what did he know? Having grown up in the sheltering shadow of his grandfather, he'd always known the finer side of living, and dealing with questionable people had never been part of it.

Now, against his will, here he was living in Port Ireland, running a subsidiary mining brokerage. He hated Port Ireland, hated Terra Four . . . hated the brokerage, for that matter.

He could still hear his grandfather's words: "Young man, if you want Wheeler Explorations when I retire, you'll settle down and prove yourself worthy to take over."

He groaned at the memory. *Worthy* meant coming to Port Ireland and spending two damn years of his life running a small brokerage and proving he was capable of turning a profit.

It wasn't an easy task, but so far he'd managed to land several highly profitable contracts, yielding large commissions. So what if his methods were a little unethical? The figures he'd just finished entering in the books were impressive. And, after all, wasn't *that* the main objective?

Yes, the name change from Cord Wheeler to Burke Sinclair had been a wise move. It had opened connections he never could have managed under the respected name of Wheeler, the name his grandfather had worked hard to build.

It was while he was living under his new identity of Burke Sinclair that he'd met Jonathan Loring; with the charisma of a snake oil salesman he'd sold Loring on both himself and the reputation of the brokerage. Before long,

Sinclair found himself sitting across from Loring and offering his bid for a large commercial mining contract. The very contract his grandfather had been striving to secure. The final decision, of course, would be Loring's, but he felt sure his grandfather would be awarded the contract.

Yet another fringe benefit to meeting Loring had been meeting Loring's daughter. Tressa turned out to be an unexpected edge in his quest for "worthiness." What better way to satisfy his grandfather's wish, than to settle down and take a wife? And a wealthy one, at that. The only problem was, he'd spent the last six months courting Tressa, and he was still seething that she needed time to think about his proposal of marriage. Back home there were dozens of women who would jump at the offer with a man of his standing, not to mention his looks and charm.

No, the entire plan was irritating, and if he had his way he'd pack up and leave this blasted place now, head for home, and slip back into the luxurious life he'd been used to. But since he couldn't do that, he'd devised a little insurance plan.

Just this morning he'd made the final arrangements with Tressa's future kidnapers. Sinclair smiled at the thought of how grateful she would be for his timely rescue—how indebted, even, Loring himself would be for the display of heroism. It was all so simple. He'd win Tressa's undying love and no one would be the wiser, least of all his grandfather.

Randy by nature, courting Tressa properly was taking its toll on Sinclair. Yes, he would continue his display of perfect gentlemanly manners, but dammit, he'd allow himself an occasional visit to a certain brothel where discretion was guaranteed.

He'd been going there a lot lately, and tonight he was headed there again. It was risky, he knew. He didn't dare screw up now. But dammit, a man had his needs. Besides, a celebration was in order, and this particular high-dollar palace of pleasure offered him just what he needed.

"Mr. Sinclair?"

Burke drew in a sharp breath at the sound of the raspy voice intruding on his thoughts. Turning abruptly, he faced a middle-aged man who looked as though life had been one rough and rugged road. Unshaven and filthy, he wore little more than rags in Sinclair's estimation. Steely gray eyes peered out from beneath bushy gray brows, and he appeared as if he hadn't seen soap and water in a disgustingly long time. Burke was intensely repelled by the man.

"Yes?" he responded impatiently.

The man snatched his cap from his head and clutched it to his chest. "Name's Toby McIntyre," he said, extending a grimy hand.

"Yes? What is it?" Burke wasn't about to touch that hand on a bet.

McIntyre retracted his outstretched hand, shoving it into a pocket. "Mr. Sinclair," he began again, "wasn't sure what t' do. I'm not one to be sellin' information, you understand, but got some news you just might be interested in knowin' . . ." He deliberately allowed his words to trail off.

In spite of himself, Sinclair's interest was piqued. He hesitated for a moment, assessing the man, looking past the dirt and rags. He was definitely lower class, judging from his demeanor and language alone. He couldn't help but wonder what information the old man could possibly have that would interest him. "Let me guess: You feel you've got something I'd be willing to pay for, right?"

"Oh, no. But if'n you decide it's worth somethun' . . ."

Sinclair pointedly raked him from head to toe. "Why should I be interested in the first place?"

A grin began to spread across the man's pasty face, exposing badly decayed teeth. "Because it involves a certain little missy leavin' in a big hurry."

Chapter Four

"Who?" Sinclair demanded anxiously.

The man grinned. "I thought you might be interested. Done some askin' around, and I know of a couple stops they'll be makin' 'fore headin' off planet."

Payment was offered, and McIntyre gladly told what he knew.

"The *Victorious*..." Sinclair mused, frowning. "The *Victorious*. I've heard of it."

"She's piloted by a man named Banner," McIntyre continued. "And, for what it's worth, I hear he's no one to tamper with."

It was Sinclair's turn to grin. "I have just the friends in mind. Four against one ought to do it, wouldn't you say?" As far as he could see, there was no problem; just a matter of a few changes.

Mere moments before Nick would have risen to get Tressa from the galley, she silently came forward, took her seat, and fastened the safety harness. Determined to ignore the brute, she immediately turned her face toward the viewport.

The main computer had already been in contact with Port Canada. Basic identification, navigational data, and clearance had all been exchanged by the time Nick switched the controls over to manual.

As they neared the space port, Tressa could see a large ring of pulsing blue lights outlining a designated L.Z.

It wasn't long before Tressa gave in to her curiosity. Turning to watch Nick work the controls, her traitorous eyes began tracing every line and contour of his profile. Despite her annoyance with him, Nick Banner was still the most gorgeous man she'd ever laid eyes on.

Within moments the *Victorious* was being gently lowered onto her landing jacks. After shutting the engines down and securing the ship, Nick took a minute to sweep the scanners across the surrounding landing field. A few ground runners scurried to and fro on assorted errands. One ship was just lifting off, and three others were sitting unattended on the field. No one seemed especially interested in the *Victorious,* and that was just the way he liked it.

He swiveled around to face her. "Tressa, I want you to stay here while I'm gone."

"You mean I can't go with you? Why not?"

Nick rose from his seat, towering above her, as he continued. "Because some of these backside ports aren't very nice places. All I have to do is drop off one small package and arrange for a shipment of liquid fertilizer to be unloaded. I'm setting the security so whatever you do, don't open the main lock for anyone. Got it? No one!"

He had her undivided attention now, and he paused while his last words sank in. "I'll also set the exterior surveillance camera so that it will remain on for you. Should anyone come within a designated range of the ship, the proximity alarm will go off and you'll be able to see who's out there by looking right here." He pointed to the monitor.

Retrieving a small package from the ship's hold, he

strode to his bunk and reached for the gunbelt hanging just inside the berth.

Tressa watched, wide-eyed, as Banner strapped the gun low on his thigh and tied it down. Withdrawing a small black object from his utility belt, he checked the energy level of the weapon, then replaced it. Finally tucking the package under his arm, he turned to face her. "When I return I'll let myself in. By checking the monitor you'll know it's me before I even get here. Okay?"

Tressa nodded, following him to the main lock.

"Remember. Don't touch anything in the cockpit." His tone was somewhere between a command and an entreaty.

His words were still ringing in her ears as the entry cycled closed. Why couldn't she just go with him? What harm could it possibly do? She'd been around Port Ireland enough to know how rough spaceports could get. It was irritating being treated like a child.

Still fuming over his refusal to take her with him, Tressa made her way back to the galley. It was funny how she was old enough to be needed for a high security release, and yet too young and inexperienced to walk across the landing field with him. He didn't want her with him. That was it. He'd certainly made it clear that he didn't want her going with him, any more than she wanted to go.

Entering the galley, Tressa made her way to the octagon viewport. There she stood for several long moments, watching the bustle of activity going on outside the ship, including the lifting of a large freighter on the other side of the landing zone.

So, this was Port Canada. It certainly wasn't much to look at, judging at least from the starboard viewport. She watched a robo loader making its way across the landing field toward the ship. Before long, it was wheeling to a stop and two men got out directly below, disappearing beneath the ship.

Soon she heard the electronic sound of cargo bay doors rumbling as they cycled open. The consignment of liquid fertilizer, Tressa realized. And looking straight down through the contoured window, she watched as the men loaded several bulky containers onto a freight sled. Within minutes, she heard the doors close and watched as the robo loader made its way back to the terminal. With a sigh, Tressa took a seat in front of the viewport.

Tressa never heard the soft chime go off as Nick entered the proximity range of the ship. Nor did she hear the main lock hiss open as he came aboard. She'd never intended to fall asleep. Having finished her entry, she'd merely closed her eyes and leaned her head back for a brief moment. "Tressa?" Nick quickly scanned the cabin for her as he came aboard. Frowning, he turned to replace his utility belt on the hook just inside his berth, then made his way to the galley.

There, his eyes fell upon her.

Quietly stepping into the galley, he greedily took the liberty of observing Tressa while unfastening the leg ties and buckle of his gun belt. He carefully studied her delicate features, noting her thick, long lashes, her flawless complexion, the pout of her mouth, and the dimple that was even present during sleep.

A *rake,* she'd called him. An unexpected chuckle rose in his throat at the memory, and he was forced to stifle it for fear of waking her.

Instinctively, his gaze slid downward to the dipping neckline of her lavender jumpsuit, and naturally, being the rake she'd accused him of being, he didn't miss the cleavage before it discreetly disappeared beneath the cut of the garment.

Emitting a sigh born of raw desire, he clamped down on the rampaging thoughts his mind had begun to entertain. A muscle jerked in his left cheek as he quickly reminded himself just whose daughter she was.

Reaching into his pocket, Nick removed a small stone, held it in the palm of his hand, and carefully examined it.

Creamy white in color, the rock was smooth and oval in shape. And as he continued to hold it, the color gradually began changing to a soft blue. Slowly he cupped his fingers over the object, and when he opened his hand again the stone had changed to a vibrant shade of pulsing cobalt.

Banner wouldn't have admitted to the twinge of guilt he was feeling. The lack of discretion he'd displayed earlier in the galley was bad enough; the fact that he'd enjoyed every minute of it was worse yet. He pondered his plan to offer the stone as a peace offering. Whether she'd accept it was another thing. One thing for sure—he would have to keep a tight rein on sarcasm.

Ever so carefully Nick laid the stone in Tressa's upturned palm. Lingering for a moment in fascination, he watched as it slowly changed from cobalt to purple to violet and finally to bright crimson, all in a matter of minutes.

Nick remained a moment longer, drinking in the sight of her. Finally he turned and made his way for the cockpit; one more stop to make before putting into space.

Since Jonathan had said nothing about Acacia to Tressa, Nick wondered just what he was supposed to say to justify the trip. He'd think of something, and hopefully she'd buy it.

Once again the *Victorious* lifted, and within seconds left nothing more than a vapor trail.

Tressa awoke with liftoff, unconsciously curling her fingers about the stone she hadn't yet acknowledged. "Ohhh," she mouthed at discovering the crimson treasure in her hand. Never taking her eyes off the stone, she started for the helm.

"We should hit Port France in about two hours," Nick said without glancing up. "Then I intend to put this baby into space as fast as possible."

Tressa quietly padded toward the passenger's seat. "Nick . . ."

"Hmmm?"

"Did you give this to me?"

54

"Hmmm? Oh . . . that? Yeah." He hated moments like this. Hated, number one, having to admit that an apology might be in order. Hated making a big deal out of apologies, number two. And three, as far as apologies were concerned, this was about as far as it was going. If she was looking for a speech, she was out of luck.

"Ohhh, it's beautiful," Tressa breathed, settling into the seat. "Thank you."

Nick completed the process of turning control over to the main computer; then, swiveling around to face her, he patted his pockets for a cigar.

"You're welcome," he responded, noting her childlike wonder as she scrutinized the stone in her hand.

"What is it?"

"The slang term for it is a sympathy stone. Supposedly, it changes colors with your mood."

"Really?" Her eyes sparkled with excitement. "And why does it pulse like that?"

Nick chuckled. "It pulses, I suppose, from energy trapped inside." He paused to light the cigar. "Just why it changes color is beyond me, but I'm sure there's a logical explanation for it."

"Would it change to a different color if someone else were to hold it?" she asked, looking at him with gleeful anticipation. Before he could respond she was out of her seat. "I want to see what happens when *you* hold it," she said excitedly, pressing the stone into his hand.

Nick shoved the cigar in his mouth as Tressa's small hands molded his fingers around the stone.

"There. Now what do we do, count to ten or something?"

"I'm not sure," he said softly, suppressing his unexpected reaction to her innocent touch. "You're the one callin' the shots."

"All right then. Ten it is." With that, Tressa began counting slowly. "One . . . two . . . three . . ."

With his cigar still firmly clamped between his teeth,

Nick winced against a trail of spiraling smoke as he held eye contact with Tressa. She was so engrossed in her experiment that he doubted she even realized she was still tightly clasping her hands over his fist as she counted.

Maybe Tressa wasn't tuned in, but he was acutely aware of her; the feel of her warm hands, in particular. So much so, that the effect was playing total havoc with his emotions and sending his wall of immunity tumbling. As it was, he was hard pressed to keep from pulling her into his arms and running an experiment or two of his own. Nevertheless, her enthusiasm was contagious; Nick found himself surprisingly curious as to just what color the stone would be when he opened his hand.

"Ten!" Her voice broke into his thoughts. "Okay, now quick, open your hand."

He could tell she was holding her breath as he teased her with deliberate slowness, peeling his fingers open one at a time.

"Oh . . . Nick!" she gasped before he'd even completed the process. "Why, it's . . . it's emerald!"   Nick released a stream of smoke toward the ceiling. "Hmmm, wonder what that means?" he drawled, failing to keep the smirk off his face. He placed the stone back into Tressa's small hand and leaned back in the pilot's seat, watching her, totally mesmerized by her enthusiasm.

With fixed fascination, Tressa held open her palm. "Watch," she said as the stone, by degrees, gradually changed back to crimson again.

After a while Nick rose to his feet and stretched with a loud yawn. "I don't know about you, Irish," he began, "but this has been a long day. I'm going to bunk out for a while before we reach the next port." With that, he headed for the sleeping berths and dropped into the lower bunk.

Clasping his hands behind his head, Nick lay there awhile, watching Tressa work with the stone. Her mass of rich brown hair shone with mahogany highlights as she sat

56

beneath a high-intensity reading beam. She looked very young and soft curled up in the seat, and Nick drank in the sight of her.

Only problem was, it didn't take much on the part of his over-active imagination to envision just how perfect that heart-stopping body would feel pressed beneath him.

Ten seconds of creative fantasy was all it took. Then Nick was acutely aware of his body's rising response. With an inward groan and a small measure of self disgust, he closed his eyes and set his mind on something other than Loring's intriguing daughter.

Tressa slid the stone into her pocket. Remembering that Nick had said Tenga tea was good cold, she rose from her seat and quietly made her way past the bunks into the galley.

Okay, this is day one, she mentally told herself. Four more days to get to Shaiel and five days to get back. Brooding over her prsent predicament, Tressa filled a tall mug with ice-cold water and stirred in a spoonful of crystals. With a sip she tested it then turned to survey the small galley. A number of log sheets lay strewn across the table where Nick had left them. Two unemptied ashtrays were shoved up against the wall, along with a half-filled mug of coffee that looked like it had been there for a while. With another sip of iced Tenga tea, Tressa quietly made her way out of the galley and back to her seat in the helm.

Hundreds of gauges, switches, and lights spanned the width of the cockpit, more dotted the ceiling above the pilot's seat. Tressa was just contemplating how anyone could remember which one to press, when a low, agonized moan drew her attention.

Nick was still sleeping. A frown now creased his brow and for a long moment Tressa sat there quietly observing him. His body flinched as a tremor shot through him. He gasped, then grimaced and his eyelids fluttered in response to some inner struggle. A nightmare.

It was subtle, so faint that Tressa barely noticed the odd sensation that swept through her own body at the same time another shudder racked Nick's. Again, he moaned and swallowed hard. Perspiration was beginning to bead his upper lip.

The decision was quick. Pushing her own curious reaction aside, Tressa rose from her seat and approached him, driven to release him from whatever hellish war he was fighting inside.

"Nick?" she called softly. "Wake up. You're having a—"

Chapter Five

Nick flew off the bunk so fast Tressa never saw it coming. With a muscular twist that wrung a gasp from her lips, he flipped her around in one agile movement. Tumbling her onto the bunk, he rolled her beneath him, dropped his weight onto her, and pinned her soundly upon the mattress. One hard knee pushed into her soft abdomen, driving the air from her lungs.

Daring not even so much as a single breath, Tressa froze as an excruciating second passed before Nick's eyes flickered in recognition.

Drawing a breath of outrage, Tressa uttered each word on a separate gasp. "Get . . . off . . . me!"

With a muttered oath, Nick drew back, pulling himself half off her. "What the hell are you trying to do?" he shouted.

Tressa blinked back instant tears as she lay pinned beneath him, sprawled wantonly across his bunk. He was furious with her. No apologies, no regard or concern. Instead, he towered over her with open hostility.

He wasn't letting her up. Tressa couldn't even move out from beneath him. And his gaze was focused on her mouth with an intensity, a masculine hunger that unnerved her.

At last, he eased off of her entirely and stood up. "What the devil were you doing, anyway?" he asked with just a little less volume.

"You were . . . having some sort of a . . . a bad dream," she stammered, reluctantly accepting his offered hand.

Silence fell between them. Time was suspended as his sapphire eyes observed her with such intensity that it brought a deeper flush to her already heated cheeks. His gaze drifted back to her mouth again, and she swallowed, sensing a barely leashed passion within him.

"I get 'em every now and then," he replied in his low-timbered voice. It's a souvenir from a nice place called Steel."

Tressa hid her trembling hands in the folds of her gown. "Nick, you don't have to suffer with nightmares. There are things you can take. . . ."

"Yeah, well they don't work for me."

"Then you haven't tried Seton Three," Tressa persisted. "It's what they use in the hospitals when the miners suffer from what they call digger's fever."

"I've tried them all, Tressa. The only thing that works is getting good and drunk."

"Well, I would hardly consider that a solution, under the circumstances." she replied.

"Hardly." His grin only affirmed that Nick Banner could be dreadfully persuasive when he wanted to be.

Banner raked his hand through his hair. "You all right?" he asked almost in afterthought. His tone had definitely softened.

"I'm fine." She pulled away from him, struggling to readjust her outfit. "I just wanted to wake you from your bad dream, that's all. I'm sorry I startled you."

"I can imagine you are." Stepping forward into the cockpit, Banner groaned. "Anyway, you have that backwards. I'm the one who owes you an apology.''

"And your apology is accepted,''she replied.

Eyeing the console, he searched his pockets, found a cigar, and then bent his head to light up. Tressa stared at his
back as he leaned a forearm against the soffet of the cockpit. He studied the control panel in silence.

Tressa came forward, still trembling. Chewing her lower
lip, she watched him work the controls, allowing her eyes
to move slowly over his powerful, well-muscled body. As
always, he radiated a sensuality that drew her like a magnet.
The memory of his weight upon her and the heated intensity of his gaze brought back all the old butterflies of infatuation; all the feelings she'd worked so hard, over the
years, to bury.

Sending a lazy stream of smoke to the ceiling, Nick
reached down and depressed a red-lit indicator, watching
as the light turned green. Next he dropped into the command seat, shifting his gaze to the vidscreen. "Tressa," he
said, never taking his eyes from the controls, "better strap
in. We're going to hit dirt in about five minutes.''

Tressa had no sooner taken her seat then a crack of static
snapped out over the speaker. Nick engaged the vidcom,
revealing the face of a very pretty blonde.

With cool formality she began providing not only verbal
clearance and landing coordinates but current temperature,
weather conditions, and docking assignment. Once the es-
sentials had been routinely dispatched, the conversation became more personal.

"Nick, love, you're early . . . or did I misunderstand? I
thought you said you'd be in tomorrow night.''

Grinning, Nick sent a stream of blue smoke plunging
toward the floor. "Lissa . . .'' he began, "you're not going
to like this.''

"Don't tell me, Nick. You're not staying. Right?''
Though her voice held a mixture of disappointment and
sarcasm, her expression was staid.

Tressa listened as Nick effortlessly offered a quick and

not-too-detailed explanation for the sudden change in plans. Though clearly let down, Lissa appeared to take it all in stride. It obviously wasn't the first time he'd pulled this on her.

Within moments the *Victorious* began gently banking into a turn. Banner reversed the thrusters. Turning toward the window, Tressa watched as the ground rose up to meet them. The landing beams flooded the area, offering a glimpse of the port as Banner danced the ship mere inches off the surface toward their assigned docking bay. Cupping her face, she pressed closer, taking in the sights.

Similar to Port Ireland, Port France contained a wide variety of ships ranging from very large interplanetary freighters to small private jobbies, with everything in between. The space port consisted mainly of docking bays— dozens of them, each defined by large iridescent numbers.

Rooster tails of dust, stirred up by the thrusters, coiled about them as the *Victorious* progressed toward its destination. At last Banner eased the *Victorious* into its predesignated bay. Feathering the thrusters, he lowered the ship onto the deck with a gentle thump.

Tressa watched as he ran through the final steps of securing the ship. Finally he rose to his feet and, in a smooth baritone, once again instructed Tressa on such things as surveillance cameras and proximity alarms, warning her not to open the main lock to anyone. He concluded by reminding her again not to touch anything in the cockpit.

Having once again secured the gun on his thigh, Nick retrieved a small envelope and headed for the main hatch. "Uh, Tressa," he began, turning about to face her, "about . . . what happened back there; I'm uh, sorry. You sure you're okay?"

It was an unexpected moment of tenderness. "Yes, I'm sure," Tressa said, rising from her seat. Nick's eyes swept over her. "I'll hurry," he said. "It shouldn't take as long this time." He turned and palmed the lock, the main hatch cycling closed behind him.

Tressa watched the monitor until he was out of sight. Drawing in a long, shuddering breath, she closed her eyes and tried not to think about the feelings stirring to life inside her. More than that, she struggled to deny the desire that had shot through her as she lay pinned beneath him. It had been short-lived, however, with him shouting at her the way he had.

Reaching into her pocket, she withdrew the stone he'd given her. It pulsed in her palm as she settled into the passenger's seat.

A half hour had passed before a soft chime drew her attention. It was the proximity alarm, announcing an intrusion into the ship's security parameter. Glancing up at the control panel, Tressa's attention was drawn to the flashing red indicator. Her eyes shifted to the monitor. Instead of seeing Nick, as she'd hoped, four shadowy figures emerged on the screen. Although the scanner was equipped with night vision, it was hard for Tressa's untrained eyes to decipher just what was happening outside.

A surge of raw panic sliced through her when another alarm sounded. This one different, louder and more insistent. At the same time another red light snapped to life on the control panel, and a glance at the monitor confirmed her worst fear: Someone was tampering with the main hatch.

By now Tressa's senses were on full alert as she recalled Nick's stern orders: *Don't open the main lock for anyone!*

Frowning, Tressa leaned forward, studying the monitor. Clearly seeing a man's face, she shrank back at the long jagged scar that started at the outer corner of his left eye and ran down the length of this cheek.

Trouble!

Anxiously, Tressa's eyes flew across the instrument panel, searching for some way to warn Nick before he returned. If only she were more knowledgeable about the ship.

Her eyes locked onto a touch pad with the words "Landing Lights" inscribed above it. Turning them on might scare the men away as well as warn Nick, she thought. But then another pad, marked "Security," caught her eye. There were three positions of use: *off*, *manual*, and *automatic*. It was presently resting in the *off* position.

Was it some sort of siren or warning device? Nervously reaching out, fingers hovering above the pad, Tressa debated using it. As she glanced back up at the monitor, Nick's final orders echoed in her ears: "don't touch anything up here in the cockpit, and stay out of trouble."

Biting her lip, she sank back into the pilot's seat. It was either do something and hope it was right, or just sit back and wait. Weighing her options, Nick's orders again thundered through her head, and Tressa slowly withdrew her hand, her eyes fixed on the monitor as she waited.

Outside, hidden among the shadows, four men also waited.

From the opposite side of the landing field, the landcraft glided to a halt. Sliding his credit plate past the scanner, Banner paid the fare and stepped out. The *Victorious* sat beneath a heavy shadow. Increasing clouds now hid Terra Four's twin moons, darkening the field. He noticed that two other ships had docked nearby during the time he'd been gone. Scanning the field, he quickened his stride and hurried toward his ship. It was probably nothing, but he couldn't seem to shake a growing feeling of apprehension.

Ahead, against the shapeless patterns of darkness and reflected floodlight, a shadow moved near the *Victorious*. Banner fixed his sights on that spot and waited. The shadow moved again.

Quickly working his way around the area, he moved in directly behind his target, silently withdrawing a thin wire garrote from his utility belt as he moved.

Remaining motionless, he pressed in tightly against a stack of freight pallets and quietly waited, twisting the ends of the metal strands around each hand.

Suddenly Banner shoved off. Swiftly reaching the man in one lithe movement, he slipped the wire over the victim's head and tightened it with a twist of his wrist.

The man struggled, reaching up to grab at the contracting device, but Banner kept the wire tight. A knife slipped from the man's hand in the process, hitting the surface with a reverberating clang.

"All right," Banner growled, his voice low, deceivingly calm. "Who are you?" He released the garrote just enough to allow his victim to reply.

The man shook his head in negation. Banner again twisted the device. "What are you doing here? Who sent you?"

Banner jerked the man's head around and noted the terror in his eyes. Leaning closer, his face only inches from the stranger's, he continued his interrogation. "I'm not asking you ag . . ."

Muscular arms suddenly grabbed Nick from behind. Struggling to free himself, the wire slipped from his hands. From the scraping of footsteps, there were others involved. At least two, maybe three.

Inside the *Victorious*, the alarms were still sounding. Faithfully remaining at her vigil, Tressa noticed a flurry of movement on the screen, but it was hard to see more than rough outlines of figures.

Frantically studying the instrument panel, Tressa noticed a small control lever located near the bottom of the monitor. From the marked positions of X50, X100, X200, X300, she felt certain it was some sort of magnification device.

Up until this point she'd followed Nick's orders and touched nothing, but her interest in the magnification device was rising.

One of the moons suddenly slipped out from behind the cloud cover, flooding the landing field in soft light. Tressa's eyes searched the screen with desperation. The moonlight not only made it easier to see what was happening, it confirmed her fear—there was a brawl going on out there.

Searching for Banner's tall, distinctive form, she anxiously studied the screen. But it was impossible to distinguish him from the others.

Finally, in a rush of panic, Tressa forcefully pushed his explicit orders to the back of her mind. Without reservation she reached out and slid the control lever to X50. The screen wavered for just a moment, then refocused with a magnified version of the image. What had been overshadowed and confusing before suddenly became clear-cut and precise. Immediately she caught sight of Nick. He was struggling against two men who were in the process of locking his arms behind his back.

Tressa gasped. Again her eyes rapidly flashed to the command console, searching for some means to interfere as a third man, rubbing his throat, staggered to his feet and aggressively advanced toward Banner. Lunging out with a booted kick to the man's groin, Banner sent him sprawling to the ground. Unable to break free, however, he remained defenseless as an enormous fourth man appeared on the scene.

Tressa watched in horror as the fourth man came forward and without hesitation delivered two sharp, crippling blows to Nick's midsection.

''Nooo!'' Tressa let out a distressed cry as Nick buckled and sank against his captors. Without second thought her hands flashed to the security system she'd noticed earlier. She selected the pad labeled *Manual* and pressed.

Nothing could have prepared her for what happened the moment the system engaged. What she had taken for a alarm turned out to be much, much more. She was instantly immobilized, every nerve ending ablaze, as if her entire body had been suddenly torched. Never had she suspected the human body could endure such pain, such agony.

Chapter Six

Suddenly released from his captors, Banner hit the deck hard, facedown. For a brief moment he simply lay against the cool surface of the decking, expecting at any moment to be jerked to his feet and exposed to a fresh tide of raw pain. When it didn't happen, he began gathering his dazed senses. His belly ached, he felt nauseated and it hurt just to breathe.

It didn't take more than a moment, however, to decide it was *pay back time*.

And that meant getting up.

Feeling as though he'd just been kicked in the gut by a *pakagodian,* Banner painfully rose to his knees. From there he staggered to his feet, stifling a groan against the searing pain that gripped his lungs and rib cage.

With his palms braced upon his knees, he fixed his attention on the simple act of dragging air into his deprived lungs and the excruciating pain that went with it.

The realization that his assailants were slumped on the ground forced his muddled brain into action. Nick straightened, frowning as he looked about. Collapsed about him were the limp, weakened bodies of four men, who only moments ago had been more than able to overpower him. Now they lay sprawled on the ground, faces contorted in anguish, one moaning incoherently.

''What the . . . devil?'' Instinctively, his eyes riveted on his ship.

The *Victorious*. There was only one logical reason for everyone lying about moaning at his feet when, in reality, it should have been him lying at their feet.

Quickly releasing the ship's seal on the main hatch, he charged through the entry, deactivating the unique defense system with a flick of a switch just inside the inner hatch. The resounding proximity alarms were still blaring their loud cadence as Banner's gaze frantically swept the cabin in search of Tressa's unconscious form.

He checked the bunk area first. Then, turning to face the cockpit, he discovered Tressa's slumped body on the floor in front of the pilot's seat. ''Tressa!'' Uttering a string of oaths she mercifully never heard, he flew to her side.

Tressa moaned in response. Nick. She could hear him, but he sounded so far away . . . so strange. And he was shouting at her. Why was he angry? Oh, she hurt.

''Tressa, can you hear me, babe?''

She moaned again and it sounded so foreign, almost as if it were someone else. He was at her side now. She could feel his light touch at her throat. Thank God he was there. Nick. She wanted to say his name . . . but couldn't form the word.

He was prying her hand open and muttering something about that damn sympathy stone.

Another moan escaped. Why did she hurt so bad?

''What the devil were you doing, Tressa?'' he shouted. Why did he sound so angry?

And then she felt herself being lifted up and carried as though she were a small child. He smelled so . . . good.

Every sensation was so oddly acute—touch, smell, hearing. She felt the coolness of a pillow against her heated cheek as she settled onto the bunk. Even in her stunned condition, Tressa knew instinctively it was his pillow, his bunk.

"Tressa, can you hear me?" Another involuntary moan burst through her wall of oblivion. "Dear God, Tressa, what the devil were you doing up here in the cockpit." he ranted. "This is exactly why I told you not to touch anything."

She felt his cool hand on her face. Every nerve ending was still ablaze, even the slightest touch was felt with painful exaggeration. She tried opening her eyes, but couldn't make her body obey even the slightest command. Another try and this time her lids fluttered open to meet Nick's deep sapphire gaze.

"Tress! Can you hear me? It's all right, honey. You're safe now. It's over."

Tressa squeezed her eyes shut again, "Nick . . . " her voice was little more than a broken whimper, "will . . . you please . . . stop . . . shouting."

Through slitted eyes she watched a grin spread across his face. "Tressa," he said more tenderly this time, "It's all over."

"You already said that."

She heard him chuckle. "I guess I did."

"Two or three times," she whispered. Opening her eyes futher, Tressa struggled to focus on his tormented face. Finally, she locked on. "Those men . . ." her whispered voice trailed off as she winced against the pain. "Had to do . . . something." In agony, she closed her eyes again.

"Shhh, we can talk later, Tress."

She felt him caress her face with a touch.

"Close your eyes, babe."

"Nick—"

"Shhhh."

"But—"

"Later, Tressa."

But she wanted to tell him about those men. She felt him arranging a blanket over her. At least he wasn't still shouting. Oh, her head hurt so bad.

He strode to the cockpit and deactivated the security sensors, silencing the resounding proximity alarms. Speculating about the men outside, he turned and headed for the main hatch. He could have sworn he recognized one of them.

Taking off across the landing field, Nick glided to a halt before the man he thought he recognized. With a nudge from the toe of his boot, he rolled the unconscious man onto his back.

Lee Bryant: one of his ex-partner's mercenaries. Dropping to one knee, Banner rapidly searched through Bryant's pockets, hoping for some clue as to what they were after. Checking the others in much the same manner, he found no hint of their motive.

Tressa. She had to be it. Especially since he wasn't carrying anything of value in the hold. The *why* eluded him.

Within thirty minutes the *Victorious* lifted for the long voyage ahead. One more stop, then on to Acacia.

He should never have allowed Loring to talk him into this little escapade. It not only had interrupted his plans, it sure as hell had brought an abrupt end to his idea of peace. Dammit. He'd had his future all mapped out; everything had been going smoothly.

What the hell did she think she was turning on, anyway? Nick's anger gradually ebbed, giving way to compassion and a twinge of gratitude. He couldn't ever remember a time when a woman had laid her life on the line for his sake. Without a doubt she'd spared him a lot of pain and suffering, if not actually saved his life. He cringed at the agony that lay yet ahead for her as a result of her heroics. The recovery was often as agonizing as the initial assault, and she still had a long way to go.

Six hours later Tressa awoke feeling as if her head was in a giant power vice. She couldn't have prevented the moan that escaped her if she'd tried.

"So, you're finally coming out of it. Just lie still and I'll get you something for the pain," came a familiar voice from somewhere nearby.

Wincing against the agony, Tressa moaned again and opened her eyes, only to squeeze them shut again. Her whole body throbbed, especially her head. Even the ends of her hair felt on fire.

"This will knock you out again," Nick said as he returned to her side. "I hate doing this to you, but at this point escape is the only way to beat it."

With that, Tressa felt a firm grip on her upper left arm, followed by a strange tingling sensation.

"I promise to do my best to help you through this, Tressa."

"I'm sorry," she gasped, closing her eyes.

"For what?"

"You told me not to touch anything in the cockpit. . . . "

Nick gently laid her arm back at her side. "Hush. Don't try to talk. Just relax and allow the medication to do its work."

Tressa nodded, too weak to do anything else. Feeling suddenly strange, she slowly lifted her lashes to find herself staring directly into Nick Banner's luminous blue eyes. Lowering her gaze, she emitted a sigh that was more moan than anything else. "Sapphire . . ." she breathed.

Banner knelt beside her bunk. "What?" He took hold of her hand.

Tressa blinked heavily. "How long . . ." she swallowed hard, "have I been asleep?"

Nick glanced down at the gold Rolex on his wrist. "About six hours now."

The watch had belonged to his great-great-grandfather and was technically an antique. As a boy, Nick had discovered it amid some of the family's keepsakes. Though he'd never voiced the interest he'd taken in it, the watch was suddenly presented to him on his seventeenth birthday. Eventually he'd modified it to accept his interplanetary lifestyle. And aside from a few scratches here and there and countless face-crystal changes, the watch still sparkled like new and was still as dependable as it had been for his great-great-grandfather.

"Are we in space yet?" Tressa asked.

"A little over five out of Port France."

"Ohhh . . ." She turned her head as a single tear slipped from the corner of her eye.

"I know the hell you're going through right now," he said softly.

Tressa managed a weak smile and quickly blinked back another tear. "Had I known the consequences, you might have been at the mercy of those men."

Banner offered a sympathetic grin. A long moment of silence passed as he continued to observe her closely. Under normal circumstances he knew exactly what to expect from the drug he'd just given her. The trouble was, he'd never seen it given to someone of her weight before. Having given her only half a dose, he wasn't sure if half was enough or still too much. He waited for the effect to kick in.

Loring would have his hide if he knew. Nick's head jerked up in surprise when Tressa emitted a soft giggle. She was peering at him with one eye closed. "There's three of yew." She frowned thoughtfully. "Now why is there three of yew?"

Stifling yet another giggle, she gave an unrefined snort. "It's bad enough shust being locked away with *one* of yew. I don't stand a rat's shance in h . . . oops!" She giggled again, placing her hand to her mouth.

Nick couldn't help his chuckle. Interesting; Loring's little angel had another side. Under different circumstances, he might be tempted . . .

72

"Wanna know a s-s-serect?" she slurred, looking up at him with dreamy eyes.

Nick indulged her. "Sure, Tressa." The drug was definitely kicking in—not only faster than he'd anticipated, but with an undeniable side effect.

Tressa started to raise up on her elbows but instantly fell backward onto the bunk in uncontrolled mirth. Her tousled hair splayed across his pillow. Several locks fell across her forehead.

"Ohhh, I feel sooo funny." With that she crooked her finger at him, and he dutifully bent his head.

"Ashually," Tressa began in a husky voice that was becoming more slurred by the minute, "this ishn't s-s-so bad afferall. I could rescue you again. Juss say when."

Her eyes suddenly became hooded, and she smiled wistfully. "Do you know, Capt'n Banner . . . *Ssrrrr,* you have the sestiest . . ." She frowned and tried again. ". . . Seshe-est . . ." Tressa closed her eyes and chuckled. "*Sex-ti-est* safar eyes I ever met?" Her profound statement was followed by a distinct hiccough that promptly sent her into another round of boisterous, unladylike laughter.

With one eyebrow raised, Nick listened with undivided interest as Tressa continued to ramble on about his physical attributes—mumbling more to herself than anyone else. "Y' juss canti'magin what those eyes do t' me. And that smile . . . Stars, when y' s-smile, my lil' heart skips so many beats that I . . ." Yawning, she left the sentence hanging and settled back against the bunk.

For a moment he thought she'd fallen asleep; then her eyes lifted slowly, silently searching his features. "And . . . yer hair, too." She lifted her hand and ran her fingers through his dark hair. "It feels s-so s-silky and soft, juss like it looks.

"And when y' talk," she purred, sliding her hand down his cheek and grazing a finger across his lips, "yer voice, it sounds like velvet and . . . and steel all swirred t'gether."

Tressa's voice was laden with desire, and Nick was sure

she didn't have the vaguest idea of what she was saying. Though unbidden as it was, it was a definite turn-on. He swore softly. The thoughts he was entertaining at the moment would shock the slippers off her. Damn, he shouldn't have agreed to do this.

". . . and that body, that gorgeous muscled body—all bronze like a . . . like a s-sun god . . . long legs poured into shnug-fittin' black trousers, huggin' every curve . . . and muscle they cover." Tressa paused, as though a wave of sleepiness had swept over her. "Leaves nothin' . . ." She yawned, finishing her sentence in the middle of it, "to the imashinashin."

Nick frowned at her last comment, mumbling beneath his breath as he glanced down at himself. What the hell did she mean by that?

A long moment of silence passed before Tressa made another effort to rise. Making it only as far as her elbows, her heavy lashes lifted seductively and she stared up at him with pure longing. "Did I ever tell y', yer eyes . . . they're like safars?"

"Yes," he answered tightly.

Tressa blinked heavily. "I did? Ohhhh."

He jerked his fingers through his dark hair. Would he survive this experience? Somehow he doubted it. What he wouldn't give right now to get his hands on Loring!

"Do y' want to hear my shecret?" she cooed, nailing him with a look of unadulterated passion.

"No!" he ground out. Grasping her by the shoulders, Nick pushed gently until her elbows buckled and she fell back onto the bunk. "Tressa," he began in a commanding voice that was beginning to sound hoarse, "I want you to lay back and *stop* talking. Besides, I doubt you're going to want to remember any of this."

Suddenly Tressa's expression sobered, "Are you mad at me?" Her slurred speech seemed to mock her sincerity. "I dint know what t' do. There were four of 'em . . ." She drew in a ragged sob, "and . . . and I couldn't shust . . ."

"Hush. It's over now. We can talk about it all later." He brushed a lock of hair from her brow. "Let go and quit fighting the medication." With that, Tressa closed her eyes, succumbing to the drug and the deep timbre of Nick's easy voice.

Banner remained at her side until he was sure she was out. Rising up off of his haunches, he felt the unfamiliar yet unmistakable sensation of heated cheeks. He'd never considered himself a modest man, and had never known a time when a woman had made him flush—including his first. Just why he'd found Tressa's appraisal so damned embarrassing, eluded him. Anyone else but her and he would have had no problem proving himself worthy of her praise. But with Tressa it was different. For one, he *couldn't* respond—period. Tressa was off limits. And two, under the circumstances it would be major advantage-taking. Even for him.

He just hoped she didn't remember any of this. It was bad enough that *he* would. *Snug-fitting trousers that left nothing to the imagination.* Hell, he'd been in one continual state of semi-arousal from the moment she'd first set foot aboard the ship.

For a mere half a second he contemplated changing into a pair of old baggy sweats. Upon second thought, he immediately blackballed the idea. There were only two ways to look at it: She either liked his snug pants or she didn't. If she did, why change? And if she didn't, who gives a damn?

"Help . . . please . . . somebody!" From behind a freight sled, a mixture of soft groans and pain-filled pleas drew the attention of a passing Port France security guard. With his help, three angry men emerged complaining of excruciating headaches and a relentless determination to find a person named Banner.

"What about Hansen?" one of them spoke up. "Where's Hansen?" It wasn't long before Jess Hansen's lifeless body was pulled from behind a maintenance platform.

An hour later, three men entered the local port bar, feeling and looking only slightly better than when they were first found.

Chapter Seven

Sam DeVries stepped through the door first. He was the big man who'd bruised Nick's ribs. "I'm through playing games. Now it's serious," he said, wincing against a stab of pain.

Lee Bryant was right behind DeVries. "I don't know how the hell he did it, but when I find him . . ."

"I tell ya, he's on his way to Acacia," James Catlin added. "If he's got the girl, I'll lay you odds that's where he's headed."

"He's got one more stop," Bryant interjected, "and I say we put a tracer onboard. There'll be no guessing, just following." He shrank against another agonizing stab of pain.

DeVries strode insolently to the bar, ordered a drink, and then turned to Bryant. "And I know just who to contact to get a tracer onboard. Banner wants to play rough," he said reaching for his ale, "then rough it . . . will . . . be!"

Mat Kelly sat alone at a corner table, silently observing the haggard trio as they filed through the door. "I hate to interrupt your party, boys . . . but would one of you mind telling me where you've been? You were supposed to have been back here two hours ago." A long moment of silence followed as he slowly assessed the three bedraggled men. "So, where's the girl?"

Without answering, DeVries took a large gulping swallow of brew. Turning to face Kelly, he wiped his mouth with the back of his hand. "Hansen's dead," he said, as though discussing the weather, but his grim look belied his casualness.

At that point Catlin took over. "Never had a chance," he began, explaining to the best of his ability what had happened.

Kelly's eyes narrowed. "Wait just a minute; run that by me one more time. You mean to tell me I sent four men to come back with one little girl and instead you all end up in shipping crates, and one *dead*? I don't like sloppy work. You see," he continued. "sloppy work leads to trails, and trails lead to Sinclair."

Lee Bryant instantly crossed the room with predatory swiftness. "No! *You* wait just a minute, Kelly," he growled, slamming his mug of ale down onto the table. "Nobody told us we'd be dealing with some kind of stunning device!" He gritted his teeth against another stab of pain. "We'll get the girl. Our way! And Banner's going to regret the day he was born."

Kelly rose to his feet, meeting Bryant eye to eye. "What you do with Banner is your business . . . *after* you get the girl."

The cabin lights had been dimmed, and slowly reality came back to Tressa in small doses as she recognized the cockpit of the *Victorious*.

Only the soft lighting from the control panel illuminated the cabin, casting fluttering reflections upon the ceiling. Other than the constant hum of the drives and the steady hiss of the ventilation, all was quiet.

The last thing she remembered was intolerable pain. No, the last thing she remembered was . . . was sapphire. Sapphire? Shreds of memory rose to the surface, only to vaporize into nothingness.

Frowning, Tressa tested her strength, slowly raising up on one elbow as she glanced around the cabin. Nick was asleep in the pilot's seat, his back to her, his chin resting on his chest and his long legs stretched out before him. A twinge of remorse washed over her. How long had she had his bunk?

Tressa eased herself into a sitting position and, from there, stood. The intense pain she remembered had dwindled to a mere dull throbbing.

Glancing at Nick again, the thought of waking him to offer back his bunk crossed her mind. But she quickly banished the notion. Not after the last time she'd tried waking him. Once was enough. She'd deal with the guilt of his stiff neck anytime over that experience. Right now all she wanted was to stand beneath the soothing hot spray of a shower and, quietly withdrawing one of her travel pacs from under the bunk, Tressa padded barefooted to the lav.

Having to lay the seat back down on the commode before she could use it only served as another startling reminder of exactly whose ship she was on, and the intimacies of sharing such tight quarters. With every turn she was becoming more aware of this man and his domain.

Tressa was working at the delicate buttons of her jumpsuit when his pointed warning hit her. *Given the lack of privacy in general around here, along with my lack of modesty, I'd say we have a potential problem.* Tressa remembered his words with precise clarity. There was a wealth of possibilities in that statement alone. One thing for sure, it left little doubt as to how he managed in tight quarters such as the lav. He probably left the privacy panel open, or something equally obnoxious.

Standing in nothing more than her lavender high-cut panties, Tressa eyed the spigot warily, wondering what magic it would take to get it working. Within seconds she had it figured out and was stepping out of her remaining underthings and into the shower. The soothing spray was relaxing, and Tressa luxuriated beneath its soft, steady warmth for a few brief minutes before finally reaching for her cleanser, its heady fragrance adding to her bliss. After rinsing Tressa pressed another pad, and warm jets of air shot at her from all directions, blow-drying her entire body in a matter of minutes.

Tressa dressed quickly in an ivory-colored gown and emerged from the lav. A glance toward the cockpit told her that Nick had changed positions, yet still appeared to be sleeping. Silently padding across to the galley, she took a seat on the small lounge in front of the observation window. There, clasping her arms about her legs, she drew her knees up beneath her chin and let her mind reflect on the events of the past two days—in particular, this disturbing fascination she had with Nick Banner.

Having long denied that she might be the type that was fascinated by dangerous men, Tressa thought she'd outgrown her girlish attraction to him. But there was just no getting around it; the mere thought of him put butterflies in her stomach.

Between his distinctive, rich voice and his luminous blue eyes, there was no denying he was handsome enough to charm and literally *take* any woman he desired.

And he was just unscrupulous enough to do so, she quickly reminded herself.

One thing for sure: the girls at LorTech, with their batting eyelashes, were living proof of the intoxicating effect he always had on the fairer sex. They giggled like schoolgirls, making total fools of themselves whenever Nick was waiting for a shipment to be processed.

But what tormented her more than anything was the clouded memory of a recent dream in which she had made some highly provocative statements to Nick . . . or was it a dream? Her memory, though foggy, was enough to cause an unwelcome heated blush to her cheeks.

Searching for answers, Tressa tried to remember the events that had occurred after Nick had left the ship: the proximity alarm, the men outside, the magnification device. And when she saw Nick in deep trouble she remembered reaching for the touch pad on the defense system. And then . . . excruciating pain.

Tressa's memory from that point on was aimless and jumbled. She vaguely recalled Nick at her side, hearing his voice but remembering nothing of what was said. Fragments of memory drifted up to tease her, only to disappear again.

The word *sapphire* surfaced several times, and Tressa wasn't sure anymore what was reality and what was illusion.

"Beautiful, isn't it?" It was a deep, velvet-edged voice that jolted her from her thoughts. The same voice that only moments ago she'd decided had the natural ability to melt even the most frigid barriers of resistance.

Tressa drew a startled breath and turned to see the very subject of her thoughts lounging in the doorway, as though he'd been standing there for some time. Her traitorous pulse leapt at the very sight of him.

"Yes, it's incredible! I don't think I could ever tire of such a view."

Nick chuckled. "Nor I."

His jaw was darkened by a couple of days' growth and he'd obviously just raked his hand through his dark hair. Tressa felt a sting of remorse at the look of deep tiredness around his eyes. He probably hadn't slept more than a few brief hours in the last two days. And in the chair, at that.

Suddenly conscious of exactly where her gaze had traveled, Tressa dragged her eyes from the black trousers straining over taut thighs and quickly returned her gaze to the viewport. Hot color stained her cheeks as she tried blocking out the memory of something about snug-fitting . . . Oh, dear, she couldn't have said such a thing. Could she?

Tressa felt his eyes on her back. She didn't dare turn to face that lazy smile of his—or was it a *knowing* smile? It didn't matter, though, for he crossed the room and sat down next to her on the lounge.

Seeing the gleam of interest in his eyes, it was obvious he'd already noticed her flushed cheeks.

"So, how's the noggin?"

"Much better. Thank you." Tressa hid behind a warm smile of forced composure, but it was the way he gazed at her that made her breath catch in her throat.

"Good. You gave me quite a scare for awhile, you know that?"

Adjusting his posture slightly, Nick suddenly sobered and froze. He was nursing badly bruised, if not fractured, ribs; she was positive of it.

"And how about you? I saw what that man did to you," she responded, eyeing him sympathetically.

Nick shrugged. "I've crawled away from worse."

She'd just bet he had, too. Under the surface there was a barely leashed wildness about him, but it was the tender and compassionate side that confused her the most.

A long moment of silence passed before Banner finally spoke again. His voice was soft and compelling. "Do you understand *now* the importance of following instructions, Tressa?

She swallowed. "Yes, but . . ."

"But nothing! You could have been killed by that device you so innocently engaged. In fact, that is exactly how I expected to find you when I first came onboard."

Her head jerked up at the impact of his words.

"Seriously, Tressa," he continued, "some people don't live through the effects of the Ripper."

"The rip-per?" she repeated, slowly testing the syllables. "But I thought I was turning on an alarm to scare them away, and stop them from beating you."

"I understand. But, it turned out to be much more than just an alarm, didn't it? You zapped literally everyone, yourself included, within a designated radius of the ship, lady. Thank God no one else was caught in that little fiasco.''

Tressa's eyes widened. ''Then . . . I could have killed you, or maybe even one of those men?''

Nick gave a snort. ''Everyone was still breathing when I last saw them . . . not that I give a damn.''

Tressa frowned. ''I wonder what they wanted.''

''I don't know. It's hard telling.'' He hesitated, then grinned. ''You sorta took care of 'em before I had a chance to find out.''

She felt her face flush again. ''I'm sorry. I know you told me not to touch anything . . .''

''You're damn right I did, and more than once too. But we'll discuss walking the plank for disobedience later. You hungry?''

''No thank you. The way my stomach feels right now, I'm afraid it would come right back up.''

Banner nodded knowingly. ''I've got just the thing for that. You wait right here.'' He rose to his feet and headed for the kitchenette along the aft wall.

It was obvious Nick was covering pain. Actually, he was doing a valiant job of it, too, but Tressa wasn't fooled for an instant. She'd been observing him ever since the first time he froze and his voice caught in the middle of a sentence. She'd noticed each time he fought a grimace, was keenly aware of each time his stomach muscles tightened in protest to a change in positions, each time his breath hissed softly through clenched teeth.

Tressa was also perceptive enough to know that her compassion and sympathy would neither be welcome nor appreciated . . . but taken as pity.

''Nick?''

''Yeah?''

''Could I ask you something?''

''Fire away,'' he said, taking a small container from the shelf.

A puzzled frown crossed her face. What she really wanted to ask was "What's a plank?" She had been troubled by it ever since he'd made the statement. However, half afraid to find out, she proceeded onto her next question. "Well . . . since you were knocked unconscious by the Ripper, I was just wondering how you were able to turn it off?"

"I never said I was knocked unconscious," he offered casually, stirring two spoonfuls of crystals from the container into a mug of hot water.

"You mean you weren't?" She twisted around to stare at him in disbelief. "How come? I mean . . ."

"Simple. I'm protected against it's effects." He filled a second cup with coffee.

"Ohhh . . ." she breathed, still wanting to ask why and how and a million other questions that were buzzing around in her mind right now. But before she could launch her next question Nick returned to her side and handed her one of the mugs. It was filled with something orange.

"What's this?" she asked, wrinkling her nose as she sniffed at the rising steam.

"Don't ask. Just drink it . . . all of it," he ordered, setting down his own steaming mug of coffee. "I tried not to make it too hot, so you should be able to drink it right down."

Tressa eyed him warily. "This isn't going to make me feel all funny inside, is it? 'Cause if it is, I'm not drinking one drop. Not one single drop!"

Banner stared at her, then burst out laughing. "No, Tressa, I promise it won't make you spaced. Just drink it."

Tressa wasn't at all sure she liked the way he laughed—as if he was laughing at something she should know about but didn't. The truth was, she didn't even want to explore the possibilities of what he'd suddenly found so entertaining.

Making a grimace, Tressa hesitantly took a tiny sip. "Y-u-k . . . this is awful! This is supposed to make me feel *better?''* Her voice was as distorted as the face she was making.

"Quit stallin', Tressa, just drink it. Plug your nose if you have to."

Taking the cup from her hands, he raised it to her lips. "Now drink."

The last two-worded directive brooked no argument, and after a moment of gathering her courage Tressa took another sip of the warm, acrid liquid.

"All of it, Irish, not just a couple of sips."

She took another swallow obediently, her eyes held by his.

"More. Trust me, the tea will help that queer feeling in your belly."

With a sigh of resignation, Tressa tossed the vile brew down her throat. "Ohhhh . . ." she moaned. "Now I *am* going to be sick."

Nick grinned. "In that case," he said with a nod toward the doorway, "the head's just across the cabin."

Tressa cast him a baleful eye. "You're finding this all quite amusing, aren't you?"

The grin disappeared. "To the contrary. I find no amusement in this at all. What I find is a little girl who's just learned a dangerous lesson on the importance of following rules."

He brushed her cheek with the back of his knuckles; then, with an exhausted sigh, he stood and walked to the viewport. Bending his head, he lit up a slender cigar, releasing a stream of smoke into the air.

Tressa sat rigidly still, staring at his wide back. "So, do I take it we're going to discuss the *plank* now?"

"The what?" He turned to face her.

Tressa cleared her throat. "The plank. You said we'd discuss walking the plank later."

She had absolutely no idea what a plank was, but for the past ten minutes her mind had been working overtime, concocting all sorts of barbaric versions of *illegal* torture devices. One scenario after another had been played out mentally, bringing her to one major conclusion: Whatever the plank was, she damn well wasn't going to walk it.

"Ah, yes . . . the plank," he said, grinning down at her. Shaking his head, he added, "Never a dull moment with you around, is there, Irish?"

"And just what's that suppose to mean?"

"Simply that you sure have a way of takin' the doldrums out of a routine cargo run."

Tressa folded her arms and, after a few moments of silence, attacked the question again. "Well . . ." she asked, too preoccupied to notice that her queasiness was all but gone.

"Well what?"

"The plank!" she repeated sharply.

Nailing her with his gaze, Banner took a slow drag from his cigar, inhaling deeply. "That, Irish, depends upon you," he answered with staid calmness, allowing the smoke to escape with his words.

His bold, steady stare was unnerving, yet Tressa thought she saw his mouth quirk. "Does that mean you're not going to make me walk it?"

"Not unless you think I should."

Tressa was sure, this time, that she saw his mouth twitch, and her back stiffened in response. While she'd been worrying over the plank, he'd been teasing her. His eyes were glittering with suppressed laughter. Though she wanted to be mad at him, just recalling a few of her conjured-up scenarios of punishment brought forth a giggle, and resentment gave way to infectious laughter.

Nick regarded her with amusement at first; then his low, throaty laughter joined hers. "I take it you're feelin' better?"

"Yes. I am." She had needed a few brief moments of diversion to keep her from tossing up the vile mixture he'd made her drink—a moment of interference he'd been most willing to provide.

"Scoundrel," she murmured, stifling another giggle.

He shot her a sharp glare. "What was that?"

"You heard me." She giggled, noting the amusement still lurking in his fire-blue gaze.

That amusement, however, soon turned to pure devilment. "Do you know what I do with insubordinate crew members, Tressa?" There was a soft huskiness in his tone now, and this exciting new twist sent a shiver down her spine. It was like playing with something very dangerous, and a small part of her found it exciting.

"Of course I do. You make them walk the plank." She bit her lip to stifle another giggle and waited for his rejoinder, finding the playful sparring intriguing.

"Ah, but that's only the beginning, Irish," he advised her softly, watching her closely as he drew on his cigar.

Chapter Eight

Tressa found his arrogance enticing, the silken thread of warning in his voice, captivating. Like a moth to the flame, she was drawn. "Oh, come now," she teased, urging on the game, "surely it can't get much worse than 'walking the plank.' "

"Somehow I don't think you *really* want to know."

"Yes I do. Tell me," she begged, pretending not to understand.

"Very well," he said, returning to her side and sitting down, his large frame seemingly taking up the entire seat. Tressa thought of pulling back when his leg pressed intimately along the length of hers.

Banner lowered his voice, being purposefully mysterious. "For minor violations," he began softly, "I make them walk the plank first, then I truss 'em and toss 'em in the hold for two, sometimes even four days," he said with an air of cool detachment.

"Oh, that sounds perfectly awful. I suppose it's very

dark and scary in the hold?'' She was barely able to keep the laughter from her voice.

''Very,'' he said with quiet emphasis.

''And cold?''

''Extremely.''

''And let me guess—you only give them water to drink and crumbs to eat, right?''

''Not even that.'' His tone remained cold and exact, but Tressa didn't miss the amusement in his eyes.

''And that's just for minor violations?''

''And if that isn't enough, I have my own version of keel hauling.''

''Keel hauling?'' She couldn't imagine what that could be and wasn't sure she wanted to ask.

Shaking her head in mock disbelief, she released a heavy sigh. ''And just when I was beginning to think that maybe you were a gentleman beneath the rough exterior.''

Nick hesitated, measuring her for a moment. ''I never once said anything about being a gentleman, Tressa, and I suggest you keep that in mind.''

A warning cloud settled on his features, the amusement gone from his eyes, as was the gentle camaraderie. For an instant Tressa wasn't sure if she had just been warned or threatened.

Nick reached for the mug of coffee and skillfully changed the subject. ''So, tell me a little more about yourself.'' The game had been brought to a halt.

Having found his playful high-handedness exhilarating, she wondered what had brought the teasing to such an abrupt end.

''Actually,'' she said with a shrug, ''there's really not much to tell.''

''Is that right?'' His lips twitched. ''I find that hard to believe. I'll bet there's lots to tell. What are you good at? Word has it Jonathan's grooming you to take over Lor-Tech.''

Tressa laughed. "Not hardly." She released a heavy sigh. "Actually, it's a toss up between LorTech and medicine. I've taken some premed classes, and for the past two years I've volunteered my time at Port Ireland's medical facility. And yet . . . I've always wanted to work at my father's side."

Nick stopped his mug halfway to his lips. "I see. And now you're not so sure that's what you want anymore?"

"Oh, I love LorTech, don't get me wrong. It's just that . . . well, I feel so inadequate. You know what I mean? Take this trip, for instance; it doesn't take any brains or special aptitude to pass clearance on a high-security parcel. All it takes is the right security code. Any robo could do that."

"Maybe," he agreed. "But in order to hold a high-security position there is a certain amount of responsibility—in particular, free thinking, and that's where the robo falls short. You have a lot ahead of you yet to learn, Tressa; don't judge your worth so soon.

"So you're interested in medicine and LorTech. Anything else?"

"Well, I'm good with animals. My father used to say that I had a natural gift of taming wild things." She looked away for a moment, then turned soft eyes on him. "You see, we used to live right at the edge of a forest. I remember always finding something that, in my opinion, either needed taming or doctoring." Tressa laughed softly. "I also remember always getting into trouble for wandering too far from the house."

"Hmmm . . ." His eyes glittered with amusement. "You had a hard time following rules even then."

Before she could produce an appropriate response Nick changed the subject again. "Feel like eating anything yet?"

"Oh, please don't even mention food. Maybe a little later."

He nodded. "Well, if you don't mind, I'm starved." And with that he turned for the froster and selected two com-

90

mercially prepared meals for himself.

"By the way, in case you're wondering, I keep standard hours onboard. Gets too confusing, trying to keep track of the time at each port."

A long moment of silence passed before Tressa finally spoke up. "Nick?"

"Yeah?"

"What's Echo like?"

"Echo? What put you on that subject?" he asked, placing his selections into the warmer.

Tressa shrugged. "Oh, I don't know; just wondered."

He refilled his mug and returned to her side. "Echo's hard to describe. Let's see; the ports of entry aren't much different from any other port. But once you leave civilization it's another story. For one, the flora and fauna are like nothing you've ever seen before. Some beautiful and some not, but almost everything deadly in one form or another."

Tressa shuddered. "Isn't there anything cute and cuddly, or is it all sharp teeth, claws, and poison?"

Nick's lips twitched. "In the jungles you might find a few cute and cuddlies, but unfortunately, Tressa, they also have sharp teeth and claws. The flora is also different from anything I've ever encountered before. Trails have to be treated with Ranite or the undergrowth will end up growing back in less than two days. Never seen anything like it. Then, of course, there's the Echo swamp version of a butterfly."

"Oh, yes!" Tressa's eyes widened. "That's that bug with a six-foot wing span, isn't it? Even on the holotape they're spectacular. Their colors almost appear iridescent."

"They *are* iridescent. Beautiful to look at, but I'm afraid deadly to touch."

Tressa sighed. "Yes, everything seems to be deadly on Echo. Is there nothing good to say?"

"Sure, there's the new fuel source they're extracting right now. And . . ." He grinned, showing perfect white teeth. "Echo's noted for the best ale in the Sector. I won't bother telling you what it's made from."

Tressa looked at him curiously. "Surely it can't be very good for you when it's made from a poison, Nick."

His roguish grin became even wider. "It's not."

Tressa shot him a sidelong glance and shook her head in mock reproof. Before long a soft tone from the warmer announced that his meal was ready.

Banner removed the platter from the warmer. "You have pets at home, Tressa?"

"No. Not anymore. I used to, when I was little. But with being away at school and all, it got to be too hard."

"I see." Banner nodded in understanding as he headed for the table with a food tray in each hand.

A long moment of silence passed between them as he claimed a seat and began sawing away at his Koji steak. Stuffing a bite into his mouth, he poked at the mound of parsos, the white rootlike vegetable that was commonly used in commercially prepared meals.

Tressa suddenly added, "Oh, I do have a small aquarium with a few fish."

Still chewing, Nick glanced up, halting his fork midway to his mouth. "Oh, yeah? What kind of fish?"

"Nothing really fancy; just a few roans."

"Roans, huh? I hear they're kinda hard to keep." He shoveled another forkful into his mouth.

"I don't seem to have any problem with them."

Nick reached for a crust of bread. "I'd say fish hardly fills the bill when you prefer cute and cuddlies."

Tressa laughed. "True."

As soon as he'd finished both meals, Nick rose from his seat, tossed the empty trays into the recycler, and stepped out of the galley. When he reentered his holstered gun was slung over his shoulder, and he had a small metal box in his hand. Stopping first to refill his mug, he turned and made his way to the table, where he set the box aside, removed the gun from the holster, and began working the action to assure himself that the weapon was empty before taking it apart.

The rasp of metal brought Tressa's head around, and she watched as Banner released the trigger mechanism. His very actions, and the grace in which he handled the gun alone, spoke of his ease with violence.

"Nick."

He was wiping the weapon down with an oily rag. "Yeah?" His eyes remained on the gun.

"Do you anticipate more trouble?"

"Not necessarily," he mumbled. "I just don't like being caught unprepared."

Tressa was silent for a thought-filled moment. "I don't think I could ever kill *anything.*"

Banner stopped his work long enough to hold an instant of eye contact with her, then returned to his task. "Sometimes guns have their place, Tressa," he offered with quiet emphasis.

"I understand that. I'm just saying I don't think I could actually pull the trigger and take someone's life."

Holding the bore of the weapon up to the light, a half smile crossed Banner's face. "Killing someone isn't exactly something you get used to. But I can assure you, if your life depended upon it, you'd do it. And if you were smart, you'd aim to *kill.*"

An oily metallic odor permeated the air as Tressa continued to watch him work. Pondering his words, several moments of silence passed before she spoke again.

"Nick?"

"Yes, Tressa." His tone held the faintest hint of mockery.

"Just what is a ripper? I mean, I don't think I've ever heard of such a device."

Nick's lips twitched. He placed a drop of lubricant onto a moving part. "There's only one place I know of you can get your hands on one."

Why didn't that surprise her? "Well, just exactly what

is it?'' she probed, becoming annoyed at his obsession with the gun and vague answers.

Releasing a heavy sigh, Banner stopped working and lifted his head. ''Ripper,'' he said, ''R-I-P-P-R, is an acronym for Radial Impulse Primary Protector Relay.''

''Impulse Primary Protector Relay,'' she repeated slowly. ''Ripper. That's a good name for it.''

''It's an extra-fancy stunner, an electronic watch dog,'' he said flatly, returning his attention to the gun and sliding something home with a solid click. ''And it bites.''

''You don't have to tell me,'' Tressa added ruefully.

Banner chuckled, tested the trigger mechanism, then picked up the cloth again. ''And you're damn lucky you came out of it as easily as you did, Irish. Some people don't, you know.'' Without looking up , he continued methodically wiping down the weapon. Finally he laid the gun and rag aside and reached for his mug of coffee.

''And I suppose it's illegal?''

He grinned. ''You might say that.''

Tressa was silent for a long thought-filled moment. ''I'm just curious about one thing, Nick. How come you weren't affected by it?''

Nick chuckled softly, ''You're sure full of a lot of questions, aren't you?''

Tressa shrugged, ''I was just wondering.''

Grinning, Banner slid her a sidelong look of skepticism. Returning his attention to the gun, he tested the action. ''The answer is,'' he began, ''I've got a micro implant at the base of my spine that protects me from the effects of the main system.''

''Then . . .'' she said thoughtfully, ''then when I turned on the Ripper you weren't affected by it at all?''

''No, darlin', not in the least.'' With the ease of proficiency, he tested the action once again.

''Are you also protected from someone else's Ripper?''

Mouth quirking, he finished reloading the weapon. ''No, just the unit that's been installed aboard this ship,'' he said, slipping the gun back into the holster and tossing it over his shoulder. "If all you had to do was get a micro, everyone would be running around with one and it wouldn't be much of a defense system then, would it?" Flashing her an irresistibly devastating grin, he picked up the cleaning kit, turned and headed for the main cabin.

Within moments he was back at her side. "Come 'ere. I have something to show you." Reaching for her hand, he helped her to her feet.

Tressa obediently followed as Nick headed out of the galley. She waited while he opened the inner hatch to the ship's hold. With a hiss the door slid open, and interior lighting sparked to life the instant he stepped over the threshold. "Well, come on."

Tressa followed, playfully eyeing him with suspicion, not missing his grimace as he gingerly lowered himself to one knee.

"Ohhhh . . ." she breathed, peering over his shoulder into an open crate.

Banner reached in and gently lifted a golden ball of fur that had been tightly curled up in a bed of shredded rags. Tenderly cradling the animal in his arms, he rose to his feet and turned to Tressa. "Didn't you say you liked pets—especially the soft and cuddly kind?"

"Yes. How beautiful. What is it?"

"He's a Lyrin Desert Cat. Name's TiMar."

"Oh Nick, he's precious."

Nick chuckled. "Don't let *him* hear you say that. He thinks he's ferocious."

Tressa looked at Nick expectantly, hesitating for a moment before asking, "May I pet him?"

"Better yet, want to hold him?" There was genuine warmth in Nick's smile as he transferred the squinting, sleepy ball of fur into Tressa's waiting arms. She laughed with delight at the soft mewing sounds TiMar made in protest.

TiMar's sleepy eyes popped open the instant he realized

Nick was no longer holding him.

"Just look at his long eyelashes," Tressa exclaimed, stroking his silky coat. "Oh, Nick . . . he's so soft."

"Um. Why don't we go back in and sit down?" With his hand resting firmly at the small of Tressa's back, Nick gently guided her back into the galley.

No sooner had she sat down when TiMar proceeded to arrange himself on her lap. Curling into a ball, he wrapped his long, fluffy tail neatly about his head, shielding his eyes. Only once did he peek out from behind the furry plume to inspect Tressa; then, yawning, he settled back down.

Tressa's eyes widened in astonishment. "Nick, his teeth!"

"Yeah. I've got a nice scar where he sank those teeth into my arm."

"He bit you?"

Banner shook his head. "It happened the night I rescued him."

"From what?"

"Bunch of drunks in a port bar. At the time, he had no reason to trust me anymore than the rest of them."

"Poor little thing."

"Who? Him or me?" he said with a wink.

Tressa laughed gently. "Why, *him,* of course." Glancing back down at TiMar, she took a moment to observe him more closely. His size was only slightly larger than a Terran house cat's, but that was where the similarity ended. The color of honey, his coat was thick and velvety, and Tressa absently buried her fingers up to the knuckles in its satiny depth. His elongated face ended in a flat black leathery snout, and his enormous round eyes appeared to be almost too big for his face.

TiMar's tail was long and feathery and golden in color, gradually darkening to black at the very tip. Four long furry black legs ended in lethal-looking feet. They reminded Tressa of bird feet. Three toes pointed forward and one pointed back, each toe flaunting a dangerous claw. Though soft and furry, judging from his feet and teeth, TiMar was definitely equipped to take care of himself.

"You two seem to be hitting it off quite well," Nick said upon entering the galley.

"Yes, I think he likes me. Oh, Nick, he's so sweet."

"Yeah, the little guy keeps me company," he said. "I'm beginning to believe you just might have some special talent with animals, after all. TiMar's not one to take to strangers. In fact, I hesitated bringing him out for that reason."

"But I'm glad you did. As you can see, we're doing just fine."

He chuckled and shrugged dismissively. "Well, I thought his presence might help break some of the boredom around here for you."

Tressa laughed. "Boredom? What boredom?"

"Don't forget, we still have three weeks ahead of us yet. TiMar just might help fill those hours for you."

Tressa gave TiMar a squeeze. "Thank you."

"You're welcome." Amusement lit his eyes as he crossed the room with that easy gate. The man was magnificent without even trying. In doing nothing more than simply walking across the cabin, he had her full wide-eyed attention.

Nick stopped before the froster and removed a bottle of Echo Extra Dark. Discarding the cap, he hesitated. "I don't suppose you drink, do you?" His masculine gaze left her uncomfortable.

"No, thank you."

Nodding, he released an audible breath. "I didn't think so." He turned and headed for the door. "Smart girl," she heard him mumble softly as he rounded the corner.

Before long the cabin lights dimmed, with the exception of those in the galley. Yawning, Tressa glanced at the chronometer, mounted above the observation window. The time read ten-forty.

Nick had been totally up-front with his comments about

the lack of privacy in order to better prepare her for shipboard life. Yet somehow Tressa had a funny feeling she wasn't quite prepared for the reality of it.

Technically, she had already spent her first night onboard the ship. But remembering nothing of it, tonight seemed like her first, and a sudden wave of anxiety swept over her.

Rising to her feet, Tressa gently placed TiMar on the seat beside her, then made her way to the door. Entering the main cabin, she glanced in the direction of the cockpit and saw Nick sprawled out in the command seat. His hands were clasped behind his head, and his long legs were stretched out, crossed at the ankles and propped against the bulkhead. A rainbow of tiny lights winked on and off from the command console, and watching him stare out into the endless night, Tressa had the distinct feeling that this was a familiar post for him. Retrieving one of her travel pacs from beneath Nick's bunk, she disappeared into the lav.

Several long minutes later, she timidly emerged, wearing a liquid-soft sleeping gown—one she suddenly wished she hadn't brought. What was she thinking?

Dashing to the berths, Tressa climbed the small ladder to the upper bunk and quickly slid under the covers. Within minutes TiMar joined her in one agile leap from the deck.

"Well, hello, little guy. Who invited you?"

"I forgot to tell you: TiMar has a bad habit of sleeping on the bunks." Within seconds, Nick was at her side and reaching up to take TiMar off.

"He's okay, Nick. Really."

"You sure? He can really be a pest if you let him."

"He's just fine," Tressa assured him, giggling as the cat nestled down by her feet. "See? Already he's made himself comfortable. I honestly don't mind if he sleeps up here."

Banner couldn't help but think of just how comfortable he'd be up there, too, and had a most improper suggestion on the tip of his tongue. He settled, instead, for simply telling her to sleep well and that he'd see her in the morning.

Striding back to the cockpit, Banner punched a red-lit indicator, then again assumed his sprawled position. He was exhausted from the events of the past twenty-four hours and, with hands interlocked behind his head, he welcomed the tranquility of the moment.

He'd worked hard, very hard, over the last few years, building up the dependable reputation of Banner Enterprises. One of the sweet benefits had been landing a service contract with LorTech Equipment that made him their first choice.

He remembered the first day he'd laid eyes on Tressa, a little over six years ago. Banner grinned at the thought of what a little twit she had been back then. It had been only recently that he had begun to see more of her, catching glimpses of her drifting in and out of the shipping department. Although he couldn't keep his eyes off her, she always seemed totally unaware that he even existed; a new experience for him, and one that immediately stirred his interest and competitive nature.

He guessed her to be about nine to ten years younger then himself. Tressa was pretty, but he'd known prettier women without being drawn to them like this. No, it was more than that; there was something about her expressive brown eyes that seemed to draw him into their depths.

Actually, everything about her interested him. She was different than the rest, and he was beginning to find her too intriguing for his own peace of mind.

Remembering the doubts he'd experienced when Jonathan first had approached him about this mission, Banner now firmly believed that there had been good reason to question Jon's wisdom. The minute he'd walked out of Loring's office, he knew he'd made a mistake. Something had told him then that this entire trip was going to be nothing but one long stress-filled experience. The ship was just too small to be sharing it with anyone, let alone a woman he couldn't touch.

Bending his head, Nick lit up a cigar and inhaled deeply. And yet . . . there weren't many women he knew, if any, that would have tried rescuing him, as Tressa had.

From there Nick's thoughts easily moved on to how soft she had looked a moment ago, having glimpsed her dashing from the lav to the bunk in that silky gown. The liquid-soft material clung to her body flawlessly, outlining her feminine attributes in exquisite detail. Though he had only seen her reflection in the viewport, Nick was sure he hadn't missed one luscious item of interest. He found himself wondering if Loring was aware of exactly what his little angel had packed to wear on the trip. Somehow he doubted it, and secretly wondered what other interesting little surprises she had in store. A corner of his mouth rose at the prospect.

Aware of his body's rising interest, Nick tamped his thoughts. Perhaps a cold shower was in order, if he had no more control than this. Seeing her dashing across to the bunk had been his undoing.

God help him, he wanted her.

An hour passed before Nick finally rose from the command seat and made his way to his bunk. From her even breathing he was sure Tressa was asleep. As though in mockery, TiMar lazily lifted his head and peered at him through contented sleep-drugged eyes. The little cat was curled up in Tressa's embrace, and Nick eyed him with pure envy as he stripped off his shirt and tossed it in a heap near the foot of the bunk. Next his boots and socks were added to the pile.

Reaching for his trousers, his hands stilled on the fastenings when he noticed TiMar still watching him. "What are you lookin' at?" he whispered harshly with a hostile glare. With a muttered oath, he flipped open the fastening studs of his trousers, and they, too, joined the collection.

Banner rolled into his bunk, turning his face to the outer hull, reminding himself that Tressa was just another job, a mission for Jonathan and nothing more. Just another woman passing through his life.

Twenty minutes elapsed before he restlessly turned onto his back. Wide awake, with a hard knot centering in his groin, Nick Banner lay in the darkness. Staring up at the bunk above him, he groaned inwardly at yet another two and a half weeks of *this*.

Chapter Nine

The morning of the third day, Nick awoke to the aroma of coffee in the air. A nice bonus, he thought, closing his eyes again and inhaling the freshly brewed coffee.

What time was it, anyway? A glance at the digital chronometer mounted into the wall of the command console told him it was 09:14. How the devil had he slept so late, and how'd she manage to get up without waking him? But then, it was really no mystery; he couldn't quit thinking long enough last night to get much sleep.

Finally sitting up, he yawned and reached for his trousers. Pulling them on, he fastened all but the top stud, then crossed the cabin barefoot to poke his head in the door of the galley. '''Morning.''

Tressa looked up. "Well, good morning." She was smiling and radiant . . . and how could anyone be so damned cheerful in the morning? Hell, even her coffee smelled better than his own.

"I sorta slept in." Nick raked a hand though his hair.

Tressa's eyes lit up with amusement. "Well, isn't that

part of the privilege of being captain?''

He gave a snort. ''Not hardly. So, how was your first official night onboard the *Victorious*.'' His voice was still husky with sleep.

''Never woke once.'' Lifting her mug for emphasis, she asked, ''I made a pot of *fog lifter;* you want some?''

Nick rubbed the back of his neck. ''Sounds good.'' He started to turn away. ''Go ahead and pour me a mug. Uh . . . please.

''Glad somebody slept well last night,'' he muttered, as he entered the lav and, out of habit, left the privacy panel open. A moment passed before it registered that he was no longer the only one onboard. Swearing softly, he reached over, sliding the panel shut.

Up until now he hadn't thought much about discretion—with her sleeping off the effects of the Ripper and all. One thing for sure, having to remember modesty every time he turned around was going to make one hell of a long run out of the next couple of weeks.

Making his way from the lav, Nick passed the galley sporting no more than his black trousers and a towel thrown around his neck, which he clung to with both hands. Within moments he was back, fully dressed, the edges of his hair still damp from the water he'd tossed in his face.

Judging from Tressa's concerned look there was little doubt but that she'd seen it, the fresh bandage he'd just finished fiddling with. It was a good thing she hadn't seen the bandage he'd just taken off. Her eyes would have really grown round. Nick groaned inwardly, knowing that the fierce blows he'd taken the other night certainly hadn't helped matters. His painful midsection now bore two purple bruises. Thanks to the handiwork of Lee Bryant and his thugs. The only thing he couldn't figure, though, was why would Bryant be after Loring's daughter? What was the connection? And who was behind it, hiring Bryant to do the dirty work?

He knew it. Tressa was just dying to ask him something.

He could see it written all over her inquisitive little face. All he knew was, whatever she was about to say, it better not have anything to do with his injuries. He was in no mood to be explaining anything to anyone, much less her. Just one more reason to fuel his fire of contempt for Quint Kendyl. He groaned inwardly at his next thought. Just one more reason for regretting his decision to take Loring's little piece of baggage off-planet.

And then she smiled. Damn, she looked beautiful this morning. Too bad she was Loring's . . . the thought trailed off as quickly as it entered his mind.

"Here," she said, handling him a mug of freshly brewed coffee. "I thought you might enjoy a mug of the real stuff this morning rather than tea.

"Thanks."

Picking up her mug, Tressa took a tentative sip, then chattered on. " I found TiMar's cat food while I was rummaging around for the coffee. He was begging to eat, so I went ahead and fed him. I hope it was all right.

At that, Nick grinned. "I have no problem with you feeding him, but let me warn you. TiMar loves to eat and you're going to find that every time you enter this galley, he'll be right on your heels begging for something.

Tressa laughed. "I think I sort of suspected that. He appeared to be acting out of habit rather than impulse."

Nick nodded in agreement. "Oh, I can assure you he was. When he's not eating, he's sleeping. He's good for nothing when it comes right down to it."

At that they both laughed and once again Nick found himself drawn to the sound of Tressa's gentle laughter and radiant smile.

No doubt about it, Nick Banner was curiously intrigued by Tressa. She baffled him, to put it mildly. One minute she was practically baiting him with what appeared to be childlike innocence. The next minute, he'd catch her studying him with a look that spoke of untethered desire, an expression that was anything but childlike.

Banner was still finding her provocative assessment of his physical qualities most intriguing. Even though she'd been tranquilized that night, the way he saw it the drug had only surfaced thoughts that were already there. He couldn't help but wonder just how much passion there actually was hidden behind that cloak of innocence. One way or another, he vowed he'd find out without completely breaking his word to Loring.

"Don't worry; we'll come up with something to keep you outta trouble," he said upon reentering the galley.

After breakfast time passed quickly with small talk and laughter. Banner liked her, even felt surprisingly relaxed around her. Actually, they had been getting along quite well, including the times his sarcasm had surfaced.

Over coffee, Nick shared a few hair-raising stories of his adventures as a cargo pilot and thoroughly enjoyed her reactions to some of his favorite versions.

Tressa, too, shared a little about herself, explaining that she'd lived for a while on Sequoi. Banner knew the place; had been there once or twice on delivery. She smiled wistfully and gently blew steam from her mug. "I loved it there. That's where the lake is I was telling you about."

Banner lit a cigar and leaned back. "So, LorTech had its beginnings on Sequoi. Interesting."

"It was a wonderful place to live. I had the forest, the pond, my animals . . . what more could I have wanted?"

Nick leaned forward to flick a lump of ash off his cigar. "You were nine when you came to live on Terra Four?"

The next two days went by without incident. Tressa settled into shipboard life, and Nick even taught her how to play a couple of games. One of them, Justice, was a miniature version of a holograph game found in most port bars. To his surprise, Tressa caught on easily. She even beat him once or twice.

"Better take a seat, Tress; we'll be makin' the jump out of hyperspace shortly." His mouth quirked with amusement. "You were unconscious when we slipped into it, so you missed out on the stimulating sensation of nausea that comes with transition."

Tressa stared at him in bewilderment. "Are you saying I'm going to be sick? If you think that I'm going to drink any more of your concoctions, you can just forget it."

He flashed her that famous Banner grin. "As we enter Shaiel's atmosphere," he continued, "I'll be disengaging the artificial grav, and you can expect another wave. Don't panic; neither incident will last more than thirty seconds, if that."

Stepping forward, Tressa took her seat and began fastening the safety harness. "Wonderful! I can hardly wait!"

Her sarcasm elicited a chuckle from him as he fluidly ran through the practiced procedures.

"We're making the jump . . . *now!*" he said, depressing a button on the console.

Instantly a wave of dizziness swept over them, leaving them both momentarily weak. But, as promised, it passed as quickly as it came.

"You all right?" he asked without taking his eyes off the command center.

"I think I'll live, if that's what you mean."

He laughed gently. "That's what I mean. Now . . . in about forty minutes I'll be switching off the grav, and you'll experience a similar effect before we hit dirt."

"That's terrific, Nick." Ignoring the resulting chuckle, Tressa chose to remain seated for the remaining leg of their approach to Shaiel. Fixing her gaze, she watched as the planet slowly became larger and larger until at last it completely filled the viewscreen. For Nick it was just an everyday event, but for Tressa the sight was awesome.

Shaiel appeared as a blotchy gray-and-tan marble suspended in blackness. The closer they got, the better Tressa could see that the darker spots on the planet's surface were actually large craters.

She listened intently to the verbal communications between Nick and the space port. When clearance to land was given Nick began entering the designated coordinates. The ship shuddered in response, and with eyes trained on the screen Banner cautioned Tressa for the next wave of dizziness as he switched off the artificial gravity. It, too, passed quickly, just as he'd promised.

Soon they were skimming over barren, moonlit dunes that spread out beneath them for as far as the eye could see. Then, suddenly, without warning, the landscape changed, and they were crossing an ominously dark canyon that appeared to be several miles wide, very deep, and slashed across the landscape to disappear over the horizon. Shaiel wasn't a very pretty place, Tressa decided. It was awesome and rugged, however, with its formidable dunes and black craters with craggy edges.

Within minutes the *Victorious* was being gently eased onto her landing jacks at the space port of a small mining town called Mirror. Tressa watched as Banner powered down and secured the ship. Rising to his feet, he headed for the bunk, reached for his holstered gun, and began to strap it on. Throwing his utility belt over his shoulder, he turned, narrowing his eyes on Tressa.

"I want you to stay right with me, you understand? I'm going to have enough to do as it is without havin' to worry about you. I just want to collect the equipment, load up, and put into space as soon as possible."

"I understand." Nick's tone and mood had definitely changed, and with that end-of-discussion look in his eyes only a fool would have crossed him. He had the appearance of a man who intended to see his wishes carried out.

Banner palmed the main lock and stepped out first. Turning, he offered his hand to Tressa, who was covering her ears at the descending whine of the *Victorious*'s powerful thrusters. Maybe to Banner this was just part of the job, simply another day in the life of a cargo pilot. But to her, the sights, the ear-piercing sounds, and the stench of hot metal, exhaust, and raw fuel were an overwhelming assault on her sheltered feminine senses.

She took a sweeping glance at her surroundings. It was nighttime, and bright floodlights illuminated the landing zone. The tiny settlement of Mirror was nestled in the base of an enormous crater, high walls surrounding them on all sides. A rising moon on the horizon detailed each shadowy crevice in a dozen shades of gray.

Tressa's eyes rose to the velvet backdrop of space, where the very spiral of the galaxy itself, the Milky Way, lay stretched across the night sky from one horizon to the other.

"Let's go!"

She'd barely heard Banner's impatient command before she found herself being abruptly ushered down the ramp and toward the nest of buildings across the L.Z.

It was a hasty walk to the terminal. Tressa practically ran to keep up, forced to take two steps to his one. A set of double doors slid open as they approached the entrance. Turning left, they progressed down a long, echoing corridor that eventually opened out into a large room. The words above the open doors read "LorTech Equipment—Shipping and Receiving."

Tressa stood off to the side as Nick approached the counter, presenting Loring's high-security documents for processing. Curious at his sudden display of impatience, she watched him with interest while moments of silence slowly passed. Occasionally a muscle would twitch in his left cheek. Periodically he would scan the room in a casual glance before returning his attention to the counter.

"See if you can hurry it up, Jackson."

"Just cool your thrusters, Banner." The young man, whom Nick appeared to know by name, was quickly processing the information into the computer. He lifted his gaze to meet Tressa's, then looked back to the terminal.

"I'm on a time schedule, you know."

"You and everyone else," the man drawled. He cast Tressa an approving glance and grinned. "I'll tell you what, Banner. Why don't you just leave her here and go have a cup of coffee or something. That way the two of us can take care of things and I'll let you know when the shipment's all cleared and ready to load.'' He winked at Tressa. ''What do you say?''

Banner ignored his suggestion with a muttered oath. ''Just get me the damned clearance, Jackson. And I mean it or you're going to find me on the other side of this counter authorizing it for you. I haven't got time to be standing around here and I'm not going to wait much longer.

''Hey, you want to give it a try, pal? Be my guest.'' Jackson laughed. ''I'll tell you what. Me and your friend, here, will go have that cup of coffee and you can let me know when the clearance is ready.''

''Like hell.''

The young clerk smiled and looked up from the terminal. ''We've been through this before, Nick. Like I've said, it's all the red tape you have to go through just to get a high-sec clearance.'' Returning his attention to the computer, he entered another series of numbers and waited. ''You got that security code?''

''Right here,'' Nick replied with a nod to Tressa.

Hoping to cool Nick's rising irritation, Tressa quickly stepped forward and placed her palm on the security pad. Within moments a soft tone signaled confirmation.

Nick smiled blandly when the computer responded with the long-anticipated paperwork. Reaching completely over the counter, he ripped the final papers right out of the computer as they emerged.

''Tressa, all we need now is your final endorsement and we'll be on our way.''

Once again Tressa stepped forward and fullfilled her part in the transaction.

''Jackson,'' he said with a clipped nod. ''You keep up the good work, now.''

Jackson grinned and slid another glance Tressa's way. ''You too, Nick. Hey, I've been meaning to ask you.

What's going on with Slater these days? I haven't seen him around in almost a year.''

"Zeke? He's around." Stuffing the release papers into his pocket, Nick caught Tressa by the arm. "I just ran into him last month on Echo," he added over his shoulder as he escorted Tressa toward the exit. "See you around, Jackson."

"Yeah, next time."

In a matter of moments they were once again stepping out onto the landing field and heading toward the ship. Five more days, just five more days and she'd be back home and—a surge of panic cut off her thoughts. She didn't recall anyone saying what was to happen after they picked up the shipment. Would she be brought back home? Or would she be expected to go on to Echo?

As they approached the ship, Tressa tamped down her anxiety. For the moment she'd keep her thoughts to herself; just wait to see what he intended to do.

Releasing the lock, Banner strode up the ramp. With a broad sweep of his hand, he waved Tressa onboard. Once inside, he slipped the utility belt over the hook just inside his berth. From there he headed for the cockpit, still wearing his gun as he sprawled into the pilot's seat.

Nick quickly entered a series of numbers into the computer, and a bank of lights snapped to life on the console. While waiting for Loring's bogus shipment to be delivered, he began entering coordinates into the NAVCOMP. It was twenty minutes before a roboloader finally came wheeling across the L.Z.

"About time," he grumbled, reaching over his head to depress a switch on the control panel, opening the exterior entry to the cargo hold. Exterior lights snapped to life at the same time.

Banner had returned his concentration to the NAVCOMP when another man appeared at the main lock, poked his head in, and said something about needing a signature before he could release the equipment.

Groaning, Banner gave Tressa that you-know-what-to-do look, along with a curt nod toward the man. "Won't be long now," he drawled, his words dripping with sarcasm as he returned to the controls.

Chapter Ten

No one noticed the pock-faced man in the terminal who had quietly slipped into a com-booth, withdrawn a crumpled piece of paper from his pocket, and keyed in a number.

"Yeah, it's me. They're getting ready to lift now."

"And the transmitter?" the voice at the other end asked.

"All taken care of. It went on with the equipment. He'll leave a trail you can follow with your eyes closed."

"Good."

"Consider yourself lucky. From what I hear Banner's got automatic sensors mounted just inside the cargo bay. I can't believe they weren't set off."

The voice merely laughed in response. "That's the beauty of this little baby; no matter how sophisticated his equipment is, there's no way Banner could detect its presence."

It wasn't long before Banner was sealing the ship. "Tressa, see that everything's secured in the galley, will you?" he said without looking up from the controls.

112

A frown crossed her brow. "You mean . . . ."

"*I mean,*" he interrupted with a roughness that wasn't necessary, "secure the latches, dump the coffee, and put away anything you happen to see lying loose."

The dictatorial tone in which he'd ordered her about sparked Tressa's anger, and for a moment she simply stood there staring at his back.

"Aye, aye, Captain!" she finally clipped out. With a mocking salute he never saw, she pivoted and stalked toward the galley to secure every latch and stuff everything loose into a compartment. Checking the lav in much the same manner, she returned to her seat and strapped herself in.

Again, Banner's fingers tapped in the necessary directives, resulting in the vibration and muted whine of power-up.

Only then did he turn to face her. "This lift is going to be rougher than what you've experienced so far," he began. "We're heading directly off-planet. We'll be pulling quite a few more *G*s with this one," he explained. "You may experience some light-headedness, and you may even black out, but don't panic; it's a normal reaction and passes quickly."

"Wonderful," she muttered, her head swimming with questions she instinctively knew not to ask.

Within moments the *Victorious* was responding to his commands, and Tressa felt herself being pushed down into her seat as the ship roared skyward. As the pressure grew stronger, light-headedness began washing over her, but to her relief, she never lost consciousness.

Tressa refused to budge from her seat until they had not only cleared Shaiel's atmosphere but Nick had activated both the artificial grav and Stellardrive.

As soon as the last wave of dizziness passed, she rose and headed for the galley. Maybe if she made a fresh container of coffee and fixed the beast something to eat, his mood would improve, especially now that the equipment was safely on board and they were back into space.

For the remainder of the day and into the evening, Banner stayed at his post. There was a brooding quietness about him, and from the rigid set of his shoulders Tressa decided it would be wise to leave him alone. Even TiMar seemed to be keeping a safe distance.

Though she continued to wonder at his mood swing, what was really still bothering her was their destination. So far Nick had made no mention of his plans. In the pit of her stomach was a hard knot that said they weren't headed back to Terra Four.

Taking a seat in the galley, Tressa reached over and scooped TiMar into her arms. "You're leery of him, too, aren't you, little man? He's just a little edgy, that's all." TiMar circled twice, then dropped down in her lap.

Leaning back against the lounger, Tressa wished she could believe her own reassuring words. Everything had been going so well earlier that morning. They were actually becoming friends, laughing and sharing stories from their pasts. Tressa sensed, however, that the things he shared with her were guarded.

Gazing out the viewport, she wondered about the complex man who, for the time being, commanded her world.

Nick remained in the pilot's seat long into the afternoon, occasionally leaning forward to check coordinates. What Tressa didn't know was that it wasn't the cargo or his own safety that had him concerned. The high-security cargo that had him worried didn't happen to be safely tucked away in the ship's hold. With a heavy sigh he raked a hand through his hair. No doubt about it; Tressa Loring would make a nice prize for any renegade lucky enough to make it past him.

Suddenly a mug of hot steaming coffee materialized next to his hand and he looked up to find Tressa searching his face with concern.

At last she smiled. "I'm starved. How about you? Would

you eat something if I fixed it?''

Before answering, Nick straightened and rubbed the back of his neck. ''That depends. Are you here to take my order, or do I get cook's choice?'' he asked with a glimmer of humor in his eyes.

Relieved to see the change in his dark mood, Tressa quickly played the role. ''Why, Captain, sir, I'm here to take your order, of course.''

''Then in that case I'll have whatever it is you're having,'' he responded, unconsciously rewarding her with that infectious grin.

''Yes, sir!'' With eyes sparkling, she turned for the galley.

Nick's smile slowly faded as he watched her leave. Halting his mug halfway to his mouth, he found himself paying particular attention to the cute little sway of her backside— the realization bringing about another silent groan. This trip was nothing but major trouble, in more ways than he cared to even consider.

Regret was a new experience for him. At first it was subtle. He knew he'd been impossible to be around today. But, dammit all, he had a gut feeling whoever was after them wasn't about to give up easily. In fact, half expecting a ''greeting party'' to be waiting for them on Shaiel, his nerves had been on edge from the moment they'd hit dirt.

With a heavy sigh Banner rose from his seat. A decision had been reached. Determined to set his dark mood aside and to enjoy this woman who had suddenly invaded his life and his thoughts, Banner rose to his feet and headed for the galley.

Tressa had steak dinners in the warmer and was presently setting the table. The coffee smelled wonderful and . . . and . . . *set . . . ting . . . the . . . table!*

Nick stood blinking in total disbelief as he recognized two of his antique navigational star charts currently adorning the table as placemats and knives and forks sitting prettily in their places.

115

"Well? What do you think?" she asked, beaming up at him with total satisfaction.

Still speechless over his star charts, Banner never noticed the *centerpiece* until she began to light what resembled an old-fashioned candlestick jammed into an empty ale bottle.

"Tressa!" Instant perception of what she was about to do sent him lunging toward her, knocking the tiny laser from her hand and sending it skidding across the floor.

"What did you do that for?" Tressa sputtered, choking on her words and regaining her balance at the same time.

"Do you have any idea what you were about to light?" His tone was raw with desperation.

Tressa eyed Nick sharply. "I was merely lighting an illumination wand, Nick. You didn't have to attack me like that. *Talk about overreacting!* I wasn't planning to set the galley afire, you know! I simply thought it would be nice to . . ."

Banner's raised voice cut her off. "As a matter of fact, lady, setting this place on fire is a gross understatement." Nick took a deep breath, releasing it in a labored sigh. "What you were about to light, sweetheart, would have done a helluva lot more than just set the galley on fire. It would have blown this entire ship out of existence! If I hadn't come in when I did . . ." He left the sentence hanging.

Tressa planted her fists defiantly on her hips. "Now why . . . doesn't . . . that . . . surprise me?" she bit out. "Everything else you seem to do is on a grand scale. Every weapon you own is twice as deadly as the next guy's; even your alarm system is lethal." In direct contrast to her heated words she smiled blandly. "Why, it only stands to reason that lighting one of Nick Banner's illumination wands wouldn't just cast a light on the dinner. Hell no! It would blow the entire damn ship up in one glorious display!"

Nick rubbed his nose, hiding his amusement as Tressa continued.

"This . . . this *thing* I almost lit . . . I suppose it's illegal, too?"

"It's not illegal, Tressa." His eyes grew openly amused as he plucked the object of their discussion out of the empty ale bottle. "It's a THJ-17 Emergency Beacon."

"Well, just how the hell was I supposed to know that? It was shoved in with the placemats, Nick. Of all the stupid places to put it."

Nick was half grinning now. "Your language, Irish!" he admonished, shaking his head in feigned astonishment. "It's rapidly deteriorating."

"I don't give a damn about my language, Banner; you scared me to pieces. And don't call me Irish!"

His smile turned into a chuckle. "You come from Port Ireland, don't you?"

"That doesn't make . . ."

"And by the way," he continued, "those uh . . . placemats, as you call them, happen to be navigational star charts. And it just so happens I had them exactly where I wanted them . . . along with the emergency beacon, a first-aid kit, and a few other items."

"Star charts? Those are *real* star charts?" she asked incredulously. "Aren't they a little unnecessary when everything's stored in computers? What in stars would you need those antiques for?"

Nick brushed past her, replacing the beacon into the storage bin. "In case of an emergency, Tressa. In case the computer fails and dumps its memory, I have a backup."

"But doesn't your computer . . ."

"I have 'em," he bit out, "simply because I happen to want 'em, Tressa. Now how's that dinner comin'?" he said, claiming a seat at the table. "I don't know about you, but I'm starved."

Tressa started removing the charts from the table when Nick reached out and caught her hand. "Leave 'em be." He grinned. "We'll use our dainty manners tonight."

After their meal they cleared the table and played another

game of Justice, then Nick listened with interest as Tressa again opened up about her plans for the future. She'd attended the finest of schools, and it was apparent that Jonathan was offering her every opportunity to pursue her own avenue in life—be it LorTech, the medical field, or marriage to a man Banner wasn't so sure Tressa was in love with. The way he saw it, any woman in love—*truly in love*—didn't wonder about her career when there were marriage plans in the making. But that was her business, and far be it from him to get involved.

"I left home when I was twenty-one," he said, skipping over the part about Linnae and the pain that had him tempting death for nearly two years on Echo. He mentioned that he was twenty-three when he'd earned enough credits for a down payment on the *Victorious*. Though he touched upon the failure of his business venture with Kendyl, he chose not to elaborate on the reasons.

Tressa finally asked about the half-healed scar she'd noticed the other morning, to which he shrugged, passing it off as nothing.

"Nick?"

"Yeah?"

"Would you at least allow me to tend to the injury? I can tell it's still painful, and . . . well, you see, I have this special salve that has remarkable healing powers. I know it would help you."

At the promise of speeding the healing, Nick reluctantly agreed, and with a sigh of resignation began undoing the buttons of his shirt.

Tressa headed for the bunks to retrieve her *miracle* salve from one of her travel packs. The highly medicinal balm was made from oil extracted from the leaves of the *Acuel* tree, a rare shrublike plant that could only be found in the relatively unexplored highlands of Terra Four's Southern Hemisphere.

Nick Banner's muscular chest was the first thing Tressa

saw as she reentered the galley. He was just removing his shirt, presently rolling the left side off his shoulder. With both arms still in their sleeves, the procedure was pulling the shirt taut across his back in a lopsided fashion. The result: one gloriously exhibited torso. Tressa's breath caught at the sight.

Clean but timeworn, the white long-sleeved shirt clung to Nick's body, flawlessly molding itself to his frame. Draping partway down his left arm, it hung on a bulge of muscle as he wrestled with the sleeve.

Muscle. She swallowed hard, acutely aware of Nick Banner's corded contours, every muscle and sinew defined in exquisite detail. But at the sight of the makeshift bandage that didn't quite cover the angry wound on his left side, Tressa hid her alarm.

"Nick, hold still for a moment," she said, approaching him with a sudden finesse born of her medical training. "Let me help you with that." Easing his arm out of the sleeve, Tressa gently, carefully began peeling away the improvised bandage. Nick's skin was hot to the touch, indicating infection. As the last of the cloth came free, Tressa clamped down on a gasp at the sight of the ragged half-healed wound that was much too inflamed for her peace of mind. It appeared even worse than she had remembered, and explained why she'd sensed him in pain.

When she first suggested this little "errand of mercy" Tressa had anticipated a routine dressing of a wound, a task she'd performed hundreds of times when working at Port Ireland Medical Center. All too soon, however, came the realization that the "errand" she had taken on was to be anything but *routine*. Her stomach clenched as he jerked the remainder of his shirt out of his pants, tossing it down beside him.

A small golden medallion hung from Banner's neck on a narrow chain, bearing an insignia unlike anything she had ever seen.

"I'm going to need hot water," she mumbled, turning for the sink. Closing her eyes, Tressa drew in a steadying breath and began scrubbing her hands. Stars, even her hands were shaking! What was wrong with her? He was wounded and feverish and had done nothing, *surprising as it was,* to illicit her present awareness of his masculinity.

Premed had educated Tressa long ago in basic anatomy. Even her volunteer work at Port Ireland's Med Center had exposed her to men in various stages of undress, but this was different. Under other circumstances there would have been no trouble keeping her mind on her task, but as always this man unsettled her, making her acutely aware of his powerful body, his very maleness.

Brushing a lock of hair away from her face with the back of her hand, Tressa filled a container with hot water. Within moments she returned to his side, placing the water at his feet.

"Now, where did you say you kept the med kit?" she asked distractedly.

"In the storage bin with the emergency things."

"Right." Tressa turned toward the bins while Banner, now seated on the end of the lounge, released an audible sigh. "Let's just get this over with."

Grabbing the salve from the table, Tressa returned to his side. A sudden wave of dismay swept over her as she knelt at his feet. The gesture was not only slavish, it put her at eye level with his hard, flat belly that still bore testimony to the punches he had taken the other night.

Nick sat forward on the edge, palms resting on spread knees as she busied herself with the supplies. Moving to his side, she breathed a silent prayer of thanks that she didn't have to kneel between the man's legs to do this. Already she could feel the heat emanating from her cheeks, or was it from him?

Upon closer inspection, Tressa saw that the blows he'd suffered had visibly aggravated the wound. "Oh, Nick . . ." she whispered brokenly, "why didn't you *say* something?"

No longer distracted by his striking masculinity, she reached for a cloth and dropped it into the pan of hot water. "One section has nearly reopened," she murmured.

He breathed an exasperated sigh, "I've survived worse, Tressa."

Silence hung heavy between them, broken only by the sounds of water trickling back into the pan as she lifted the cloth and wrung it out.

"How long ago did this happen?" she asked, busily removing a container of liquid cleanser from the med kit and applying a small amount to the cloth.

"Hell, I don't know. A month ago, I guess." The unmistakable edge to his voice clearly said the subject was closed.

Ignoring the curious sensation of warmth presently coiling in the pit of her stomach, Tressa fixed her gaze and set to the task before her. The hard muscles of his abdomen tightened when she gently laid the hot cloth to his side and the angry red wound started bleeding.

"I'm sorry. I know this is painful," she murmured, never pausing in her task, yet keeping her touch as gentle as possible.

"Just get it done."

Struggling desperately to remain detached, Tressa forbid her eyes to wander, deliberately concentrating on the wound. But it was hard, especially when several tiny rivulets of soapy water coursed down his torso, following muscular valleys that ran down his side and into the waist band of his pants.

Holding the cloth in place with one hand, she quickly reached for a soft towel, gently mopping the excess water from his side and stomach. Even as she steeled herself, her traitorous eyes shyly stole glances at the taut muscles of his powerful biceps, his wide shoulders and hard, flat belly. He was . . . magnificent. There was a deep, jagged scar on his left forearm and several less obvious ones across his abdomen. He was clearly no stranger to violence.

Again his muscles tightened, and this time he drew in his breath with a hiss as she, again, laid the cloth to his side and held it in place. Though she tried not to—oh, how she tried—her gaze wandered. After all, what choice did she have? In kneeling at his feet, she barely came up to his chest.

Poor excuse, a small voice echoed.

Tressa quickly averted her attention to his lower back, where the wound initially began. Her cheeks were already scalding, and just when she thought it couldn't get any worse, her eyes widened in dismay as she saw the puckered, angry-looking scar dipping beneath the waistband of his trousers.

Nick wasn't outright grinning, yet Tressa had the distinct impression he was beginning to find the scenario entertaining, despite the pain and discomfort. There was no mistaking that faint gleam of deviltry in those blue eyes of his. For the moment Tressa wasn't sure which was worse, dealing with his foul mood or his intimidating arrogance.

She willed herself to ignore him, focusing her attention on getting the project over with as quickly as possible. Catching her lower lip between her teeth, she dipped the cloth once again into the steaming water. Soft mounds of suds floated on the surface like miniature icebergs as she wrung out the cloth.

Slowly, Tressa became aware that under his intense study, every movement, every touch was beginning to take on the intimacy of a caress. Never had she been so aware of a man's body. Stars, he smelled of leather and cold steel and . . . and a scent that was blatantly masculine—unquestionably Nick. Just being close to him, observing him, touching him, catching his scent as it mingled with the soap, ignited a flame that began in her belly and radiated throughout her body. Even as she tried not to feel it, a surge of white heat shot through her as she touched his skin.

Having cleansed and rinsed his inflamed side, there was only one place left, and Tressa had no choice now but to finally ask the question she'd been dreading most—and the very question the arrogant beast had no doubt been waiting for.

She opened her mouth to speak but quickly gulped back the words. Again—this time clearing her throat softly and licking her lips—she began with a note of nonchalance that she clearly wasn't feeling. "Would you loosen your waistband a bit so I can reach the rest of this?"

At first Nick hesitated, then reluctantly stood to tower above her. Still kneeling at his feet, her mouth dropped as her gaze followed his hands to his belt. Mesmerized, Tressa watched as he casually unfastened the buckle, allowing both ends to dangle loosely from their loops. She lost her breath when, with suggestive leisure, he slowly began flipping open the top two studs of his black trousers. The resulting gap put a serious strain on the remaining three rivets.

Tressa tried to swallow and failed. Her heart was pounding so loudly, she was certain he could hear it. It was good she was already kneeling, for surely her legs were jelly by now.

With agonizing slowness, Nick proceeded to nudge down his trousers, baring the sleek skin of his left hip and exposing the remaining portion of the jagged wound.

But Tressa's gaze was not locked on his injury at the moment. The entire act had been performed with such blatant suggestiveness, she had become thoroughly lost in the sensuous mechanics of it all.

"Is this far enough?"

It was a deep satin drawl that suddenly broke the spell as Tressa caught herself following a dusting of crisp black hair down a corded belly. At his navel it began tapering, forming an arrow that disappeared into the gap of his straining, partially opened fly.

Tressa blinked and drew in a quick, fevered breath. Nick was grinning at her when she glanced up at him. It was a slow, roguish grin that was so brazenly indecent, it had her heart and stomach colliding with a jolt.

"Are you *quite* finished?" she demanded firmly.

Banner chuckled, his knowing eyes dancing with deviltry. "I was just about to ask you that same question, Irish." Still grinning, he reached for the third stud on his trousers, "Would you prefer me to . . ."

"Sit down!" she snapped, cutting him off midsentence.

Nick chuckled again and dutifully obeyed as Tressa began cleansing what she discovered to be the deepest and angriest portion of the wound.

It was a pleasant scent that filled the air when she at last opened the container of Acuel salve. The ointment was smooth, the color of black pearls, and it smelled of mists and woods.

Just as she figured, Nick's suggestive teasing came to an abrupt halt once she began applying the salve. Secretly taking delight, Tressa watched his expression change from a seductive gaze to that of a set jaw.

Pain was the one drawback about the salve. On an infected injury it burned like hell, and she knew it. Oh, she could have pretreated the area with Nervatrite, numbing the area before applying Acuel. But, dammit, he deserved this, and her still-flaming cheeks justified her reasons. Besides, she told herself, the burning effect wouldn't last too long.

With private pleasure Tressa continued to glaze on the initial application. There was no doubt but that the salve was working. She felt Nick's stomach muscles jump, instantly tensing beneath her fingers. And he was being so very gallant, too, trying not to show his reaction. But no matter how hard you try to stifle it, there's just no mistaking the sound of air hissing through clenched teeth.

Several tense moments passed with Tressa in total control. Oh, it wouldn't last long; she knew that. But for the moment she was loving every second of victory.

"What I don't understand," she muttered, smearing another glob into the wound, ''is why a robomed didn't see to this for you.''

Silence. Then, ''Because Port Ireland . . . is one of the few places that . . .'' he stiffened, ''have such luxuries as robomeds, Tressa. I wasn't at Port Ire . . .'' His voice broke again with another hiss of air.

Tressa was all business. ''I see. Lift your arm a little.''

Holding his breath, Banner complied, his body rigid.

''This should never have been left this way,'' she mumbled, frowning as she worked. She smoothed more of the burning salve into the angriest section.

Nick sucked in his breath again; there was just no hiding it this time. ''Tressa!'' he finally ground out between clenched teeth. ''You're mad at me. Right?''

''Nick,'' she began, peering up at him with wide-eyed innocence, ''why would you say such a thing?''

As if understanding her game, his mouth quirked. ''Because you're a mite rough with your touch, darlin'.''

Tressa feigned a look of anguish. ''Oh, I'm so sorry. I know this is painful.'' Miraculously, she kept the grin off her face. Oh, how she wanted to burst out laughing. His lordship was finally getting his just dessert.

''I'll live,'' he groaned. ''Just lighten up a little, okay? This stuff burns enough without the heavy hand.''

Tressa nodded and lowered her gaze. Finishing quickly, she carefully bound his entire midsection, including his bruised ribs.

Having had the wind sufficiently taken from his sails, Nick Banner was totally submissive. A fine sheen covered his body as he sat stock-still, jaw set, silently waiting for her to complete the task.

''There,'' she pronounced with a note of satisfaction and a final tug that brought a gasp from his lips. ''You should notice a great improvement by tomorrow,'' she proclaimed cheerfully.

Turning a baleful eye on her, Banner made no comment,

but rose to his feet, grabbed his shirt, and tenderly made his way from the galley.

By the time Tressa entered the cabin the lights had been dimmed and Nick was in his bunk, facing the outer hull. Quickly grabbing her nightshift, Tressa headed for the lav.

Nick Banner was just about the most complicated man she had ever met, tender and understanding one moment, rude and demanding the next. Furthermore, since he obviously wasn't in the habit of apologizing for anything . . . neither would she.

Quietly climbing up into her bunk, Tressa remembered the day Nick first strode through the doors of LorTech. There was a natural grace and charm about him that women found irresistible, and Tressa was no exception. At the time she had been fourteen and boy crazy.

Tressa smothered a giggle, recalling how her best friend, Sara, had rushed up to her, breathless . . . *"Tressa! I've been looking all over for you!"* Then, in a dreamy voice, she continued, *"There's the most handsomest guy I've ever laid eyes on, waiting to see your father! Hurry, or we'll miss him."* She grabbed hold of Tressa's hand. *"Well . . . come on! I promise, you won't be disappointed."*

Sara turned and rolled her eyes to the ceiling. *"Oh Tress,"* she breathed, *"he looks just like a . . . a sun god. Tall, dark, sun-bronzed skin, the most magnificent blue eyes you've ever seen, and that voice . . . that deep voice of his . . ."* Releasing a breathy sigh, Sara continued in her normal voice. *"I just happened to be coming down the hall when he stopped me to ask directions to 'Mr. Loring's office.' I swear, Tress, I thought I was going to lay down and die right there on the spot!"*

Tressa rolled onto her side, wondering what Sara would say if she knew her best friend was sharing the tight quarters of the *Victorious,* not to mention doctoring that gorgeous body of her ''sun god.''

Nick moaned softly, turning restlessly in his sleep. There was little doubt but that his side was still on fire. With a twinge of regret, Tressa recalled seeing a small container of Nervatrite in the ship's first-aid kit. She probably should have used it.

But, dammit, he'd earned this!

Chapter Eleven

Jonathan Loring finished signing his name on the last of a stack of purchase orders. "Anything come in from Nick Banner through the night?" he asked, gathering the papers in an orderly stack.

Liz stood by faithfully. "Nothing on a personal nature, Jon, but a memo-torp from Shaiel did come through just this morning with a message confirming the release of a Security-3 Clearance. I placed it right on top for you."

"Good," he said, snatching the memo from the stack of mail. "That means they were there two days ago, I trust with no problems. Now for the remainder of the trip," he added, his face growing somber as he handed the signed purchase orders back to Liz.

The prim middle-aged secretary was one of the very select few who even knew that Nick Banner had taken Tressa away. "She's in good hands, Jon," Liz offered encouragingly. "He's never let you down yet, you know."

"I know, Lizzy. It's just not knowing anything." He dragged a hand through his hair. "Drives a man crazy."

128

Liz smiled in reassurance. Clutching the stack of papers to her breast, she turned to head for the door. "You'll hear. Just a soon as they arrive at their destination, you'll hear."

From the very first day Banner had set foot in his office Loring had been amusingly aware of Liz's affection for the incorrigible rogue. Though it was always expressed in a motherly fashion, there was little doubt that she was just as enamored with the man as the rest of the women around the place.

Stopping in the doorway, Liz turned to face him once again. "Mr. Banner is a very capable young man, Jon," she added with a note of confidence. "I'm certain he has things under control."

Jonathan smiled. "Thank you, Lizzy."

Oh, yes, Banner was more than capable of protecting Tressa from harm. The question was, who would protect her from *him?* Loyal or not, three weeks was three damn long weeks.

By the end of the eighth day Nick's mood had changed again, the tension hanging heavier than ever. Things had taken a turn, and as near as Tressa could tell it had begun two nights earlier, right after she'd dressed his wounded side. The socializing they had once enjoyed had come to an abrupt halt. No more talks. No more games. No more shared laughter. Instead Banner's time was spent entirely by himself, and his evenings were spent stargazing from the pilot's seat, a mug of ale for companionship and a bottle at his elbow for easy refills.

Tressa had tried to approach him several times, but nothing seemed to work. Tonight he was quiet—too quiet. His mood was dark, and he'd started drinking much earlier than the nights before. Tressa and TiMar had retired early. The best thing to do was leave him alone.

The cabin lights had been dimmed for some time to low, indirect lighting. There was an almost mystical glow to the cabin. Nick Banner's now hardened features were softly illuminated by the faint lights of the command console. A two-day shadow darkened his jaw, the rakish look mirroring his thoughts and emotions perfectly.

Banner remained at the helm, sprawled in the pilot's seat with his long legs stretched out before him. A second bottle of ale had been opened and he'd dispensed entirely with the formalities of a mug.

It had been a long time since he'd last allowed himself to drink in this manner. After the heartbreak of losing Linnae, drinking had become a way of life, his escape from reality. Trouble was, Banner didn't hold liquor well. A few drinks to get high was one thing, but full-blown, overindulgence was quite another. It had a tendency to make him mean, besides stripping him of his pride, his dignity, and most of all, his reason.

But tonight he needed this. Tossing back another burning gulp of the strong ale, he laughed softly. No, what he *needed* was a woman. Tressa was driving him insane. Oh, he hadn't missed the way she looked at him. He'd seen that look often enough to know exactly what was going through her pretty head.

So, you thought you'd simply harden your heart against her, didn't you? But all of that resolve of yours disintegrated the instant you allowed yourself to look into those beguiling brown eyes. Come now, Banner, quit fooling yourself. That wide-eyed innocence is merely a smoke screen. Maybe she hasn't come right out and said it, but there're other ways of sayin' it without using words.

And you learned to read that language years ago.

Shoulders set, staring dead ahead, Nick took a slow drag from his cigar.

You know she wants you, so what are you waiting for— an invitation? Hell, a girl like that doesn't offer invitations; she waits for you to make the move.

Once again Banner vividly recalled Tressa's drugged assessment of his physical qualities. Yes, he numbly reminded himself, she'd been under the influence, but those thoughts didn't just materialize out of thin air. He was convinced they'd been there before he'd ever given her the injection. Then there was the other night, when she'd tended his wounded side, and how he'd managed to arouse her interest with his seductive theatrics. Once again he'd seen that look of desire. But he'd also sensed naive curiosity.

Banner tossed back another swallow of ale, grimacing as it burned a trail to his gut. Loring! Damn him! How the blazes was he supposed to remain in this self-imposed celibacy while that little piece of baggage wormed her way into his life, unlocking the doors to emotions he thought had died years ago.

Forget Loring. You know what she wants, so what's stoppin' you? Admit it: You're afraid to let yourself feel again, aren't you, old man?

"Shut up!" he hissed into the darkness. Raking his hand through his shaggy dark hair, Banner rose from the pilot's seat and stood before the viewport, staring out at the diamond-studded blackness that surrounded the ship. Just what the devil was he suppose to do now? Hell, even staying away from her wasn't working.

He reached for the bottle again and drained the last swallow. There was nothing he wanted more right now than to have her naked beneath him, to breathe in her soft fragrance, to kiss her, to taste her, to see her face flushed with passion. He wanted . . . oh, hell.

Nick shoved his hand through his hair again. One thing he knew for damn sure—he was doing one helluva fine job at getting disgustingly drunk. He smiled crookedly at the echoing words of Sam Taylor. A seasoned cargo pilot who had taken a liking to Banner during the time when he'd lost all direction in his life, Taylor had taken him under his wing and eventually put Banner in touch with Jonathan Loring. "Banner," he'd say with a sly grin, "there's just not much that'll take the place of a woman warmin' yer bunk at night, but I can tell ya' this—'' he lifted a bottle of Extra Dark for emphasis—''When it gets rough, you'll find a bottle or two of this stuff sure beats playin' five-fingered-stud between ports.''

Banner's smile slowly faded. Setting down the empty bottle, he turned and headed for the galley. ''Unless the woman's warmin' the bunk above yours,'' he muttered in renewed frustration.

Go on, look at her, the voice whispered as he passed the bunks. *Go on. It won't hurt to just look. So what if she wakes. You're drunk. That excuse hasn't failed you yet.*

His eyes came to rest on Tressa's sleeping form.

That's right . . . go on. Look at her.

TiMar lifted his head and curiously watched Nick for a moment before yawning and settling back down. Tressa was sleeping on her back, her hair fanned out in a tangled mass across the pillow. The liquid-soft nightshift she wore had slipped slightly off one shoulder and, entranced, Nick watched the steady rise and fall of her breasts.

This one's different, the voice whispered. *Not like the others . . . not like Linnae.*

She seemed so childlike as she lay there. One arm curved palm up over her head; the other was tucked protectively around TiMar. But Tressa was far from a child. In truth, she was more woman than he cared to dwell on at the moment.

Waitin' for that invitation again? Go on . . . touch her. Breathe in her scent. She'll never know the difference.

Banner reached out, touching her hair with just the tips of his fingers at first. It was soft, like spun silk. Gently he rubbed a glossy lock between his thumb and fingers, then closed his eyes as he breathed in the scent of her. Soft and clean, reminding him of soap and fresh air. The heady bouquet was like incense to his already overloaded senses.

Remember her touch? What it felt like when her small hands tended your wound? Just imagine what kind of magic the rest of her is capable of.

132

You want her. Go on, take her. She won't fight you . . . not if you're gentle. Not if you take it slow and easy. She wants you, remember? You've seen it yourself; she wants you as bad as you want her. Then the whispered voice seemed to laugh. *And you want her so bad right now it hurts, doesn't it?*

With lust churning in his gut, Banner jerked back his hand, turning on his heel and heading for the galley. Gliding to a halt before the froster, he withdrew a third bottle. Making his way to the booth, he dropped into one of the seats, braced his elbows on the table, and buried his head in his hands.

You're afraid, aren't you? Afraid of this little slip of a girl. Admit it; she's already breaking through your defenses, already worming her way into your protected world. She's fanned to life a tiny spark of emotion in that frozen heart of yours, hasn't she? And it's scaring the hell out of you.

He swiped out at the table-game that sat poised before him. Game pieces flew across the room and scattered about the deck. A mug crashed into the bulkhead, sending rivulets of cold coffee streaming down the wall.

Wide-eyed, her hair in disarray, her voice soft and drowsy, Tressa stood in the doorway. "Nick? . . ."

Nick's shoulders were set, his back rigid. "Return to your bunk, Tressa," came his gravelly reply, without so much as turning to face her.

Rubbing her eyes, Tressa hesitated, then took a step forward. "What's wrong?"

But she stopped again when all six-foot-four-inches of him slowly rose from the chair. On legs spread slightly apart, he turned to face her, a lock of dark hair spilling over his forehead as his narrowed gaze leveled on her. "Your bunk, Tressa!" he repeated in a low, uncompromising voice.

She should have been frightened by the raw savageness he presented. But, strangely, she wasn't. Keeping her eyes locked on his, Tressa bravely stood her ground. "And you should be in bed too, Nick."

At that, Banner's eyebrow arched and a crooked grin slowly emerged. "Is that right." His bold stare frankly assessed her. "And uh . . . are you offerin' to join me, Irish?" His gaze slowly slid downward, taking in her skimpy nightshift, noting particularly how her breasts almost spilled out over the top of the low-dipping neckline, how the lace-trimmed side slit exposed the entire length of her right thigh. If he hadn't been so filled with hot desire at the moment, he would have found it funny that she was standing there still clutching a matching wrapper. Obviously grabbed in haste, only to be forgotten in her distraction.

A long moment of silence hung between them as she hurriedly donned her wrapper.

He watched with silent interest as she fumbled with the tiny clasps. "Need any help?"

Tressa's back stiffened as she met his gaze. "You're drunk."

"Not drunk enough," he muttered.

Tressa shifted uneasily, as if she was finally realizing that she should have stayed in bed. With a glance down at her feet, she noticed the scattered game pieces. As if suddenly needing something to do, she began picking up a few that lay nearby.

"Leave 'em be!" he growled.

Obeying numbly, Tressa dropped the pieces and straightened up. "Nick . . . please, tell me what's wrong."

What the hell are you stallin' for now? You've given her fair warning; now take her. You're burnin' for her. Go on, take her.

Tressa stepped closer. "Nick, I'm a good listener if you'd like to talk." Her voice was soft and compelling. "Sometimes it helps . . ."

Nick stopped her in midsentence. "Helps what, Tressa?" he inquired tauntingly, watching her face flood with color.

"I . . . I only meant that I would be willing to listen if

134

you needed someone to talk to.'' She took a cautious step backward. ''But I can see that now's not a good time.''

''No kidding,'' he drawled, reaching for the unopened bottle he'd set on the table and working at removing the seal.

Tressa took another step backward. ''Maybe we'd just better forget it. We can talk tomorrow, when you're feeling better.''

''Smart girl, but don't count on it, 'cause what I have to talk about, I don't think you wanna hear.'' He raised the now-opened bottle in a mocking salute to her. Placing it to his lips, he swallowed a generous portion of the brew in two burning gulps.

Banner's eyes narrowed, his gaze menacing. Beyond the skimpy attire, Tressa's somber dignity drew him, and he found himself aching to find out just how much woman there was beneath that cloak of naïveté. He'd even be willing to bet there was a wildcat hidden behind that facade of respectability.

Tressa started to turn, then hesitated. ''Nick,'' she began, ''sometimes all a person needs . . .''

He slammed down the bottle with such force, it sent a geyser of spray into the air and a cascade of foam running down its side to the table. He moved so swiftly that Tressa gasped when he shackled her wrist in a iron grip.

''You haven't the vaguest notion of what I need right now or you wouldn't still be standing here.''

Tressa looked up at him in wide-eyed alarm. ''Let me go!'' She struggled to wrench herself free, but she was no match against his superior strength.

Gripped by a primitive need to possess her, Banner's heavy-lidded gaze focused on her full-lipped, sensuous mouth.

Slow down, old man. You're scaring her. Say something nice.

Fighting for control, he loosened his tight hold without completely releasing her. His gaze flickered lazily.

"Tressa..." he began softly. "Honey... you have any idea how pretty you are."

Thaaaat's right ... seduce her.

He felt a shudder course through her. Her large brown eyes were looking up at him with apprehension ... or ... was it anticipation? He was so spaced, his mind so foxed right now, it didn't matter. He pulled her intimately against his steel-hard frame. His senses reeled with the touch of her body in direct contact with his, the heady scent of her filling his nostrils, urging him on. His hooded gaze dropped to the gaping neckline of her nightshift, and another intense wave of raw lust swept through him.

"I need you," he said brokenly.

He groaned, fighting his desire to have her right then and there. She was so small and fragile, he thought, noting that his splayed hand at her back nearly spanned the width of her waist.

A heartbeat passed before he felt the jolt of comprehension chase through her. He watched her throat work as she choked back a convulsive swallow. "Please ..." she whispered, unconsciously teasing him with her dimpled cheek.

This woman-child had walked into his life and blown his entire existence to hell and back with her smile, her flashing brown eyes, and her damned dimple. He'd never been so driven to possess a woman as he had been over this last week. Even Linnae had never had him aching like this. And the worst part of all was that he was helpless to do anything about it.

Banner's glazed eyes continued to hold her captive as an eternity of silence passed between them. Slowly his gaze slid back to her mouth.

"A kiss ... that's all I ask. Just a kiss."

Before she could protest he'd gathered her into his arms, lowering his head and capturing her lips in a kiss that was both tender and shockingly seductive. He felt Tressa's body jerk in response when he touched the tip of his tongue to the corner of her lips, seeking entrance. Tentatively, her mouth parted, allowing him access, and with a groan he thrust his tongue inside her mouth.

Tressa squirmed, struggling to break free, but he wouldn't let her go. With hot desire overriding his attempt at seduction, he bent his head lower and kissed the pulsing hollow at the base of her throat, nibbling at it even as he, with practiced skill, unfastened the tiny clasp that secured her wrapper.

"You should have gone back to your bunk when I told you," he said so seriously that there was no mistaking his intent.

"Nick . . ."

Her answer came immediately as both of his hands swept down her back, pressing her into intimate contact with his hard body. With a groan, he drew back and gazed down at her. "Don't be afraid. I just want to hold you. That's all." Again his mouth captured hers, his tongue tracing the line of her lips, seeking entrance.

Leashing his rampaging emotions was not on the agenda. He wanted to ravish her, to make passionate love to her. He groaned her name, and Tressa stifled an answering sob.

Suddenly she relaxed. As if some unseen force had taken control, she melted into his embrace.

Sensing the change, Nick reacted immediately. "C'mere," he said hoarsely, guiding her to the lounge. Easing himself down, he gently pulled her onto his lap, capturing her chin, holding her still as he again tenderly claimed her mouth.

That's right . . . don't frighten her. Be gentle.

"I've been goin' outta my mind with wonderin' about you," he confessed. With a growl low in his throat he blazed a trail of soft, slow, and agonizingly long kisses across the arch of her cheekbone to the sensitive curve of her ear. "I need you," he whispered roughly, and felt her tremble when his strong dark hand came up and gently outlined the fullness of her breast. The liquid softness of her gown presented only the slightest of barriers, and when he cupped her completely Tressa moaned, offering no resistance as she buried her face in the hollow of his shoulder.

Capturing her face, he held it gently, reclaiming her mouth, deepening the passion of his kiss while subtly easing the wrapper off her shoulder. With skill born of experience he took the strap of her nightshift with it; breaking the kiss, his gaze slowly slid downward as he bared her breast.

"Nick . . ." she whispered on an indrawn gasp when his thumb passed lightly over the peak. He sucked in his breath, watching it harden beneath his touch. Then, drawing back, he gazed into her eyes. "I'm not going to hurt you," he vowed silkily. Encircling her waist, he pulled her even closer, entrapping her as she sat across his lap. "I promise," he whispered.

With agonizing slowness he kissed a path down her neck, then lower, brushing her sensitive flesh with a light caress of his stubble-roughened cheek. When his hand slid down across her silken belly, coming to rest upon her thigh, he felt her tremble.

"I just want to hold you," he rasped, hoping he could honor his declaration. With the dangerous combination of lust and ale in his blood, Nick's defenses were crumbling fast. But he waited until he'd leashed his raging desire. Calming Tressa with soft murmurs, he waited until she'd once again relaxed in his arms.

Tressa never noticed the insignificant yet deliberate pressure being applied as Nick slowly drew his hand along the length of her thigh. Nor did she notice that the hem of her soft gown was skillfully rising with it. In fact, it wasn't until he lazily slipped his hand between her legs that he felt her tense.

Sensing her flash of uncertainty, his hold tightened. With a low murmur he began subduing her, only faintly conscious of just how naive and inexperienced Tressa was to the heated desire that he was deliberately stirring to life.

Slow down. Remember, she won't fight you if you take it slow.

"I want you, Tressa," he murmured softly against her hair, adjusting her weight on his lap. "Just for tonight, honey." And it was another moment before his hand began to move again.

Tressa tensed, this time reaching down to grasp his encroaching fingers. "Please . . ."

"Don't," he groaned. Drawing a ragged breath, Banner again willed himself to slow down, stilling the hand that was presently trapped in the cocoon of her tightly clamped thighs.

Tressa tried to rise, but a gentle pressure was all it took to keep her pinned.

"Don't pull away now." He tilted her chin with his free hand. "Let me," he commanded hoarsely, grazing her mouth with a tender kiss. She smelled of flowers and tasted like heaven.

Tressa moaned softly; then with a submissive sigh, she buried her face in his neck in sweet surrender.

Lured on, Banner gently nipped at her, wanting to taste her, feel her, to touch every inch of her.

"I won't hurt you," he assured her again.

Unresisting, Tressa moaned his name as he introduced her to his alternative to talking. With a sudden sharp intake of breath she wrapped her arms about his neck, entangled her fingers in his silky dark mane, giving in to the magic of his touch.

Her weight, her delicate structure, her soft curves—she felt so good, so damn right in his arms. She was designed, he knew, to fit him to absolute perfection.

The fullness of her breasts pressing against his chest tormented him. Dimly aware that Tressa was holding her breath, Nick felt her nails flex into his shoulders. Her pulse beat nearly as hard and as fast as his.

"You like that, don't you?" His voice was deep and resonant.

Tressa clung tighter. Nick knowingly placed a tender kiss on her forehead. Without breaking the rhythm he'd begun, he dipped his head lower, capturing her parted lips.

"Nick . . ." Again Tressa moaned his name.

Go on. She's ready for you. What are you waitin' for, idiot?

The vivid mental image of taking her right then and there swamped Banner's heated thoughts. It would be so easy . . . so good. With her gown already rucked up to her hips, it'd be a simple matter of freeing himself and repositioning her on his lap.

She deserves better than this, Banner.

The cold voice of reason just barely cut through his drugged senses. Ignoring it, he went for his pants. With one arm wrapped about Tressa, he fumbled single-handedly first with his belt, and then on his fly. He'd managed the first two studs and was flipping open the third when his movements triggered a wave of reality in Tressa. Her mood suddenly changed.

"No!" Tressa made an attempt to scramble off his lap, but the arm of steel that was wrapped around her waist held her tight.

"Let me go," she demanded, twisting in his arms.

Banner tightened his hold even more. "Tressa . . . don't." The flame that had ignited in his loins was now pushing for release. He blinked heavily. "Honey, just let me . . ." But his thought was lost in her protest.

"No, Nick! I didn't come in here for this."

One jet brow rose in query. "What *did* you come in here for, if not this?"

She shoved against his chest, determined to be free. "Let me go! I won't be one of your on-board trollops!" she hissed.

Banner froze. In fact, nothing could have killed his mood more quickly. "One of my *what?*" he asked. Little did she know his convictions about bringing women on board the *Victorious*. He could count the number on one hand.

And there was Tressa. Pinned on his lap. Struggling with the shift that was bunched up around her waist. Banner's eyes flickered as perception slowly emerged through the fog. He'd practically taken the damn thing off, he realized. Her gown was hanging off one shoulder, exposing her breast. Her hair had fallen about her face and shoulders, and her dark eyes were wide as she stared at him in confusion.

The curses were soundless as he uttered them through clenched teeth. Neither his need nor his desire had lessened, but his sense of reason, at least, was beginning to burst through the mindless barrier of intoxication. With a muttered oath he loosened his hold on her.

Hell, at the rate he'd been going, one more minute and Loring's little angel would have lost her innocence crudely straddling the lap of the *Victorious'* crocked captain. Just what the hell did he think he was doing anyway? Fondling, of all people, Loring's daughter.

His expression grew serious as he regarded her quizzically for a moment. At the base of her throat her pulse thumped erratically. A rush of pink stained her cheeks, and there was no denying the wonderment in those liquid brown eyes staring up at him.

She had responded to him. He *knew* she had. He dimly recalled her moaning his name, clutching his shoulders, her soft gasps of pleasure, her answering kisses.

And for one savage moment he hadn't cared about anything but burying himself in her silky depths—with or without her consent.

He'd never forced a woman in his entire life, but he'd come awfully close to it just now with Tressa. Shock and confusion were evident in her expression, but so was something else. Drunk or not, he hadn't missed the undisguised passion in her eyes. Cupping her face with both of his hands, he sighed heavily. God help him, if he didn't let her go now, he'd never be able to pull away from her a second time. Never.

Banner's tender gesture seemed to subdue Tressa, as if interpreting the anguish in his eyes as regret and self-disgust. Now that his arm had loosened she no longer struggled for freedom. No doubt coping with her own private war with passion, she slipped into what could only be termed a false sense of security.

Tressa might have thought him remorseful. But in truth Nick Banner was no more accountable for himself now than when he'd first pulled her onto his lap. Self-disgust hadn't even entered the picture as yet. Still on the edge, Banner was struggling with only two things: overwhelming lust and the startling realization of whose daughter he was lusting after.

Oh, he'd eventually get around to feeling wracked with guilt. But for now, in his present benumbed state, the fact that she was innocent and that he'd frightened her hadn't quite registered.

With another sigh, Nick pushed her away from him. Her wrapper had fallen to the floor at his feet. Cursing softly, he retrieved it, shoved it into her hands, and set her back on her feet.

"Go on," he said harshly, never taking his eyes from her face. "Get back to your bunk 'fore I change my mind."

Chapter Twelve

Tressa remained standing when Nick had released her. At first his desire had been a heady lure. His kiss, tender, tentative, as if tasting a new wine. Then, suddenly, it had turned possessive.

He'd warned her more than once to get out. And now he was giving her still another chance. Common sense told her it was foolish—crazy—not to take his advice and run as fast as she could. To stay out of his sight until he'd sobered up.

Propriety told her that she should be angry and upbraid him for the liberties he'd just taken. Ah, but passion . . . passion told her differently. Passion told her she wanted more. And with her body still humming from his attentions, Tressa found herself dazed, unable to move.

At first she hadn't questioned the strange yet overwhelming emotions that had flooded her mind. She'd never thought to wonder at what point her thoughts had turned from honest concern to blatant lust for a man she knew so little about—yet strangely understood. The easy submission

143

he had elicited was so unlike her—as if something—no, someone—was overriding her own sensible judgment. And it all happened so mysteriously. Not until he'd stopped to open his pants had reality hit her.

Now, as her breathing began to return to normal, a wave of overwhelming need swept through her. Not the lustful need she had experienced in his arms, but the emptiness of longing. A feeling so strong and so foreign to her that for an instant Tressa felt as if she were someone else. For an instant the unfamiliar emptiness had become hers.

Nick was watching her with curious interest. Maybe she should try talking to him again, try reasoning with him. Maybe this time he would listen.

"Nick . . ." She paused for a meaningful moment, hardly recognizing her own voice. "Why won't you tell me what's wrong?"

"Cause you wouldn't want to hear it, Irish."

The intensity of his gaze was intimidating. "Yes, I would," she persisted. "Nick, please, has something happened?"

Swearing softly, Banner looked away. "What did I ever do to deserve this," he muttered dejectedly. Slowly his gaze returned, revealing twin sparks of glittering flame. "Tressa, my little innocent," he began, "I've come to a conclusion. No, make that two conclusions. One, you talk too damn much. And two, you assume everyone else likes talkin' as much as you do. Particularly me."

Tressa's back stiffened but, before she could speak, he went on. "Just for the record, sunshine—what's *happened*, talkin' won't cure."

Calling upon every ounce of willpower he possessed, he rose from the lounge and swept her into his arms.

Tressa gasped, clutching at him for support as he staggered, striving to maintain his balance.

"Nick! Let me go!"

Ignoring her struggles, he headed for the door.

"Nick! This is *not* funny. You put me down at once!"

"Don't tempt me, Tressa. I'm having a hard enough time with this decision as it is."

She tried to squirm free, but it was useless. He had no intention of releasing her.

They were approaching the bunks now. "Nick? Please . . ." Her voice broke. Keeping one arm wrapped about his neck, she pounded with the other against his shoulder. Ignoring her futile efforts, he seemed to be concentrating more on keeping his balance than anything.

"Consider this your lucky night," he said, coming to a halt before the tiered berths, " 'cause I can't believe I'm doin' this."

Cradling her in his arms, Nick swayed on his feet, gathering his strength for God only knew what. "Nick! Put me down!" Stars, he was going to fall with her!

Wavering slightly, he transferred her weight to his hands. With a surge of power he stiff-armed her above his head.

"Nick!" she cried out. But before she could launch any further protests, she'd cleared the guard rail and was toppling unceremoniously out of his hands and onto the upper berth.

Tressa pulled in a stunned breath as a growling, hissing TiMar rushed to the edge of the bunk, flashing four rows of lethally sharp teeth in warning.

"Ah, shut up," Nick growled back. And for an instant Tressa wasn't sure just who he was glaring at—her or TiMar.

Leaning an arm against the upper bunk for support, a long thought-filled moment passed before a slow, suggestive smirk stole across his face. "Hell," he added hoarsely, "you returned my kisses, lady, whether you care to admit it or not."

"You're drunk, Nick. Good night!"

"Damn right," he mumbled. "But not *that* drunk."

Tressa slowly burrowed beneath the covers, pulling them protectively under her chin. Her cheeks burned at the truth of his words. She opened her mouth to speak, then clamped it shut.

"I can't help but wonder"—his lazy drawl was beginning to take on a definite leer—"what ol' Burke baby—"

"Good night, Nick,"

"What's the matter, Tress, don't ya wanna' talk now?"

"All right," she hissed, her temper flaring, "we can talk. And after we've thoroughly discussed Burke's reaction we can move on to discuss my father's. Now, that should prove to be interesting, wouldn't you say?"

Nick frowned, his hand falling away from the bunk as he mumbled, "I'd say that's a severe understatement."

Tressa felt the jolt as Banner's weight hit the lower berth. A long moment of silence followed in which she hoped he'd passed out. But, as if in reply, his gravelly voice once again broke the silence. "By the way, Irish, off hand I'd say you weigh just a trifle more than a feathery one-hundred and ten, as listed on your security plate."

That just about did it! Who in stars had given him access to her security records? Indeed who?

"You returned my kisses, Irish . . ." He snorted once again, and then there was silence.

Miraculously Tressa kept her mouth shut and was thankful when that was the last she heard from him. What had started out as concern and kindness on her part had been misconstrued somewhere along the way. As a result, the feelings Nick had set into motion were more than Tressa wanted to face. Her body still tingled where his unshaven jaw had grazed her flesh. She could still taste the ale he'd been drinking—still feel the blatant differences in their anatomies.

Never in her life had she felt the way he'd made her feel. Never had she been kissed the way he'd kissed her. Even Burke had never taken such liberties.

And when he touched her! Tressa didn't even want to think about *that,* nor the feelings that had coursed through her as a result of his intimate touch. Her face heated at the memory.

How many times over the years had she literally dreamed of being held captive in Nick Banner's embrace—of being kissed senseless by the notorious rogue. Even drunk there was an air about him, an arrogance that fascinated her.

Tressa's breath caught at the memory of the smoldering flame she had seen in his eyes and recalled that her friend Sara had referred to him as a mythological sun god.

Having now seen and experienced this seductive side of him, Tressa was convinced that, drunk or sober, Nicholas Banner, if given the opportunity, was quite capable of seducing Venus herself.

But what concerned her more than anything was the fact that there was no rational explanation for the overwhelming lust that had raced through her while in his arms. Whispers of unfamiliar emotions assaulted her mind. Feelings she had never before experienced or known. In truth, it was as if she were someone else, not Tressa Loring. As if an experienced lover had somehow taken over her emotions, desires, and body. Someone so practiced and versed in the art of love, she knew what she wanted, and exactly what he wanted.

Nick was right. She *had* returned his kisses, in full measure. Why, he'd have taken her right then and there—and she would've let him without so much as a whimper of protest if something hadn't snapped her out of the spell she'd fallen into. Tressa's face clouded as his words echoed in her mind: *What I need, talkin' won't cure.* It was so clear. She meant nothing more to him than an easy take. Another conquest.

With a tiny separate part of her brain, Tressa numbly wondered what it would cost to totally win the heart of a man like Nick Banner. What could she possibly have to offer? He had girls in every port, and she'd bet every single one of them knew not only what he liked, but just how he liked it.

It was then, as she lay there in the dark, staring up at the ceiling, that the full force of reality hit her. He'd released her *not* out of honor. He'd dumped her back in her bed because he'd lost interest in her!

Tressa's breath caught in her throat. What a laugh it must have given him. He as much as said so himself when he teased her about Burke.

Closing her eyes, Tressa vowed that no matter how unpleasant it would be to face him in the morning, he would not have the satisfaction of humiliating her further. In the meantime she silently wished Nick Banner the very worst hangover of his entire life.

Sprawled across the top of his bed, still fully dressed, boots and all, Banner awoke with a low moan. Slowly opening his eyes, he squeezed them shut again in unbearable agony. They felt gritty, and his tongue felt like a flap of dried leather when he tried to swallow. He managed to open his eyes again, gingerly this time, to mere slits. Wincing against stabs of pain, he stared motionlessly at the bottom of the upper bunk.

He was disoriented at first, but reality slowly came back by degrees, bringing with it distorted images of Tressa and unfulfilled desire. Groaning, he rolled onto his side. He should have known the momentary lapse of memory was too good to last. No one to blame but himself for this morning's high price. Damn . . . it'd been years since he'd tied one on like this.

He braved the task of sitting up, burying his head in his hands just as Tressa breezed in from the galley.

"Well, good morning. You're finally awake I see! Stay right there, and I'll get you some coffee."

Suppressing another moan, he ignored her. Her cheerful, let's-pretend-nothing-happened attitude was enough to set his teeth on edge. Damn, his head hurt!

Tressa had just disappeared into the galley when he managed to whisper, "And some pain tabs . . ."

The next thing he knew, a mug of coffee was being shoved into his hand. Again Nick made an attempt to gain her attention. "Tress . . ." he croaked, turning a pain-filled gaze upon her.

"Yes, Nick? Is there something else I can get you?"

As if she didn't know. "Some pain tabs . . . please."

"Of course." He was certain he heard a muffled giggle.

"Bring me . . . three," he added, but she'd just rounded the corner into the lav and his whispered voice was so soft, it was doubtful she'd heard him.

He set the cup down on the shelf inside the berth. Leaning forward, he braced his elbows on his knees, buried his head in his hands, and waited.

"I don't know how you managed to get your hands on a supply of these," he heard her mutter from the lav. Within moments she'd returned to his side.

"Two is *all* you're getting."

Belatedly, and with agonizing slowness, Nick uncovered his face and held out a hand while Tressa dropped two tiny green pills into his palm.

"As it is, this is borderline toxic, Nick."

Banner gratefully accepted the pills and ignored her ongoing flow of objections.

"You know, all it would take is some enthusiastic Customs Officer . . ."

Raking both hands through his hair, Nick clenched his teeth and groaned. Even his hair hurt. "Tressa . . . can we discuss this later?"

It wasn't the words, it was his tone that brooked no argument. Tressa's insistent chattering stopped immediately, and Nick settled back onto the bunk, gritting his teeth against the throbbing pain that was stampeding through his head.

He closed his eyes. Maybe if he stayed perfectly still and didn't move, didn't even breathe, maybe it would just go away.

"Do you want me to help you with your boots?" Tressa was flitting about him again.

"*No*," he moaned. "Just . . . leave me alone."

As an anchor in the middle of a spinning cabin, Nick braced his booted foot against the back wall of the berth and held on.

Four hours later he stirred. The pain had eased to an almost tolerable level and he lay perfectly still, afraid to move for fear it would return. Slowly coming awake, his gaze slid from studying the bottom of Tressa's bunk to the cockpit, where he read the time off the command console. Between last night and now, time had ceased to exist for him.

He swung his feet over the edge of the bunk. His body parts responded to his brain's commands in slow motion. From there he climbed to his feet, clutching the edge of the upper bunk for stability.

With a sigh and grim determination he reached for his mug and made his way to the galley. Better to get an unpleasant job over and done with. Leaning against the doorway, he stood there awhile, quietly observing Tressa as she sat on the lounge. TiMar was curled in her lap and she was talking to him.

As if sensing his presence, she turned, flashing him a smile. "Feeling better?"

He should have known it would be one of the two—either the too-cheerful scenario or the ever-popular silent treatment. He didn't know which was worse.

Gritting his teeth against a sudden wave of pain, he ran a frustrated hand through his sable hair. He'd been doing a lot of that lately—raking his hand through his hair.

"Uh, Tressa," he began in a stilted voice, not quite up to its full, rich volume, "I owe you an apology for . . . um . . . what happened last night. I was outta line, and you have my word it won't happen again."

A moment of heavy silence followed his noble apology before Tressa rose to close the distance between them, her expression inscrutable. "You're apology isn't necessary, Nick." She took the mug from his hand.

"Like I said, it won't happen again."

Nodding in acknowledgment, she turned for the sink.

Banner's eyes narrowed, assessing her mood. She was much too calm when she should have been furious with him for last night's little performance. In fact, he'd braced himself for it.

He stared long and hard at her back as she busied herself near the cook center. At last, shoving away from the doorframe, he approached her. "Would it help if you slapped me?" he asked softly. "I deserve it, you know."

"Yes!" she said, turning abruptly to face him, "you *do* deserve it."

"All right . . ." he said in compliance. "Do I sit down first or afterwards?" He offered a lame grin and added, "I've never done it quite like this before."

"You're not funny." Tressa turned her back to him again.

"Look," he began, "I *said* I'm sorry. I don't know what else to say."

Tressa turned and faced him square on, "There's nothing else to say. It's obvious you're sorry, Nick."

He stared at her, baffled.

"And what's that supposed to mean?"

"Nothing. Not a thing."

A muscle jerked in his jaw. "Damned if I know what you're talkin' about."

"Oh, I'm sure we understand one another perfectly. But please . . . don't worry, because as far as I'm concerned . . . last night never happened." Tressa turned away and began wiping down a small counter.

Frowning, Nick continued staring at her rigid back while she scrubbed furiously. Trying to make sense of it all, he watched her for a long moment. Then, swearing softly, he turned and headed for the shower.

Standing beneath the spray, he came to one very sure

conclusion: No matter what, he was going to have to put a tight lid on his consumption of ale right along with everything else he was being forced to censor in his life.

Hell, there was no excuse for last night. He knew it. And now more than ever he knew he was going to have to come up with something to occupy that little girl's time. It was either that or lose his sanity entirely.

Little girl? He wanted to laugh at his choice of words. She was no little girl. Tressa was affecting him more than he'd ever dreamed possible. He didn't *dare* allow his mind to conjure up the image of her responding to him last night. As it was, her very presence was pushing him beyond his limits of endurance.

As drunk as he'd been, he should have been spared the memory, but somehow he had a sinking feeling that the image of last night would be with him for a long time.

He was just buttoning his shirt when he stepped out of the lav, clean and freshly shaven. His dark hair, still damp, was swept back, curling over the top of his collar.

Tressa was still fussing about in the galley as he passed by. "There's a fresh pot of coffee, if you want some." Her tone was as cold as ice water.

With a sigh, Nick entered the galley and accepted the mug of steaming coffee she wordlessly handed him.

Taking a seat at the table, he blew steam from his mug and watched her over the rim.

"If and when you feel like eating, I'll . . ." she began, but never had the chance to finish. Up and on his feet, two long strides was all it took to reach her. Catching her by the arm, Nick spun her about to face him.

"We need to have a little talk," he growled. "You and me. *Now!*"

Strained silence filled the cabin. Every curve in her enticing body spoke defiance as she twisted out of his grip. "You're the one who needs the talk, Nick. Not me."

He jerked her back so fast, her head snapped with the effort. "I was drunk last night, lady. *You weren't!*"

"I see," she said, her chin raised as she met his icy gaze. "And being drunk gives you an excuse, does it?"

Banner caught her chin firmly. "I'm not just talkin' about last night, damn it." Whether you realize it or not, sweetheart, we have a serious problem here.

"This relationship is turning into far more than it should be. Just for the record, Tressa, you're not my mother!" he all but shouted. "Nor my wife or even my mistress, for that matter."

He rolled his eyes toward the ceiling, exhaling in frustration. "Oh, God, what did I ever do to deserve this?" he moaned.

Tressa tried to look away, but his grip on her jaw prevented her from moving her head. He bent his face close to hers. "I'm only going to say this once and you'd better listen. This . . . relationship, if that's even the word for it, is strictly employer-employee-based. Do you understand what I'm saying? You mean nothing more, nothing less. I'm on contract to pick up a high-sec shipment. The reason, and the *only* damn reason you're along, is because I didn't happen to have the authority to release the shipment *and you did.*"

With a heavy sigh, he glanced away. "How did I ever manage all these years," he mumbled to himself, "without you around to fix my meals, bring my morning coffee, and mother me like you've been doing . . ." His sentence trailed off with another exasperated sigh.

"Are you implying . . ."

His deep voice was no more than a whisper of warning. "The next time you decide to encourage a man, you'd better be damn sure you're prepared for the results."

Tressa's expression was crestfallen; nevertheless he continued. "The next guy might not let you off so easy. Are you with me, Tressa? Is it beginning to sink in?"

Tressa swallowed hard. Her face had drained of color. "For your information, I was not trying to encourage you."

"Oh, yeah? And just what have you been trying to do?

I'm curious. Did you have a particular goal in mind, or were you just playing house for a while?''

He heard her quick intake of breath and felt a twinge of regret at the harshness of his words. He was hurting her, but damn it all, something had to be said or next time he wouldn't be able to stop himself.

''It's a dangerous game you're playing, Irish.'' His voice had turned low and husky again. ''I'm willing to play if you are. However, I suggest we go over the rules first.'' He frowned mockingly. ''Somehow I got the impression you weren't quite ready for last night's consequences.''

Chapter Thirteen

Nick released her chin and took hold of both of her hands. His voice softened. "Tressa . . . please stop mothering me. I'm begging you, stop looking after me as if there's more between us than there is. Quit worrying whether I've eaten or not, or if I'm staying up too late. Don't even put salve on my damned wounds. I'm *not* going to survive at this rate."

Tressa set her jaw stubbornly. A moment of silence passed between them.

"Just don't . . . do . . . anything!" he added, enunciating the last three words and staring at her long and hard. Tressa unconsciously sucked in her upper lip, bringing into full play that damned dimple again. It was almost his undoing, and he found himself hard-pressed to keep from taking her into his arms.

"Do I make myself clear?" he asked.

Up went her chin. "Clear as krystaline, Captain."

"Good." He turned and made his way to the cockpit.

Outraged, Tressa darted for the lav and leaned back against the closed privacy panel. "I'm not going to cry," she whispered "I'm not going to cry."

Her eyes narrowed furiously. How dare he accuse her of being the one at fault? How dare he blame her for *his* weakness? Of all the arrogant . . . The echo of Nick's maddening words marched through her mind. "Just . . . don't . . . do . . . anything."

Fine. If that's the way he wanted it, that was exactly what she'd do; absolutely nothing, least of all speak to him. "Swamp rat!" she muttered.

With the morning's lecture still resounding in her ears, Tressa made a deliberate effort to keep out of Nick's way. With nowhere to go, she isolated herself in the galley, ignoring him whenever he came in for coffee or something to eat.

For the past ten minutes she had been standing before the viewport. The *Victorious* had been gaining steadily on a comet that was following its own parallel course. Though separated by millions of miles, they were presently abreast of it, the sight breathtaking, its fiery head completely engulfing the viewport.

A wave of nostalgia swept over Tressa. Not all that long ago she had dreamed of being just such a comet at LorTech, working at her father's side.

Jonathan had always left the door open for Tressa to change her mind, had always encouraged her to sample and investigate other careers. In fact, it was he who had encouraged her to volunteer at Port Ireland's Med Facility and to eventually take premed. She'd taken the course just to please him, not really thinking she'd ever be interested. But to her surprise she'd begun showing a genuine interest in the medical field, and eventually she found herself torn between the two careers. Meanwhile, her father continued acquainting her with the various levels of the corporation, including the position of company medTech. At last--a chance to combine both fields. Even her sparking interest in Burke Sinclair wasn't enough to dim the lights of her bright future at LorTech.

Yet, here she was trapped aboard a small cargo ship with an arrogant, overbearing, belligerent brute who blamed her for *his* lack of control. Staring sightlessly out the viewport, Tressa swiped away another tear. She'd been blinking back tears most of the day, despite her promise not to cry.

Typical rake, her mind shouted, not wanting to admit that there was absolutely nothing *typical* about Nick Banner, neither his looks nor his conduct. In truth, his innate sensuality had totally addled her brain the moment she'd first stepped aboard.

In her mind's eye Tressa relived the first few moments when she'd faced him in the galley last night—the wide shoulders, those long black-clad legs, that gloriously handsome face framed in dark, silky hair, and that seductive gaze that had set her heart pounding. She tried not to think of his touch, that slow magic that had awakened frightening new sensations and emotions she only half understood.

How could she feel this way about him when he made her so furious? He certainly made it clear she was no more than a nuisance, an inconvenience that he felt nothing more than lust for. She supposed she should be thankful that he had dumped her in her bunk—*untouched*. The experience had been humiliating; being carried to bed like a child. She recalled how effortlessly he'd lifted her up over his head, depositing her into the top bunk. The act in itself was impressive, but considering his blood alcohol level, at the time, the achievement was awesome and had to be much harder physically than he'd made it appear.

Tressa wondered what would it take for him to think of her as something else besides ''Loring's cargo.'' A small part of her wished that somehow she was prettier or maybe more experienced in love. But then, why should she care? Nick Banner would never commit to anyone but himself.

''Taylor's Comet . . . in case you're wonderin'.'' Nick's deep voice broke into her thoughts.

Totally committed to her plan to ignore the swamp rat, Tressa refused to even acknowledge his presence, let alone the offered information. And she didn't need to turn around to see him. In her mind's eye she knew just what he was doing. He was standing in the doorway, probably leaning against the frame in his usual stance. He seemed always to be leaning or slouching or sprawling on something. Tressa knew that wasn't entirely true, but she was in no mood to admit that the swamp rat had about the most sensuous way of carrying himself of any man she knew.

"When you get a moment, Tressa," he continued, "would you come up front? Please." Not waiting for a response this time, Nick turned and headed back.

What was it about that man that could make her forget what was most important in her life? And why was it her pulse raced every time he entered the same room?

Just as the comet, now dropping rapidly astern, seemed to be running a losing race against the *Victorious*, Tressa's plan of attack was running a losing race against her heart. With a sigh she turned and headed for the cockpit.

"I've decided to give you something to do to keep you busy," he said as she came forward.

A gleam of mischief lit Tressa's eyes. "Oh? Did you forget that I was specifically told I wasn't to do *anything*."

He looked at her so hard, Tressa felt a jolt course through her. "Have a seat," he said with tight control, motioning for her to take the pilot's seat. "I've decided to teach you a few cockpit basics."

Instantly forgetting her anger and her plan to be obstinate, Tressa's face lit up. "You're going to teach me how to run the *Victorious*?"

Nick's mouth quirked with humor. "Not exactly, just a few basics. I'm assuming you know how to pilot a landcraft."

"Yes, of course."

"Good; then you have a working knowledge of what I'm about to show you."

Beginning with power-up, much of the afternoon was spent with Nick leaning over Tressa's shoulder, patiently explaining the difference between that switch and this button. What it means when this light turns red and what to do when that one turns green.

"See that lineup of toggle switches overhead?"

Tressa glanced up. "You mean these?" she asked, pointing.

"Yes. Flip the first four straight down."

Tressa did, then watched in amazement as another section on the command console suddenly sparked to life. A diagnostic schematic materialized on the screen, depicting the entire ship from stem to stern. Below was the notation "Pilot Information".

"Now, before you go any further," Nick continued, "you're going to ask the computer to do a basic systems check. Tap in the words 'System Overview.' "

Tressa did, then looked up in anticipation.

"Okay. Now flip that fifth switch."

She did and instantly, the schematic of the ship snapped to life. To the left, beside the illustration, was a progressive read-out of every detail about the ship, from the life support system, to the security.

"See this list?" he asked, pointing to the screen. "As each feature is monitored, this list will highlight exactly what the computer is checking. Over here, the corresponding area on the schematic will light up in red. If it checks, the color will change to green and the list will move on to the next detail. If it doesn't, that section will remain in red on the schematic. The objective is to wind up with a completely green diagram of the ship at the end. Anything still in red, needs fixing."

Tressa caught on quickly, but not without a certain amount of awkwardness. Banner was thorough and surprisingly unhurried with her, continuing to go over the same thing until he was satisfied that she understood it completely.

A couple of times she became confused, like when she was learning to enter coordinates into the NAVCOMP. Still, Nick continued to show extreme patience with her while carefully keeping things on a no-nonsense basis.

He was doing it again, causing that peculiar tingling in the pit of her stomach. And he wasn't even trying. She refused to admit that it took nothing at all to stoke a smoldering fire inside her, bringing back memories of last night's kisses . . . his touch. Just the scent of him as he leaned over her, the way he said her name, or even looked at her was all it took. Wasn't it odd, she thought, his male arrogance, the very thing that infuriated her the most about him, was what drew her like a magnet.

"This gauge here relates to temperature," he said, pointing to a panel headed by the title CLIMATE CONTROL. "It displays both interior and exterior temperatures." He leaned over and touched a pad marked INT. TEMP. "Right now the temperature is seventy."

Tressa nodded. "And this one, here," she pointed, "tells the exterior temperature?"

"That's right."

"Would it give the outside temperature reading right now?"

"I've never tried it in space before," he said. "If it registers at all, it will be reading the temperature off the hull. Go ahead. Press it and see what happens."

Tressa touched the pad labeled EXT. TEMP. and was instantly rewarded with an answer.

"Minus two hundred four? Now that ought to chill your Extra Dark."

"That ought to chill something," he muttered.

By the end of the afternoon he seemed genuinely impressed that she'd passed two tests he'd set for her. "Tomorrow," he told her, "I'll teach you about Stellardrive." He referred to the very mode of travel that was making it possible for them to get to where they were going in just a few short weeks rather than years.

160

Over the next couple of days Tressa breezed through each step of instruction. But when she wasn't occupied with her new lessons Tressa kept her vow about staying out of his way. She continued to make coffee but no longer brought him his. And conversation, unless it pertained to the workings of the ship, had been brought to a grinding halt. True to her vow, she neither spoke nor acknowledged him unless he spoke or initiated the conversation, and even then her responses were short and to the point.

Lee Bryant activated the ship's tactical screen. With another entry, a simulated star system appeared, complete with major planets. A solid green dot represented their own ship; a flashing red delta symbolized their target.

Bryant's lips twisted into a sinister smile. "Gentlemen, looks like we've just caught up with the *Victorious.*" He entered instructions into the on-board computer, then smugly puffed a fat cigar stub to life. All three men watched in fascination as a pulsing amber line measured the distance between the green dot and the red delta, then computed the distance into time. "We should have the Loring girl in eighteen hours and be on our way back to collect payment."

"And Banner will be wishing he was never born." De Vries sneered.

By midmorning of the next ship day, Banner was growing weary of the game Tressa was playing. Oh, he was well aware of what she was doing. After all, he reasoned, it was far safer than to have her continually underfoot, driving him to drink with her nearness.

Banner took a sip of his coffee and reflected on the other night. Drunk out of his mind or not, the memory of her responding in his arms was vivid. But in his intoxicated drive to have her, slow and easy wasn't part of the game plan; a mistake that had frightened her into pulling away.

He could see her now, breathless with the desire he had

stirred to life, yet too inexperienced to fully understand what was happening. But *he* knew. He knew exactly what was happening to her, and in his rush to have her he'd blown it.

And thank God he had! *Loring's daughter!*

With a sigh, he patted his pocket for a cigar, found one, lit up, and blew smoke into the air. If given a second chance, he'd never be able to pull away—in spite of who she was.

Sad thing was, his plan to keep her busy and out of his way had failed miserably. He wanted to laugh. No, he wanted to cry. He'd spent the last two days hovering over her, breathing in her sweet scent and touching her while patiently mixing physical with verbal instruction. His entire plan had backfired, leaving him in almost worse condition than when he'd started the noble endeavor. Further defeating his purpose, the thoughts he was presently entertaining would shock the socks off her.

Silently cursing, he chided himself for his weakness. It was madness, and there was only one solution to his self-inflicted torture. He would simply have to put the girl out of his mind for the remainder of the voyage. The responsibility was his, and it wouldn't be easy. He leaned back in the pilot's seat, pondering the unbelievable fact that his desire for her was stronger than ever. He missed their talks and the sound of her warm laughter. But he'd given his word to Jonathan, and by God, he meant to keep it.

Hardening his heart, Nick closed his eyes in an effort to relax. Damn it, Tressa wasn't even within sight and his entire body was in a state of torment. Steeling his mind against his desire for her, he clamped his cigar between his teeth, clasped his hands behind his head, and stretched his long legs out before him.

It was early on the fourteenth day. Nick had just stepped out of the galley with a mug of coffee in his hand when suddenly a host of Klaxons and proximity alarms began sounding.

What he saw when he activated the ship's vidscreen brought him up short.

"Ho . . . lee shhhit!" There was no mistaking the fast-approaching ship, and no escaping either.

Tressa came tearing from the galley. "What's wrong?"

"Nothing. Yet," he answered as he strode across the cabin for his gun and began strapping it on.

"Nick . . . what's happening?"

"Tressa, c'mere." Grabbing her by the arm, he propelled her toward the bunks. Dropping to one knee, he began pulling out the stored articles jammed beneath his berth. "I don't want any arguments and we haven't got time for questions. Just crawl under the bunk," he ordered.

"What?"

"It's not a suggestion, Tressa. *Just do it!*"

Tressa slowly lowered herself to the floor. "What is it?" she asked, her eyes wide with alarm.

Banner hunkered down beside her, catching her chin affectionately and then searching her face, as if committing every detail to memory. "I don't know what's going to happen, but I have a gut feeling you're not going to like what you see or hear." He brushed his thumb tenderly over her lower lip, then caressed her mouth with a gentle kiss.

A moment of silence passed before he spoke again. "It's imperative that you stay hidden until I say otherwise, you understand? Above all, do *not* draw attention to yourself in any way. It will be all I can do to defend this ship without having to worry about you too."

Tressa nodded and obediently crawled beneath the bunk, sliding clear to the back at his coaxing. Reaching above the bunk, Banner withdrew a small handgun from his utility belt. "Here," he said, pressing it into her palm. "If for any reason I don't make it through this . . ." he paused meaningfully. "*Use it!*"

Tressa stared at the weapon in her hand. It was heavy and cold. "Nick?"

"*You use it!* Just aim and press the trigger." With that he commenced replacing as many of the boxes and travel packs as possible. As soon as Tressa was hidden from view, he stashed the crate of ale into the ship's hold, along with a few remaining boxes that wouldn't fit back under the bunk. From there he stood and shoved the upper bunk back into place against the bulkhead.

"Nick . . ."

"Just remember what I told you about keeping quiet, no matter what happens. And Tressa . . . should anything happen to me, you have enough knowledge to get this ship out of here. The coordinates are already preset," he said, scanning the cabin for any other telltale signs of a companion on board.

"Nick, you're scaring me. What's happening?"

Another alarm sounded, this one with more urgency, as the *Victorious* shuddered under a heavy jolt.

Recognizing the sensation, a heavy rock landed in the pit of his gut. "Damn," he mumbled softly, turning for the cockpit. There was no mistaking the grab of a tow beam.

With a crackle of static, the comset snapped to life, and Nick was face-to-face with a familiar enemy: Kendyl.

"Kill your drives, Banner, and prepare to be boarded."

With a heavy sigh, Nick leaned forward and reluctantly tapped in a series of keys. Within seconds the drive system began shutting down. The ensuing silence was penetrating, leaving only the soft hiss of the ventilation.

It was then, for the first time since Tressa had come aboard, that the ship's main computer broke the silence, and did so with a seductively feminine voice.

In one of their earlier conversations Nick had told her about the time he'd had the computer overhauled and, as a practical joke, it came back with a voice change—from dull monotone to sensuously female. Though he'd intended to return it for an adjustment, he just never got around to it, and in the meantime had programmed the computer to use "voice" only in the event of emergencies.

In breathy undertones the "voice" began analyzing the ship's situation and logically deducing Nick's best maneuver. "Nick, darling, I think you should know that we are being held by a tow beam."

"No kidding . . ." Banner responded dryly. "I hadn't figured that out yet." He reached overhead and activated yet another series of red-lit keys.

The sensuous voice continued. "As a result of the ship's current tactical status, as well as the lack of sufficient weaponry, the probability of a successful engagement and/or escape is zero, love."

"Right . . ." he drawled, preoccupied at the controls.

"Therefore any decision to engage will be considered improper and abnormal use, invalidating the hull warranty. In no event shall the manufacturer be liable for loss of profits, loss of business, interruption of service, or any indirect, special, or consequential damages arising out of any breach of this warranty."

Banner ignored the provocative voice and its flow of legalese. A soft chime sounded, and he depressed a pulsing red-lit button.

"Nick, darling, under these conditions if you should elect suicide over surrender, I will dump the ship's atmosphere at your command."

"Thanks, I think I'll give surrender a try. Now, will you shut up so I can decide what I'm doing after that?"

A second jolt traversed the ship. Nick rose from his seat and stalked toward the main entry port. "Tressa, remember what I said. Not a word, *not a single sound.*" There was an edge of desperation to his voice.

Life-sustaining air could be heard hissing into the small chamber between the outer lock and the inner hatch. Removing the safety thong from his gun, Banner waited until a Klaxon sounded and a red indicator turned green. Palming the lock, he stepped back, the heel of his hand resting on the butt of his gun as the doors cycled open and three men boarded the *Victorious*.

"Well, well, Banner. Fancy meeting you clear out here in the middle of nowhere."

Quint Kendyl was aiming a hand weapon directly at Nick's chest, his words deceivingly friendly, his tone clearly lethal.

Reminiscent of a nineteenth-century Terran high seas pirate, Kendyl was about Nick's age. His medium-brown shoulder-length hair was swept back and tied at the base of his neck. Though he wasn't as tall as Nick, his muscular build spoke of a potency all its own.

"Yeah, what a small galaxy," Nick said dryly, allowing his gaze to slide to the two thugs standing behind Kendyl. "You sure three of you are enough, Quint? Maybe you ought to send for a backup or something."

The man's eyes narrowed. "If my guess is right, the backup is well on its way." And without explaining anything, he turned. Giving a curt nod to one of the men standing behind him, he sent the man advancing toward Nick.

Nick slowly raised his hand from the butt of his gun, allowing the man to lift the weapon from its holster.

"You know, now that I think about it, it's a coincidence meeting you at all." Kendyl continued his meaningless play at casual friendliness. "Why, the last I heard . . . you were dead." He frowned, shaking his head in mock discouragement. "Just can't seem to find good help nowadays."

"Got that backwards," Banner replied. "It goes: 'You can't keep a good man down.' " Nick simply stood there in his usual laid-back manner, emanating an air of total boredom. The deceptive laziness was belied only by the contempt in his eyes.

Kendyl's smile was smug. "That reminds me; my compliments on the way you handled those men back at Port France."

"Yeah? They were your men?"

" 'Fraid not, but you left one of 'em dead." Kendyl

laughed. "It seems you're even more popular now than you were before."

"Is that right?" Nick said, continuing to watch Kendyl with idle interest. "Shame someone didn't warn them about messing around the *Victorious.*"

A moment of intense silence passed before Kendyl changed the subject. "Word's out you have some high-security cargo onboard."

Frowning, Banner looked confused. "What cargo is that? I wasn't aware I had anything with a high-sec tag on it."

Quint threw back his head and laughed. "Oh, but you do, Nick, ol' partner. And unless I miss my guess, or you've changed an awful lot over the past few years, I'd say you're very much aware of exactly what's sitting in your cargo bay."

Kendyl's face grew serious. "I'm giving you a choice. Either open the ship's hold willingly, or buckle under a little uh . . . shall we say, motivation? The choice is yours."

The corners of Nick's mouth rose in a humorless smile. "Just curious, Kendyl; how'd you find me?"

Kendyl grinned. "You're glowing brighter than the double stars of Triton right now. Looks like some thoughtful person put a tracer on your hull. You must be growing careless in your old age."

Kendyl wouldn't have had any way of knowing that he'd just answered the two questions that had been bouncing around in Nick's head for the past ten minutes. Number one, he now knew that Kendyl was after the Shaiel shipment, and not Tressa. And number two, he knew exactly how Kendyl had tracked him down. If there *was* a tracer on the *Victorious,* it sure as hell wasn't on the hull as Kendyl suspected. With the Ripper for security, there was only one way a tracer could have been placed onboard the ship. Despite his sophisticated sensing equipment, it had to have been smuggled on with the cargo he'd picked up on Shaiel. Banner grinned inwardly . . . the very cargo Kendyl was now so anxious to take off his hands.

Skillfully masking his speculation behind a casual facade, Banner smiled. "Well, in that case I suppose I'd better check the hull as soon as I hit dirt."

Kendyl chuckled. "That's if you even make it to the next port. Now . . . are you going to open the hold or do you need a little incentive?" He gave a faint nod to the man who had taken Nick's weapon, and in response Nick felt the bore end of his own gun resting against his ribs.

Skilled at masking his emotions, no one would have guessed the concern racing through Banner's mind as they passed the berths. One noise: That was all it would take.

"So, what do you plan to do with the shipment?" Nick asked casually.

"Depends on what it is, first." Kendyl replied. "One thing's for sure; I can sell it on the market for a hell of a lot more than you're delivering it for."

"So, you've gone pirate all the way, is that it?"

The grin faded and Kendyl ignored the comment.

"Why doesn't that surprise me?" Banner continued softly.

"Just open the hold, Banner, and cut the crap."

The equipment was not only bulky but heavy. It took Nick and one of Kendyl's men a good ten minutes to move it from one ship to the other. Once the mission was accomplished Banner was escorted back at gunpoint, where he turned and faced Kendyl, his expression unreadable as his gaze slid from Kendyl's face to the small black weapon in his hand, then back to his face again.

"I'm sure you can understand that we can't afford to have you following us. I should just kill you right here and now, but I think I'll leave that amusement for your fan club. They shouldn't be too far behind." With that he laughed as his thumb depressed a small button.

Chapter Fourteen

Choking back a cry as Nick collapsed to the deck, Tressa felt the fury of the stunner rip through his body just as if the two of them were linked somehow, sharing the same emotions. Unable to see more than his extended arm resting palm up, anguish nearly overpowered her. Sheer will kept her silent.

She was experiencing . . . Nick's pain!

Suddenly the sensation died to dull spasms, and with it Tressa sensed Nick had lost consciousness.

"Been a pleasure seein' you again, Nick ol' buddy." With an unmerciful smirk of satisfaction, Kendyl began backing into the air lock. The inner hatch cycle closed, and then there was silence.

Too stunned, too scared, and much too smart to move, Tressa remained hidden for what seemed an eternity. The only sound was the pounding of her heart and her own ragged gasps for breath. Only when she heard the sound of Kendyl's ship disengaging from the *Victorious* did she scramble out from her hiding place.

"Nick," she sobbed, rushing to his side. "Oh, Nick . . ."

But there was no response. Sprawled on the deck of the ship, Nick Banner lay motionless, his body limp and deathly still. Dropping to her knees, Tressa placed a trembling hand to his pulse point, relived to find a strong, steady thud beneath her touch. She brushed a dark lock of hair off his face. "Nick . . . please . . . can you hear me?"

Tressa's eyes brimmed with tears as she assessed his unconscious form. Noticing the stilted angle of his leg, she straightened it. Then, unable to think of anything else to do, she grabbed a pillow and blanket from his bunk and tenderly covered him, cushioning his head against the cold hard deck of the ship.

Sensing it would be many long hours before he would come around, Tressa rose to her feet and drew in several calming breaths. But a fresh lance of panic shot through her when her gaze rested on the silent, empty cockpit.

The *Victorious* was drifting aimlessly in the dark void of deep space, awaiting God knew what to catch up with them.

Tressa swallowed hard.

Establishing her priorities was easy, but finding the strength to carry them out was another matter. If Kendyl was right, trouble was on its way, and Tressa knew Nick Banner wouldn't be sitting around waiting for it to arrive.

There was only one course of action to take—power up and get out of there.

Promising she'd return to tend to him, Tressa made her way to the cockpit, taking her place in the pilot's seat. She could never remember feeling quite so small as she did at this moment . . . or quite so lost. Another wave of panic swept over her as she glanced at the complex command console.

"Dear God," she whispered.

With a deep breath, Tressa's shaky fingers began entering information she had only recently begun to learn. In response, a host of indicators snapped to life on the instrument panel, and Tressa's eyes were drawn to a brightly lit section, a diagnostic data center linked to the on-board computer. It featured a full display of digital readouts. She remembered Nick briefly going over this with her.

Headings such as FUEL CONSUM and WATER CONSUM were self-explanatory. She moved on to others, finding RANGE CODE, BOOSTER DELAY, DRIVING THRUST and OR-BITAL TRAJEC not only confusing, but leaving her with no idea how important they were. He'd never explained them to her.

Blinking away tears, Tressa leaned back, trying to remember what came next. A soft chime sounded, heralding the illumination of a single panel of orange indicators. A pulsing notation on a small vid screen read: SOURCE OF POWER?

Tressa's mind spun.

There are two drive systems, Tressa. Nick's voice echoed in her mind. *Standard jets and Stellardrive.*

The soft chime sounded again, and the tiny notation winked off, then repeated itself. SOURCE OF POWER?

Tressa reached out and depressed her selection, watching as the notation instantly cleared.

She waited expectantly. Nothing.

Imagination clawed at her brain, kindling her worst fears.

What if she couldn't get the ship running?

What if those men caught up?

What if Nick should die? That one was the worst of them all. Biting her lower lip, Tressa stole a look at him. "Don't you dare die on me," she breathed, glancing down at Nick and feeling overwhelmed by the mixture of compassion, terror . . . and a sudden empty void she couldn't explain.

With a deep breath she studied the controls. *Relax and think, Tressa. Think about what Nick taught you.*

Tressa emitted a nervous giggle at suddenly remembering the next step. Reaching out, she depressed the final key in the sequence of ignition, flinching as the *Victorious* responded to her command with a shudder and a low growl.

By now she was holding her breath and reaching over

her head to press yet another key. In return, the low-pitched whine began building, and Tressa emitted a soft gasp when all sorts of digital readouts began climbing rapidly. Indicators on the console winked from red to amber.

With a new sense of urgency, Tressa called upon her memory. Facing the console, her back rigid, she watched the display of lights change one by one from amber to green. When the cycle was complete, she proceeded to turn to the NAVCOMP. Thank God the coordinates for their destination were already loaded.

She entered yet another series of numbers, and within a matter of minutes the readings indicated that they were indeed underway.

As soon as Stellardrive had engaged and the wave of dizziness had passed, Tressa swung around with a heavy sigh of accomplishment, her gaze lighting upon the helpless captain as he lay half on his stomach.

"First we need to get you to the bunk," she murmured, considering the task of getting him off the cold decking. She rose and went to him.

Once again her training at Port Ireland's med facility came into play. Removing the blanket she'd placed on him earlier, Tressa purposefully began rolling up one edge until she'd rolled up approximately one-fourth of it. From there she commenced tucking the rolled section up against the length of his back, spreading out the unrolled portion.

With that done, she knelt behind him, hooked her fingers through his belt loops, and pulled. Two strong tugs rolled Nick's almost lifeless body onto his back, but it also entrapped her folded legs beneath him in the process. Tressa squirmed free of his weight and Nick slid off her knees and onto the blanket, moaning softly when his head hit the deck with a thud.

"Nick . . ." Tressa's heart pounded with anticipation. "Nick, can you hear me?"

No response.

Tressa studied him speculatively, looking for a sign, any

indication that he would soon regain consciousness. At the realization that it wasn't going to happen, disappointment welled in her and a cold knot formed in the pit of her stomach.

Tressa touched his face, her hand cupping his jaw. "Nick . . ."

Refusing to give in to tears, she clambered over him to the other side. The rolled section of the blanket was now pinned beneath Nick's back; several hard yanks and she had it free. The end result, as she unrolled it, left Nick just where she wanted him—lying somewhere near the center of the blanket.

"Now to get you to the bunk," she muttered with determination.

Grabbing both top ends of the blanket, it took Tressa ten of the most strenuous minutes of her life to drag Nick's inert body over to the bunk. From there she angled him into a sitting position, with his back against the bed and his head dropped forward onto his chest.

Tressa blew at an unruly curl of dark hair that was tickling her forehead. He was much heavier than she'd anticipated. Pausing, she allowed herself a minute of rest before tackling "phase two" of the project.

Next she climbed up on the bunk behind him. Sitting on her knees, she reached down, grasping him beneath his arms. "Here it goes," she muttered, straining against his weight.

It took all of her strength and several unladylike tries before she'd managed to even budge her unconscious companion. Leaning back, jaw clenched in determination, Tressa continued her struggle as Nick's body slowly inched upward.

"I could sure use . . . a little . . . team effort about now," she ground out between clenched teeth.

Tressa was so caught up in her efforts, she failed to note that the procedure was actually dragging him up on top of her. The realization didn't set in until a final lunge knocked her back onto the bunk, where she smacked her head against the back wall and was left helplessly pinned beneath Nick's formidable body.

Exhausted from her efforts and trapped beneath Banner's dead weight, Tressa couldn't move. It was hard to even breathe. Her chin nestled into the hollow of his shoulder and his sable hair tickled her cheek. The male scent of him filled her nostrils, and for an instant Tressa could almost picture that cocky grin of his and hear his low chuckle.

"Oh, you'd just love this, wouldn't you?" she muttered, working her arms in between their bodies until she had the palms of her hands braced against his back. Even unconscious, his back was an immense slab of muscled steel. His buttocks snuggled into the gap of her slightly parted knees and to Tressa's dismay, every move she made, every wriggle, separated her legs even more.

Cozy, isn't it darlin'? She could almost hear his taunting voice and see that lazy smile.

Now the trick was to roll him off her and not have him slide right back down onto the floor. Tressa was just gathering her strength for the endeavor when a deep purring interrupted her concentration. Turning her head toward the sound, she found herself peering into huge green cat eyes.

TiMar had joined them on the bunk and was presently kneading his front paws in her fanned-out hair, contented at the cozy arrangement.

"I don't want to hurt your little kitty feelings, TiMar, but this . . . is definitely a temporary situation and you're right in . . . my way," she said, gasping between words.

With his tail held high, TiMar lazily sashayed up onto Nick's belly. In so doing the tip of his tail was all that Tressa could see from her limited point of view. Peering over Nick's massive shoulder, she watched the end of TiMar's fluffy tail going around and around in a tight circle; then it suddenly disappeared. Loud purring in the middle of a yawn told her that he had made himself quite comfortable on top of Nick.

"I'll remember this, TiMar. You traitor."

With a giant breath Tressa heaved herself up, tugging until Nick's body slowly slid off onto the bunk and TiMar jumped to the floor. It was just a matter of arranging Nick's legs on the bunk now, removing his boots and positioning the pillow beneath his head. At last she covered him with a blanket and sat down on the edge of the bunk.

She was exhausted. Her head throbbed. Her arms ached, and she was sick with worry over Nick, over the men following them, and over some sort of tracking device that Quint Kendyl said was on the hull.

"So what now, Captain Banner?" she whispered imploringly, unable to draw her eyes from his face. Stars, that face. He was so handsome, he could melt a woman with a glance, make her acutely aware of his masculinity and leave her panting with desire—all in the space of a heartbeat. And it wasn't just *her*. Nick Banner seemed to addle the wits of just about every woman he came near.

Quickly assessing her own appearance, Tressa swiped at an unruly lock of hair and tried smoothing the wrinkles from her wilted jumpsuit. At the moment she hardly felt a "catch" in anyone's book. Now that the ship was finally underway and she'd successfully maneuvered Nick onto the bunk—the shower beckoned her.

Chapter Fifteen

Banner stirred as frightful visions and images rose up to torment him. Brief flashes of memory surfaced, only to dissolve again into uncertainty. Entrapped in a deep void of darkness, he was restrained by unseen bonds, poised on the edge of reality while fiendish monsters tore at his flesh, clawing and scratching. The pain . . . he bit back a cry of agony as another intense thrust of it shot through him. His thoughts blurred and he felt himself drifting, deeper and deeper into a beckoning black hell. He felt intense heat, could hear it crackling and almost smell the stench. Ah, God, death would be mercy.

Suddenly there was a presence at his side and he felt a cool caress on his face, a soft voice.

"Linnae?" he called out. He needed her so desperately now.

Though temporarily repelled by this unseen ally, the monsters weren't about to give him up without a struggle, and he cried out again in torment before they were driven back, their eyes glittering in the dimness.

There it was again, that soft sound. He strained, riveting his attention on the gentle voice that offered refuge and hope. Feeling a cool touch on his hand and gasping in relief, he hung on, desperately forbidding this angel of mercy to leave his side.

Suddenly he was alone again!

Inching their way back, his tormentors returned. Banner's throat worked convulsively. He'd never survive, not alone!

Tressa paused as a strange sensation swept through her. An image rose in her mind. Struggling through layers of white pain and enshrouding blackness, it surfaced briefly, then dissipated.

"Nick," she whispered, her face paling with realization.

A low moan broke the silence, and Banner tossed his head in torment.

Rushing to his side, panic curled within her as she watched his chest heave with a broken gasp. His fists clenched and unclenched as they twisted into the blanket.

"Nick," she called, studying him closely. "Can you hear me?" she pressed her palm to his cheek. "Please . . . wake up."

"Linnae?" he gasped.

Tressa stiffened.

Banner moaned again. ". . . need . . . you . . ." he mumbled brokenly, his throat working between words.

"Linnae?" Tressa repeated. By his own declaration Nick Banner loved someone named Linnae. It was as a knife to her heart. He'd never mentioned someone special. She'd even recalled asking him once if he'd ever been in love and his answer had come on a burst of humorless laughter. "Love?" he repeated mockingly, "Love is for fools, Tressa. Here today, gone tomorrow." She distinctly recalled his cynical tone. No . . . *angered* was more like it.

A low, guttural growl dragged her from her thoughts. Banner's breathing became ragged.

In an effort to offer comfort, Tressa caught his hand, only to have her forearm captured in a vicelike grip that all but cut off her circulation.

"Let go!" she demanded, working to pry his fingers loose. "Nick! Let . . . go!"

Banner's chest rose and fell with broken gasps as he desperately clung to her. Forgetting her arm and the pain he was causing, Tressa shuddered as an unexplainable fiery current passed between them. Icy black fear shot through her and she inhaled sharply as once again she sensed the link between them—and frightening, unfamiliar emotions became hers.

His frightening emotions.

"Nooo!" Wrenching her arm from his hold, Tressa stumbled backward, nearly falling in the process. For a brief instant she knew his emotions—knew the excruciating pain he was enduring, the agony and panic of being imprisoned in darkness. Alone.

She had experienced his fear, as if it were her own.

Her heart pounded and tremors racked her body. Panting, Tressa stared at him blankly, rubbing at the fresh bruises on her arm.

Go to him, a small voice inside her urged. *He needs you.*

"Nooo!" Recoiling at the thought, Tressa looked away, pushing back the fearful images, the blackness and the staggering pain.

Look at him. Tressa. He's alone and afraid.

"I can't," she whispered, backing away. "I *can't!*"

Yes. You can, the small voice calmly assured her. *You must. He won't make it through this alone.*

Banner emitted a low, husky cry, and Tressa's eyes were drawn back to him. Frightened, she watched as his body jerked hard against unseen bonds—shackled in hell by elusive tormentors.

Go to him, Tressa.

Instinctively she knew Nick would not be able to hold on much longer. Swallowing hard, she hesitated, then took a small step forward, then another . . . and another, until she was again at his side, her heart pounding.

"Nick," she began, her voice shaky, "can you hear me? I'm here." Sensing his response to her closeness, she hesitantly reached for his hand and continued talking.

Ever so slowly Banner succumbed to Tressa's touch, her soft voice and meaningless words. Though he remained unconscious, his struggles seemed to ease, his moans and ragged breathing calmed. There was no doubt but that he knew she was there.

Still holding his hand, Tressa sat beside him on the bunk, struggling to make sense of it all, but there was none to be made. It was as if some sort of channel had opened up and she'd just had a firsthand glimpse of hell.

His hell.

Tressa continued to murmur soft words to him, and slowly Banner's strong fingers clamped about her hand, but not unbearably tight this time. She watched as he relaxed, seemingly pacified, and drifted into a restless sleep. Now, strangely afraid to leave his side, Tressa alternated between murmuring meaningless words and humming softly.

Smoothing back Nick's dark hair, she wondered at her feelings for this man. What would it be like to have him love her? She tried to imagine a life with him, but her imagination failed her; she'd already decided that Nicholas Banner would make a terrible husband. He was rude and uncivil, and she seriously doubted that he could ever commit to one woman.

Tressa's thoughts were prompted to speculate about the woman whose name he'd called out. She pondered the name Linnae, trying to envision the face and body of the one woman who'd obviously captured the heart of this notorious rake.

"So, you're not as immune to love as you'd like me to believe, are you?" she murmured. Tressa stayed at his side long after his breathing had returned to normal and his fingers had gone lax in her hand.

Ten hours passed. Banner awoke slowly in a cold sweat, reality seeping back by degrees. Where was he, and why the devil did his entire body feel as if he'd just been hit by a freight sled? Swallowing hard, he lay still for a long moment, feeling as weak as a baby. He was never weak. What the hell had happened to him, anyway?

Reality wasn't quite reachable. He vaguely remembered Kendyl intercepting the ship, but whatever happened after that was a blank. He struggled for memory. Kendyl was after something.

Just then another memory flashed before him—he'd hidden Tressa.

Tressa . . . !

The thought brought his eyes open, and with it came a wave of agony. His sight blurred and his eyes rolled involuntarily. Suppressing a groan, he squeezed them shut again as blackness threatened to pull him back under.

Banner swore silently, fighting against the pain and light-headedness. It was all he could do to hang on to consciousness. The pain and flashes of memory continued. He remembered the stunner Kendyl had used on him and the resulting agony before he blacked out. But Tressa? Had Kendyl discovered her? Was she still safely hidden?

Banner ordered himself to open his eyes again and uttered a silent oath when his body wouldn't cooperate with his brain. He wanted to call out her name, but the effort was beyond him.

Oh, there was no mistaking the problem; he understood all too well why his body failed to respond to his commands. Pain had nothing to do with it. The problem was a little matter of dispersion. Somehow he was scattered about in every direction, and in order to accomplish anything, even the smallest thing, he needed to concentrate on gathering himself back together. *Then* he could focus his energies on doing one thing at a time.

Arranging the confusing pieces of memory into some

semblance of order, Nick set his mind to the task at hand. Pulling himself together, bit by bit, he focused on his senses first and became increasingly aware of his surroundings.

He was on a bed, he realized. Gingerly peering through slitted eyes, he discovered he was on his bunk. How the devil did he get on his bunk? he wondered, recalling that he'd collapsed somewhere near the main entry port.

Hearing came next as he centered his attention on the constant hissing of the ventilating system and the familiar hum of the ship's drives.

. . . ship's drives? The memory of shutting down was vivid, and with unrelenting determination Banner again opened his eyes, wincing against stabs of pain. Who the hell was piloting the ship?

Frantically setting his gaze on the cockpit, his breath caught at the sight.

Tressa was sitting in the pilot's seat, monitoring the controls, just as she'd seen him do so often. He watched in silent astonishment as she reached up, depressing an overhead button on the console.

Banner continued staring in mute shock at the scene before him, mesmerized as Tressa, with agonizing slowness, tapped in a code to the computer. The screen blurred, then cleared to reveal a close-up of the *Victorious'* exterior hull.

What was she doing?

Another flash of memory surfaced, bringing about a lopsided grin. She was scanning the ship's exterior, he realized, inch by inch, looking for that damn tracer. Initial shock became instant admiration. There was more to this little slip of a girl than he'd ever dreamed possible. Not only had she managed to get the ship underway, she'd somehow figured out how to do an exterior hull check as well. He continued watching in silence, absorbing every detail of the drama before him.

The cabin lights had been dimmed, yet Tressa's dark fire-brown hair glowed beneath a narrow beam of light. Banner's gaze was soft as a caress as he lazily devoured her.

She was wearing another one of those sexy shifts, he noted, and if he hadn't felt so lousy, he would have been content with hours of simply lying there watching her.

The pain wasn't as bad now, but the battle was far from over. He moaned faintly as his gut roiled with spasms.

The low moan brought Tressa's eyes around. "Nick!" She was at his side in an instant. "You're awake!"

Nick was sitting on the edge of his bunk, looking none too steady. He blinked hazily, licked his lips, and then glanced slowly up at her. "How..." He paused, as if speaking was difficult for him, "how long have I been out?"

"Almost ten hours now." Tressa frowned. "You shouldn't be getting up, Nick. Please, lie back down and I'll get whatever it is you're after."

Banner ignored her gentle reproach. "I doubt I'll be able to stand on my own," he said. There was another long pause and then, "I'm going to need your help, Tressa."

"You're too weak to be..."

"If you won't help me, I'll manage by myself." With that, Nick stood up, swaying on his feet just as Tressa steadied him and eased him back down.

"You are the most stubborn man I've ever met," she bit out.

Banner sat motionless on the edge of the bunk, eyes closed, mouth set in irritation. Finally he turned a baleful eye on her. "As dizzy as I am right now, Tressa, I'm not so sure I'm going to make it to the lav in time as it is, much less sit here arguing with you about it."

Tressa simply stared at him as comprehension sank in. "Oh, you're sick. Why didn't you say so?"

The corner of his mouth twisted in exasperation and he shot her another penetrating look.

This time Tressa supported him as he rose to his feet. She slung his arm across her shoulders and grasped him about the waist. "Lean on me," she instructed, somewhat surprised when he did exactly that. Despite his weakened condition, Tressa was acutely aware of the hard muscle beneath his clothing as he hugged her from hip to shoulder.

The trip of a few steps seemed to take hours. With his free hand Banner clutched at the bunk and storage unit along the way, and Tressa continued assisting him until he shrugged out of her embrace and stumbled into the lav, closing the privacy panel behind him.

She hovered near the closed panel, wanting to help, yet respecting his privacy. Finally grabbing clean linen from the storage unit, she made her way back to the berths and proceeded to strip his bunk. At last she took a seat on the edge and waited until the panel slid open and Nick emerged, braced in the doorway. His color was ashen, his mouth, a grim line of determination.

Racing to his side, Tressa offered him her assistance. But instead of stopping at the bunk Banner continued on to the cockpit. There was no use arguing with him; it was perfectly clear he was a man bent on his own will.

Banner was silent as he surveyed the command console, his features unreadable as he stood, bracing his weight on the back of the pilot's seat.

"For a while I wasn't sure I was going to be able to get this thing powered up," she said softly at his side.

Without responding he reached out and made a couple of minor adjustments, then stood studying the instrument panel for several moments longer.

Tressa saw him sway on his feet and reached out to support him. "And unless you have a valid complaint about the way I've been running things around here, Captain, I suggest you get back to bed until you're able to take over."

Banner silently complied, allowing her to assist him back to the bunk.

"Nick, can I get you something? What about that stuff you gave me when I was recovering from the Ripper? Tell me where you keep it and I'll . . ."

"No!" He released a labored breath. "I can't afford to

be sleeping for hours. I want you to wake me in two. Unless something unusual happens. In that case, wake me immediately.''

Tressa blinked at him in confusion. ''Something unusual?'' she repeated softly.

Banner eased himself down onto the bunk. ''Yeah. Just keep a close watch on things up there. I've set all the sensors on max. They'll let you know if anything's goin' on.'' His eyes slid closed. ''Oh, and Tress?

''Yes?'' She leaned closer to hear him.

''You did good.'' With that, his voice trailed off.

Chapter Sixteen

Lee Bryant sat hunched over the scanner. "According to these readouts, gentlemen, it appears our boy's no longer headed for Acacia."

"What are you talkin' about?" James Catlin came forward to peer over Bryant's shoulder.

"Just what I said. Take a look for yourself. We've been tracking him on this new course for about three standard hours now."

Sam DeVries, the meanest of the three, whirled around. "All I want to know is one thing. Is he in range yet?"

Bryant was already entering the series of numbers that would answer the question. With the tap of a final key, a pulsing arrow danced across the ship's tactical vidscreen, measured the distance between the two ships and calculated the range for a direct hit. Within seconds the information appeared in the lower right corner.

"He's in range," Bryant answered levelly.

DeVries's lips twisted into a cynical smile. "Then I say let's waste 'im. Now."

Catlin cleared his throat. "What about the girl?"

"She goes with 'im," DeVries interjected coldly.

Bryant eased back into his chair. "I don't think so."

"And why not?" DeVries challenged.

Catlin spoke up. "There's no profit if we blast the girl too. I say, collect our earnings, *then* deal with Banner."

"And just how do you propose to do this?" DeVries asked. "It isn't likely he's going to sit back and just let us take her."

Bryant sat forward. "We cripple his ship first. Let's see if we have him on visual." Bryant's hands flew to the controls.

DeVries squinted and leaned closer. "Can't you boost this thing any further?" He continued studying the screen. "Banner's not one to go down without a fight, you know."

"Let's hit him now and ask questions later," Bryant said, sliding a protective cover back on the console.

"Do it."

Without further delay Bryant thumbed the red button. In response the ship shuddered, and three sets of eyes gravitated to the the the screen, tracking the path of a small torpedo.

Somewhere at about the halfway point the torp suddenly exploded into a ball of fire.

"What the . . ." His words were drowned out by the sudden blare of Klaxons. Glancing down at the console, flashing indicators confirmed Bryant's fears. Enemy weapons were being locked onto their ship. Now they were the target.

The comset sounded, Bryant flipped the switch, and the vidcom snapped to life, filling the monitor with Quint Kendyl's enraged face. "This is the *Renegade,* and before I blow you the hell out of existence I just thought I'd introduce myself."

"Damn!" Bryant groaned. "Kendyl. How the hell . . ."

"I *knew* it," DeVries muttered, stepping closer.

Bryant cleared his throat and hit the com button. "*Renegade,* this is the *Starcutter.* Bryant here. Our sensors are picking up one of our tracers onboard your ship. Sorry doesn't exactly cut it, I realize, but we took you for someone else.'' Kendyl's scowl eased. ''Let me guess. The *Victorious,* right?''

''Yes. I don't understand how you . . . where the devil is Banner?''

''You should have come upon him long ago. I left him slumped on the deck, with the ship's main drives down,'' Kendyl offered.

Bryant sat back. ''There's been no other ship on our scanners except for you. Did you by any chance lift something from his hold?''

A warning cloud settled on Kendyl's features. ''Let me guess: You smuggled the tracer onboard his ship with the equipment. Am I right?''

''That's right, and you wouldn't believe the trouble we went through.''

Bryant frowned at his next thought. If Kendyl took the equipment, chances were he had the girl too. Which meant they could kiss good-bye their whole deal with Sinclair. ''What about the girl?'' he asked, trying for a note of cool disinterest.

He had Kendyl's undivided attention now. ''What girl?''

Bryant's brow quirked in surprise. ''Banner's got a girl with him.''

''I saw no girl . . . unless—'' Kendyl smiled. ''Unless he had her hidden somewhere.'' Kendyl paused. ''You boys wouldn't happen to need any help, would you?''

Bryant grinned. The Klaxons were still screaming in the background. ''If you want to disengage your weapons, Kendyl, I'm sure we can work out something for your services.''

James Catlin simply stood there shaking his head. ''While we've been traipsing halfway across the galaxy after the wrong ship, Banner's on his way to Acacia, just like I figured in the first place.''

"Nick?" Tressa gently prodded Banner awake. She'd let him sleep longer than the two hours he'd requested, and besides, she sensed he was struggling again with a nightmare.

She shook him again. "Nick, wake up."

Banner struggled from a deep sleep, his heart pounding, his body slickened with sweat. He'd been back in that black void again, with those creatures, and they were inching forward, threatening to resume their torture.

There it was again: the voice of the guardian who had stayed by his side when the pain was at its worst. The one who had held his hand, had protected him, and had driven the creatures away.

"Nick, can you hear me?"

Banner struggled through layers of fog. Sensing the soft voice calling to him and the aroma of food in the air, he opened one eye at a time and peered up to find Tressa hovering over him. Tressa.

She was smiling at him. "How are you feeling?"

He groaned. "Lousy."

"Stay right there. I'll be right back." With that, Tressa disappeared into the galley.

With a heavy sigh Banner shook the dream aside and shoved himself up on his elbows, his gaze sliding to the cockpit.

"I let you sleep just a little longer than two hours," she called from the galley. He glanced over at the clock. It didn't tell him much, since he couldn't remember when he'd fallen asleep.

"I hope it was all right." She was at his side again. "For a while you were sleeping so soundly, I hated to wake you, but then you started getting restless. Here, I made some coffee." Holding a steaming mug, Tressa waited patiently as Nick slowly eased his legs over the edge of the bunk and moved into a sitting position.

It was *her* voice he'd heard in his dream. *She* was the

guardian who had protected him and given him hope when all seemed hopeless.

"Are you hungry? I made soup." She laughed gently. "No guarantees, but at least it's hot."

Nick blew the steam from his mug before taking a sip. "Maybe a little later. Just how long *did* you let me sleep, anyway?"

"About four hours," she replied.

Banner nodded and scratched his stomach. "Homemade soup, huh? What'd you find to make that out of?"

Tressa laughed. "Believe me, it wasn't easy."

"Yeah. I'll bet." He stood and gingerly made his way to the command console. Four hours had passed since he'd set the sensors on maximum. Machines had their place, but though they all seemed to be doing their job, Banner was a hands-on kind of man who preferred doing things personally rather than relying on machines to do it all.

Rubbing the back of his neck, he wondered if Kendyl was still out there somewhere. What about the tracer and the men tracking it? Were they on Kendyl's back now? He hoped so.

Finally he turned and made his way to the galley. "I'm going to take a quick shower; then I'll try some of that soup of yours," he said, popping three pain tabs into his mouth and swallowing them with a gulp of water.

A short while later Nick emerged from the lav, showered, shaved, and his towel-dried hair still damp. Making his way to the table, he took a seat just as Tressa placed a steaming bowl of soup and a plate of bread in front of him. Pouring herself a mug of coffee, she sat down across from him. "Can I get you anything else?"

"No," he said, picking up his spoon. "Thank you."

"Nick," she began, "I overheard about the tracer."

"Uh-huh." Banner took a sip of the savory liquid.

"Well," Tressa went on, "I tried to run an exterior check on the hull, but I didn't know what I was looking for. So of course I didn't find anything."

Banner reached for a crust of bread. "If my hunch is correct, it's no longer onboard."

Tressa sat back, momentarily rebuffed as he continued. "With a little luck it went onboard the *Renegade* with the cargo Kendyl pirated from us."

"You mean it was in the cargo hold? But what about the men following us?"

"Assuming they're following the tracer, they're on Kendyl's tail now." He gave a nod to the soup. "By the way, this isn't bad."

Tressa ignored the backhanded compliment. Her expression stilled and grew serious. "But what happens if they catch up with him and discover they're following the wrong ship?"

Dipping a chunk of bread in his soup, he stuffed it in his mouth. "One of two things," he said, chewing. "One, they'll annihilate him before they notice the difference. Or two, they'll discover their mistake, in which case they'll *all* come after us."

"That sounds encouraging."

He studied her over the rim of his coffeecup. "We still have one helluva lead, Tressa."

It was early on the morning of the twentieth day. The ship's screens blurred briefly as the *Victorious* slipped out of Stellardrive. Banner felt and ignored the resulting moment of nausea and scanned the readouts. All systems were green. Opening the COMLINK, he tapped in a frequency and spoke into his mic. "This is the *Victorious*, Delta Beta, six-niner-four, requesting a planetary approach vector."

Tressa awoke at the sound of Nick's voice, yawned and stretched. "How long before we arrive?" she asked sleepily.

" 'Mornin' Tress." It was said without taking his eyes off the screen. "We should be hitting dirt in about four hours."

Rising, Tressa slipped into her wrapper. Coming forward, she took her seat, tucked her legs beneath her, and stared at the green planet in the viewscreen. "Is that Echo?"

"No," he responded without looking up. Just that one word—flat and final.

Tressa stared at him. Finally she cleared her throat. "Well, if it wouldn't be too much trouble, would you mind telling me where we are?"

"We're four hours out from Acacia," he said, making another minor adjustment.

"Acacia" she repeated. Her chin lifted. "Why are we going to Acacia, and why didn't I know about this?"

"Probably cause I already had the coordinates locked into the NAVCOMP," he said, still without looking up. "Everything engages automatically with power up; the only way you could have known our destination is by specifically calling up the information. And that takes a security code."

Tressa rose from her seat. "That's *not* what I meant, and you know it, Nick. Why wasn't I consulted about this?"

After finishing an entry he turned to face her. "Because, number one, I'm not in the habit of consulting with passengers about my destinations."

"Excuse me?"

"It's a long story, Tressa; I'll tell you about it sometime. In the meantime I want you to get your travel pacs ready to bring with you when we land."

Tressa's eyes widened. "We're staying?"

Nick returned to his task at the controls. "*You* are. I've got some business to attend to. You'll be staying with Delta. A neat lady. You'll like her."

"If you think I'm budging from this ship, you've got another think coming."

Banner glanced up at her, his expression held a note of mockery. "I'm not offering you a choice."

Tressa's fists were firmly planted on her hips. "Does my father know about this?"

"He knows." It was said smoothly, with no expression.

A heavy moment of dead silence passed. "Long story
... or short," she ground out, "you've got exactly two
minutes to tell me what's going on or . . ."

That brought his head around, his half scowl flickering
with amusement at the very sight of her. "Or what,
Tressa?"

"Nick Banner, I'm sick to death of Rippers and stunners
and tracers and pirates and guns and . . . and trying to fly
this damned ship on my own while you're passed out on
the bunk.

"I'm *not* getting off this ship to stay with your . . . your
friend," she stammered. "I want to go home, Nick, you
hear me? *I . . . want . . . to . . . go . . . home!*"

Banner released a heavy sigh, withdrew a cigar, lit it,
and puffed it to life.

Then he sent a ribbon of smoke toward the floor. "Have
a seat."

"I'm *fine.*"

He gave a nod of compliance. "All right. I'll make this
short and to the point."

"Please do."

He looked at her hard. "Jonathan asked me to take you
off-planet for a while. He has reason to believe there's a
threat on your life, and until he gets to the bottom of it he
wants you safe."

Tressa released a short burst of laughter. "Safe?" she
repeated. "Safe from what? Let me see . . . I've watched
you get beaten up. I've been zapped senseless by something
illegal. I was damn near raped because you can't control
your lust or your drinking."

Banner jerked his cigar from his mouth. "Now wait just
a damn minute!"

She didn't. "Then, of course, I had the distinct pleasure
of squeezing beneath your bunk so that I could watch three
men hold you at gunpoint while they stole equipment from
your hold. I overheard talk about something called a tracer

and that we're being tracked by men with murder on their minds. And, finally, I watched *you* being zapped senseless."

Nick expelled a stream of smoke toward the ceiling. He couldn't avoid the smirk, just watching that damned dimple of hers.

Tressa went on. "And as if *that's* not enough, in order to escape the mean men following us . . ."

Banner grinned, shaking his head in amusement. "Mean men?" he murmured.

". . . I had the responsibility of piloting this ship, which, I might add, I know nothing about. And all the while you're passed out on the bunk for God only knows how long."

Tressa paused for breath and folded her arms across her chest. "Now, if that's what *you* call safe . . . I'll take my chances at home, thank you!

"All right, all right. I admit things have been a little harried."

"Harried?" Tressa glared at him. "Listen, Banner, harried doesn't even begin to describe it. And furthermore, I'm not some empty-headed adolescent, to be protected from the truth. Why wasn't I told about this in the very beginning?"

Banner leaned back in the pilot's seat. "I'm afraid you'll have to talk to Jonathan on that one; I just work for him." He paused. "But I think he figured you wouldn't leave if you knew."

Tressa's eyes narrowed. "He was right. I wouldn't have."

"Well," he turned to face the console again, "there ya go." Tressa opened her mouth, then clamped it shut again. Turning on her heel, she stomped off barefooted toward the lav.

Two hours later she was showered, dressed, and packed. Coming forward into the cockpit she observed Nick sprawled, as usual, in the pilot's seat and staring at the monitor. Occasionally he'd lean forward for his mug of coffee or to make an adjustment of some sort.

Without so much as turning to address her, Nick's satin baritone calmly broke the silence. "It's a damned good thing we don't have any more days left on this run," he began. "With your lengthy showers everyday you've managed to put our more than sufficient water supply into the red."

Tressa raised her chin. "I'll have you know that I've not been taking lengthy showers. In fact, I've been conservative."

Banner smiled slowly. "Yeah, well, we've got a flashing indicator here that says differently."

Tressa cast a glance at the console, then made her way to her seat. "Well, I can assure you that's not *my* fault."

"No, of course it isn't," he said sarcastically. "It's TiMar's."

Although the on-board computer had already transmitted the necessary information to the space port, Nick opened the COMLINK for verbal communication. Tressa listened in. It was different this time; now she understood much of what Nick was doing.

The closer they got to Acacia, the larger the swirly green planet became on the viewscreen, until it filled the screen entirely. Tressa eventually turned toward the small observation window at her left.

The comset buzzed, and a voice announced, "Please initiate your descent."

"Understood," Banner replied, and assumed control from the ship's computer as the *Victorious* entered the planet's atmosphere.

"Hang on. It's going to get a little rough. The computer's registering high winds up ahead."

When it came to tricky landings Nick Banner preferred doing it manually. Nothing against computers, but to Banner's way of thinking humans have an ingrained ability to *sense* things and *guess* how to handle the situation. Years ago, they used to call it "flying by the seat of your pants."

The ship veered off course as a gust of wind came out of nowhere. Banner tapped in the correction, then swore beneath his breath when, moments later, the wind suddenly fell off, requiring yet another correction.

Tressa quietly watched as he fought his way down through the various layers of unsettled air. Finally they were coming in on the final approach. Banner cut the speed, felt the response, booted the nose up, then goosed the thrusters to slow their decline.

As they came in, a vast blue ocean spread out beneath them. Soon they were skimming over a flat plain. A range of mountains stood beyond. At regular intervals a soft chime would sound, breaking the silence as it signaled designated drops in elevation.

"That settlement up ahead is Imperial, Acacia's capital," Nick said, drawing her attention to the master screen.

Within minutes Banner was killing the ship's forward motion and firing reverse thrusters. Next came the sound of the proximity alarm as the ground rose up to meet them. With a gentle thump, the *Victorious* settled onto her jacks, the whine of her powerful turbines still winding down.

The comset chimed, and Banner reached overhead to flick it on. "Nick Banner, here."

"Well, ain't seen your handsome face around here in a long while. What brings you home, darlin'?" The voice and image belonged to a middle-aged, heavy-set woman with laugh wrinkles framing her eyes.

"Shara. Good to see you again. I'm here on business, so I'll only be staying a day or two at the most."

"Hun, you know what to do. The drone should be pulling up in front of you any moment now. Then, darlin', if you can spare a moment, stop by the Outbounder. Dinner's on me and you can tell me all that's been happening to you over the past few months."

"Plan on it."

"Do you want me to let Glori know you're in, or are you planning on surprising her yourself?"

Nick cleared his throat. "Shara, I won't have time to see Glorianna this trip. It's best if you don't say anything about me being here, okay?"

Shara raised a curious eyebrow, "Whatever you say, hun, but you'd better plan on keeping a low profile while you're in port. I'm not the only source of information around here, you know. I'll see ya later tonight." The screen went blank.

Discreetly choosing to disregard the look of puzzlement on Shara's face, Nick switched back to the exterior vid. As promised, the small robosphere was just drifting into place, the words "This Way" flashing in bright neon. Nick fired the thrusters, lifted the ship mere inches off the scarred surface, and slowly began trailing after their bouncing robotic guide. It had been a while since he'd set down in this port. It felt good to be home.

Tressa watched in fascination as they advanced. Jets of air from the thrusters sent roosterlike tails of dust high into the air about them. From the gray outbuildings nestled at one end of the port to the freighter sitting out on the L.Z., Tressa took in every detail.

Suddenly the robosphere came to a stop and Banner followed suit, noting that they were now resting on the deck of an enormous elevator. Banner gently lowered the *Victorious* onto the scarred decking and killed the thrusters. After a brief moment of waiting, there was a marked jolt and vibration as the metal platform slowly began sinking beneath ground level.

Underground hangars were nothing new to Banner. Many ports preferred this type of set up. Putting the ships belowground not only served as protection against inclement weather conditions, it helped to compact the space port.

Tressa's eyes grew round as the rock walls slid upward around them. Suddenly the walls ended, opening up to a massive, lower-level hangar with rows of ships for as far as the eye could see.

Banner fired the thrusters once again and lifted the *Vic-*

torious inches off the decking to follow the robosphere down a long, wide isleway. At last they were led into a sizable berth of their own where Nick killed the drives, and eased the *Victorious* down on her jacks.

With a click, Banner released the latch and shrugged out of his harness. Rising to his feet, he turned and made his way toward the bunks.

Tressa watched as he removed the holstered gun from inside the berth and strapped it on. It hung low on his right thigh and he wore it so naturally, it was as if it were an extention of his leg.

Banner seemed completely unaware of the breathtaking sight he made, totally unconscious of his rampant sexuality. He was dressed in black leathers today, his collar flipped up and his dark hair, having grown three weeks longer, spilling down over the edge. He was just securing the leg tie on the holster when he glanced up, his luminous eyes meeting hers briefly before Tressa looked away.

Nick withdrew the gun and checked the chamber. Satisfied, he holstered it again and snapped the safety in place.

"You ready?" he asked, throwing the utility belt over his shoulder.

Tressa pulled her travel pacs out from under the bunk. "As ready as I'm going to be."

Banner gave her a sidelong glance. "Trust me on this one, sunshine. Besides, something tells me you and Delta will get along great."

"But . . ."

Banner cut her off. "I've already explained it, Tressa. Now remember, stick close to me." With one final sweep of the cockpit, he reached for Tressa's travel pac, shouldered it, and palmed the main lock.

"But that's just the trouble," she went on indignantly.

Ignoring her protests, Banner extended a hand to her, his sapphire eyes raking her admiringly. Tressa was dressed in a soft gray jumpsuit made of supple leather. It included a matching jacket that came to her hips.

He was glad they'd finally arrived. It had been sweet hell, and the truth was he wasn't sure he could have lasted another day. He'd promised Loring he wouldn't touch her, and by God, he hadn't . . . almost.

The main hatch cycled open.

"Oh, Nick, TiMar!"

"He'll be fine, Tressa. He's used to this. As long as he's got water and food, he's happy."

Dismay was written plainly upon her face.

"Oh, hell." Banner released a heavy sigh. "Go get him."

Chapter Seventeen

Once again the fumes and sounds of a space port battered Tressa's senses as Nick assisted her down the ramp and onto the scarred metal surface.

"Watch your step," he shouted over the whine of turbines as they picked their way over fuel and service lines strewn across the decking.

Upon reaching the open passageway, Nick caught her elbow and propelled her toward the terminal entrance. Tressa hurried along, trying to keep up with his long strides, ignoring the possessive pressure he was exerting on her arm.

Banner's eyes scanned the hangar as they made their way toward the terminal. Confident of where he was going, he appeared oblivious to the flashing arrows embedded in the decking.

It was a quick trip across the hangar, through a set of doors, up a flight of stairs, and finally to the terminal. Through another door, and they were outside standing beneath a covered entry.

Vendors were everywhere, hawking their wares, from handcrafted items to flowers.

"Wait here," Nick instructed.

Tressa drank in his swarthy good looks as he stepped forward to hail a taxi. He'd shaved, and something about the smoothness of his jaw caught and held her eye.

On returning, Nick stopped and purchased an armful of flowers, the color of a sunset and intoxicating in scent. Selecting another single, long-stemmed vibrant red bud, he paid the man and returned to Tressa. Wordlessly he handed her the flowers, then bent to retrieve her travel pacs off the sidewalk.

Were they hers? she wondered, inhaling their sweet fragrance.

Nick stepped forward, catching the door of the vehicle for her. A soft breeze whipped around the corner, teasing his dark hair, tossing it down across his forehead and ruffling it at the back of his neck. He helped her inside, then followed, leaning forward to instruct the driver.

TiMar tensed and anxiously climbed up onto Tressa's shoulder. Juggling both flowers and cat, Tressa coaxed TiMar back down onto her lap, where he finally relaxed under a murmuring of soft words and a gentle hand stroking his back.

"Oh, here," Tressa said, realizing Nick was empty-handed and she was still holding the flowers for him.

Nick retrieved the single red bud. "Those are yours," he said, nodding to the bouquet.

"They are?" Tressa never noticed the desire rising in Nick's eyes as he watched her nuzzle her nose in the bouquet. He was learning all too fast that Tressa never did anything halfheartedly.

"Thank you," she said, glancing up from the flowers.

"You're welcome." He grinned and leaned closer, gently brushing a hint of yellow pollen from her nose. "By the way, Irish," he added silkily, "I remember more of that night than you think I do. And just for the sake of keeping the records straight, it wouldn't have been rape.''

Tressa's mouth parted in shock and she cast a quick glance toward the driver.

Nick continued. ''Whether you care to admit it or not, I . . .''

''Nick, *please!*'' she hissed. Nick's idea of a whisper left much to be desired. Cringing, she cast another distraught glance at the driver, then turned her gaze toward the window. Her cheeks burning. ''Imperial's quite different from Port Ireland,'' she said, abruptly changing the subject.

''Quite.'' His mouth quirked with suppressed humor.

''That seems like a nice place, Nick. Why can't I just stay there?'' she said, looking at a building.

He dipped his head to glance out her window. ''Uh-huh,'' he said, masking his grin. ''As I remember, it's not exactly a hotel.'' He turned his face, hiding his amusement.

''Really?'' She turned to glance out the back window. ''What is it then? It sure looks to me like one.''

''It's a high-dollar . . .'' He cleared his throat. ''It's uh, sorta like uh . . .''

''And what is that building?'' This time Tressa's gaze was directed out Nick's window, to an elegant building surrounded by artistically sculpted gardens.

''That? That's the general headquarters for the Port of Imperial.''

''It's beautiful. Have you ever been inside?''

''Once or twice.''

Suddenly she saw it!

''Don't even ask, Tressa.''

''But Nick, it's the Imperial Hilton.''

''No.''

''But . . .''

''The answer is no.''

Before long the city was left behind them as a winding road carried them higher into the foothills. At last, after twenty-five minutes of endless questions and nonstop chatter, they were moving down a long, tree-lined drive.

Carole Ann Lee

Pastures flanked them on both sides. Within minutes they were pulling around a circular drive and stopping beneath the portico of a massive building.

A doorman hurried to catch the door for them. "Good to have you back, sir."

"Thank you, Jordan. Delta around?"

"She's inside, sir."

Grabbing the travel pacs, Banner extended a hand, assisting Tressa from the taxi. With TiMar nestled in the crook of her arm and her flowers clutched in her other hand, Tressa made her way up a short set of stairs, where a double-doored entry swung inward and another doorman greeted them with a smile and a nod to Banner.

Nick handed over the travel pacs and instructed the man to place them in one of the guest rooms. "Oh, and Dawson . . ." He turned to Tressa and gently took the bouquet from her—"put these in water."

"Yes, sir." The man turned and headed for the wide green-carpeted staircase.

Tressa gazed about in awe. The entry was an atrium with a vaulted ceiling. The walls were paneled in a rich wood that resembled Terran oak, and several large planters had been placed about, containing rather unusual-looking trees, one nearly reaching the ceiling. The effect was rustic and masculine.

"Nicky! I thought I heard that voice of yours."

Nick caught Delta in an embrace that lifted her feet off the floor. "You look prettier every time I see you, you know that?" he murmured sensuously.

Delta's laughter was infectious. "Oh, you say that to all the girls."

Banner's satin baritone was lowered an extra notch as he handed her the single long-stemmed flower. "For you."

"Oh, Nicky. It's beautiful."

Delta rose up on her toes and placed a quick kiss on Nick's cheek. "Thank you."

"You're welcome."

She stepped back and proceeded with what appeared to be a motherly onceover. "You look good," she said eyeing him critically. "A little skinny, maybe. Things been going okay for you?" She included Tressa in her welcoming glance, and her eyes sparkled with approval as she cast him a curious look.

Nick shrugged. "Can't complain. By the way, I'd like you to meet Tressa. Tressa, Delta. Tressa will be staying for a night or so while I take care of some business here in port."

Delta extended both hands to Tressa in warm welcome. "It's good to meet you, Tressa. Your company will be refreshing. And TiMar . . ." Delta caressed him between the ears. "Why, little guy, you haven't come visiting for a long time." TiMar closed his eyes in sheer ecstasy, cocking his head to direct her caresses just where he wanted them.

It was hard to judge Delta's age. She was exceptionally attractive. Her soft blond hair was pulled up off her face into a cluster of curls at the back of her head, and her green eyes were dancing with both humor and intelligence.

Tressa liked her but found herself curious. What was she to Nick? Just a friend? An aunt? A friend's mother? A sister?

"Come on in and let me get a better look at you," Delta said, leading the way into a drawing room off the main entry. With TiMar still in her arms, Tressa stood to the side and took it all in.

"Thank you for allowing me to intrude like this," Tressa offered, her tone apologetic.

"Nonsense." Delta's laugh was warm. "To be truthful, I welcome the female company. It gets tiring being surrounded by arrogant males all the time."

Tressa smiled and nodded in agreement. One arrogant male was enough for her.

Delta motioned for them to sit down. Tressa did, though Nick chose to remain standing. "I was just about to have a cup of tea. Would you like to join me?"

"Yes, please," Tressa said, arranging TiMar on her lap. "How about you, Nicky?"

"No, thanks. Actually, I'm not stayin'. I need to get back and try to locate Slater. Oh, and tell Clint I picked up that case of Extra Dark for him. I'll bring it back with me."

"That's just what he needs," Delta grumbled, eliciting a grin from Nick.

Glancing up, Tressa noted that the ceiling was transparent, and again potted plants were everywhere, ranging in size from very large to exceptionally tiny, producing a gardenlike effect.

Most of the plants were unusual, different from anything she'd ever seen on Terra Four. "I've never seen such beautiful plants. Are they all native to Acacia?" As she spoke, Tressa's eyes grew round. The very plant she was eyeing changed color before her eyes, turning from milky white to transparent in a matter of seconds.

Delta smiled. "You were looking at it."

"What?"

"You were *looking* at that plant," Delta went on to explain. "It sensed your eyes on it and went into camouflage."

Tressa laughed gently. "Really?"

"It's called an Illusion plant, and yes, these particular plants happen to be native to Acacia."

Nick broke into the conversation, his eyes sparkling with amusement. "While you're here, make sure Delta takes you out to the greenhouse and shows you some of the *real* stuff." He was leaning against the wall in his usual negligent stance, hands shoved into the pockets of his open jacket and one foot crossed over and toed to the floor. "Delta's on staff at McCade Botanical Research," he continued.

"You are?" Tressa's smile broadened in approval. "I've always been interested in the research reportss that come out of that organization."

Nick's mouth quirked with humor. "Especially when it's

about plants with healing abilities, huh, Tressa?'' He turned to Delta, with that Banner grin overtaking his features. ''Tressa has a jar of stuff that cures everything. *Real* quick.''

Before Tressa could respond a young woman appeared with tea and a plate of sweet cakes. ''Thank you Annie,'' Delta said.

The girl dipped her head, cast Banner an appreciative glance, and disappeared.

Not missing the wistful glance, Tressa's curious eyes followed the girl from the room.

Delta handed Tressa her tea. ''Now,'' she began, sliding a glance toward Nick, ''what about this jar of 'stuff' that supposedly cures everything?''

''It's made from oil extracted from the leaves of the Acuel bush,'' Tressa offered.

Delta thought a moment. ''The Acuel bush. I was just reading something about that the other day.''

''I wouldn't doubt it. The medical world is just now beginning to recognize its healing qualities. It's wonderful.''

''Yeah, if it doesn't kill you first,'' Banner interjected with a wink to Tressa.

Tressa set down her cup of tea, then turned to Delta. ''I'm afraid it's rather unpleasant on an open wound; even more so if there's infection present.''

Delta nodded. ''But couldn't you apply something like Nervatrite to the area first?''

''Yes. In fact, Nervatrite is always used as a precau . . . tion . . .'' Her voice trailed off. Tressa tried ignoring the deafening silence suddenly coming from Nick's direction. Her gaze wandered about the room, not daring to glance at him. Stars, she could feel his eyes boring into her as it was.

''And I take it, Nicky,'' Delta said, ''you've had firsthand experience with this magic salve?'' Her bright countenance slowly faded at the sight of Banner's intent expression. ''Is something wrong?''

"Oh, nothing I won't take care of later," he said in a tone that held promise.

Tressa's head jerked up, and she found herself riveted by his steady gaze. She thought she saw amusement lurking in his eyes, but then it was gone.

No explanations were necessary as far as she was concerned. The brute knew exactly what he'd done that night to deserve it. Refusing to be intimidated, Tressa raised her chin, locked gazes, blinked, and smiled innocently, her dignity intact.

Delta cleared her throat and set down her tea. "Well, Tressa," she began, in a voice that was almost too cheery, "if I may be so bold as to ask, how did you happen to meet Nicky?" She laughed warmly. "Forgive me, but you don't seem the type to hang out in his sort of places."

Nick feigned a yawn and shoved himself away from the wall. "Well, if you ladies will excuse me, I've got important things to do." He directed his sapphire gaze at Tressa once again. "I'll return as soon as I can, but it could be a couple of days. If you need anything, just ask Delta."

Tressa nodded, and he turned to leave, only to stop in midstep. "Oh, and Tressa, I don't want you leaving the grounds without an escort."

Delta raised a curious eyebrow, but Nick's eyes were trained on Tressa. "You hear me?" he said.

"I hear you."

Nick frowned slightly, then turned to Delta, who was busily taking it all in with unmasked amusement. "I shouldn't be gone more than a day or two at the most."

"That's fine. We'll be here," Delta replied, still smiling.

He glanced at Tressa, then back again to Delta. "I'll see you when I get back, then." With a final glance at Tressa, he turned and stalked from the room.

A long moment of quiet followed Nick's exit. Delta took a sip of tea, regarding Tressa quizzically for a moment. "It's not often Nicky takes passengers onboard the *Victorious*."

Tressa reached for her tea. "That's what I've heard."

Delta laughed warmly. "You'll have to forgive me for my curiosity, Tressa. It's just that, well . . . actually, it's not often Nicky shows up with someone respectable."

Tressa couldn't suppress a giggle. "I understand. He's earned quite a reputation on Terra Four as well."

"I can imagine."

Tressa glanced around the room. "This is certainly a beautiful place," she continued, absently stroking TiMar as he snuggled deeper into her lap.

Delta's smile broadened. "I'll take you on a tour after we've finished our tea, if you'd like."

"I'd like that very much." Tressa sat back. "You've known Nick for some time, I take it?"

"Oh, yes," Delta said. "I can honestly say I've known Nicky quite intimately for a very long time." She chuckled. "I can't begin to count the numerous baths I've given him, the countless times I've tucked him into bed or cooled his fevered brow."

Tressa's mouth parted before she caught the glint of humor in Delta's eyes.

"I'm Nicky's stepmother, Tressa."

"Oh." Color touched Tressa's cheeks. "Forgive me, but I never would . . . never would have guessed."

Delta laughed softly and waved her hand in dismissal. "Nicky's mother died when he was five. As a friend of the family, I'd offered to help Max with the boys until he found someone permanent."

"Nick has brothers?" Tressa asked incredulously.

"Two. Nicky's in the middle."

Tressa's eyes widened. "I'll bet *that* was an undertaking."

Delta laughed. "It certainly was. Max and I married two years later. Five years after that we had a child of our own, a daughter, Rachel. I take it Nicky didn't tell you he was bringing you home."

"No. He just mentioned your name and said that I'd be staying with you."

Delta shook her head. "When he left home he had some crazy notion to prove himself—something about forging his own way and making it on his own. Which he seems to have done, but . . ." Delta sighed. "But that's another story. Anyway, tell me, what brought you two together?"

"Well . . ." Tressa took a fortifying breath. "Nick's worked for my father for about six years now." Tressa briefly explained about the alleged threat, and that Nick had been asked to take her off planet. "I don't know how long it will be before I can return to Terra Four," she said, "but with all we've been through lately, I'm just about ready to take my chances back home."

Delta set down her cup. "Do they know who's behind this?"

"I don't know," Tressa answered. "Nick doesn't tell me much."

"And you say you've had problems along the way too?"

Tressa sighed. "That's an understatement. Nick's life has been threatened at least two times that I know of. Someone smuggled some sort of a tracer onboard his ship. Then Nick's ex-partner pirated a shipment out of the hold at gunpoint and ended up using a stunner on him."

Delta gasped. "Where were *you* while all this was going on?"

"Hidden beneath his bunk." Tressa frowned. "Somehow I don't think it's over. Nick never leaves the ship without that gun strapped to his thigh."

Delta looked stunned. "I noticed the gun." She paused. "So, does Nicky think his ex-partner's in on this?"

"I don't know."

"But you're sure it was Nicky's ex-partner who came aboard the ship? Were you able to see him at all?"

"Yes, I caught a glimpse of him through a tiny slit between the boxes Nick had me hid behind," Tressa said.

"He's not as tall as Nick. Long, medium brown hair, pulled back and tied at the nape."

Delta nodded at her description. "That sounds like Kendyl, all right."

"Kendyl. That's the name I remember Nick using." She took another sip of her tea. "There certainly seems to be a lot of hostility between them," she said. "Nick mentioned one time that Kendyl wanted to transport contraband. I suppose that must be why the partnership dissolved."

"Well, I'm afraid it goes a little deeper than that," Delta explained. She shook her head bleakly. "Quint blames Nicky not only for the break-up of their partnership, but for the break-up between him and a young girl named Aria Morgan.

Tressa's eyebrows rose. "Nick wanted his partner's girl?"

"No. It was the other way around, I'm afraid. Aria wanted Nicky; was madly in love with him, or at least had a severe case of infatuation. They met when Nicky and Quint formed their partnership."

Delta leaned back. "I saw it for myself. Nicky brought Quint and Aria with him on one of his trips home. Aria managed to find one excuse after another to corner Nicky."

"And he wasn't interested in her?" Tressa asked, her curiosity piqued.

"No." Delta shook her head. Her faint smile held a touch of sadness. "At that point in his life commitment to anything was the last thing Nicky was interested in. No, he'd made it perfectly clear he wanted nothing to do with her. But Aria apparently broke off her relationship with Quint anyway, and for a long time continued to follow Nicky around like a shadow."

Sitting forward, Tressa asked, "So what happened?"

"Well," Delta said, pouring more tea for both of them, "it ripped their partnership apart, plus Quint put full blame on Nicky and vowed to destroy him because of it." Delta sighed heavily. "Rejection like that sometimes does horrible things to a man's ego." Her face clouded. "Nicky was a classic example of just that after his break-up with . . ." Delta left the sentence hanging.

Tressa glanced away, aware that a boundary had been reached.

"Has Nicky told you about himself at all?" Delta frowned. "I mean . . . about his past?"

"A little." Tressa hesitated. "He told me about Echo."

Delta slowly nodded, her face slightly flushed. "Please forgive me, Tressa. I'm wondering if maybe I'd better not say anything more."

Tressa lowered her eyes. "Of course; I understand," she said politely. And she *did,* but stars, it was just getting good.

"So," Delta said, abruptly changing the subject, "three weeks aboard the *Victorious* with Nicky." She laughed infectiously and shook her head in mock dismay. "I'll bet you were ready to get off by the time you landed."

Tressa glanced down at TiMar, who was curled up, asleep, in her lap, and began stroking him. "The *Victorious* is a little cramped. Let's just say I learned *when* to stay out of his way."

"I'm sure you did," Delta responded with understanding. "I can imagine you were pushed to your limits."

Tressa laughed. "Actually, I think Nick was the one pushed to his limits." She smiled and cleared her throat. "Besides, there's someone named Glorianna I think he's going to want his privacy with."

Delta rolled her eyes heavenward. "Oh, yes . . . Glorianna. She's still after him? Those boys . . . they're so much alike. Lots of girls, but never anyone serious. They learned much too young that if their damnable good looks didn't get them what they wanted, their distinctive Banner voice would."

A flash of feigned horror crossed Tressa's face. "Are you saying they're all alike?"

Delta laughed softly. "Well, I'm afraid Nicky and Clinton are, in particular."

"Oh, my." Tressa shook her head in mock dismay. "Three weeks with one Banner is enough to send me over the edge. How did you manage three of them and still keep your sanity?"

Delta laughed openly. "Seriously, they've been good boys, and after twenty-five years of 'mothering' I can honestly say I don't have any regrets."

Tressa's expression grew solemn. "Actually, you can be proud of him, Delta. I can't speak for anyone else, but I *will* say that during my time aboard the *Victorious* Nick conducted himself quite . . . *gallantly*." Her eyes sparkled with amusement as she added, "Most of the time."

Delta's laughter was responsive. "Why, this is becoming more interesting by the minute," she said, her raised eyebrows conveying total amazement. "I'm afraid Nicky's been called many things, but to the best of my knowledge I don't *ever* recall 'gallant' being one of them." She laughed again. "If I didn't know better, I'd say we were talking about two different people." A double peal of feminine laughter escaped into the main entry.

Chapter Eighteen

Tressa was on Banner's mind the entire trip back to Imperial. Conflict raged within him, and he found himself at a loss as to what to make of his feelings, much less what to do about them.

One thing he knew for certain—leaving her like this was making him painfully aware of the fact that she was becoming more than just a job. What had started out as just another assignment, a favor to Loring, had taken on a new twist—one he hadn't expected or welcomed.

With the exception of the hologames and the luminous glow of the indirect chem lighting, the Outbounder was reminiscent of a swank 1800s saloon, as one might have seen in San Francisco during the height of the Gold Rush Era.

A large mirror hung on the wall behind the bar. The surface of the bar itself was made of polished marble. Along its base ran a shiny genuine brass footrail. The aroma of food mingled with the scent of tobacco and liquor, and to complete the atmosphere, waitresses, clad in nostalgic trappings, moved among the patrons, delivering food and drinks.

Shara's eyes lit up as Banner, looking every bit the dark and handsome gunslinger, pushed through the swinging doors. Excusing herself from a group of patrons, she met him halfway. "Nick, come on over into the light and let me get a good look at you, darlin'."

He chuckled. "You sound just like Delta."

"Well, what do you expect?" she replied, leading the way to a table along the wall. "It's been months since we've seen you."

Nick held out a chair for Shara, then eased into one across the table from her.

"You're lookin' good, Nick. So how's everything goin' for you?"

He shrugged. "Can't complain."

"I take it you're still workin' for LorTech?"

"Yeah, still working for LorTech." He searched his pockets for a cigar, found one, and lit up.

"I hope your cancer shots are current, hun," Shara said, wrinkling her nose at him.

Nick simply grinned and blew a stream of smoke high into the air.

"So tell me," she began "what sounds good? Tonight's special is fresh Keimbo, grilled to absolute perfection with . . ."

"Just coffee for now, and some pain tabs."

"Headache?"

Banner nodded. "One that's about ready to take the top of my head off."

Shara hailed a passing waitress. "Two coffees, Jen, and bring a couple of Soma tabs." Shara glanced over at Nick. "You sure you don't want somethin' to eat? A sandwich maybe?"

"Just coffee will be fine. I'll eat a little later."

Shara nodded, returning her attention to the waitress. "That'll do it for now."

A moment of silence passed in which Shara studied Banner with intense curiosity.

"What . . . ?" he said, capturing her eyes.

"Oh, nothing." Shara's eyes twinkled with amusement. "Just wondering what's so important that you don't have time for Glori this trip."

Nick's left eyebrow rose a fraction. "Shara, I've told you before, there's nothing goin' on between me and Glori. We're friends. It's that simple."

Shara threw back her head and laughed uproariously. "Nothing's ever simple with you, Banner." Her amusement slowly faded. "Ah, Nick . . . you know I'm just anxious for you to find someone to tame that roguish heart of yours and settle you down.

Nick smiled blandly. "But I don't *want* my roguish heart tamed, Shara. And I sure as hell don't *want* to settle down. I happen to like my life just the way it is."

"Uh-huh, and I'll say it again. You're making a big mistake letting Linnae haunt you like this . . . wallowin' in your solitude like you do. Why, if I were a few years younger . . ." Shara let the thought trail off.

Nick took a slow drag from his cigar. Studying her with suppressed amusement, he blew a lazy stream of smoke toward the floor. "What does age have to do with anything?" he asked in silky challenge.

"Ah, pooh, she said with an unladylike snort and the faintest hint of a blush. "You should be taking advantage of these sweet young things batting their eyes at you and . . ."

"Oh, but I do," he said emphatically, his grin becoming broader, "every chance I get."

Shara hesitated a moment as the double meaning sank in. "I give up," she said, shaking her head in mock disgust.

"Good! Now can we drop the subject?"

Banner let almost an hour slip by, enjoying laughs and bringing Shara up to date on the last few months of his life. He purposefully left Tressa's name out of the conversation. Shara would never let it rest. Besides, he wasn't ready to admit or explain his feelings to anyone, let alone himself.

Nick glanced up at the chronometer. "I'm going to have to get going," he said, adjusting the second time zone on his Rolex to match Imperial's. The first zone was always set for standard hours—ship time. He'd taken the watch in when he first got it and had both the bezel and face converted so that it could work with any time zone, anywhere.

Despite its age, the burnished gold Rolex wasn't just a conversation piece; it was as accurate today as it had been for Nick's great-great-grandfather back in the late 1900s.

"I can't believe you're not hungry. Can't I talk you into eating something before you go?"

He grinned boyishly. "I just haven't got much of an appetite with this headache and all."

With a final draw on his cigar, Banner leaned forward and crushed it out in the ashtray. "I've still got a few things to do before I can call it a day," he said, rising from his chair.

"Nick, darlin', you look drained. Why don't you come on back, have dinner here, and sleep in a real bed tonight? Do what you have to do, and when you get back, why . . . I'll have dinner, a room, and even Glori waiting for you," she added with a wink. "Come on, what do you say?"

Banner sighed, resting his hand on the back of the chair. "Sounds tempting, Shara, but I . . . think I'll pass on it."

"Are you sure, darlin'?" Shara rose to her feet. "You'd wake up more rested in a real bed rather than staying onboard that ship. And think of the breakfast this place puts out." Her eyes glimmered with anticipation as Nick pondered her words.

"All right," he said, laughter in his deep voice. "You've talked me into it. In truth, I haven't had a decent night's sleep in three weeks. But just the bed. No Glori, okay?"

That earned him another raised eyebrow that he, again,

chose to ignore. But Shara continued to study him intently, her eyes sharp and assessing.

"I should be back in about an hour," he said, grabbing his jacket. "Save me a couple bowls of that house stew and I'll have it when I get back."

"You got it," Shara answered.

"Oh, I've left a message for Slater. If you see or hear from him, tell him to stick around. It's important I talk to him."

"Got it. Stew. You'll be back in an hour. And Zeke's to stay put," she repeated.

Banner nodded wordlessly, then turned for the door.

"What's her name, Nick?" Shara asked with casual confidence.

"What?" He turned to face her smug expression.

Shara repeated her question. "What's her name?"

"Who?"

"The little girl that's got a hold on your heart," she said, smiling confidently and closely watching his reaction.

He gave her a sidelong glance of disbelief. "Damned if I know what you're talking about now, Shara."

"And damned if you don't," she said with conviction. Humor twinkled in her green eyes as she continued, "At first I wasn't sure I was readin' you right." Her face broke into a wide grin. "But I wasn't born yesterday. I've been around too long not to recognize the symptoms, Nick." She chuckled happily. "And damn if you aren't just about the most bit man I ever saw."

Nick scowled. "Well, this time you're wrong, Shara. Now, will you let it rest?" With a muttered oath, he turned and strode toward the door, leaving her thoroughly delighted with herself.

Nick headed for the underground corridor that ran between the Outbounder and the lower-level hangar. The air was tainted with the fumes of fuel and exhaust, despite the ventilation. Chem strips brightened the way, and neon advertisements on the walls promoted the local hotels, restaurants, points of interest, and Imperial's various forms of entertainment. Then, of course, there was the ever-present graffiti, none of which was especially enlightening.

Before long Banner was entering the hangar, making his way toward the *Victorious.* A hundred yards from the ship, he withdrew the remote from his utility belt and released the ship's security. With the touch of another button, he tapped into the primary on-board computer and scanned for messages. A tiny vid screen on the remote indicated that there were four. Nick thumbed yet another button and began a verbal playback as he continued making his way across the hangar.

"Hey, Banner, Taylor here. Couldn't help but notice the *Victorious,* pal. It's about time you hit port. If you get the chance to join us for a few drinks, me and the boys will be at the Porthole."

Pause.

"This is Space Port Ship Maintenance confirming computer payment authorization. Fuel comes to thirty-six credits, fresh water, fifteen, and routine servicing, five, for a total tab of fifty-six credits. Imperial wishes you a nice stay and that you return again soon."

Pause.

"Nick? Slater. Got your message. Called the place, but Delta said you'd left. You can reach me for the rest of the night at four-four-eight-thirty-two."

Pause.

"Banner, ol' buddy, Tom Rist. Hey, you wouldn't happen to be interested in . . ."

Thumbing a small button, Banner discontinued the messages and headed for a bank of com-phones housed just inside the terminal.

Before he could release the safety on his holstered weapon, they were upon him—three men hidden in the shadows.

The first man lunged forward, but Nick effectively dodged his attack. The second man grabbed Banner's left arm, but Banner swung hard with his right, crashing his fist into the attacker's face and sending him sprawling to the deck.

The first man returned, this time throwing himself at Nick's back, looping his arms through Nick's and locking them behind him with such force that for a desperate moment Nick thought his shoulderblades would snap.

Banner kicked out at a third man, landing a hard blow to his thigh. Finally he was restrained long enough for someone to deliver an uppercut to his jaw, and his mind exploded into stars. With brute force, someone else rammed a hammy fist deep into Banner's midsection, expelling the air from his lungs with a whoosh. Banner swayed on his feet, his gut in spasms.

By now the second man had recovered from Nick's right fist and began assisting in the restraint. Nick was hit again, this time so hard, his feet left the ground and he vaguely heard ribs crack under the force of the blow. The jolt of pain that shot through him was so intense, his vision blurred, his legs buckled, and he sank against his captors with a groan, sliding halfway to his knees before he was forced to stand again.

"Get him up!" one of them said gruffly. "Take him inside and secure him." Someone grabbed Nick's remote and opened the hatch of the *Victorious*.

The incident was over before it even began. It took two men to hoist him to his feet. Dazed, Banner struggled futilely against his assailants as they removed his gun and dragged him onboard the *Victorious*.

He was slugged hard in the side for the trouble, and his body went limp as blackness threatened to pull him under. There was a horrendous roaring in his ears, his gut roiled with nausea, and his ribs hurt so bad, just the simple act of breathing was limited to shallow panting. Each breath was so excruciating, it felt like hot pokers slipping into his lungs.

They took ropes used for stabilizing cargo and tied them

to Nick's wrists, then stretched his arms straight out from his sides, lashing him to tie-downs along the bulkhead. He couldn't prevent the husky cry of pain that tore from the back of his throat as a final yank pulled the ropes so taut, he felt the wrenching of his arm sockets. Weakened by shock and pain, he hung helpless, his muscles and tendons savagely stretched to their very limit.

Within seconds all feeling had left his hands, and he struggled to hide the agony of his cracked ribs. Ah, God, it hurt just to breathe, but he'd be damned if he'd give them the satisfaction of knowing it.

He glared insolently at his captors, trying not to think about their plans for him. Most likely he'd be asked questions he wouldn't care to answer. They, in turn, would give it their best shot to persuade him. He knew he'd be damned lucky to survive the ordeal, whatever it entailed.

One man was in the process of wiping the blood from his mouth, compliments of Banner's right hook.

Escape was impossible. As best he could tell there were three, maybe four of them. Banner knew their kind. Lord knows he'd met his share during the two years he'd spent on Echo. Brutal men, the kind who were capable of anything for easy money, including murder. Nick didn't know all of their names, but he sure as hell knew one: Lee Bryant. They were the same men who'd jumped him at Port France. Odds were they were after Tressa.

"Hello, Banner."

Nick looked up through a blurry haze, his eyes dulled with pain. His lip was swollen and blood dripped from his mouth in a steady trickle.

"Bryant," he gasped, "see you . . . haven't changed. Still the same good-for-nothing, lousy scum . . ." The words were broken and uttered between gasps.

Bryant's face drained and became sullen as he drew back his fist and planted an impulsive blow into Nick's already bruised abdomen. "Let's see, Banner, we can do this two ways. Easy or hard."

Choked by the force of the impact, Banner coughed once, his lungs convulsing, his gut coiling and knotting around the blow. The world dimmed for just an instant, then exploded into white-hot agony as a jolt of pain surged through him.

"I'm only going to ask this once," Bryant said in a menacingly soft voice. "Then it's going to get nasty."

"You mean I haven't . . . seen nasty yet?"

Bryant ignored Nick's taunt. "*Where's the girl?*"

Nick managed a cynical sneer. "So you're the one Loring's worried about. And here I thought we might be up against something."

That comment earned him a backhand across the face. "Are you going to answer the question, or do you need a little more persuasion?"

"Go to hell."

The grin that swept over Bryant's face was slow and chilling. "Somehow I figured you'd say something like that." He turned and gave a clipped nod to the large, burly man with the hard eyes and the ugly scar running down his left cheek, Sam DeVries, the one who'd already cracked Nick's ribs earlier with a single blow of his fist.

"Citizen Banner, here," Bryant began in a sniveling voice, "seems to be having a little trouble remembering. Seein' how you like being helpful, how would you like to help him with his memory?"

A massive fist slammed into Banner's jaw, snapping back his head with cruel force. The ropes bit into his wrists and his knees sagged.

"Too bad, Nick. I'm afraid this is one time your size and strength are going to work against you," Bryant stated with a contemptuous smile. "I can see it now. A man your size . . ." He shook his head in mock sadness. "It's going to take some serious abuse to bring you down.

"Why don't you put a stop to it, Nick. Tell us where the girl is. Otherwise . . ." Bryant leaned forward and spoke in lowered tones. "DeVries, here, gains pleasure in torture."

"Suck vacuum . . . Bryant!" Nick gritted out.

Banner saw it coming even before DeVries raised his hammy fist. Though he tried to brace himself for the blow, pain exploded in his jaw and he saw stars. Thousands of them.

"Careful of his pretty face," someone said.

"I think if I were you, Nick . . ."

Banner was just barely aware of Bryant's wheedling voice as he drifted on the edge of consciousness.

". . . be to answering the question real soon. Besides . . . pretty face won't be so pretty anymore. If nothing else . . . save yourself a lot of . . . and pain."

Banner was in no position to argue with the man. The suggestion, he thought dimly, did seem to make sense. After all, it didn't take a genius to figure out that hurting wasn't good. But . . . telling wasn't good either. Banner heard a moan of distress coming from somewhere, hardly recognizing the sound of his own voice. One thing he knew for sure: If they punched him one more time in the gut, throwing up was going to feel awfully damn good. As it was, he'd already swallowed back the rising gorge twice.

"Mulling things over, are you?" Bryant taunted.

Banner didn't answer, but his defiant gaze plainly reiterated "Go to hell." Drawing upon what little strength he had left, he lunged with a booted kick to Bryant's groin, narrowly missing the vulnerable area. The physical effort cost him dearly, as an explosion of white-hot pain shot across his cracked ribs.

Bryant's jaw ticked with suppressed rage. "Time for further persuasion, I see." His voice was dangerously soft, and with a nod to DeVries, he stepped back.

Nick tensed, bracing himself for the blow, but it did little good. DeVries's doubled fist connected viciously with his side. Banner's face became devoid of all expression as the shock of raw pain surged through him, shattering into layer upon layer of echoing agony. He sought the refuge of the beckoning darkness, but it wavered just out of reach.

It took two more punches before the pain faded, the nausea passed, and he slipped into the sweet oblivion of unconsciousness, his head resting against his chest.

Bryant stepped forward, gripped Nick's dark shaggy mane in his fist, and wrenched his head up. "He's out."

"I say let's bring him back around," DeVries growled.

Bryant motioned to two men standing just inside the main hatch. "Unshackle him and transfer him to Kendyl's ship."

Sam DeVries stepped forward. "Did you hear what I said?"

"I heard you."

"You're not going to get answers this way," DeVries warned, following Bryant into the cargohold. "I tell you, you've got to keep at him with no breaks inbetween."

"We're going to let him rest while we transfer ships," Bryant said firmly, scanning the inside of the hold for anything of interest. "There's only so much a man can take at one time," he continued, "and you'd do well to keep that in mind when working him over. The boss isn't going to pay us for a dead man."

DeVries growled in disgust. "More torture is the only way to get an answer out of him. I say we wake him up. All you're doing is allowing him time to gather his strength." Curses fell from DeVries's mouth as he strode across the cabin to where Banner was tied up. He studied him critically. "I wouldn't be surprised if he was pretending right now." He slugged Nick hard in the shoulder.

Aside from a muffled groan, there was no response.

Bryant rounded on DeVries. "Let's get one thing straight: As long as I'm in charge, I give the orders. Understood? What I want is the girl. What I *don't* want is to have Banner dying on us. Once we get our information, you and Kendyl can decide who gets him first. Until then we do things my way."

"Tressa? Are you all right?" Delta was winding up the tour of the Banner home. But for the past ten minutes she'd been silently observing Tressa's strange behavior.

In the beginning the young woman had bubbled over with questions and comments. Then suddenly she changed, becoming strangely quiet. No longer was she eagerly listening as Delta touched on the highlights about the Banner heritage, or marveling at the history behind many of the points of interest.

And now . . . Tressa was distant, preoccupied, her breathing erratic, her color pale and her expression grave.

"Tressa, dear, why don't we go over and sit down." Delta had no sooner made the suggestion when Tressa placed a trembling hand to her mouth, gasped, and dropped to her knees.

"Noooo! Noooooooo." Her voice trailed off into low, agonizing sobs.

Frantic, Delta went to her knees beside her. "What is it? What's wrong?"

Tears ran unchecked down Tressa's cheeks. "Noooo, pleeeeeze."

"Dawson! Someone, help!" Delta screamed. "Tressa, what's wrong?"

Gathering her strength, Tressa drew back, her body still trembling, her words broken between sobs. "Del . . . ta, it's . . . it's Nick! Something terrible's happening! He's in p-p . . . ain! I can feel it!"

"*Dawson!*"

Tressa struggled to get up. "I've got . . . to go to him! He's hurt."

"Tressa, please calm down and . . . *Dawson!*"

"He needs help! We have to go," Tressa cried, rising to her feet. "Please."

Dawson ran into the room. "What the hell's going on?" he demanded between gasps for breath.

Delta nearly collapsed with relief at the sight of him. "It's Tressa."

"Please, we must go to him," Tressa continued.

Dawson scanned the room for signs of an intruder. "Will someone tell me what the hell's happening?" For the first time ever, the prim head butler spoke to Delta in a less than subservient manner.

"Delta," Tressa suddenly clutched at the woman's arm and dropped to her knees again.

By now several servants, clustered in the doorway, were peering in for a better look.

"Dawson, help me get her up. Annie! Annie, bring a pot of herb tea to the guest room."

The girl nodded, running off.

"And . . . and call the medics!"

"Yes, ma'am," Annie tossed over her shoulder.

Dawson drew Tressa to her feet.

"Noooo!" she cried, pushing them both away. "Please, I must go to Nick! Pleeeeze!"

"What is she talking about?" Dawson demanded.

"She feels Nicky's been hurt."

"He *is* hurt," Tressa insisted. "We must . . ." Her voice trailed off in a moan.

Delta turned to Dawson. "See? Try to get hold of Zeke; tell him it's urgent."

Dawson nodded, turned, and disappeared down the hall.

"Tressa," Delta said softly, trying to rein in her racing heart and appear calm, "I want you to know I believe you and I *am* sending someone to find Nicky," she said, slipping a comforting arm about Tressa's shaking body and heading her down the hallway toward the guest room.

"No! Not just one . . . of the servants, Delta. This . . . time he's in a lot of trouble."

"Don't worry, Tressa. The person I have in mind can handle himself and will know just what to do when he finds Nicky. But right now you need to concentrate on relaxing."

"I don't want to lay down!" Panic returned to her voice.

"All right. You don't have to." Delta ushered Tressa to a sitting area in the bedroom. "I've got some nice hot tea on the way," she said, guiding Tressa into a chair.

Delta struggled to maintain her fragile control. "Tressa," she began as casually as she could manage, "I don't understand how you . . . how you know all this. How can you be so sure that Nicky's hurt?"

Tressa's face clouded with uneasiness. "Because I . . . I *feel* it," she whispered.

"What are you saying? You mean you think the pain you're feeling is . . . is actually *Nicky's?*" Delta regarded her quizzically.

Trembling, Tressa lifted her eyes to meet Delta's. "Yes, but I . . . I can't explain it."

"Tressa, have you ever felt anything like this before?"

A long moment of silence passed before Tressa slowly shook her head in response. "No," she said in a small, frightened voice, her body still trembling. "Once, when Nick was suffering from the effects of the stun gun."

Delta drew back in silence. "You physically *felt* . . ."

"Delta, please, I need to go to him." Her hysteria was building.

Delta looked up as the young housemaid hurried in with the tea. "Oh, thank you, Annie."

Tressa sat in the chair, nervously fingering the neckline of her jumpsuit, as Delta began pouring them each a cup.

"This will help you to relax, Tressa."

"Please . . . don't give me something to make me go to sleep. I . . . I don't want to go to sleep," she pleaded softly, frantically wiping the tears from her face. "I promise, I won't cause any more trouble."

"Nonsense. You're not any trouble, but you do have us worried. This tea will only relax, not drug you. What are you feeling now? Anything?" she asked, steadying the cup in Tressa's trembling hand.

"I don't feel the p-pain so much now, but I'm c-cold. I just . . . want to hold . . . him," she answered between sobs.

Chapter Nineteen

Banner was dimly aware of being carried by rough hands and unceremoniously dumped onto a hard, cold surface. He fought to regain consciousness but lost the battle as tendrils of darkness reached out, enveloping him once again.

He awoke several hours later to the metallic taste of blood in his mouth.

Commanding his body to get up, he swore silently when it refused to obey. His hands were still numb from being tied up. It was his own stupidity that had brought him to this pass, and his wits were all he had now to save him.

Lying perfectly still, he slowly gathered himself. Finally, in what he considered to be an awesome feat of heroics, he managed to maneuver himself into a kneeling position. From there he concentrated his efforts on crouching and finally he stood.

Every muscle in his body ached and throbbed from countless bruises; his eyes were all but swollen shut and the nausea was was ever-present. As best he could, he inventoried his injuries. There was a cut on his face, another on his lower right side. His left arm dangled helplessly, and the agony in his shoulder was excruciating. He was sure of a broken rib, probably two; the pain in that area was deceiving. In truth, his entire rib cage felt crushed. He didn't think his nose had been broken, and although his jaw ached fiercely his teeth remained intact.

Banner was eased back against the wall, surveying his surroundings, when the door suddenly opened. He glanced up through blurred vision to see Quint Kendyl once again facing him, his lips twitching with amusement.

"Well, well, sleeping beauty is awake." A sardonic grin slowly swept across Kendyl's lips as he took in Nick's battered form. "You look a little worse for wear." Kendyl's smile faded; with a nod from him, two men came forward.

"I understand you forgot to introduce me to your shipboard companion," Kendyl continued with mock casualness. "That wasn't polite, Nick. Not at all."

Banner's right arm was thrust upward and the back of his open palm slammed against the wall with more force than was necessary. He choked back a gasp as his wrist was secured in shackles. Flames of fire shot through his rib cage.

Kendyl spoke with continued with nonchalance. "I'll find her, you know."

Banner's left arm was grabbed and slammed against the bulkhead. Gritting his teeth against the white-hot agony of his wrenched shoulder, he wouldn't give them the satisfaction of knowing how badly it hurt.

Hooking his thumbs into the waistband of his pants, Kendyl went on with deceptive casualness. "This one's special, huh, Nick?"

Banner barely comprehended the questions being fired at him. But the water that splashed in his face shocked him back to awareness.

"Have I got your attention now?" Kendyl's grin was cruel.

Choking, Banner looked at him with hooded eyes.

"Let me see . . . where were we? Oh, yes, I believe we were discussing . . . *Tressa.*" He grinned. "Now, you can either make it easy on yourself or . . . well . . . you know. Either way we're waiting right here until that little piece of baggage of yours is found."

"You're welcome to 'er. I guarantee she doesn't know the . . . first thing about pleasing a man," Nick lied between gasps.

Kendyl threw back his head, laughing arrogantly. "Then it will be my pleasure to teach her. You always did lack patience."

Kendyl's voice hardened. "Where is she, Banner?"

"Your guess is as good as mine," he rasped. "She stormed off ship the . . . minute we hit port." It sounded believable, for it was common knowledge that Banner's rough edges always managed to get him into trouble when it came to women.

A cynical smile spread across Kendyl's face. "Well, that means we'll just have to go find her now, won't we? By the way, we're taking her to Steel, Banner." He grinned. "*My* idea. I figure she'll warm my bunk on the way, and by the time we get there . . . I assure you, she'll be worth something."

Without comment, Banner lifted his swollen, hate-filled eyes. All he could envision was Tressa being forced into Kendyl's bed. Dear God, just thinking of it shattered him. He struggled against his bindings, cursing his inability to break free. If only he could, the forces of hell wouldn't be able to stop him from tearing that sonofabitch apart, limb by limb.

"What's the matter, Nick, don't like that idea?" Kendyl laughed. "You want to know what our plans are for you?"

"I'm sure you're just dying to tell me."

Laughter danced in Kendyl's eyes. "You're right, I am. Once DeVries is through with you we're dropping you off on Jewel. Only we're going to skip the formalities of orientation. Sorry, ol' pal, 'fraid you'll be without supplemental oxygen. If Jewel's low oxygen level doesn't get you, the heat will.''

Banner didn't respond; never even heard Kendyl, for that matter. He was too busy envisioning Tressa in Kendyl's bed and . . . Steel, one of the most corrupt and degenerate places he'd ever been. He closed his mind to the mental torment.

Kendyl turned and with a nod dismissed the two men waiting by the entry. Stepping forward, he grabbed Nick's bloodied jacket and pulled him forward against his bonds. ''This is for Aria, partner,'' he said in a harsh, raw voice.

That was all the warning Banner got before Kendyl's knee slammed up into his groin. Buckling under the crucifying pain, Nick fell forward against his bonds, his gut in spasms, vaguely hearing himself groaning out his distress before he blacked out.

Port Ireland, Terra Four

The built-in comset on Jonathan Loring's desk chimed. ''Yes?''

''Mr. Carson is here to see you, sir.''

''Send him in.''

Within moments the door opened. ''Tom, what can I do for you?'' Loring said, putting down his pen and looking up.

''I need to speak with you, sir.''

A slight frown creased Loring's brow. ''Certainly. Have a seat.'' Loring leaned back, steepling his fingers. ''What's on your mind?''

''I'm not sure just where to start,'' Carson began, his tone apologetic.

Jonathan grew serious. ''Maybe you ought to start at the beginning then.''

''Yes,'' Carson said, awkwardly clearing his throat. ''To start off, I suppose I should tell you that I'm the one who wrote that note about a possible threat on your daughter's life.''

A muscle quivered in Loring's jaw. "It was *you* who wrote the note?''

"Yes. I'm the one who overheard the conversation.''

A long moment of silence passed. "Please, don't stop now,'' Loring urged.

"Since then,'' Carson continued, "I've been keeping my ears open, and I've learned a few more things.''

A cold knot formed in the pit of Loring's stomach. "Like what?''

"What I originally overheard was, if the marriage didn't go through, the plan was to force your hand.''

"Force my hand? What do you mean?''

"I'm not sure, but Tressa's name was brought up twice during the conversation, and that was when I decided to get a note to you. Since then I've done some checking around.''

"Yes?'' Loring's expression was one of pained tolerance.

Carson took a deep breath. "Well, sir, I was just wondering . . . how much do you know about this Burke Sinclair?''

"Sinclair?'' he stammered, nailing Carson with a narrowed gaze. "What the devil does Sinclair have to do with anything?''

"It's my understanding that he's asked for Tressa's hand in marriage. Am I correct?''

"Yes. So have others. Duane Harris, Matt Dreyer. Sinclair isn't the only one who has shown serious interest in Tressa.''

"Harris and Dreyer are not a concern,'' Carson said. "Sir, I strongly believe that this Sinclair isn't who he says he is. I believe he could be associated with Tyron Wheeler. Maybe even related.''

By now Jonathan's nerves were at full stretch. "Wheeler? What the devil are you talking about?''

Carson rose from his seat. "The brokerage, Mining and More, Incorporated? I found out it's a subsidiary of WheelerEx."

"Who the hell did you hear that from?"

"I didn't hear it from anyone. It took four days of research to dredge up that information. I'm not saying I'm positive he's related to Wheeler—that part's only speculation—but Mining and More is definitely a subsidiary of WheelerEx. And as for Sinclair not being who he says he is, so far everything supports my belief."

Jonathan leaned back in his chair. "How?" His voice was a hushed rasp. "Why?"

Carson moved forward. "Think about it!" he said, splaying his palms on Loring's desk. "If the marriage doesn't go . . ." he said with exaggerated slowness, "that statement alone narrows our subjects down to only those who have asked for marriage. Right?"

"Go on."

"I've done an identity search on everyone who's even looked sideways at Tressa." Carson straightened. "Sinclair's the only one without a past."

"Now wait just a minute . . ."

"I know, I know," Carson interrupted. "You checked him out long before Tressa even knew he existed. Right? And his record's impeccable. He came from a perfect family, got perfect grades in college, and is running a successful business." Carson shook his head. "It all sounds great until you have reason to question it. And I decided to delve a little deeper."

"Yes?" Jonathan asked expectantly.

"A routine check disclosed perfect backups for every aspect of his personal identity. The schools, his parents . . ." Carson shook his head. "Everything checked out. Even the business is doing great. But . . ." Carson's voice turned ominous, "go beyond that and there's nothing."

Momentarily stunned, Loring sat motionless. "I don't understand. What are you saying?"

"I'm saying that the computer should be able to back-track the personal records on anyone, as far back as necessary, including great-great-grandparents and further.

"In the case of Citizen Sinclair," he continued, "there is no backup beyond his immediate stated identity. In other words, Burke Sinclair doesn't exist beyond the surface."

A tense silence enveloped the room.

"For instance," Carson continued, his voice hard, "I ran a computer search on his supposed parents."

"And?"

"There's no information on either of them: where they were born, who their parents were, and so on. They don't exist. Period." He waved a hand. "I don't know who this Sinclair is, but he sure as hell isn't who he says he is."

Loring rose from his chair. "Then I've played right into their hands by approving of Sinclair in the first place."

"Possibly. This is the way I see it: If the marriage goes through, Wheeler's grandson—assuming that's who he is—would have his foot planted right in LorTech's front door."

Carson leaned forward, his voice a harsh rasp. "And there's more. Sinclair hasn't been seen for going on three weeks now. Why is it I feel he knows Banner has Tressa?"

Jonathan ran a hand through his hair, his expression grave. "And he's gone after her."

"It's likely. But what concerns me is that Sinclair's not stupid. If he *did* go after her, he'd know Banner wouldn't just hand her over." Carson's mouth spread into a thin-lipped smile as he continued. "Somehow, I just can't envision Burke Sinclair confronting Nick Banner at gunpoint and demanding he turn over Tressa. He'd have thugs doing his dirty work for him."

Jonathan's face paled as he dropped back into his chair. "If what you're saying is true . . . instead of getting Tressa off planet to safety I may have placed both of their lives in danger."

"It's speculation, sir, but I thought you should know."

Deep in thought, Loring nodded. "Yes. Thank you, Tom."

"If there's anything else I can do . . ." Carson left the sentence hanging as he turned for the door.

"I'll let you know," Loring said, grabbing for the comset.

The door to the drawing room opened quietly. "Mr. Slater is here. Would you like me to show him in?"

Delta rose to her feet. "Oh, yes. Please."

A loyal friend from Banner's childhood, Zeke Slater was about as tall, almost as handsome, and equally as well-built. His shiny blond hair, usually flowing recklessly about his shoulders, was pulled back and tied at the nape of his neck.

Zeke entered the drawing room with a rigid set to his shoulders and a distinct crease of worry between his deepset blue eyes.

"Oh, Zeke, thank God."

He stepped forward, enfolding Delta in an embrace. "I would have been here sooner, but I just got your message."

Delta felt a wave of relief sweep over her now that Zeke had arrived. He was like a son to her. Though he'd been closest with Nick, he and the three Banner boys had all grown up together. Delta had lost count of the many times Zeke's feet had been planted beneath their table for meals with the rest of the family.

"Start from the beginning," he said, guiding Delta to the couch. Removing his jacket, he sat down across from her as Delta began unfolding the story of why Nick had brought Tressa to Imperial. She went on to relate Tressa's unusual behavior, explaining how she had sensed—no, literally *felt*—something terrible had happened to Nick.

Zeke listened with an intent frown as the story unraveled. "Where's Tressa now?" he asked.

"She's sleeping. Do you want me to wake her?"

"No. Let her sleep."

Delta nodded in agreement. "I'm afraid she didn't sleep well at all."

Zeke gazed at her speculatively. "And neither did you, I take it?"

Delta smiled at him. "No, I didn't. I spent most of the night in a chair next to Tressa's bed. Poor little thing, she sobbed herself to sleep."

Zeke stared at the floor, deep in thought. "I left a number where I could be reached on Nick's message center. Never heard back, so this morning I went looking for him." Rising from the chair, he walked to the windows, presenting his back to Delta. His voice flat, he continued. "I stopped at the Outbounder first, figuring Shara might have seen him. Nick had been there, all right. Shara talked him into staying off-ship. Apparently he had a few things to do first and said that he'd be back."

With a heavy sigh, Zeke paused. "Only he never came back."

Delta's eyes closed.

"I checked out the *Victorious* next. Not only found the security off the main hatch . . . I found traces of blood inside."

He turned to face her, his expression grim. "I don't know how she knew, but the girl's right. Something's happened."

Breathing Nick's name, Delta sank back against the couch, her eyes brimming with tears.

Zeke returned to her side and sat down. "Can Max be reached?" he asked, taking hold of her shaking hands.

Delta looked up expectantly. "You have an idea?"

"Only the beginning of one, and I'm going to need help."

A spark of hope lit Delta's eyes. "I talked to Max yesterday, before all of this happened. The boys are with him. I expect them back sometime around midday."

"Good." Releasing her hand, he rose. "I'm posting several guards around this place, and neither you nor Tressa are to leave the grounds. Agreed?'' He touched her arm.

Smiling bleakly, Delta nodded and wiped the tears from her eyes. "That's just what Nicky said before he left."

Zeke reached for his jacket. "I'll be back by the time Max gets in, and I'll want to talk with Tressa then, too."

Chapter Twenty

Port Ireland, Terra Four

Jonathan reached for the small control pad built into his desktop and depressed a button. "Lizzy, get WheelerEx on the vidcom for me immediately."

"Yes, sir. Anyone in particular?"

"Wheeler," he gritted out.

"Yes, sir."

Loring spun his chair about, facing the glass wall behind his desk. Stretched out beyond it lay a network of buildings, parking lots, and warehouses. Leaning back, he waited, steepling his index fingers and placing them to his chin.

He'd personally taken the rest of the morning and part of the afternoon double-checking Carson's claims, finding everything he'd said to be true.

Jonathan's features hardened at the thought of being suckered. Wasn't it interesting, he thought, that Wheeler just happened to set up his grandson as a mining broker, right when a very large contract happened to be surfacing? It surprised him that Tyron Wheeler would stoop to such a plan. But the thought of Tressa being involved in the scheme enraged him beyond belief. Jonathan's thoughts were interrupted by the intercom. "I've got Mr. Wheeler on the vidcom, sir."

"Thank you," he said, swiveling around again and engaging the large comscreen on the side wall with a flip of a switch. The screen flickered briefly, then focused to reveal Wheeler's face.

Tyron Wheeler was a work-hardened man in his early sixties with a stocky build and thick silver hair, thinning at the temples.

"Jonathan, it's always a pleasure." Wheeler seemed genuinely pleased. And why wouldn't he be, Loring thought; he probably thinks I'm calling to discuss the upcoming contract.

"Cut the crap, Wheeler. I just want to know one thing. Is your grandson running a mining brokerage here in Port Ireland?"

Wheeler's smile faded. "My grandson? Yes . . ." he said slowly, "I've got him managing a small subsidiary. Why?"

Loring's face suddenly went grim. "What in a renegade's hell do you think you're doing? Is this how you're operating now? And dragging my daughter into it was a mistake you'll regret."

"Dragging your dau . . . I don't know what you're talking about!"

"I'm talking about sending your grandson here under a fictitious name. Using him to secure a mining contract you *probably* would have been awarded anyway. And how does Tressa fit in to it? Thinking of merging our companies, Ty? It would be a nice advantage for you."

Moments of silence passed in which Wheeler nailed Jonathan with his steely gaze. Finally he spoke. "I have no idea what you're talking about, Loring."

Jonathan would have almost believed the look of innocence if he wasn't so furious. "You're denying you sent your grandson here under an assumed name to secure the mining contract for the silicon crystals?

"What assumed name? Yes, I sent my grandson to Port Ireland to run Mining and More, but I didn't . . . Assumed name? What the hell are you talking about?"

"Friendly warning, Wheeler," Jonathan said levelly. "If anything happens to Tressa, I'll crush you." He paused meaningfully. "And that's a promise."

A drawn-out moment passed in which both men glared at each other in silence.

"Loring," Wheeler began calmly, "we can sit here trading threats and flexing our muscles all day. But I guarantee it won't get you any closer to finding out who's really behind whatever it is you're accusing me of."

Wheeler's image wavered, then cleared again. "If my grandson's been running Mining and More illegally, I will deal with him. Meanwhile, as a sign of goodwill, and my innocence, I'm offering my assistance. What do you say? Between the two of us and our combined resources, I guarantee—"

"I don't need your help, Wheeler," Loring ground out. "And furthermore, if I find out you've had any involvement in this, you and your grandson are going to wish you hadn't."

Nick . . .

Awaking with a start, Tressa bolted upright. A quick glance at the clock on a nearby stand told her it was almost noon. *Nick* . . . the memory of last night's experience lingered.

Folding back the covers, she swung her feet over the edge of the bed and took in her surroundings. The chamber was light and cheerful as shafts of bright sunshine streamed through the skylight, but Tressa had neither the time nor the inclination to enjoy it. Rising quickly, she grabbed a travel pac and headed for the lav. After a quick shower she would seek out Delta and find out about Nick.

Her damp hair hung in a single braid down her back as

Tressa closed the door to her room and stepped out into the hall.

There it was again. Earlier, she'd thought she'd heard voices drifting up from below, but it was Nick's voice she heard this time. Quietly moving to the wide staircase, Tressa stood at the top of the landing for one breathless moment and listened.

"Nobody spills Banner blood and gets away with it! *Nobody!*" One angry voice rose above the rest, and with it Tressa's heart skipped a beat. Nick!

Starting down the stairs, Tressa drew to a halt as a man stormed from the drawing room into the entry. Their eyes met and Tressa found herself frozen in place. He was older than Nick by several years but just as strikingly handsome, and he possessed those same luminous blue eyes.

Tressa swallowed hard, unable to break free of his riveting gaze. Slowly the man's anger and hard expression softened. "You must be Tressa." His voice was low and smooth, and he sounded exactly like Nick.

"Yes," she replied, slowly descending the stairs. "And you must be one of Nick's brothers."

His answer was an unexpected rumble of laughter. "Darling, you just bought the universe with that one. I'm Nick's father, Max Banner."

"Oh . . ." A blush immediately heated Tressa's cheeks.

As she neared the bottom step, Max came forward, extending his hand. "No wonder Nick's keeping an eye on you."

"Is he here?" she asked expectantly. Before he could answer Delta and three men burst into the foyer.

"Tressa, how are you feeling?" Delta asked, rushing to Tressa's side.

"Better." Her gaze searched the faces surrounding her. "Where's Nick? I thought I heard him talking."

Delta sighed. "They all sound alike. You've met Nicky's father; let me quickly introduce you to the rest of the family. This is Clinton, Nicky's older brother."

"My pleasure, Princess." Clint's gaze skillfully captured Tressa's as he caught her hand and held it a little longer than necessary. She only needed ten seconds to know that Delta was right; Clinton was gifted with that same cocky arrogance Nick possessed.

Next came Marc, the youngest of the three and the one who looked the most like Nick.

"Tressa," he said with a wink and a clipped nod of acknowledgment. Though Marc appeared self-assured, he didn't seem nearly as arrogant as his two older brothers.

Finally Zeke was introduced, along with a brief explanation of his friendship with the family. Zeke greeted Tressa in much the same manner as Marc, with an extended hand, a nod, and the gentle mention of her name.

Tressa was suddenly the center of attention—mainly Clint's. Marc and Zeke weren't quite as blatant in their inspection. Nevertheless, she was beginning to feel like pirate's loot just unloaded from Nick's ship.

"Where's Nick?" she asked, hoping for an answer.

Delta finally spoke up. "Why don't we all go back in and sit down."

Clint immediately sauntered forward as Tressa's self-appointed escort.

The family resemblance was strong among the Banner men. There was certainly no mistaking them for anyone but Banners.

"I told them what happened last night," Delta said as they sat down. "They're going back out now to try to find Nicky, but first they need to ask you a few questions."

Tressa's eyes widened in astonishment. "No one's gone after him yet?"

Zeke spoke up. "We've tried, Tressa. I spent the morning retracing his steps and questioning port security, but it all dead-ends at the *Victorious*. We're hoping you might be able to help us."

"Of course I'll help. I'm going with you," she stated firmly.

Max sat forward. "It will be best for you to stay here."

Although his words were kindly spoken, Tressa recognized that Banner end-of-discussion look. She'd certainly seen it enough in the last three weeks.

Standing before a large floor-to-ceiling window, Zeke turned and came forward. Hunkering down before her, he placed himself on eye level with her and began speaking in a slow, gentle manner. "Do you remember what you experienced last night?"

"Yes," she replied, clasping her hands tightly in her lap.

Zeke paused, then slowly asked, "Are you telepathic?"

Tressa lowered her gaze, making an attempt to straighten nonexistent wrinkles from her shift. Slowly she lifted her eyes to meet his. "I . . . I don't think so," she stammered.

"I see." Zeke paused for a moment. "Do you read minds?"

Tressa shook her head. "No."

"What about visions?"

Again, "No," she said with conviction.

As if having run out of ideas, Zeke cast a questioning glance to Clint.

"How about emotions, Tressa?" Clint asked. "Do you experience feelings that aren't yours—happiness, sadness . . . pain?"

Tressa hesitated. "Yes. No . . . that is . . . not until Nick." She glanced up. "I *felt* his pain," she said helplessly. "I didn't just *know* it, I *felt* it. He was cold and I was . . . *cold*."

"All right," Zeke said slowly "Then you must have some sort of empathic tendencies."

"My mother is part Creohen," Tressa offered.

That got a raised eyebrow from Clint, but he said nothing.

Zeke nodded and took her hand. "Do you feel up to just a couple of questions? It might help us find Nick sooner."

Nodding, Tressa let out a shaky sigh. "Yes. I'll do my best."

241

"Good girl. First of all, Delta tells me Quint Kendyl came aboard the *Victorious*.

"Yes. Nick's ex-partner."

Max spoke up. "And other than informing Nick about the tracer, Kendyl mentioned no names, gave no indication at all about who had put the tracer onboard?"

Tressa shook her head slowly. "Just that he'd picked up on the tracer. I really don't think he knew who had put it there."

"That rules him out as being part of this," Delta murmured.

"Not necessarily," Zeke said, pushing himself into a standing position.

Clint immediately took the seat beside her. "What about now? Do you feel or sense anything now?"

A wave of panic flashed through Tressa at the question. Suddenly she wanted to run, to escape their probing questions—to evade the strange sensations of pain and fear that weren't hers.

Ever since the night Nick had tried to seduce her, she had denied the occasional waves of unfamiliar emotion that connected her so intimately with him. Though naive in the ways of love, the raw passion she had felt that night was that of a practiced lover, not a naive young woman. And Tressa found the intoxicating sensation both frightening and exhilarating.

Then there was the time when he was unconscious from the stunner; again foreign sensations had assaulted her mind. Frightful things she didn't *want* to feel—*his* pain, *his* panic, *his* aloneness.

Even now, her ribs ached with his agony. Anxiety coursed through her with his panic, and a cold knot formed in the pit of her stomach with his isolation.

Clint's warm hands suddenly wrapped around hers and tightened in reassurance. "You're sensing something right now, aren't you?" he asked.

Tressa squeezed her eyes shut against the terror that

welled up deep inside. She fought back the waves of fearful emotions, unfamiliar and confused feelings that weren't her own.

Terrified to delve deeper, Tressa denied the intrusion on her thoughts and frantically sought to erect a wall of defense. She would *not* go through again what she had last night.

"Tressa," Clint said gently, "what is it?"

"Noo," she cried, snatching her hand from his grasp.

Clint flashed a quick glance at Max, then back to Tressa. "Can you tell us what it is you're feeling, little one?"

Tressa drew a shaky breath and for a moment said nothing.

"He's . . . suffering a great deal," she said at last, afraid to probe deeper.

"Hang on for just a little longer, Tressa, okay? Try to reach for Nick." Clint's *Banner* voice was low and gentle, and if she closed her eyes . . . it was Nick.

Max stopped pacing and came forward, dropping to one knee before her. "Tressa, I know you can't actually see things, but as you sense Nick's feelings . . . can you give us any clues at all as to his whereabouts?"

Zeke nodded and moved closer. "Good idea."

"Are you sensing anything else besides his pain?" Max continued.

Yes, she wanted to say. *Yes,* she was feeling a whole gamut of emotions that she neither asked for nor wanted. And other than the pain she didn't know which emotions were hers and which were his. She glanced from one face to the next, each one expectantly awaiting her answer.

"My *goodness,* boys," Delta said, fanning her hands at the four of them. "Back off. You're giving *me* claustrophobia. How can you possibly expect Tressa to concentrate on anything with all of you crowding her like this?"

They backed off reluctantly, but not far. Clint remained seated at her side. Max, his eyes never leaving her face, went only as far as the seat across from her. With a sigh of exasperation, Zeke strode impatiently to the window, leaning an arm against the frame. And belying his frustration, the youngest brother, Marc, calmly withdrew a cigar. Ignoring the look of censure from Delta, he lit it and stepped back against the wall to study Tressa, the cigar clamped between his teeth.

"Tressa, dear," Delta's voice broke the silence, "I think what they mean is . . . is there anything else you can tell them that might help them know where to start looking? Do you sense that he might be cold . . . hot? Is he alone?"

The air was charged with tension and suppressed frustration.

"Can you sense smell, Tressa?" This time Marc's deep voice penetrated Tressa's barriers. "Anything? No matter how small or insignificant, it could help us."

"He . . . He's alone, and . . ." Panic welled in her throat and she paused. "I . . . I can't!"

Clint reached for her hand again. "Yes, you can. And . . . *what* . . . ?" he prompted.

Max caught Zeke's attention, and with a jerk of his head, he strode to the far corner of the room. Zeke followed.

Tressa's fingers slowly curled around Clint's hand. She swallowed hard, searching his face, her own face grim with pain . . . Nick's pain. "He's . . . he's hurting again." A lone tear trickled down her cheek. "My . . ." She struggled to separate the two sets of emotions warring within her. "*His,*" she corrected, "ribs hurt and his arms . . . and . . ." She gasped. Hot tears began slipping freely down her cheeks. "And I think he's having trouble breathing."

Delta slipped Tressa a handkerchief.

"Tressa," Clint continued, "try not to concentrate on Nick's pain right now." His voice was rough with anxiety. "If you can, try to shut it out and concentrate on anything that might help us rescue him.

"You're all he's got right now, Princess."

Nodding bleakly, Tressa remained silent for a long time. Swallowing hard, she slowly lifted her eyes. "I sense cold and hardness and . . .'' She sensed what could even be described as a deck or maybe a bulkhead. ''I don't know why, but I think he's still at the space port.''

''You do?'' all four said in unison.

''I . . . I think he might be shackled to something.'' Tressa's chin started trembling.

Clint squeezed her hand. ''Thank you, Tressa. That gives us a starting place.''

Zeke turned to Max. ''Damn, he's still at the space port.''

''Yeah,'' Marc interjected. ''But where? It's like a small city down there.''

Clint gently released Tressa's hands with another light squeeze and rose to his feet. ''You all right?''

She nodded.

''Would you like something to drink?'' He turned his gaze toward Delta. ''. . . Maybe a cup of tea or something?''

Tressa shook her head. ''I want to go with you.''

''Pardon me?''

''I want to go with you,'' Tressa repeated with emphasis.

''I'm afraid that's out of . . .''

''But you don't understand! You need me.'' She rose in one fluid motion. ''I can help you find him. I know I can. It only makes sense that the closer we get to him, the stronger . . .''

''You're staying here, Tressa,'' Max said in a voice that forbade any arguments.

Chapter Twenty-one

Tressa had about the most expressive brown eyes Clint had ever seen, and his breath caught as he stumbled over his words. "Tressa . . ." he said gently, struggling for the right way to put it. "We *can't* take you with us."

He glanced away for the length of a heavy sigh. "Number one, it would be far too dangerous, and number two, Nick would . . ."

Tressa interrupted. "But . . . I can *help*. I *know* I can. You *must* let me go with you!"

Silence.

"Tressa." Max's voice carried a unique force all its own.

But Tressa wasn't listening. "No. You don't understand . . ."

"*Tressa!*" Max had her undivided attention now. "I want you to stay here with Delta." His tone was uncompromising, yet oddly gentle. A long moment of silence followed in which Tressa and Max locked gazes.

Her mouth thinned in irritation. "Very well," she said

stiffly, "if you are finished, then I wish to return to my room."

"Certainly." Clint rose to see her to the stairs. Tressa started to refuse his assistance, but he wouldn't be denied.

After the doors of the drawing room had closed behind them he caught her arm. "Tressa, surely you can understand the danger that will be involved here?" One corner of his mouth rose in that unmistakable Banner grin. "Besides, as I started to explain back there, I'm afraid Nick would end up feeding us all to the Greegs in bite-size pieces if we brought you along."

"Ha! That's a laugh. What makes you think he'd care? Why, I've been exposed to more danger in the last three weeks than I have in my entire life! I'm your best bet, Clinton, and you know it. *Let me go with you!*"

Clint's amusement waned. "Believe me, he'd care, Tressa. And he'd be damn mad—and that's just if nothing happened to you. We could handle his anger all right, but if you were to get hurt . . . or worse, we'd have our own regret to deal with along with his fury. Personally, that's a chance I'm not willing to take."

Tressa jerked her arm from his hold. "I can assure you, in the shape he's in right now he wouldn't know. Let me go, Clinton!"

He grinned. "Just plain Clint will work, and it's not that simple, Tressa. I know, 'cause I've had an experience with a Creohen girl myself."

A long moment passed. "So?" she said, staring at him blankly.

Clint's eyes narrowed. "So . . . what?"

Tressa frowned. "So . . . what's that supposed to mean?"

She *really* didn't know, he thought in disbelief. "Didn't . . . didn't anybody ever explain this to you, your mother or someone?"

A look of wariness crossed Tressa's face. "Explain? Explain what?"

"Your Creohen heritage, Tressa," he replied.

"My mother explained very little. I was tested when I was ten and came up negative. And until now I've never experienced anything like this."

Clint released a sigh of frustration. "Look, whatever you and Nick have shared is you're business. You've bonded with him, lady, whether you realize it or not. Nick's in this as deep as you are, and if my guess is correct he's hooked but good."

"Hooked?" Taking a steady breath, Tressa stepped back. "For your information, Clint Banner, Nick and I have *shared* nothing! And I can assure you I have not bonded with anyone!"

"Look, Sunshine, I haven't time right now to get into this, but . . ."

"Just plain Tressa will work, Clint."

His mouth twitched. "Fair enough."

Tressa nailed him with a glare. *"Let me go with you. This should be my decision, not Nick's or anyone else's."*

Clint merely shook his head. "No, Tressa."

"All right," she said at last, turning for the stairs. *"All right,* I understand. I'd probably just slow you down."

He cast her an amused glance. "Now that *isn't* what I said. I said it's too dangerous."

Tressa nodded. "You're right. I think I'm going to go back to my room and try to get some rest."

He favored her with an easy grin. "Good girl."

The rest of the men burst from the drawing room. "Clint! You coming?"

"I'll be right there."

"Hurry it up," Max called over his shoulder. "We'll fill you in on the way."

Clint simply stood there, a twinge of suspicion crossing his mind as he glanced back at Tressa so obediently ascending the stairs. Only a moment ago she had shown no signs of relenting. Now all of a sudden she was as meek as a kitten—even to the point of telling him he was right. He didn't buy it; not for a second. She was just a little too submissive for his peace of mind. And damn, he didn't have time to question it now.

He turned to catch up with the others when her voice stopped him.

"Oh, and Clint? As far as Nick being *hooked,* as you put it? He couldn't get me off his ship fast enough." With that, she turned and continued up the stairs.

Clint's roving gaze lazily appraised her. "Honey, I'll . . . just . . . bet he couldn't," he murmured, a flash of humor crossing his face as he turned for the door.

Blinking back tears of frustration, Tressa rushed to her room, slamming the door behind her. The report was as loud as the discharge of a Waring slug gun.

"Stupid, stubborn, arrogant *men!*" She leaned against the closed door, dashing away her tears with the palms of her hands. She was getting damn sick of being told what she could and could not do. First her father forcing her into this trip in the first place, withholding his reasons as if she was a small child. Then Nick, ordering her about like some member of his crew. And now . . . now his family, too caught up in their chauvinistic world to listen to reason. Couldn't they see that Nick's life was at stake?

Tressa froze, mind and body benumbed. "Nick . . ." Just breathing his name shot a lance of panic through her. She wasn't sensing anything from him now. *When had it stopped? Why? Had they taken him away somewhere? Was he unconscious, or worse?*

With a surge of determination she shoved away from the door. If they thought they were keeping her here, they were in for a surprise! No one was going to tell her she couldn't help. Tugging her shift up over her head, she threw it in a rumpled heap on a nearby chair. Jerking a travel pac from the shelf, she tossed it on the bed and pulled out a clean jumpsuit.

Suddenly a soft tap came at the door. "Tressa, it's me." *Delta.* Quickly sliding the pac under the bed, Tressa grabbed her shift from off the chair and hurredly opened the door.

"Are you all right, dear?"

"Yes, I'm fine. Just a little tired, that's all."

Delta nodded in understanding. "Can I get you anything?"

"No, actually I thought I'd just lie down for a little while." *She seemed believable as she stood there clutching the shift to her breast.*

"I think that's a good idea, and if you're still sleeping when they return with Nicky, I'll wake you."

"Thank you, Delta." Tressa forced herself to close the door gently, then quickly returned to her purpose.

Grabbing the jumpsuit from the pac, she yanked it on, then reached for her boots.

TiMar leapt on the bed, watching curiously as she hopped first on one foot and then the other, donning the boots as she went.

"You're worried about him, too, aren't you, little man?" She picked him up and squeezed him affectionately before putting him back down. Then, grabbing her jacket off the hook, she headed for the door.

The hall was empty. Tressa was halfway down its length before she discovered TiMar had slipped out with her, tail held high as he darted on ahead.

"TiMar," she whispered, extending her hand to him. "Come here, boy."

He turned, watching her quizzically, rubbing his side against the leg of a small table along the wall.

"Come here, TiMar," she whispered, tiptoeing closer.

Scampering just out of reach, he rushed to the top of the stairs and waited, hesitating as he glanced back at her. Tressa knew all too well where he was trying to lead her:

the kitchen. It was a habit he'd picked up onboard ship.

Tressa swallowed the lump in her throat. Every nerve in her body was on alert as she inched her way closer. "TiMar!" she whispered, but he wasn't about to be caught.

In frustration Tressa turned and hurried back. Maybe if she just ignored him, he'd come after her.

Deliberately leaving the door ajar, she entered her room and waited, barely a minute passing before TiMar stalked in after her. This time she dashed for the door, and Tressa slipped out into the hallway, closing in TiMar behind her.

Once again calling upon her skills of stealth, she made her way down the length of the wide, paneled hallway, her boots making not a hint of noise on the carpeted floor. Several times she paused, listening for sounds, but was met with nothing more sinister than the pounding of her own heart.

Stopping at the landing, she held her breath and surveyed the foyer. The coast was clear. Hurrying down the rest of the stairs, she made her way to the kitchen, where she recalled seeing a service entrance on her tour yesterday. A quick trip through the kitchen and she was out the door.

Tressa kept a low profile as she hurried across the parking lot. If she was lucky, maybe she'd get one of the land crafts to work. They looked similar to the ones she was used to driving back home.

"Hello there."

Startled, Tressa turned abruptly to face a young woman coming toward her and smiling openly.

"Hi, I'm Angie."

Tressa hid her anxiety behind a brilliant smile. "I'm Tressa. You wouldn't happen to be heading into the city?"

"Yes, I am. You want a lift?"

"Please." Relief swept through Tressa as she hurried around to the passenger's side. Within minutes they were heading down the long drive.

"Today's market day," Angie said, holding up the list

for emphasis. Sliding a square disk into a slot, she cranked up the music.

Deep in unsettled thought, Tressa turned toward the window and swallowed hard at the tightening knot in the pit of her stomach. *Nick*... A terrible, fierce yearning took hold of her, wrenching her heart as waves of anguish washed over her. *Would she find him? Would he be all right? What if he'd been taken off-planet... what if...*

Soon the land craft picked up speed and the scenery became a blur. Angie turned briefly to give Tressa an assessing glance. "So, who's friend are you?" she asked boldly over the blare of the music, "Clint's or Marc's?"

Tressa was startled by the question. "Uh, neither. I guess you could say I'm here on business. Nick hauls cargo for my father and..."

"Nick?" With a sharp intake of breath, Angie cast a quick glance at Tressa. "Nick's back?" she asked in pleased surprise.

"We got in late yesterday afternoon."

A thoughtful smile curved Angie's mouth as she returned her attention to her driving. "That ought to stir up some gossip."

"Why do you say that?" Tressa asked.

"Imperial's a small town. Nick's already known as the family rebel. You're bound to stir up talk."

Turning her attention to the passing countryside, Tressa's brows drew together in a thoughtful expression.

"So where's home?"

"What?" Tressa asked, turning to face the young housemaid.

"Home," Angie repeated. "Where are you from?"

"Terra Four," Tressa answered. "It's a little over two weeks from here."

Angie looked at her with exaggerated shock. "Two weeks? *With Nick?*" She groaned. "I feel sorry for you."

Tressa smiled wistfully. Returning her attention to the window, she struggled to tune out Angie, her questions, and her thundering rock music. Any other time, she would have found the girl delightful. But the knot in the pit of her stomach was growing tighter by the minute. Nothing mattered anymore, nothing but Nick and finding him . . . alive.

Soon they were entering the city limits.

"Would it be too much trouble to just drop me off at the space port?

"Sure. Hang on. I know a short cut," Angie said, swinging a hard right.

Within minutes they were entering a circular drive and pulling up to the main terminal at Imperial's space port.

"I really appreciate this. Thank you," Tressa said.

"No problem. You have a ride back?"

"Yeah, I do. Thanks." Stepping out, Tressa traded the sound of rock music for the echoing roar of the space port.

Making her way through the terminal, Tressa hurried below to the lower hangar. The *Victorious* sat several rows ahead. But it wasn't the *Victorious* she was seeking. Tressa was certain that somewhere on this lower deck Nick was being held captive.

The hangar was enormous. Overwhelming was more the word, she thought, pausing to gather in her awareness of Nick.

Finally honing in on what could only be explained as Nick's weakened life force, Tressa galvanized herself into action, cautiously making her way across the burn-blackened surface of the deck, picking her way over fuel lines and sidestepping maintenance platforms. The air was heavy with what was now becoming the familiar stench of a hangar and its ever-constant whine of turbines.

Passing beneath a ship that was still emanating heat, Tressa narrowly dodged a hot jet of vapor that suddenly surged from a vent.

Without conscious thought of where she was going or what to look for, she continued. A roboloader beeped, and she scurried out of its way.

Suddenly, off to her left a loud Klaxon sounded three

short blasts of warning. Moments later, Tressa's eyes were drawn upward as two enormous floor-to-ceiling doors began sliding open with a bone-jarring rumble. Shafts of daylight streamed in around the perimeter of a huge platform that was positioned at the top of the opening.

Tressa glanced at the overhead sign flashing STAND CLEAR OF BLAST AREA. She was a good hundred feet away. Deciding it was far enough, she remained, transfixed, her head tilted back as a ship slowly moved into place on the platform, its navigational lights strobing, its thrusters screaming.

Covering her ears against the deafening roar, she watched as the ship eased down onto its jacks, then killed its drives. At the brief reprieve she released her ears, watching as the platform, with a deep hydraulic growl, slowly began descending.

Upon reaching the bottom, a robosphere hopped off and glided ahead, just as it had yesterday when Nick had docked the *Victorious*.

Tressa remained sheltered behind a stack of cargo pallets, watching as the robosphere moved ahead, its message, FOLLOW, flashing. Again she covered her ears as the ship powered up. The rumble of the closing hangar doors soon became lost in the high-pitched scream of the ship's thrusters. Cowering lower, Tressa covered her head as a wave of heated exhaust washed over the area, the vibrations pummeling her body.

Once it had passed she stood up, staring in disbelief at the retreating ship. Turning, Tressa pressed on, stepping over maintenance hoses, avoiding landing jacks, and dodging freight sleds along the way.

Then she saw it, off in the distance. She didn't question how she knew—she just knew. There it was, the ship she'd been seeking.

It sat low on its jacks, with a short set of stairs reaching down to touch the ground. The main lock stood open, unguarded.

Darting in behind a stack of cargo modules, Tressa crept closer, her empathic senses reaching out for Nick's presence. It was weak, and she steeled herself against the distraction of panic. What he *didn't* need right now was an overemotional female on a self-appointed mission of mercy. If she lost control, she'd most likely end up shackled next to him.

Inching forward, Tressa cautiously ducked behind the landing jack of a nearby ship and waited, watching, deciding whether to take advantage of the unprotected entrance.

Suddenly a large hand clamped over her mouth as an arm snaked about her waist, jerking her up tightly against a steely length of hard muscle and bone. Tressa's heart nearly stopped beating before she heard the low-whispered voice against her ear.

"What the hell are you doing here, sunshine?"

Tressa relaxed immediately, and with a muscular twist, Clint whirled her around to face him. "You surprised me, love," he said in a whispered tone that was almost conversational. "You've got a rebellious streak in you."

He tipped her chin so that her eyes met his narrowed gaze. "If we were anywhere else but here, I'd turn you over my knee and heat that shapely little backside of yours for coming here."

It was her face that heated instead. "You wouldn't dare!"

"Oh, wouldn't I? You underestimate me, sweetheart."

Judging from his grave expression, there was little doubt but that he most certainly would dare. Tressa's gaze slid to Max, Zeke and Marc, who didn't appear any more pleased with her than was Clint. They all wore identical scowls.

Swallowing a surge of rage, Tressa met Clint's glare head on and responded in a heated whisper of her own. "Your childish attempts at discipline are *hardly* the issue here. Nick's inside that black ship and I really don't think now is the time or the place to argue over my defiance."

"What are you saying?" Max interrupted.

255

Clint released his hold. "You think he's on *that* ship?"

"I don't think. I *know!*" Tressa exclaimed.

Chapter Twenty-two

"What are we waiting for? Let's go!" Max said.

"I'm coming with you," Tressa clipped out stubbornly..

"No. You're not!"

"*Yes!*"

"Not this again," Zeke groaned.

Max grabbed her by the arm and spun her to face him. "Dammit, woman!" His voice was a harsh whisper. "This isn't some damn game! It's my son's life we're dealing with here!"

"And you think I don't know that?" Tressa shot back.

"What I know, young lady, is that you've become a liability. And I will *not* jeopardize this mission or the lives of my boys by having to rescue you from your misguided heroics.

"But you don't understand."

"Oh, but I do. And unless I miss my guess these thugs are the same ones that have been after you right from the beginning."

Tressa's eyes widened in stunned silence.

"Max." Zeke's whispered voice interrupted. "Looks like our guard's returned."

Without so much as an acknowledgment, Max continued to hold Tressa's gaze. "Do we understand each other, Tressa?"

Swallowing hard, she nodded slowly.

"Say it!"

"... *Yes!*" The word stuck in her throat.

Max hesitated, still holding eye contact. "You'd better," he added levelly, releasing her arm.

"Damn, this changes everything," he said, turning back to the others. "One of us is going to have to keep an eye out for her now."

"You want me to take her back to the land craft?" Marc offered, watching Tressa closely.

"No. We don't have time."

For the moment Tressa obediently remained standing where Max had left her.

"What about the guard?" Zeke asked. "Someone's going to have to take him out."

Tressa's eyes followed theirs to the man standing watch. He was armed and looked impossibly despotic, lounging against a crate near the entrance to the ship. Her gaze slid back to the Banners.

"Marc, I want you to . . ." They were huddled together in conference. Clint glanced up, captured her gaze for several breathless heartbeats, then returned his attention to the on-going discussion.

This is not some damn game! It's my son's life we're dealing with here! Max's words pounded through Tressa's mind again and again.

Her gaze returned to the guard. What they needed was someone to distract him. And who better to do it than her? It was the one thing Tressa knew for a fact she could do better than any one of them. The only problem was, they'd never go for it. And they were keeping a close eye on her. If she was going to do anything, it needed to be either very quick or so subtle, they wouldn't realize it until it was too late.

With her eyes still fixed on the men, Tressa opted for slow and subtle, and took one tiny step backward. She paused, then took another small step . . . paused, then another. Again Clint glanced up, and their eyes met. Returning his look innocently, Tressa assumed a relaxed pose, knowing her chances of escape depended upon their arrogant belief that she wouldn't dare to disobey them a second time. Seemingly satisfied, Clint glanced away again.

"When we get to the ship . . ." Max's voice became lost in the backdrop of whining thrusters.

Now was her chance!

With her heart in her throat, Tressa slipped out of sight, once again dodging servicing equipment, fuel lines, and roboloaders as she quickly made her way along the row of ships. Within moments she was directly across the passageway from the sleek black yacht. The name *Renegade* was inscribed on the hull near the entry port.

Tressa kept herself hidden from view. In order to play decoy and do it right, she would need to go beyond the *Renegade,* so that when she approached the guard it would force his back to the encroaching rescue party.

Edging her way over, between and around various pieces of equipment, she quickly covered the distance of two more ships. Pausing, she appraised the guard, gathering her courage for the task ahead. He seemed young, yet there was a hardness about him that left no question in her mind that he wouldn't hesitate to use his gun on anyone, including a woman. The thought sent a chill up her spine.

With a fortifying breath and shaking hands, Tressa opened the neckline of her jumpsuit, exposing a generous portion of cleavage. Stepping boldly from the shadows, she found herself looking directly down the business end of a Sheldon mini-blaster.

"That's far enough!"

Tressa stopped in midstride. "Oh, my!" Her hand fluttered to her breast as she played the role of a vapid female who was too dumb to know she'd stumbled into wolf's territory.

"What are you doing here, lady?" came his gruff response, the gun still trained on her.

"Oh . . ." She swallowed. "I . . . I was hoping you could help me."

A long moment of silence passed before he spoke. "That depends on what you need help with, babe." His gaze was riveted to her gaping neckline.

Tressa moistened her lips. "I think I'm lost," she cooed in her best imitation of an oversexed echo-brain. "You see, I thought I knew the way back to the ship, but . . . well . . ." With a wave of her hand, she took in the expanse of the hangar. "This place is so big, and so many of the ships look alike." Frowning, her tone turned indignant. "and a moment ago I was practically run down by one of those . . . those roboloaders, or whatever they're called."

The gun lowered just a notch, though he still didn't appear to trust her. "And just what ship is it you're trying to find?"

"The *Westar*," she offered, grabbing at a name. "Have you heard of it?"

He shook his head. "Don't recognize it."

"Oh."

She didn't know what to do next. Acting the part of a space-port whore wasn't exactly a rehearsed role. She knew she had to come on to this guy and do it with such finesse that it would leave no doubt about what she was offering, or the skill with which she offered it.

Suddenly she recalled Nick's seductive performance that night onboard ship, when she'd cared for his wounded side. How he'd slowly unbuckled his belt and aroused her by provocatively toying with the studs on his trousers; and how with deliberate ease he'd nudged the waistband down his narrow hips. He'd skillfully ignited a slow fire in Tressa that night, and with that memory in mind she determined that, given a modification or two, she could mimic the performance.

Swallowing back a wave of fear, she sauntered closer, her tone silky. "What are you guarding with that great big gun of yours? Something real valuable I bet, huh?" She rested one hand suggestively on a cocked hip. "I assure you, I'm not a threat. I don't have a violent bone in my body."

A muscle jumped in his jaw, and Tressa lowered her lashes, pleased at his response.

She stepped closer, her hand moving to the opening of her jumpsuit, where she deliberately toyed with the zipper, suggestively flipping the pull. "I'd be grateful to you if you could help me find my way back."

A long moment of silence passed before he finally said coldly, "I'm on duty."

Tressa took in the muscled contours of his body with a look of deliberate approval. Though unshaven and grimy-looking, she decided that beneath the filth was probably a face that had no trouble attracting female companionship. And in a way that was good, for it made it all the more believable that she could be attracted to him.

"You look like a guy who knows his way around. I don't think it would take long at all. I'd make it worth your while," she added suggestively.

"Oh, yeah? What do you have in mind?"

"A trade, maybe . . ." Her voice trailed off. A tidal wave of apprehension swept through her with that one, yet she managed a seductive smile.

The guard hesitated. Raw passion lurked in his gaze as he assessed her boldly. Finally he grinned wickedly and holstered his gun. "Maybe I can help you after all, honey."

Max looked up just in time to witness Tressa stepping out of the shadows.

"That little fool!" he hissed.

Even from four ship-lengths away there was no doubt of

her intent; it was boldly written in her body language. The Banner men watched in shocked disbelief as Tressa cleverly coaxed the guard away from the ship's main hatch.

"You know what she's doing," Zeke stated matter-of-factly.

Max nodded slowly. "I know exactly what she's doing. And it's the fact she's doing it that I'm having trouble with."

Clint grinned. "Sure's a good thing she's Nick's headache, huh?"

Ignoring Clint's mockery, Max turned to his youngest son. "Marc, I'm going to need you to keep an eye on her."

A look of disappointment flashed across Marc's face, leaving no doubt that he'd been looking forward to the prospect of a little action.

"And no heroics. Understand? You do nothing unless she gets in over her head."

"She's already in over her head," Clint muttered.

Max returned his gaze to the ship. "Boys, time to move." With weapons raised, they darted from one cover to the next, and in a matter of minutes they were crouching behind an empty freight sled, close enough to the yacht now to actually see inside her open hatch. Soft light spilled out from the inside.

"Notice the name?" Zeke whispered.

Max nodded slowly. "Yeah, I already did." The *Renegade*. His expression grew hard. *Kendyl*.

Silently assessing the surrounding area, Max wondered why they would post only one guard at the entry. Two would have been harder to distract. As it was, it was taking no more than a little slip of a girl to render the ship defenseless.

From his point of view that meant one of two things: The people they were up against were either very stupid or very confident about whatever defenses they had.

A curt nod from Max sent Marc veering off to the right in search of Tressa. Then, closing the distance between them and the yacht with predatory swiftness, Max, Clint, and Zeke ascended the ramp.

Pausing at the threshold, Max quickly scanned the entrance for electronic eyes or signs of any other types of security devices. Seeing none, he led the way onboard, easing his way back against the bulkhead just inside.

Strangely, the ship appeared deserted. Only a few winking lights on the command console greeted them. He couldn't believe the lack of security. Either people weren't doing their job or Kendyl was awfully damned sure of himself.

Max slowly scanned the area. To his right an empty and highly sophisticated cockpit spanned the entire bow of the ship. To his left a side corridor led the way to the stern. At Max's signal the three of them began edging their way down the narrow corridor.

Scarcely aware that he was all but holding his breath, Max found himself acutely aware of how noisy it is just trying to be quiet. Every chain, every buckle and clip suddenly seemed to rattle and clink with each step.

Even the rasp of metal as Zeke cocked back the hammer on his gun sounded like a clap of thunder. Both Max and Clint turned on him with scowls. Meeting their looks with a sheepish shrug, Zeke eased the hammer back in a series of tiny nerve-jarring clicks. Max rolled his eyes heavenward, thanking God that at least he and Clint had stunners.

Though not denying the advantages of the high-tech stunner, Zeke, like Nick, seemed to prefer the heaviness in his hand and the dead-set accuracy of the slug gun to that of its silent counterpart.

Expelling the breath he'd been holding, Max again started down the corridor. Bringing up the rear, Zeke slowly eased around, rechecking the entry and ramp area, gripping his gun in a two-handed hold as he made a wide sweep of their backtrail before proceeding.

The aroma of food drifting up the corridor suggested that somewhere ahead was the galley. And if Max's guess was correct, that door at the end led to the hold—and his son.

Long before he'd boarded the ship he'd decided that if anywhere, he'd find Nick in the ship's hold. Anything as messy as dragging information out of someone sure as gravity wouldn't be performed in the living quarters.

Suddenly they paused, stopped by the sounds of deep voices drifting out of an open doorway. Backs against the wall, weapons drawn, the Banner party prepared for trouble. In silence they waited until, satisfied there was no immediate danger, Max gave the signal to commence. Step by step they moved down the passageway until Max raised his hand once again, bringing them to a halt.

The time for mercy was long past.

A soundless command left Zeke standing guard in the corridor while Max and Clint swiftly entered the galley, weapons silently belching invisible beams of nerve-jamming impulses.

"What the—" Words were cut off in midsentence as Clint dropped to one knee and fired again.

Silence.

It was over before the punks even knew what hit them. One man lay sprawled on the floor beside a dining booth. Clint's gaze rose slowly to find an overturned cup of steaming hot coffee trailing across the surface of the table, spilling over the edge and forming a dark puddle near the man's face. Another crewman, still sitting in his seat, was slumped over a scattered deck of cards. Weapon poised, Max cautiously advanced further into the galley. To his left, a third and final crewman lay crumpled at the base of the food service center; his meal remained untouched on the counter above.

Another tense moment passed as Max silently surveyed the remainder of the galley. At last satisfied, he turned for the exit. Clint exchanged a confident glance with Zeke as they followed Max out into the corridor.

Max drew in a long, steady breath as he pulled to halt before the closed door at the end of the passageway. The thought of his son lying just beyond filled him with anguish. Nick, his middle son, was as independent and bullheaded as they come. He couldn't even remember the last time Nick had turned to him for help. And now . . . now, at the time when his son had needed him the most, he hadn't been there for him. None of them had! His guts churned with remorse and fear. But what terrified him more than anything was the realization that they might be too late.

Somehow it wasn't surprising when they discovered a security device on the door to the hold. Whether it was engaged or not was another question.

Zeke brushed past Clint. "Security?" he whispered, directing his gaze toward the door.

Max nodded, sweat beginning to bead on his forehead.

"I want to take a look at this baby," Zeke muttered softly, visually tracing a series of electronic eyes along the doorframe. "Well . . . It's definitely manufacturer-installed." He turned and headed back up the corridor toward the cockpit, Max following at his heels.

"The first thing we need to know is whether it's engaged or not," Zeke said, coming to a halt before the controls. One glance was all it took. A tiny red indicator boldly pronounced that security on the ship's hold was activated.

Taking a seat, a long moment of silence passed as Zeke studied the command console. Finally, rubbing his sweaty hands on his thighs, he tapped in a directive to the on-board computer.

Immediately the words ACCESS DENIED appeared on screen. Zeke heaved a heavy sigh, dragging his hand through his hair as he studied the console again. Then, on a wild hunch, he began entering a series of five numbers. It was crazy, he knew, but why not? This particular little set of numbers had not only pulled him out of a tight spot on more than one occasion, they'd even been lucky at the gaming tables.

A few seconds ticked by; then, grinning, Zeke shook his

head in disbelief as the computer accepted his entry. Within moments the red-lit indicator winked out.

"What did you do?" Clint asked.

Still grinning, Zeke rose from his seat. "You remember that jet bike I used to own when we were kids?"

"The one I used to borrow all the time?"

"Let's move!" Max's harsh whisper snapped Clint and Zeke to attention.

"You wouldn't believe how many tight spots its serial number has pulled me out of," Zeke added as he and Clint followed after Max.

"If you ask me," Max muttered, nearing the cargo hold, "this entire rescue has been too easy, right down to a guard who could be easily distracted by a little girl. I just want to get Nick and get out of here before all hell breaks loose." Without hesitating, he palmed the lock and stormed into the hold as the door cycled open.

Caught by surprise, two men standing guard just inside the door went for their weapons, but not fast enough. Max dropped one of them with a fist to the jaw. Having just ducked a meaty fist aimed at his own jaw, Zeke grabbed the offender by his shoulders and pulled him down hard onto an uplifted knee. It was over in a matter of seconds, and Clint added insurance by using his stunner on them both.

". . . Nick." The whispered name was barely audible as Max rushed to his son's side.

Unconscious, his head resting to the side against a raised arm, Nick hung lifelessly from tie-downs along the bulkhead. His breathing was so shallow that it was just barely discernible.

Max's shoulders tensed visibly at the sight of his son's brawny body, now limp, bruised, and reduced to a state of helplessness.

Jaw set with anguish, Zeke stood guard at the corridor as Clint and Max tucked their weapons into their waistbands and began working to release Nick from his bonds.

"Easy! Easy with him," Max commanded, his voice choked with emotion as they struggled feverishly with the cargo tie-downs.

Nick's body sagged as the wrist Max was working on finally broke free of its restraint. Quickly supporting his son's slackened weight, he eased the tension on the other wrist while Clint struggled with the other tie-down.

"They have these damn things tight enough!" he muttered, withdrawing a knife and attempting to saw away at the reinforced metal bindings. The next minute Nick was buckling to the floor.

"I got him!" Clint gasped, bracing his brother's bulk against his own body.

Moving into position, Max accepted the weight of his son's slackened form as Clint eased Nick up over his father's broad shoulder.

"Let's get the hell out of here," Max said harshly, exhaling as he straightened under the burden.

Shouldering the body of his son as gently as possible, Max laboriously made his way back up the corridor. Weapons readied, Clint led the way, Zeke following behind.

Coming to a halt just inside the main hatch, Nick emitted a low moan as pain broke through his threshold of consciousness. It didn't take much imagination to envision the pain of cracked ribs wedged against a hard shoulder. Max gently shifted Nick's weight, but the movement only brought forth another low moan of agony.

Clint gave a quick glance outside. "Let's go!" he whispered, starting for the door. Zeke stepped in front of Max, strengthening the security as they made their way down the ramp and disappeared between the surrounding ships.

Chapter Twenty-three

Weapon readied, Marc remained hidden, watching as Tressa said something to the guard. He laughed and kissed the hollow of her neck, then thrust her roughly against a wall of loading pallets.

It was getting just a little out of hand, in Marc's estimation. Yet, there was Tressa, running her hands through the guard's hair, clinging to him as if she was enjoying herself. Just how the blazes was he supposed to know if she was over her head or not? Hell, at this rate the guy would soon be dropping his pants and getting on with it. Didn't that little fool realize what she was inviting?

Scowling, Marc worked his way closer. Hell, if she wasn't standing so close, he'd simply immobilize the bastard now and get it over with.

Willing herself to follow through, Tressa smiled seductively, running her hands through the guard's hair. "What's your name?"

He laughed. "Does it matter?"

"Just wondered, that's all."

He studied her long and hard, then bent his head to kiss the hollow of her throat again. "Name's Devon," he murmured huskily.

"Devon. Nice name," she purred, revolted by his attentions. Tressa feigned a fevered sigh as he began working his way lower. *Oh, God, please make them hurry,* she prayed. A cold sense of foreboding swept over her. She was playing with fire and she knew it, but the stakes were too high for her to back out now.

You can do this, Tressa.

Devon murmured something unintelligible against the swell of her breast, and Tressa trembled. Fighting a wave of nausea, she fixed her gaze on the *Renegade*.

Up until now she'd been very careful to keep her eyes off the ship, drawing his attention only to herself and away from his post. But now that she had his undivided attention, Tressa struggled for the composure she needed to follow through.

How much longer? she wondered. *If only she had a weapon.*

Appalled at the feel of Devon's hands on her, she wrestled with the desperate need to bolt and run. Only one other man had touched her so intimately. Tressa recalled how Nick's glance alone was enough to send her over the edge. Even as drunk as he'd been that night on the *Victorious,* there was no comparison between the two men. No contest between Devon's lewd comments and pawing hands and Nick Banner's murmured words and slow magic.

Tressa felt a hard lump in her throat as Devon's hands moved down her body.

"I want you. Now," he growled as he ravished her mouth. He tugged at her jumpsuit. The zipper broke, an open invitation to his gaze, and he lowered his head, nuzzling his stubbled cheek against her tender flesh.

When Tressa opened her eyes again they widened at the sight of Clint descending the ramp, his weapon poised.

Nick's friend, the man with the long, sun-streaked hair, came next. And then . . . She drew a sharp breath as Max emerged with Nick slung over his shoulder.

Nick . . . The name was all but audible as a cold knot formed in the pit of her stomach. *Dear God! He was hurt bad.*

Numb and unheeding of Devon and of what he was doing, Tressa stood motionless, watching as the Banner group quickly descended the ramp and disappeared into the shadows.

It was over. Her work was complete.

Devon mumbled something lusty—something Tressa wished she hadn't heard. With a sharp intake of breath she was jerked back to hardened reality and the knowledge that she must deal with this animal on her own.

And deal with him she would!

"I think I've changed my mind," she sighed.

Devon's head jerked up. "What?"

Tressa smiled sweetly. "I *said* . . . I've changed my mind."

Assessing her sharply, he pulled back, a cold smile flitting across his face. "Well, now, that's just too bad," he said, grabbing for her again.

He never saw it coming. Drawing her knee back, one swift jab was all it took. The anguish on his face said she'd scored. He doubled over in agony as her tiny, hard fist hit him square in the jaw. Groaning out his distress, he wilted at her feet.

Tressa stumbled back in shock, clasping one hand to her mouth and the other to her gaping jumpsuit.

Approaching footsteps sent yet another surge of panic racing through her. Jerking the gun from Devon's holster, she whirled toward the sound, eyes narrowing as she gripped the heavy gun with both hands, cocking and aiming it for the chest of the advancing man.

The action brought Marc to a skidding halt. "Tressa. It's me! Put the gun down!"

Hesitating, her hands shook as Marc remained frozen in place.

"Tressa! Put—the blasted—gun down!"

She lowered the weapon.

Marc strode to her side, his gaze quickly sliding over her half-clad body as he snatched the gun from her hand and tucked it safely into the waistband of his pants.

"Here, put this on," he said, shrugging out of his brown taubear hide jacket and thrusting it at her. Turning away, he regarded the man still down and moaning. "Nice knee action."

"What else was I supposed to do? He meant to have me."

Sliding her a sidelong glance, Marc didn't respond. Instead he dropped to one knee beside the guard and pressed a small black object to the man's temple. Devon's body shuddered, then fell silent.

"You just *now* figured that out?" he said at last, confiscating a knife that hung from the man's belt.

"Figured what out?"

"That he meant to have you," Marc said, rising to his feet and returning to her side. "What did you expect? The way you were coming on to him, you're lucky . . ."

"What?" Tressa's eyes narrowed.

Marc caught her arm. "Come on; let's just get out of here."

Tressa jerked free of his grasp and rounded on him. "And just how would you know how I was coming on to him?"

"Let's go!" he said, grasping her elbow for the second time and avoiding the obvious answer.

Again Tressa jerked free, her cheeks flaming. "You needed someone to distract that guard. There's not one of you who could have done it as well as I did!"

Marc grinned, raking her with his gaze. "I'll have to agree with you there," he said, stepping aside and allowing her to precede him through a narrow opening between two cargo stabilizers. "Max gave me the job of keeping an eye on you," he added.

That stopped her in midstride. "Is that what you did?" she hissed indignantly, "You . . . you watched?"

Marc muttered a silent oath, his face reddening at Tressa's accusation. "Well, not in the sense you put it."

Ignoring his flushed features, she challenged him again. "And in what sense would *you* put it, may I ask?"

"Look, we can discuss this later if you'd like. Right now I suggest we get out of here."

"I can't *believe*," she said, half running to keep up with his long strides, "that you were skulking around in the shadows."

He stopped abruptly. "I wasn't *skulking* around, Tressa,"

"Is that right? You never even lifted a finger to help."

He studied her long and hard. With a heavy sigh, he raked his hand through his dark hair—the action reminding her of Nick.

"Let's just go," he said, his tone filled with frustration as he stalked away from her.

"And tell me," Tressa called out, "did you enjoy the show?"

Marc's back stiffened, but this time he didn't break stride. "To hell with it," she heard him mutter.

Tressa hurried to catch up. "You could have at least helped me, you know."

"Oh, yeah? And just what would you have suggested I do?"

"For starters, you could have taken him by surprise and . . ."

"And what, Tressa? He would have had a gun pressed to your temple before you could even blink. Look, I *would* have immobilized him, but I was too far away for a direct hit. You'd have been hit along with him. And by the time I moved closer and was in range . . ." He shot her a twisted smile. "You seemed to have everything under control."

"Yeah, no thanks to you!"

"This way," he said curtly, guiding her to the left and up a short flight of stairs to another level, a parking area for ground vehicles.

Marc hastily escorted her toward a landcraft just backing out of its parking slot. Tressa's eyes urgently swept over the blackened windows that concealed its occupants. The car stopped, the front passenger door slid open with a hiss, and Tressa slipped into the front seat, meeting Max's grave expression as she scooted in next to him. Marc slid in beside her and the door hissed shut.

"Nick . . . Is . . . Is he all right?" she asked anxiously.

Max gave a taut jerk of his head. "In back."

As Tressa turned around her gaze fell upon Nick with an indrawn gasp. Unconscious and bruised, he was wedged securely between Clint and Zeke, his head slumped against Clint's shoulder.

Tressa's heart wrenched at the sight of him. "Dear God," she breathed, her gaze wandering over his face and body in horrified assessment.

"What did they do to him?" she asked with tears blinding her eyes and choking her voice.

"Everything imaginable," Clint ground out, his eyes glittering with rage.

Swallowing hard, Tressa reached across the seat for Nick's hand. It lay limp and unresponsive in her grasp. Brushing away tears to see, she held his hand, rubbing the pad of her thumb across the back of his bruised knuckles, studying his expressionless face and uttering broken words of encouragement.

It was subtle but there nevertheless . . . that mysterious flicker, a sudden awareness flashing across her mind. For a brief moment Tressa sensed Nick's inward response to her voice, her touch.

Then . . . it was gone again.

Refusing to release his hand, she continued holding him as they drove on. The silence was broken only by the sweetness of her gentle voice.

"We *are* going to a medical facility, aren't we?" Tressa asked, turning to Max. It was obvious they weren't heading back home.

"No. We're taking Nick to the town house," Max replied. "It's closer and a lot safer." He glanced over at Marc. "Call the Medical Center. Tell Sam we've got an emergency and ask him to meet us at the town house immediately.

Marc nodded, reaching for the mobile comphone.

The landcraft lurched as it turned off the main street. They were passing a large building, the name over the main door reading BANNER TRANSPORT, INC. Turning again, they followed a short drive to a security gate. Max hit a small sensor pad on the dash and the gate swung open. Within minutes they were driving onto the platform of an elevator. Hydraulic braces slid out from the sides and secured the base of the landcraft for the ride. With a lunge so subtle it was barely perceptible, the walls began slipping downward, large numbers indicating the floors as they advanced.

When they reached the fifteenth floor the elevator stopped, the braces glided back into their housing, and the wall in front of them began cycling open. Max guided the runner off the platform and into a spacious garage. The wall was still closing behind them as he burst from the vehicle, Marc and Zeke following.

Tressa remained inside, still clutching Nick's hand as Clint eased out from under his brother's slumped body. It wasn't until Max leaned in and began lifting his son out that she reluctantly let go. The effort of being eased out of the back seat brought forth another agonized moan from Nick as the boys rushed forward to help carry him.

"The door!" Max instructed as Tressa hurried ahead, palmed the plate on the wall, and then stepped aside as they entered the living quarters.

Edna, the housekeeper, met them at the entry, her gaze riveted on the load they were carrying. "Sir . . ."

"My room!" Max commanded.

Edna quickly rushed ahead, turning back the covers as Max lowered his son onto the crisp white linens.

At first there were no words spoken. Dazed, Tressa simply stood outside the doorway, watching in mute shock as Edna brushed past mumbling something about getting towels.

Clint quickly removed Nick's leather jacket, cutting away the bloodied crew shirt. Max unbuckled his son's belt, easing the tightness on Nick's bruised stomach.

"Damn," Marc muttered. "They beat the shi . . ." he'd almost forgotten Tressa, "out of him."

Silently Tressa stepped inside, pressing her back to the wall, her heart wrenching in anguish at the extent of Nick's injuries. Her medical training told her some of those marks could very well indicate internal injury. The flesh across the whole of his stomach and rib cage was badly bruised. Shades of deep purple marked an area where she suspected ribs had been broken. Both of his eyes were blackened and swollen shut, and traces of crusted blood trailed from his nose and the corner of his mouth.

With a moan of distress, Tressa turned away, biting her lower lip to control her sobs. *Were these welts and bruises the physical evidence of the pain she had experienced last night?*

His pain?

Tressa's thoughts were interrupted when Edna returned with an armload of towels, set them on a bedside table, and then bent to pick up the discarded jacket and soiled shirt. "I'll get some hot water," she murmured, heading for the door.

"Thank you," Tressa replied in approval, moving forward to help. Turning to Max with a sudden surge of new-found strength, she said pointedly, "He should be in a hospital."

Max nodded slowly, dragging his anguished gaze from

his son. "Yes, I know. But it's not safe. . . . " His voice broke.

"This place is a fortress, Tressa," he continued. "Both of you will be safe here."

His gaze returned to Nick. "If we have to, we'll turn this room into . . ." Again his voice broke off, and this time his jaw tensed visibly. "The medTech should be here shortly," he said, finally regaining control of his emotions.

Edna reentered the room, carefully carrying a large basin of steaming hot water.

"Here, I'll take that," Tressa said, lifting the heavy container from the housemaid's arms. She set it on the bedside table.

Edna stood by, her fingers clenching together nervously. "Is there anything else I can do?"

"First aid," Tressa said. "Do you have a first-aid kit?"

"Yes . . . yes." The woman turned and headed away.

Biting her lower lip, Tressa's gaze returned to Nick. The dried blood, the bruises . . . the pain he must have endured before blacking out. *Was* Max right? Had Nick been beaten like this because of her—because he had protected her? She squeezed her eyes shut against the stab of guilt that lay buried deep in her breast, and against the deluge of questions flooding her mind.

Get control of yourself, a small voice cautioned. *Cry later; for now you must be strong!*

"Where the devil is Grant, anyway?" Max thundered, pacing the room like a caged animal.

"I don't believe I've ever seen anyone this badly bruised," Edna said, returning with the first-aid kit.

"I have," Tressa said coldly, clenching her jaw to kill the sob in her throat. "Once."

Then the professionalism of her medical training began taking over. With iron control she separated herself emotionally from Nick and began a cursory examination, viewing the man lying before her as merely a patient.

She mentally noted a bump on the side of his head that

didn't seem too serious. It was hard to tell about his eyes; they were swollen shut. An especially dark bruise marked his left cheek.

"Well, his nose isn't broken," she said in a voice that sounded much calmer than she felt.

He was breathing raggedly through parted lips; pulling down gently on his jaw, Tressa opened his mouth further, noting his lower lip was split open and the inside of his cheeks were badly cut up from his teeth. "Thankfully," she murmured, "all of his teeth appear to be intact."

As Tressa worked her way down his neck, her determination faltered at finding his left shoulder bulging abnormally, wrenched from its socket. The raw marks on his wrists clearly indicated how his arms had been pulled to the point of dislocating his shoulder.

It was too much. Tressa's iron control wavered, and she swiped at a tear. *What bastards would do this?* Steeling herself to be calm, a long moment of silence passed as she recaptured her composure.

"His left shoulder is dislocated," she said at last in a weak whisper. Carefully probing his upper torso, she ran her hands intimately along the hard-muscled contours of his frame.

"I know this hurts," she murmured sympathetically, watching the play of pain across his face, almost feeling the twinges herself as they broke through the threshold of his oblivion.

With the slightest of pressure, Tressa moved the sensitive tips of her fingers along the arching length of his rib cage, breathing a sigh of relief that there were no displaced ribs. When she began gently probing the darkened mark on his left side, however, he emitted a low groan and sucked in his breath with a hiss. She ignored the faint corresponding twinge of pain in her own side.

"I know, darling," she whispered, "I *know* this hurts."

Despite his agony, Tressa didn't pause in her task. He flinched again. Yes . . . *there* it was. He gasped, intense pain alone confirming the fracture that she had suspected from the beginning. She probed further, and this time Nick emitted a husky growl, mumbling incoherently as he reached feebly for his side.

Tressa nudged away his hand. Maybe two fractures, she thought. She made a mental note to check with the medTech.

Max instantly came forward. "Tressa, the medTech should be here anytime." The concern and possessiveness in his voice was unmistakable. It clearly said, *leave my son alone.*

Tressa's hands stilled as she glanced up. "I *know* what I'm doing, sir. It will speed things along if I'm able to tell the doctor my findings when he arrives."

Weighing her words, Max hesitated. "All right," he said at last. "Marc, find out what's holding Grant up."

Tressa moved lower, to Nick's stomach. Although it was badly bruised, thank God it wasn't distended: a good sign of no internal bleeding. However, she could only see what was on the outside. It would take a medTech's diascope to positively say if he had internal injuries or not. She watched his chest rise and fall with another broken gasp as she palpated a particularly tender area.

"I'm going to need help turning him onto his side," she said at last.

She didn't have to ask twice. They were at her side.

"Max, over here," she said with a newfound voice of authority. "Take his shoulders. Be careful. His left one's been dislocated." At one point she'd contemplated asking for their assistance in resetting the dislocated shoulder, but she decided to leave the task for the medTech. The painful process would be harder on Max than on Nick.

"Clint, I want you right here," she continued, pointing to Nick's midsection. "And Marc . . . here," she said indicating Nick's legs. "Now, on my count I want him log-rolled onto his right side in one single motion."

Once Nick had been turned Clint steadied him, while

Tressa tugged down the loosened waistband just enough to expose his lower back. Instantly her stomach clenched at the darkened purplish mark in the area of his right kidney, obviously the result of a vicious booted kick.

"From the looks of that cleat imprint, I'd say someone was wearing Bungi cleat-toed boots," Clint said.

Zeke leaned forward, closely examining the bruise. "Don't see those much around here."

Tressa shot them both a look that plainly asked who the hell cared what kind of boot he'd been kicked with? "Any higher," she snapped, "and it would have been a direct hit to the kidney."

Gently placing her palm on the darkened mark, she checked for swelling and abnormal heat, breathing a sigh of relief at finding neither.

Tressa's gaze was drawn to a jagged scar that ran diagonally across his upper back. Obviously an old wound, but one that had been deep. She wondered at its cause.

"Okay," she sighed, stepping aside as the men rolled Nick smoothly onto his back again.

Tressa blew tendrils of hair from her forehead and turned her attention to Max. "You might want to go ahead and remove the remainder of his clothing before . . ."

A soft chime announced someone at the main gate. Marc strode to the vidcom and hit the pad. "That must be Grant, now."

But as the screen flickered to life, the worried face of Delta's head butler appeared. "Dawson! What the . . ."

"There's trouble," Dawson exclaimed into the camera as Marc released the security.

Chapter Twenty-four

Max met Dawson at the front entrance, his expression tight. "What do you mean, there's trouble?"

"Tressa's missing. We've looked everywhere for her. Delta's worried half sick."

Awkwardly clearing his throat, Max's gaze slid away, then returned to Dawson. "I intended to call Delta the instant we got here," he muttered. "We've got Tressa with us."

"But . . . You took Tressa with you?"

"No," Clint interjected. "Little Miss Rebellious left all on her own."

Wordlessly, Max turned and headed for the phone.

"There's more," Dawson said, hesitating until Max turned to face him. "I think the house is being watched."

Max's jaw tightened. "What makes you say that?"

"Somehow that doesn't surprise me," Clint said. "It only figures Kendyl would case the place, looking for Tressa." A long thought-filled moment passed before Max spoke up. "You don't suppose Nick could have been the lure to get us all out of there while they snatch Tressa?''

Overhearing the commotion from the bedroom, Tressa briefly left Nick's side and came to the end of the hallway. There was a new aura of desperation in the air. In silence, she scanned the room, gauging the mood of its occupants.

"I'm going back out to the house," Max said, replacing the handset. "I don't like the idea of Delta being alone out there. Zeke, Marc, I want you to come with me."

Tressa cleared her throat softly. "Will anyone be coming back?"

"What do you need?"

"Would you please ask Delta to get the Acuel salve and . . . also TiMar?"

Max nodded in acknowledgment. "Clint, I want you to remain here."

With a nod, Clint made his way to a nearby chair and sprawled into it with that same rangy manner Tressa had become accustomed to.

Nick . . . An odd sensation suddenly sliced through her, a beckoning she couldn't begin to explain or understand. Turning in response, she hurried back down the hall.

Nick's eyes were closed when she entered the room.

"Nick?"

He seemed agitated. Tressa approached the bed. "I'm here," she whispered, brushing back a sweat-dampened lock of dark hair from his face. With a low groan he stilled at her touch.

Reaching for a small cloth, Tressa dipped it into the basin of water that Edna had brought earlier. In mute protest, he turned his head away from her when she placed the cloth to his face.

"You're just bound and determined to make this difficult for me, aren't you?" she continued in the same measured tones. Laying the length of her palm against his stubble-roughened cheek, Tressa turned his face toward her, holding him still as she cleaned away the grime and dried blood. "No man should ever be allowed to have lashes as long as yours,'' she whispered, gently cleaning around his bruised and swollen eyes.

The chime sounded again, announcing the arrival of yet another caller.

Marc engaged the security vid to find Dr. Grant Adams, a distinguished man in his late fifties, gazing directly up at the vidcam. Tall and lean, his full beard was close-trimmed. His dark gray hair was cut in a short butch.

"It's about time," Marc grumbled, releasing the security.

Flicking a speck of lint from his navy-blue MedTech's uniform, Grant jerked his gaze back to the vidcam. "Sorry. Your message came moments after I'd gone into surgery."

The elevator door slid open, and another vidcam switched to life as Grant entered the cubicle. The conversation continued. "I came as fast as I could." He hesitated, his snappy brown eyes nailing the vidcam. "What's the emergency, anyway?"

"It's Nick," Max responded.

Sam's gray eyebrows rose inquiringly. "Nick?" he asked, staring blankly up at the camera. "You mean, *Nick,* as in the nomadic middle son?"

"Yes," Max answered tersely. "Hurry it up, Grant."

"I am, unless you have a turbo on this thing I don't know about."

Burke Sinclair shut down the com link with a doubled fist. Here he was, one day . . . just one damn day out of Acacia, expecting to breeze in, pay the ransom, rescue Tressa, and seal his future with her and LorTech, in one gallant gesture.

The plan was so simple, and it would have worked, too.

He'd have had her and her old man both eating out of his hand. But everything that could go wrong, had.

The kidnapping should have taken place at Port France, not on Acacia. He hadn't counted on her lifting off planet with Banner. Hadn't counted on some damn high-tech immobilizer zapping everyone within range of Banner's ship. Hadn't counted on having to travel halfway across the sector to pull off this fiasco.

Hell, he hadn't counted on some ex-partner of Banner's getting involved either. Especially some bastard harboring a grudge and screwing up his plans like this.

Everything had changed. Just like that, all his carefully laid plans had been vaporized. Banner was supposedly all but dead, not that he gave a damn, but Tressa was nowhere to be found. And to top it all, James Catlin had just told him that Bryant had broken off the deal. Apparently Kendyl was calling the shots now. Catlin told him that if he wanted the rest of the story, it would cost.

Sinclair groaned aloud. Like a fool, he'd agreed to meet with Catlin at the space port. And just what the hell good would it do to know the rest?

There's nothing you can do, a dark, defiant voice thundered in his mind. *Besides, from what you've heard about Banner, three long weeks aboard ship with him and you may as well consider Tressa used merchandise.*

A small, barely perceivable voice of reason broke through his barrier of frustration. *What do you care if she's used or not? What bearing does that have on attaining your goal? You're losing sight of your objective here. The attainment of LorTech alone will be compensation enough, not to mention the favor you will gain from your grandfather.*

Sinclair ran his hands through his hair. Oh, hell. Even if he did go after Tressa, what could *he* do? He'd never stand a chance against their kind.

Ah . . . but what if you go to Banner instead, personally elicit his help? If he's not dead by now, he'll go after her. 'Course, that'll mean having to answer questions. But you can come up with something. Hell, you can simply say you were approached for ransom. Yes, that'd do it.

A nagging pain in the back of her neck roused Tressa from her slumber.

Nick!

Memory returned with shocking perception as she bolted upright in the chair. Her eyes riveted to the bed and . . . Nick. She recalled Dr. Adams giving him an injection, something to help him rest. Then, before leaving, the medTech had turned to her and, in a fatherly tone, issued strict orders for her to get some rest, also.

Kneading the muscles at the base of her neck, Tressa rose from the chair, barely remembering easing into it. But she *did* remember applying Acuel salve to every scrape, every scratch, and every cut on Nick's battered body. Oh, yes, she remembered *that* with dramatic clarity.

Tressa glanced about. A soft breeze ruffled the sheer curtains to her left. Sunrise was already tinting the horizon, filtering through the wall of veiled windows, bathing the room in a soft pink, almost magical atmosphere.

A quick glance at the bedside timer told her that a little over five hours had passed since Dr. Adams left and it was time for a second application of the Acuel ointment. With that, she reached for the Nervatrite, the pretreatment that would put a pain-killing barrier against the burning effect of the Acuel salve.

Tressa's eyes drifted over the expanse of Nick's broad shoulders and muscled biceps. The small golden medallion he wore around his neck had fallen haphazardly over his shoulder. Catching the golden chain with the hook of one finger, she drew the slackened length up until the medallion was in her hand. One side was embossed with what appeared to be a family crest, the same design that hung in the entry of the Banner home.

Tressa slowly turned over the medal, frowning intently as she studied the flip side. ''Bannier,'' she whispered, recognizing the French origin of the name Banner. Had it been the original name, generations back? She wondered when the *i* had been dropped. Only after carefully examining both sides did she set the medallion down on his chest.

Nick's left arm was bound firmly to his midsection. The ordeal of resetting the displaced shoulder had been excruciating. He'd come out of it fighting, momentarily rousing from unconsciousness with a growl and a right hook that narrowly missed its target—the doctor's jaw.

"Do something!" she'd cried.

"Like what?" Clint answered, already adding his brawn to the struggle. It was evident they were dealing with supercharged strength, and it was all the two men could do to hold Nick down.

"Careful of his shoulder! Don't hurt him!" Tressa moved forward to help but quickly backed off as Nick delivered a smashing blow to Clint's stomach. Catching the full force of the impact, Clint doubled over, wrapping his arms protectively about his belly and gasping for breath. Then, as suddenly as it began, it ended. Nick collapsed onto the bed, out cold, as three panting, gasping people stood staring at each other in disbelief.

"I'm getting too old for this," Grant groaned, retrieving his diascope, along with several other items that had fallen and scattered about the floor during the brief but wild struggle.

Tressa's thoughts were brought back to the present when Nick emitted a soft moan. Trailing one lone finger along the relaxed muscles of his biceps, she contemplated the initial pain he'd endured at having an arm wrenched from its socket. Recalling her own strange and agonizing bout with pain, she wondered if the dislocation of his shoulder was the very torture that drove her to her knees while on the tour of the Banner home.

Settling hipshot on the edge of the bed, Tressa slowly twisted open the jar of salve, recalling the time she'd doctored his wounded side. He'd embarrassed her so, she'd never asked to see the wound again. Instead she'd handed him the jar with orders to apply the salve himself, strongly doubting he ever would.

It wasn't until the medTech's examination that she had seen the results for herself. No longer was it the inflamed, angry gash she'd first treated. In just a matter of days the wound had been reduced to a minor scar.

It couldn't possibly have healed to that degree with only one application, she thought, denying a twinge of guilt at the realization that he'd used the Acuel without ever knowing to apply Nervatrite first. She'd never told him.

Though at the time he'd well earned her revenge, she wouldn't dream of doing such a thing now.

Glancing down at his still form, Tressa's heart wrenched at the welts, bruises, and cuts he'd suffered in trying to protect her.

Dr. Adams had confirmed her evaluation of Nick's condition. All in all, he looked worse than he was. Only one rib was fractured, and despite the awful bruises there was no internal damage.

Twice during the examination Nick had roused from unconsciousness. Both times it had been her name he'd cried out. Tressa reveled in the thought. The notorious Nick Banner had called out *her* name, not someone else's.

Using a gentle touch, she continued smoothing salve over his scraped cheekbone. Even unconscious, there was an aura about him. The shadowy beginning of a beard gave him a dangerous appearance, the stubble rough and scratchy against her palm.

"In a day or so these bruises will be gone. I promise," she murmured.

Tressa slid the sheet lower, exposing his stomach for treatment. And the harder she tried not to notice, the more aware she became of the pronounced demarcation between the darker coloring of his upper torso and the flesh protected below his belt line—physical proof of hours spent in the sun.

Envisioning the *Victorious* docked on some hot, arid planet, Tressa could almost see him, stripped to the waist,

286

overseeing, even assisting in the transfer of cargo between his ship and the dock.

No matter how hard she tried to fight it, Nick Banner aroused her sexual curiosity as no other man ever had. As if to prove the extent of her helplessness, a heated rush surged through her as she boldly took in every muscled inch of him, her gaze following a tapering path of dark hair across his flat belly to where it disappeared beneath the low-slung cover. Unable to resist the temptation, her gaze wandered even lower, trespassing to that forbidden territory where the soft cover left little to the imagination. But then, there was no need for imagination. Tressa swallowed, color climbing high in her cheeks. She'd seen more of Nick Banner at the medTech's side than she'd wanted to.

The profound revelation went even deeper than that. She had seen much more of this man than she'd *ever* wanted to see of Burke Sinclair.

The realization stunned her. Since when had she started comparing Burke to Nick? There was no comparison. The two men were complete opposites. Where Burke was polite, Nick was rude. Where Burke was civilized, Nick was rugged. Where Burke was decent . . . Now *there* was a word— *decent.* Nick Banner was anything but *decent,* and he would be the first to agree.

So, what was it about Nick that drew her to him? Was it this rugged, dangerous side . . . his lack of decency? Tressa was rocked with the memory of just how indecent Nick Banner could actually be. How he'd awakened her senses that night onboard the *Victorious.* How he'd taught her more about herself in the space of a heartbeat than she'd learned in her whole lifetime. He'd left her confused that night, longing for something she didn't understand, for something she knew now she wanted only *him* to teach her. Tressa's gaze drifted to his bruised hands and chafed wrists, lingered for a moment, then returned to his swollen face.

The man lying before her was a hero. A man of unrelenting loyalty.

Would Sinclair have withstood this kind of abuse, or would he have sold her out? The question had tumbled through her mind before she realized it.

How do you know you're in love? It was a question she'd asked not all that long ago of her mother when Burke Sinclair had asked her to marry him.

Oh darling, Mary had said, *for each person it's different.* She had placed a loving arm around Tressa's shoulders and given her a gentle squeeze. *But there are some common signs that almost everyone experiences.*

Like what? Tressa had persisted.

Well, for instance, do you feel breathless whenever you're near him?

Tressa had shrugged. *Maybe . . . just a little.*

Dizzy?

She shook her head. *No.*

How about queasy or weak?

Tressa had laughed out loud. *No. Sounds like you're describing the symptoms of Quarax.*

Mary chucked. *In a way, it is a sickness. And . . . If I'm reading you right, I'm not so sure you have the symptoms.*

As the memory faded, Tressa opened her eyes, her gaze resting upon Nick's gloriously handsome face, now swollen and discolored.

Do you feel breathless whenever you're near him?

Yes. The answer came quickly.

Dizzy?

Stars!

Queasy? Weak?

''Yes,'' she whispered softly. ''Oh, yes.'' Just the sound of his voice made her weak. His very presence incited a myriad of scandalous thoughts and temptations within her, a recklessness she'd never known before. For what seemed the thousandth time she closed her eyes and wondered what it would be like to be loved completely by this incorrigible rogue. To have him finish what he'd so proficiently started that night. To have his satin voice murmuring love words in her ear. Would they be sweet and tender, she wondered—or would they be rough and heated?

This time it's not clinical, is it? It's not just some stranger lying there before you. It's Nick Banner.

Her eyes flew open in silent denial. She'd spent the last ten hours caring for this man, cleaning him up, nursing his injuries, never leaving his side. Not . . .

Not lusting after him? the inner voice taunted.

Tressa inwardly cringed. She was a medTech's assistant. She'd glimpsed other men before. She'd . . .

That's right. The inner voice laughed mockingly. *The word is* glimpsed. *And never one so robust, so blatantly masculine as this man lying before you.*

Because of her age and her volunteer status at Port Ireland's Med Center, Tressa had always been replaced by a resident medTech's assistant when it came to dealing with a naked male patient. Somehow textbooks and mere glimpses hadn't quite prepared her for the reality of seeing Nick in all his glory. In spite of Dr. Adams's attempts to preserve Nick's dignity, and in spite of her own sense of propriety, it couldn't be helped. Tressa gently caught her lower lip as once again a rush of heat surged to her cheeks.

With quiet determination she quickly finished applying the salve to Nick's bruised stomach, then set down the jar of salve.

A hint of a frown creased her brow as she drew the cover completely up over him. Somehow . . . he was different. It wasn't just her imagination, either. Inwardly she sensed his response to her nearness.

For a long moment Tressa simply stood there watching him, motionless, comforted by the even rise and fall of his chest. Then, driven to touch him just once more, she slipped her hand beneath the cover, pressing it to his heart.

Closing her eyes, she found solace in the warmth and the steady beat beneath her palm. Splaying her fingers, she gloried in the knowledge that he was alive, silently marveling at the wondrous combination of crisp dark hair, smooth flesh, and hard-steeled muscle that was Nick.

It was by unspoken command that Tressa's eyes flashed open. Slowly her gaze moved upward across the broad expanse of his chest, past his stubborn jaw, past the hint of a rueful smile.

. . . Smile?

Tressa's eyes widened, locking with two smoldering sapphires glowing beneath swollen lids.

"I'm 'fraid . . . you're gonna have t' wait 'til I'm feelin' a little better, Irish."

Chapter Twenty-five

"Nick . . ." Tressa's voice was a hushed whisper at finding him suddenly conscious and her hand shackled in a firm yet gentle grip. "Y . . . You're awake!"

"Very," he drawled, a mischievous grin lightly tipping the corners of his mouth.

Tressa found it difficult to swallow. Her face flamed.

A subtle attempt to slip her hand free of his grasp didn't quite do it. It took a determined yank, which she strongly suspected wouldn't have done it either, had he not been so weak.

"I'll . . . umm . . . I'll let Clint know you're awake," she stammered, tearing her gaze from his and turning for the door.

"Please . . . stay. Tressa . . ." But she was out the door.

Ignoring his husky plea, Tressa rushed blindly into the hallway, flames licking at her cheeks. Good Lord, had he read her mind? Had he been awake the entire time she . . . "Umph!"

"Hey, slow down!"

The wall she'd just slammed into was Clint. Grasping her by the shoulders, he set her back. "What's the rush, sunshine?"

"It's . . . it's Nick! He's conscious!"

"Yes. I know."

"You do?" Her reaction seemed to amuse him.

Clint released her. "He came out of it during the night."

"But . . ." Tressa watched a slow smile break across his face.

"You were asleep in the chair, darlin'."

"Why didn't you wake me?"

"There was no need. Besides, you needed the rest."

Tressa paused. "How was he . . . I mean . . ."

"In a world of pain. I gave him the injection Adams left, and he settled right down." Clint's gaze shifted toward Nick's room. "So, what prompted the hasty exit?"

"I . . . I was just coming to get you."

"Ahhh." A knowing smile tugged at the corners of his mouth. Tressa averted her gaze. If her face was as flushed as it felt, she could count on the fact that he'd not only noticed, he'd already determined his own rakish version of the cause.

"Let's let Edna know. She was brewing some sort of special tea for him. You hungry?" Clint's brows lifted in question. "When did you last eat, anyway?"

"Yesterday morning."

"Yesterday morning?" Frowning in disbelief, he reached for her hand. "Come with me, lady. If I know Edna, she has the morning meal well underway."

"But . . ."

"No buts. Come on. Edna can make up a tray for Nick if he feels like eating, and after you've finished you can take it to him."

Hesitant, Tressa glanced toward Nick's room. Dear God, he was finally awake!

"Well?" Clint released her hand and touched her elbow lightly. "You coming?"

With a forced smile and a tense nod of consent, she allowed him to guide her toward the kitchen.

The aroma of hot food and steaming coffee welcomed them as they entered the room.

"Good morning, and how's my favorite cook today?" The warmth of Clint's smile echoed in his voice as he peered over Edna's shoulder. "Ummmm, bronzeberry biscuits. My favorite."

Joy bubbled in Edna's laughter. "Oh, everything's your favorite." Her eyes softened when she caught sight of Tressa. "Good morning, dear. How's our Nick doing today?"

"Better," Tressa replied softly. "He's awake."

Edna drew in a deep breath. "So I heard. Thank God."

Clint plucked a bite of something hot out of a pan and popped it into his mouth. "Ummm . . . Perfect," he mumbled, sucking air into his mouth and rolling the fiery morsel about to cool it.

"Uh-uh-uh!" Edna good-naturedly batted Clint's hands away.

"Tell me, Edna," he said, skillfully reaching around and snatching another bite, "what will it take for you to marry me?"

"Bah!" She firmly placed a lid on the pan. "A lot more than that fancy sweet-talk you and your brothers are so skilled at." Clint grinned and picked up a frosty pitcher of bright green juice. Filling a small glass, he turned and guided Tressa to a large round table.

"Have a seat, sunshine," he said, setting the glass before her. "You ever tasted kuavo juice?"

"No. Kuavo juice? I've never even heard of it." Clint grinned. "Wait 'til you try it."

Tressa watched Clint return to Edna's side at the cook center. From there her gaze wandered. The kitchen could only be described as light and airy. Floor-to-ceiling windows flanked the exterior wall and a set of double doors opened out onto a small veranda.

Tressa's gentle laughter rippled through the air when Clint returned, setting down a plate before her. "And just what am I suppose to do with all this?" she asked in disbelief.

"Eat it, of course." He lifted a mug of steaming tea. "I'll be right back."

Past hunger, Tressa picked at her food, finding she couldn't eat more than a few bites. The desire . . . no, the *need* to return to Nick was overpowering, and worst of all, she kept hearing in her head his husky plea for her to remain at his side.

"Not hungry?"

Tressa met Edna's perceptive gaze. "I'm sorry. It's not your cooking, Edna. The food's wonderful. It's just . . ."

"I understand, honey." Grabbing a towel, Edna wiped her hands, reached for a cup, filled it, and joined Tressa at the table. "He'll come out of this," she said, settling herself into a chair.

Tressa swallowed hard. "I know. It's just that . . . it's so hard to see him like this." She blinked back tears at the memory of Nick, so proud and handsome, lying so helpless and dependent.

"It's hard on us all," Edna said. "Especially Max. But Dr. Adams said he was lucky. It could have been much worse."

Tressa took a deep breath and nodded.

Edna sipped her coffee slowly, assessing Tressa over the rim of her cup. "Have you fallen in love with him?" she asked.

"What?"

Edna smiled knowingly. "You've fallen in love with him, haven't you?"

With a sigh, Tressa looked away. "To be perfectly honest," she said with quiet emphasis, "he's driving me crazy. I've never known such bizarre feelings in my entire life as I have during these last three and a half weeks."

For a long moment Edna said nothing. She simply studied Tressa. "You may very well be the best thing that's ever happened to him." Edna hesitated, as if weighing her next words. "May I humbly offer a little word in his behalf?"

Tressa's gaze moved up to meet Edna's smiling eyes. "Yes, of course."

"Honey, I know Nick has a tendency to be rough around the edges at times, but I can assure you that beneath that protective facade lies a tender heart.

Tressa smiled, a warm rush of heat flooding her cheeks. "I already guessed that." After all, she thought, anyone who would rescue a defenseless kitten from mistreatment in a rugged port bar couldn't be all that bad. And wasn't he, at this very moment, lying injured in her defense? She loved his courage, his kindness, and, yes . . . even his rough edges.

"Right now," Edna continued, "what he needs is lots of rest and . . ." her eyes twinkled with merriment, "a good dose of TLC. But the one thing you must remember is, each day he'll be a little better than the day before. If you forget that," she said, shaking her head in mock concern, "you'll end up with more trouble on your hands than you'll know what to do with."

"That's for sure," Tressa said wholeheartedly.

"Well, if it means anything, Nick's cranky as all hell," Clint said, striding through the door.

"That's a good sign," Tressa said, gathering the dishes from the table.

Edna's mouth quirked with humor. "A very good sign." Rising to her feet, she slipped Tressa a sly wink.

"He asked about you, sunshine," Clint murmured silkily, for her ears only.

Tressa nearly dropped her plate. "H . . . he did?"

"Um-hmmm . . ."

Tressa's breath caught in her throat. Clint was amused. Stars! Had Nick told him what she'd done?

With a feigned air of composure she took her dishes to

the sink, poured Clint a cup of coffee, and returned to the table. "So, besides cranky, how is he?"

Clint shrugged. "I suppose as well as can be expected. I know one thing: That stuff you've been putting on him has already taken a lot of the swelling down."

Tressa beamed. "You think so too? The next thing you'll begin to notice is that the bruises are going away."

"Oh, yeah? That's some stuff," he said, taking a sip of his coffee.

Tressa cleared her throat. "Clint, could you tell me a little more about your experience with your Creohen friend? I mean . . ."

Clint set down his cup. "If you're looking for answers, Tressa, I'm hardly an expert."

"Not just answers, Clint. I need to talk to someone who can help me understand what's happening to me," she said softly.

He stared at her in thoughtful silence. She'd nearly given up all hope of a reply when he finally nodded.

"All right. I'll tell you what I know. But there are some things you'll have to find the answers for yourself, and some things only Nick can answer."

Tressa nodded in agreement.

"So . . . what do you want to know?"

A wave of apprehension coursed through her as the question tumbled from her lips. "First of all, can . . . is Nick capable of reading my emotions, as I read his?"

Tressa watched his mouth twitch as though he was dying to ask why. "No, love, you're safe there. You're the one with the empathic abilities."

Trying not to show her relief, Tressa moved on to her next question. "And what about this bonding thing? Why did you say that I've bonded with him?"

Clint's cup was raised halfway to his mouth when he hesitated. "Because bonding is the *only* way you could have sensed Nick's emotions as you did. It's that simple."

"I don't understand."

He set down his cup. "You see, Tressa, Creohens don't go around empathically reading just anyone's emotions. It's not even a matter of ethics. It's virtually impossible. Example: Are you sensing my emotions right now?"

"Of course not."

"How 'bout now?" He deliberately eyed Tressa with a look of scorching intent.

Tressa forced a demure smile. "It's pretty obvious, Clint."

He shook his head slowly, "No. That's just it. What you see in my eyes may not be the same as what I'm feeling inside." He grinned. "Try it again. This time close your eyes and concentrate."

"This is ridiculous," she muttered, embarrassed as she closed her eyes.

A moment of silence passed. "Well? Anything?"

"No," she said flatly.

Clint chuckled. "And I was sending you vibes like crazy. But I'll bet you don't even have to try with Nick. Do you?"

Tressa lowered her gaze.

"As I said before," he continued, "you've bonded with him."

"I don't understand."

"No one fully does, and that includes the guys in research. All I know is that there are different chemicals released into your system as a result of your emotions. Supposedly the particular chemical released into your system when you're . . ." He paused long enough to struggle with a grin. "when you're in love has a direct reaction on a Creohen's ability to sense the emotions of the person she's in love with."

"Then why did you tell me that Nick is in as deep as I am?"

"Because he *is*."

"But you said that in order for me to bond with him . . ."

"Sorry, Tressa, I don't pretend to understand it all. All I know is what I've told you. This is one of those questions you're going to have to ask someone else.''

Tressa released a sigh of frustration. "Okay. For hypothetical purposes, let's just say there's something to this bonding thing. Is it just me, or what?" Stars, her cheeks were on fire again.

"You mean, is Nick affected by it? Yes. In a way," Clint said. "Drawing from my own experience, Tressa, I can tell you it takes a willing partner. You know . . . the old Earth adage, it takes two to tango?"

"But . . .''

He flashed her a grin. "Let me put it this way; you're more than just another woman passing through his life.''

"I don't think I'd go *that* far." Tressa looked away, embarrassed.

A moment passed before he spoke again. "By the way, how much Creohen blood do you have in you?"

"My mother's half Creohen.''

Clint nodded and took another sip of his coffee, then he muttered, "I can't believe she never told you what to expect.''

"I told you, I was tested when I was ten and the results were negative.'' Her tone sounded defensive, even in her own ears. "Up until now," she added on a softer note, "I've never had anything like this happen.''

"Well, maybe the tests were wrong.'' He flashed that Banner grin again. "And leave it to a *Banner* to be the catalyst to trigger it.''

Suddenly embarrassed, Tressa glanced down at her lap. "They say it all started with the mines on Terra Three.''

Clint nodded. "The Creoh mines. The mineral from outer space!" he recited in his best announcer's voice. "Guaranteed to stretch your memory, boost your vitality, increase your longevity. Hell, they probably even claimed it would enhance your . . .'' He paused and didn't finish.

Tressa didn't ask, knowing she didn't want to hear what he was about to say.

"It's popularity," he went on, "was short-lived when

298

they discovered its irreversible side effects.''

"The empathic abilities," Tressa interjected.

Clint nodded. "When they finally figured it out they realized that even breathing the damn dust was harmful, and the mind-altering effect was almost always passed on to your children. Geeez—what we do in the name of science." Clint shook his head in apparent exasperation.

"Even grandchildren, like myself, can inherit the ability."

Clint leaned back, stretching out his long legs before him. "Yeah, it would seem so, sunshine."

A long moment of contemplation passed.

Smiling at the memory, Tressa commented, "No wonder Grandpa always read me like a computer chip." She inhaled sharply and rose from her seat. "Well, before Edna gets Nick's tray ready I suppose I should go see if he even feels like eating. Clint, thank you. Thank you for talking with me and answering at least some of my questions."

Clint straightened up. "I don't know how much help I was, but you're welcome."

"Uh, Tressa," he said as she turned for the door, "you'd better give Nick a minute. He was damn mad when I left him."

Tressa glanced back at him. "About what?"

Clint's mouth quirked with amusement. "Because I refused to help him get up."

A soft gasp escaped her. "Get up? The medTech said he wasn't to get up for at least two days."

Clint was outright grinning now. "That's exactly what I told him."

"Well, I'm checking on him."

"Better give him a minute to . . ."

"Don't worry," she tossed over her shoulder, "I can handle him."

Clint's smile broadened as he mumbled, "Suit yourself. If anyone can handle Nick, it would be you."

Tressa was halfway there when the reverberating clang

echoed into the hallway. "I'm not pissin' in this, damn it!"

With a deep breath, Tressa braced herself and entered the room.

Nick was sitting upright in bed, several pillows propped behind him.

"Who the hell took my damn pants?" he demanded, scowling with cold fury and making no effort at being polite.

Tressa crossed the room with her usual quiet composure, retrieving the makeshift urinal from the floor. "Count your blessings I'm bringing this back to you," she said softly. "When you discover you can't quite make it out of bed you'll be glad this isn't still sitting where you threw it."

"I said, I'm not pi . . . using that!"

"And off hand I'd say your options seem rather . . . limited." She placed the receptacle within easy reach, then moved to the door. "By the way," she added cheerfully, "Edna's putting a tray together for you. I'll be back in a little while with your breakfast."

Muttering a string of muffled curses, Nick despondently cast his gaze toward the window.

Chapter Twenty-six

Nick was dozing when Tressa entered the room. Determined not to be bedridden, he'd made the trip to and from the adjoining lav, gritting his teeth every inch of the way, every muscle in his body screaming in protest.

The faint rustle of Tressa's gown and the soft clinking of dishes roused him as she quietly crossed the room and set down the tray. He grinned to himself, tempted to keep his eyes closed, to let her think he was asleep. But an involuntary sigh escaped as a gentle palm checked for fever, then brushed back a stray lock of hair. Slowly opening his eyes, he blinked and focused his gaze. Tressa. Her name echoed wistfully through his mind.

"I'm sorry. I didn't mean to wake you."

"You didn't. I was just resting." He looked her over approvingly. She was a vision of femininity. The teal gown she wore caressed her body, outlining every detail from the swell of her breast to the curve of her hips. Her hair fell about her shoulders, shimmering like polished mahogany.

Nick knew what it meant to touch Tressa's hair, knew

its silky texture. Drunk or not, he vividly remembered the feel of that glossy lock slipping between his fingers, remembered the soft fragrance that filled his already overloaded senses. Oh, yes, with graphic clarity he recalled his all-consuming drive to have her that night. The need to brand her as his own.

The desire was strong but different somehow; no longer was it the detached lust he'd always experienced. No, Tressa had become more than just a sexual attraction, more than just another conquest. She'd changed.

No . . . *he'd* changed.

"Don't look at me like that." Tressa's blush deepened beneath his prolonged gaze.

Banner feigned innocence at her accusation, with widened eyes and a sharp intake of breath. "Like what?"

"You know very well *like what.*"

A crooked smile tugged at the corners of his mouth. "Sorry; I just can't help myself. You're exceptionally beautiful this morning, Irish."

Tressa gave a short laugh. "Edna warned me about you."

"She did, huh?"

"Uh-huh. She said to beware of that silver tongue of yours. As if I didn't already know."

"Silver tongue?" he repeated slowly, frowning in mock disbelief. "Why the devil would she say that?"

Tressa just laughed. "Why, indeed?"

Nick shifted positions, grimacing as a bolt of pain ripped through him. Tressa's smile quickly faded, replaced by a cloud of concern. "Are you all right?" she asked softly.

A grunt was his only response.

A moment passed before Tressa spoke again. "I can't believe what's happened. And it's all because of me, isn't it?"

Banner shook his head and lied. "It was just an old acquaintance with a score to settle."

Her gaze roamed his face, as if seeking the truth. "It was

302

more than that, Nick Banner. Here,'' she said, reaching for the hand that wasn't bandaged firmly to his side. "Let me see how your wrists are doing.''

With a frown of concentration, Tressa carefully began unfastening the med strip. "I put Acuel on them,'' she said. "Twice. There should be a marked improvement, even this soon.''

Banner gloried in the attention, welcoming the physical contact as Tressa freed his wrist of the cumbersome binding. Closing his eyes, he relaxed as the warmth of her touch filled him with a curious lassitude, feeling her fingers slide over his hand, turning it over in thorough inspection.

"Those lash burns aren't nearly as angry!'' Satisfaction pursed her mouth as she focused her gaze on his reddened wrist. "You're going to be back on your feet in no time.''

"Good,'' he said softly. " 'Cause I've got things to do.''

"I'll need to put more salve on, of course,'' Tressa babbled on, not noticing the silken thread of promise in his tone and too pleased at the results to question his meaning. Her gaze shifted back to his face. "But first you must eat.''

"Only under one condition,'' he said with a half smile.

"And what's that?''

"That you'll stay and keep me company.''

Tressa's brows drew together as if seriously considering a major concession. She leveled her liquid browns on him. "Deal . . . but only if you allow me to continue treating your injuries with Acuel.''

A slow grin begin to spread across Banner's face in arousing speculation. As if reading his thoughts, Tressa firmly added, "*Without* intimidation or harassment, Nick Banner.''

"Intimidation? Harassment? Me?'' His deep voice simmered with barely checked humor. "I'm as weak as a newborn *tamran.*''

"Uh-huh. Just as long as we understand the rules, Nick.''

He secretly gloried in anticipation. It would be sweet hell, but he could keep his mouth shut and lie there in complete submission to her touch. Oh, yes . . . he could do that.

An hour later his belly was full and the warmth of Tressa's touch still lingered. Reclining against a soft mound of pillows, he leisurely watched her gather up her supplies.

He was still trying to decide if she'd purposely tormented him or was just being excruciatingly thorough. She hadn't missed a single damn spot, and the sensual pleasure he'd so warmly anticipated quickly became a living nightmare. But other than an occasional gasp he'd remained true to his word and hadn't opened his mouth. Not once.

"Am I hurting you?" she'd asked. He groaned at the memory. Hurt him? Hell, she was killing him. But pain had nothing to do with it, for Tressa had meticulously pretreated every scratch and scrape on his heated body.

No. To his horror, it was his own involuntary response that had him fighting a losing battle. The only thing that helped was envisioning Loring's face. And even that wasn't a total cure. Dealing with his rising interest was bad enough, but the fact that he was too damn weak to even follow through was humiliating. He was as harmless as a babe and she knew it.

"You try and get some rest now, okay?" With that Tressa turned for the door, the scent of wildflowers still lingering in the air. Closing his eyes, he wondered at the strange feelings this woman instilled in him, stunned by how important she was suddenly becoming to him.

Over the next two days Tressa faithfully continued the ritual of Acuel treatments, and with each passing day Nick became stronger, the bruises less noticeable.

It was time to get out of bed.

A dull ache rewarded his efforts as he swung his legs over the edge. It took fewer muttered curses this time to get to his feet, and his movements were much quicker. It was a vast improvement over the sharp surge of agony he'd experienced in the beginning.

The image of Kendyl cut across his mind as he made his

way to the window. Even here she wasn't safe. Recalling Kendyl's promise to find her, he knew it would only be a matter of time.

It wouldn't surprise him if Kendyl already had the place staked out. And all it would take was one slipup. He shuddered, just thinking of Tressa at Kendyl's mercy.

A sharp knock roused him from his thoughts. Clint poked in his head. "Feeling better?"

"Come 'ere.

Clint stepped inside. "What?"

"Close the door."

Following instructions, Clint crossed the room.

Nick turned away from the window. "Has anyone contacted Loring yet?"

"You kidding? We left that for you."

"That's fine, I'll get a message off to him this afternoon." Nick's expression clouded. "Tressa can't stay here, Clint. Kendyl won't quit 'til he has her."

"And you have a better idea?"

"Yeah, I do. Zeke's coming back with Dad this afternoon, isn't he?"

"As far as I know. Why?"

Nick's jaw tightened. "I want Tressa outta here this afternoon."

Clint's eyes were beginning to sparkle with suppressed humor. "This afternoon, huh?"

Nick eased into a nearby chair. "I want Zeke to take her."

Clint was barely concealing his amusement now. "And just what do you plan to tell her to get her to leave with him?"

Nick's eyes narrowed. "Just get her in here. I'll worry about the rest. Have her bring me a cup of coffee or something."

Clint shook his head. "I'll get her in here, but don't hold your breath on her agreeing to leave."

Oh, she'd leave all right, Nick thought. She'd gladly

leave with Zeke by the time he finished.

Nick dressed in a hurry after Clint left the room, nearly draining every ounce of his strength just getting into his clothes.

There had been one other occasion, standing out in his memory, when he'd thrown on his clothes in even less time than today. He had been seventeen at the time, and Dawson had walked in on him and Jeannie. Nick almost smiled at the memory of himself hopping first on one foot and then the other, trying to jerk on his pants and chase after Dawson all at once. Poor Jeannie; she was a new hire, and it had taken some fast-talking on Nick's part to convince the prudish head butler not to fire her on the spot.

Nick's thoughts were jerked back to the present as he ran a hand across his stubble-roughened cheek. He glanced at himself in the mirror and shrugged dismissively at his sinister reflection. The more hostile his appearance, the better, he decided grimly.

Quickly finger-combing his hair, he'd barely made it to the window to strike a nonchalant pose when a soft knock came at the door. A hasty glance at the clock told him that hardly five minutes had passed. "Come in," he responded, keeping his back turned.

"Oh my, you're up and dressed."

As if he'd been standing there forever, Nick casually turned to face her. "Yeah."

"I brought you something to eat," she said cheerfully.

He watched her cross the room, denying the comfort her nearness gave him.

"I stole one of those delicious *zalo* jam pastries to go with your coffee," she chattered on with a hint of laughter.

"Just set it down on the table," he said, unable to stop himself from looking her over seductively and filling his senses with the sight, scent, and sound of her.

Yesterday Clint had told him about her empathic abilities, referring to his own experience in trying to explain the phenomenon. If Tressa was capable of reading emotions, as Clint had suggested, he wondered if she could sense the rapid beating of his heart. Did she know that she was the cause? And did she know her sweet scent was driving him slowly out of his mind?

The thought was so absurd, he wanted to laugh out loud. Nick Banner, beguiled by the lingering scent of wildflowers, seduced by a strong-willed, tenderhearted little . . . Banner's thought suddenly chilled, recalling how this little *angel* had seduced a guard from his post. Oh, yes, Clint had told him about that, too. Every detail. He'd been meaning to say something to her but had put it off, not wanting to spoil the sweet rapport he'd so enjoyed while recovering.

Mixed feelings surged through him when he first heard the story. First *shock,* then *anger.* Anger that she'd deliberately put her life in jeopardy, against explicit orders to stay put. He couldn't believe she hadn't learned anything from her encounter with the Ripper, an experience that could have been avoided if she'd simply followed orders and left things alone in the cockpit. Next came *rage.* That one went deep. Deeper than he wanted to admit, and it was founded solely on the fact that she'd been in another man's arms, not counting the fact that the bastard had ripped her clothing in his rush to have her. Finally came *compassion* for what she'd gone through and . . . heart-rending *tenderness* that she'd taken the risk for him.

With a heavy sigh of resignation, Banner knew what he had to do, like it or not. With a silent curse, he gathered his strength and determination, knowing her strong will and stubborn belief that she could call the shots, made a perfect target for starting an argument. And that *was* the main objective, he reluctantly reminded himself.

"I've been meaning to thank you," he began quite harmlessly.

Tressa turned to face him. "For what?"

"Everything. The all-night vigil the other night, the special care since then, the . . ."

"I did no more than anyone else," she protested softly.

"Oh, I'd say you did a *little* more. I understand you were quite the heroine the other day."

"Heroine?" Tressa paused. "Oh . . . that."

"Yeah. *That.*" Banner stepped closer, looking down at her intently. "You have a hard time learning lessons, don't you, Irish?"

"What do you mean?"

Nick used the unsettling image of Tressa in another man's arms to fuel his anger and keep him on track. "Didn't you learn anything from your experience with the Ripper? What the devil were you doing comin' on to some renegade who'd just as soon toss you to the ground as look at you?"

Tressa rolled her eyes. "Please don't tell me I have to hear it from you, too. I've already heard enough from the rest of your family to last a lifetime. If you'd just let me explain, maybe . . ."

"I'm not interested in your excuses. Whatever they were, they don't justify anything, Tressa. You were given orders and once again you chose to ignore them. But that's only half of it. You not only put your own life at risk, this time you put everyone else at risk."

Every curve in Tressa's body spoke defiance. Her voice rang with indignation. "I don't believe this! You're mad at me for helping them rescue you?"

"Hell, yes, I'm mad."

Sudden anger lit her eyes. "For your information, Nick Banner, I had your location pinpointed long before they even arrived in the area. And as for distracting the guard . . ."

Curses burst from his mouth. "Did you even stop to think what could have happened if you hadn't been able to get away from him? And what about Marc? What if he'd been discovered? Did you think about that, Tressa? What if someone had taken him down before he'd had a chance to rescue you?"

"Rescue me?" her voice rose with outrage. "I'll have

you know I had everything under control long before ..."

"Not only did you put Marc in danger," he interrupted, "you reduced the strength of the rescue party. You made them all more vulnerable."

"I-I never asked Marc ..." she stammered, anger vibrating in her voice, reddening her cheeks.

But Tressa's rising voice seemed to fade into the background of his awareness. This wasn't what he wanted. He ached to draw her into his arms, to kiss away the tears that were welling in her eyes. To tell her he really wasn't angry with her—frustrated, yes, but not angry. On the contrary, he was flattered beyond words. He'd had women, lots of them. But never had even one offered to risk her life for him.

Tressa was staring at him, waiting for his reply to her last heated retort.

He wouldn't back down now. Couldn't. And he desperately hoped that her present state of anger and confusion prevented her from sensing his feelings of regret.

Leaning forward, he purposefully lowered his voice to a steely tone, and through gritted teeth added, "If you *ever* ... try anything as foolhardy as that again while in my custody ..."

"Custody? Of all the ..."

"... I will personally see that you regret it."

Tressa glared at him. "You wouldn't dare. My father would ..."

"Don't bet on it, Tressa. We have a problem here. A big problem. You see, it's my duty to keep you safe, and I can't even trust you to follow a simple order."

"What?" she cried.

"Pack your things and be ready to go. When Zeke gets back you're outta here."

"I see," she said, her voice suddenly controlled. "In other words, I'm to lock myself in my room and stay there until your next *order*. Is that it?"

"That isn't what I said, but if that's what it takes, yes."

"Fine!" She swallowed hard. He watched her throat work, as if holding tears in check. "I won't be of any further trouble for either you or your family," she said with cool finality.

Banner's eyes narrowed suspiciously. "And just what the devil's that supposed to mean?"

Tressa turned for the door. "You figure it out."

"Tressa!"

But she was gone. Clint stood in the open doorway, grinning. "Don't tell me, let me guess. It was something you said. Right?"

The door hissed shut behind Tressa as she entered her room. Clasping her palm to her mouth, she leaned back in stunned silence.

I won't cry, she vowed silently, swiping at a determined tear. He wants me gone? Fine. I'll go—but I'll be damned if it will be on *his* terms.

Delighted with Tressa's sudden appearance, TiMar leapt from the bed and padded up to her, loudly voicing his pleasure. "Oh TiMar . . ." Her voice broke, and the name ended in a tiny sob as she reached down and gathered him into her arms. "I'm going to miss you, little man."

Hugging him tightly, she nuzzled her face against his luxurious coat. "I'm going to miss you *so* much."

Tressa swallowed convulsively, overcome with sadness and bittersweet memories. She was crushed by Nick's sudden hostility.

No . . . not just hostility. Rejection.

His words thundered through her mind. *It's my duty to keep you safe . . . when Zeke gets back you're outta here. It's my duty . . .*

With the back of her hand Tressa swiped angrily at another tear. "Consider yourself officially relieved of your duty, Nick Banner.

"I'm outta here, all right. *I'm going home!*"

Chapter Twenty-seven

Tressa stirred, reality shielded behind a thick blanket of mental fog. Slowly opening her eyes, she begged her beleaguered brain to function and gazed languidly about the room.

She should have been alarmed when her eyes rested on a large, round viewport, yet oddly she wasn't.

Concentrate on one thing at a time.

Closing her eyes, Tressa began honing in on the unmistakable hiss of ventilation and the hum of a drive system. Recognizing the sounds for what they were should have brought her upright.

It didn't.

Strange, but she didn't even care. Funny, how perfectly relaxed she felt just lying there with fog for a memory and alarming details not quite registering.

Tressa pulled herself into a sitting position, struggling to remember. Remember what . . . ? She frowned as fragments of memory surfaced briefly, only to vanish again.

The sound of an electronic door drew her benumbed attention. Slowly raising her sights, she watched as a man entered the room, carrying a tray with a carafe on it.

"I see you're awake."

His voice was distant, hollow-sounding as he spoke.

"I figured you might be coming out of it by now."

Following his movements through dulled eyes, Tressa simply sat there. Something in the back of her mind said he looked familiar, said she should be afraid . . . and yet . . .

"I trust the accommodations are satisfactory."

Even in her languid state she heard the mockery in his tone. Instinct, tranquilized as it was, said she didn't like the man, yet oddly, she felt no cause to be afraid.

"I want you to know, you've got the best cabin on-board." He turned and smiled at her. "Mine."

No alarm was being sounded with that comment either. Tressa simply watched vacantly as he set down the tray.

"So, how are we feeling? Kind of fuzzy?"

She offered no response, having neither the strength nor the inclination to do so.

"Well, that's to be expected. I brought you some tea." He turned away and began pouring something into a cup. Setting down the carafe, he came to her side. "This will help clear your head from the effects of the drug they used."

Drugs? They'd used drugs? Even *that* was no more than a dull realization.

"Here, drink this."

Tressa pulled back, avoiding his outstretched hand. She felt so . . . strange. In the far reaches of her mind she knew she should be terrified, yet . . . her body wasn't cooperating.

"Drink it, Tressa." His tone was becoming harsh.

She didn't like him. "Nooo . . ." Moaning, she turned her head away, her voice sounding strange and distant, hollow.

Suddenly she was jerked to her feet, though she was

swaying with weakness, fighting for balance as he yanked her up against his rigid body.

"I said, drink it!" Placing his hand at the back of her head, he pressed the cup to her lips, forcing her mouth open. "I want you fully awake, sweetheart," she heard him say as the liquid entered her mouth. Tressa struggled, half choking, half gulping to keep up with the flow.

"Atta girl," he murmured, releasing her and allowing her to sink back onto the bunk.

Tressa blinked lazily, watching with passive interest as he pulled up a chair, flipped it around, and straddled it backwards. "That'll clear the cobwebs from your brain," he said with a brisk nod.

Minutes passed before fragments of recollection surfaced, teasing her mind and then disappearing again. Tressa frowned, struggling to remember as the fog slowly began dissipating.

She remembered slipping out of the Banner town house, lulling them all into believing she was napping. She vaguely remembered taking the endless metal stairs instead of the lift.

A man . . . Yes . . . yes, there was a man standing near the end of the corridor. She remembered sensing danger, slowing her steps. Then the stranger burst into action, grabbing her by the hair, yanking her back, stilling her screams with a grimy hand clapped over her mouth. Next she was hit hard and after that . . . nothing.

Tressa scooted back on the bunk, putting as much distance as possible between the man sitting before her and herself. Through narrowed eyes she studied him as reality seeped back by degrees. He looked so familiar. Her eyes moved over his face, noting his high cheekbones, his steely gaze, his arrogant expression.

She took in his features, noticing his short-trimmed full beard, his dark shoulder-length hair, swept back and tied.

Emanating wealth, the man was smooth but in a sinister way. Even her half-drugged mind recognized that aspect about him. He wasn't exactly handsome, but he was a long way from ugly, and he smelled good, like expensive cologne.

Tressa would never have allowed her gaze to wander so brazenly over his body if she hadn't been so groggy. And wander it did, taking in every detail from his soft gray shirt to his crisp black trousers to his shiny . . .

"Like what you see?"

This time his voice jolted her memory.

That voice! How could she ever forget it! She inhaled sharply, as recognition set in. She'd only caught a glimpse of him from her hiding place beneath the bunk, but there was no doubt about it. He was the same man who'd forced his way onboard the *Victorious,* the same man who'd hurt Nick and stolen the cargo from his hold!

Tressa scrambled to her feet, swaying against the remaining effects of the drug, her legs nearly buckling beneath her. "You!" she cried, fighting her weakness with sheer boldness.

Rising to tower above her, Kendyl stood, too, his amusement unmasked. "You know me, Tressa?" he asked with soft menace. Sweeping away the chair, he removed the barrier between them.

Her heart pounding with terror, Tressa edged away from him. "Where am I?"

Kendyl's gaze calmly followed her every movement. "You're onboard my ship."

Looking for something to use as a weapon, her eyes darted frantically about the room. The fog was receding quickly now. Swallowing hard, she gathered her courage. "I suggest you take me back right now. When Nick catches up with you you're not going to be worth . . ."

"Banner?" Kendyl's laughter was harsh. "Your hero's dead, Tressa. I killed him myself."

Silence enveloped the room as Tressa's liquid brown eyes clashed defiantly with his laser blue ones.

"You're lying!" she hissed.

He wagged his head slowly from side to side, watching her reaction. "I slipped a knife into him. Right here." He touched the place over her pounding heart.

Tressa batted his hand away, jerking back in response to both his touch and his words.

"And this time," he continued coldly, "I didn't withdraw it until he stopped breathing."

"I don't believe you! It's not true!"

"Ah, but it is true."

His calm composure frightened her. She was stunned to momentary silence as the edges of the room seemed to fade as she digested his claim.

"I cornered the fool while he was out looking for you," he added on a chuckle.

Kendyl broke through her fragile control with that one. *Dear God, no . . .* Nothing he could have said could have brought her more pain, more despair than that last statement.

"Why?" she whispered.

"Revenge, darling. Sweet revenge."

Kendyl drew close, filling her nostrils with his scent. "Banner took something from me," he said, grasping her chin harshly. "Now it's my turn to take something from him."

Tears clouded Tressa's vision. She hardly heard his words. It didn't matter. Nick was dead and suddenly nothing mattered anymore.

Releasing her, Kendyl stepped back, watching her with idle interest. "He serviced mine." And with no vestige of sympathy, his hands moved to his belt, his thumb flicking the buckle for emphasis. "Now I'll service his."

Revenge, a small voice whispered. The very word that meant Nick was still alive. *Snap out of it, Tressa! If he's seeking revenge, Nick's not dead!*

Lifting her head, Tressa met Kendyl's gaze with cold triumph. "You won't get away with this, you know." Defiance coursed through her veins now. She didn't stand a chance against this brute, but she'd be damned if she'd give in easily. She'd give him a fight he'd never forget! Glancing past his shoulder, she measured the distance to the door.

"There's nowhere to run, darlin'," he said, as if reading her mind. A soft chime suddenly sounded, and Kendyl turned to the small panel mounted on the wall. "Yes? What is it?"

"Could I have a word with you? Alone? It's important."

"It had better be," he said.

Turning to Tressa, he said, "I want those clothes off by the time I return or I'll take them off for you."

Rage exploded within her. "You lay one filthy finger on me and I swear you'll regret it!"

Kendyl crossed the cabin to stand before her, his eyes filled with amusement. "Is that right?" he asked in silky challenge.

Refusing to show her terror, Tressa took a haughty stance. But before she knew what he was about, Kendyl's hand moved to her chin, holding it firmly as he lowered his head to take her mouth in a kiss that was both arrogant and brutal.

"Regret it?" he drawled. "I don't think so."

He must have seen it coming, for he caught Tressa's hand in midair. Their eyes locked in open warfare. "Don't try that again, Tressa. I hit harder."

Struggling vainly to free her captured wrist, Tressa finally relaxed. "You're hurting me," she said softly.

"I know." An intense moment passed before he released her. "It won't always be this way," he said, turning for the door. "By the time we get to Steel I guarantee I'll have you craving my touch." Then he was gone.

"Never!" she screamed. "Your touch sickens me!" Tressa turned away, her throat burning with unshed tears. What and where was Steel? Would she ever see home again? Her family? Would she ever see Nick again? Despair swept over her.

Tressa was standing before the viewport when Kendyl

returned a few moments later.

"You know what this is?" he asked.

Tressa turned to see a crumpled piece of paper in his hand.

"No."

"It's a memotext. You want to know what it says?"

"No."

He chuckled. "It's about you, honey. And if what it says is true, you're worth a whole lot of credits."

He had her attention now.

Kendyl studied her long and hard before going on. "Just exactly what were you to Banner, anyway?" he asked, reclining against the bulkhead.

"None of your business," she snapped.

He smiled knowingly. "Then maybe you'd like to explain what your relationship is to Burke Sinclair."

No response.

"You *do* know that his real name isn't Burke Sinclair, don't you?"

Tressa's eyes followed him as he crossed the room.

"It's Cord Wheeler," he offered casually. "I wonder what your daddy would say if he knew that." Kendyl's laugh turned harsh. "Wonder what he'd say if he knew ol' Sinclair's been behind this entire kidnapping scheme from the very beginning.

"He doesn't love you, sweetheart. All you are is a means for him to get what he's after: LorTech along with Wheeler Enterprises."

Still no response.

"Don't believe me? Ask me how I happen to know all about the contract he convinced your daddy to give to Wheeler Enterprises. Ask me how I know he's asked you to marry him." Kendyl laughed. "This kidnapping farce is just a conspiracy to make him the hero. To win you over."

Before she could respond another soft chime sounded. With a sigh of exasperation Kendyl palmed the intercom. "Now what?"

"You'd better get up here."

"What is it this time?"

"Our sensors are picking up a shadow."

Kendyl finally responded. "How far?"

"Right on the edge of our long-range scanners and closing."

"I'm on my way." Turning to Tressa, he said, "We'll pick up this conversation when I return."

The record-breaking drive down the narrow mountain road from the Banner home did little to improve Sinclair's mood. As agreed, he'd met with James Catlin at the space port, paid an exorbitant price, and listened while Catlin spilled his guts.

Like it or not, Sinclair knew Tressa's only chance in hell was Nick Banner.

Catlin's directions to the Banner home had left much to be desired. It had taken Sinclair over an hour just to find the place. Another twenty minutes passed while he argued with the guard posted at the front gate. The final blow, however, was being told that Nick wasn't there.

Fifteen minutes later here he was, arriving at the space port. His brief conversation with some woman named Delta confirmed everything Catlin had told him. Tressa was missing, and the Banner men were at the space port now, looking for her.

Well, they wouldn't find her, Sinclair thought bleakly. If what Catlin said was true, Tressa had left with Kendyl about three hours ago.

Guiding the landcraft into a parking slot, and with Banner's description fresh in his mind, he hopped out. "Now . . . to find him," he muttered, heading for the terminal building.

Nick leaned against a stack of freight pallets, his strength waning, and though the pain in his ribs was progressively getting worse, it was nothing compared to the pain in his heart over Tressa.

He'd driven her to this. In his damn haste to see her safe, he'd as good as told her to get out. Hell, he couldn't even remember all that he'd said.

Cursing softly, he raked a hand through his hair. Two hours had passed since they'd discovered her missing, and God only knew where she was by now. Nick knew well the hazards of a space port. His mind was alive with mental visions—visions of Tressa wandering into the wrong section, falling prey to some slimeball spacer—if not Kendyl himself—visions of her getting burned by a discharge of scalding vapor from the vent of a cooling ship. Or even being run down by some robotic cargo mover. The possibilities were endless.

Zeke had taken it upon himself to check with the commercial liners first, on a hunch that maybe she'd reserved a cabin on an outbound ship. But there was nothing.

Clint hit the local port bars, looking for anyone wearing Bungi cleat-toed boots and shooting his mouth off. But again, nothing came of it. From there he went to space port control, coming up with one piece of interesting news: Kendyl's ship, the *Renegade*, had left its assigned berth yesterday. To some it might have indicated that Kendyl had given up his search for Tressa. To Nick it meant nothing more than the fact that he'd simply moved his ship. There were hundreds of places outside the space port to ditch a small yacht like Kendyl's. Nick knew all too well how easily the *Renegade* could be relocated, miles away if necessary.

Nick and Max had personally questioned space port security, along with every maintenance crew in the area. But no one seemed to know anything.

Kendyl had her all right; he felt it in his gut.

Nick looked up to see Marc returning to the sight. "Anything?" he asked, rising to his feet.

"Nothing. At least nothing on the departure log that matches the Renegade's identification since yesterday."

"And what about clearance?" Nick asked.

"Again, nothing. I even had Leanne do a security check for me," Marc added. "I figured if they were stupid enough to lift without proper clearance, port security would be crawling all over them by now." Marc shook his head. "Nothing."

Nick's mind raced. Kendyl was many things, but stupid wasn't one of them. One sure way of drawing attention to yourself would be to lift without going through proper clearance procedures. It was a guaranteed method of inviting a swarm of armed security officers on to your tail.

No, Nick thought, Kendyl either hasn't left Imperial yet or he's bought someone off. Nick opted for the latter theory.

"Banner? Nick Banner?"

All five of them turned as a man, searching each of their faces, made his way across the hangar deck.

Watching him pick his way over fuel lines, Nick took his time studying the outsider before answering the question. "I'm Nick," he said at last.

"I'm Burke Sinclair. I need to talk to you. It's about Tressa."

Chapter Twenty-eight

Nick sat in the dimly lit control room of the *Windstar,* the illumination from the console softening his now hardened features. Warning indicators pulsed, digital readouts were dangerously high, and every rule in the book was being broken.

Pushed to her limits, the ship vibrated around him, rattling what seemed to be every nut, bolt, and rivet in her structure.

Though Nick had long tuned out the ever-constant noise of vibration, he refused to listen to the computer's repetitive monotoned lecture on the hazards of continuing at their present breakneck speed. They had been barely an hour out when he'd silenced the irritant by disconnecting the vocal center.

With a long, tired sigh, he looked up from the monitor, rubbing his blurry eyes with his thumb and forefinger. He was exhausted; his body demanded sleep and he ached all over, especially his ribs and left shoulder. Both were still annoyingly sore.

Gingerly rotating his upper arm, wincing as he worked with stiff muscles, Nick wondered if his shoulder would ever be the same. The Acuel salve had helped, but without Tressa the use of the ointment had fallen by the wayside.

Six days of chasing Kendyl had passed—six days since his meeting with Sinclair had confirmed his worst fears.

Having taken off across the hangar on a dead run, the Banners were onboard the *Windstar*, had coordinates set and clearance for liftoff in a record-breaking twenty minutes—four pain-filled hours behind Kendyl's illegal departure. So far, in pushing the *Windstar* to her limits, they'd sliced Kendyl's lead time in half. Sinclair, however, trailed behind, unable to keep up with their perilous speed in his smaller yacht.

The *Windstar* was not only twice the size of Nick's cargo ship, *Victorious,* she was more than twice as fast. Max had obtained the vessel several years back in trade for services. Originally she was a Terran MRV, a military reconnaissance vessel, decommissioned during a budget cutback. The previous owner, a wealthy earth-based businessman, had purchased the vessel and transformed her into a private pleasure yacht, a renovation that included both her drive systems along with a luxurious interior.

Banner's mind slid back to Tressa, who was never far from his thoughts. He'd hardly slept since they'd left port. Grief and despair tore at his guts like a double-edged knife. Guilt, in particular, rode him hard; he knew in his heart that it was his own words that had sent her running.

When Zeke gets back, you're outta here. It wasn't just the guilt that leveled him. It was much more than that. It was an ache. A shocking hunger. A need to be there for her, to draw her into his arms and kiss away the terror. To once again see her radiant smile, that intriguing dimple that never ceased to captivate him. Even more than that, it threatened his ability to think clearly.

Bracing his elbows on the console, Nick lowered his head to his hands, thrusting his splayed fingers through his shaggy dark hair. What ungodly torture had Kendyl already subjected her to? He didn't need an overactive imagination to envision her fate. He knew the kind of torture that bastard was capable of.

Dear God, *Steel.* A muscle jerked in his jaw at the very thought.

Oh, yes, he knew what those auctions were like . . . knew firsthand that among the merchandise that crossed the platform were sentient beings. Sensitive, caring people like Tressa, many of whom were grabbed right off merchant vessels, or even, in some cases, snatched from their home planets.

Banner stared vacantly at the controls, reliving in his mind the time he'd witnessed a small band of terrified children being herded across the auction platform. They'd reminded him of frightened animals. Once sold into slavery, they were doomed to live out their short lives in the bowels of some godforsaken mine on some uncharted planet.

The memory sickened him. The jagged scar that ran across his upper back bore permanent testimony to his impulsive but futile effort to try and stop their sale to some slimeball of a slaver.

In the long run he supposed mining slaves were the fortunate ones. Banner was all too aware that among the crowd of customers were a select group of buyers who came to the auctions with special needs in mind, needs requiring beautiful young women. He knew the kind. Scum with desires so dark and perverse no woman would ever submit willingly. Nausea roiled and twisted in his gut at the thought of Tressa being subjected to such treatment—at the mental vision of her being stripped, shackled, and forced to stand upon a raised platform while Kendyl held out for the highest credits from a salacious crowd.

And in the meantime had Kendyl already defiled her as a means to settle some imaginary score? An almost possessive rage welled up from deep inside. Hatred Nick had never known coursed through his veins at the idea of Kendyl even touching her.

Maybe the bulletin dispatch he'd sent out would buy her time. Maybe Kendyl would leave her alone, untouched, knowing her innocence would be worth a pretty price on the market.

There was a time when Banner could have reasonably guessed at the answer. No more. The seven years since their partnership had brought about too many changes, changes in both men as well as their motives.

The only thing Banner knew for sure was that Quint Kendyl was a dead man.

His eyes narrowed and the familiar muscle ticked in his left cheek at the intensity of his silent vow. *That bastard had damn well better be where he could find him too.*

Inhaling sharply, he cast his eyes to the overhead controls, patting his pocket for a cigar. Damn, only one left. He bent his head and lit up, blowing a stream of smoke toward the floor.

"You ready for a break?" Zeke entered the control room, dropping into the co-pilot's seat. "Anything happening?"

Acknowledging his friend with a quick glance, Banner reached for his coffee. "Kendyl's still holding at two and a half hours ahead. Sinclair has dropped to the edge of our long-range scanners. We'll be coming up on Steel's buoys in about three, and their weapons satellites shortly thereafter."

Zeke regarded him curiously. "Since you've been there, tell me, is that security system of theirs as touchy as they say?"

"Effective's more the word," Nick said. "No one gets within seven thousand kilometers of the place without an invitation."

"The ID code," Zeke interjected.

Banner nodded and leaned back. "The system consists of a ring of warning buoys. If you advance beyond those, you'd better be prepared to pass through the *Gate*—an orbiting ring of computerized weapons satellites."

Zeke smiled blandly. "And that's where you present your personal invitation."

"Or get your backside blown off." Banner fell silent as memories came flooding back across seven long years.

In serious need of a shave, he absently scratched the stubble on his jaw. "One time there were five ships backed up . . ."he began, his voice distant as he relived the memory. "All coming through one at a time. We were third in line. Everything was going fine until some renegade in front of us didn't happen to pass inspection." Banner paused. "The bastard never even knew what hit him."

Releasing a breathy whistle, Zeke shifted uncomfortably. "You ever hear why?"

Nick shook his head. "No one gives a damn on that hellhole, but I'd be willing to wager his ID wasn't valid."

Banner picked up his cigar, tapping ash into the ashtray as another thought-filled moment slipped by. Steel's security was effective. Every pirate ship had its own ID number encoded right into its very structure. "Once a ship approaches the weapons satellite," he went on, "computerized energy scanners automatically scan the ship's hull for the code. If there, and still valid, you're allowed to pass. If not . . ."

"If not, they're blown to eternity," Zeke finished.

Banner's jaw tightened. "One way in. One way out," he said, staring vacantly into his mug, watching as tiny vibration ripples danced across the surface of his coffee. Who would have ever thought that the *Windstar*'s hidden assets would someday be put to official use. Damn if she wasn't a pirate ship, complete with her own ID encoded right into her frame. Obviously her previous owner was involved in more than legitimate dealings.

Max hadn't discovered the *Windstar*'s enhanced ability until a major maintenance inspection. The discovery had brought about hoots of laughter among the Banner men, as well as a never-ending progression of jokes and fanciful scenarios of fearless pirating.

But this time the scenario was real. This time no one was laughing, and if all went as planned, the *Windstar* would be their ticket both to and from Steel. A wave of contemptuous satisfaction swept over Nick at the thought, for it was an advantage Kendyl wouldn't figure on.

Zeke's voice broke the long silence. "So . . . how do we know the code's still valid on this baby?"

Leaving the question dangling, Banner calmly stuck the cigar between his teeth, wincing against uptrailing smoke as he made a minor adjustment on the controls. Satisfied with the modification, he swiveled around to face Zeke again.

"We don't." His matter-of-fact tone belied his own emotions.

A moment of dead silence followed before Zeke finally responded, his voice a mere whisper. "Geeez, Nick . . ."

Nick grinned. "I know. Stimulating, isn't it?"

"Hell, you always did thrive on this sort of madness."

"And *you* didn't?" Nick shot back with a low chuckle, remembering how the two of them used to tempt fate beyond rational thought. Removing his cigar, he held it between his thumb and fingers, watching the smoke trail off the tip. "Just think of it as old times."

Zeke heaved a sigh of exasperation. "All I've got to say is this: Since you're the one who has been there before, you damn well better be operating with your head. I don't know about you, pal, but I don't exactly relish the idea of having precious parts of my body melded to shards of drifting fuselage."

Banner laughed openly and reached for his coffee.

"What about Sinclair?" Zeke asked.

That wiped the grin off Nick's face, stopping his coffee midway to his mouth. "What about him?"

"How's *he* going to pass security?"

Banner shrugged. "That's *his* problem."

Zeke grinned. "Did you see how furious he was when you told him he wasn't going with us? I think the fool actually would have taken you on."

"Yeah?" Nick failed to see the humor. "That arrogant bastard would've had his teeth knocked down his throat too."

A moment of silence passed before Zeke spoke again. "I take it you don't like him much."

Knowing full well where the conversation was heading, Nick busied himself with the controls again. "I don't trust him."

Zeke was grinning. "It wouldn't happen to have anything to do with the fact that he's asked Tressa to marry him, would it?"

With an air of composure, Banner took a slow draw from his cigar, releasing a lazy stream of smoke toward the vent. Finally turning toward his friend, he leveled a bland gaze on him and drawled, "Not a damn thing."

"I see."

Zeke's condescending tone was irritating. Worse yet, his knowing grin said he was well aware of just how irritating he was. With a muttered oath, Banner rose to his feet. "Back off, Slater! I'm getting tired of repeating myself. She's nothing to me. You got that? I'm not interested in her beyond the fact that it's a damn job!" Shoving his cigar into his mouth and grabbing his mug, he turned on his booted heel and stalked out of the control room—pushing down the mental image of Tressa's sweet face.

"She's interested in *you*, pal," Zeke called out, his voice laced with laughter.

Banner stopped in midstride. A heartbeat later his boots echoed down the narrow corridor.

He was getting tired of having to defend himself every time Tressa's name was mentioned. She was a temporary assignment, nothing more. No different from any other high-security payload he'd taken on for the Corporation. There were plenty of other times he'd put out just as much effort to safeguard a shipment without all the hassle of explaining himself to everybody.

The galley smelled of freshly brewed coffee as he entered. Max sat at the table nursing a cup.

Setting his mug down with more force than was necessary, Nick refilled it. Sure, he was attracted to her; he'd admit to that. Hell, he'd have to be blind not to be. But interested in her . . . as in *relationship, commitment?* No thank you. He liked his life just the way it was. Free, independent, and no commitments.

Making his way to the table, he eased into a chair and angrily flicked ash into a nearby ashtray. It missed, cascading to the carpeted floor.

His motives were no different than anyone else's. He'd noticed the way they all looked at her, grinning like idiots. Marc in particular. After all, he was the one who had given her his jacket to cover herself. An unconscious scowl spread across Nick's already disgruntled features. Not that he gave a damn, but just how much had little brother seen before handing over the jacket?

"Everything's okay up front?" Max's deep voice interrupted Nick's thoughts. Glancing up, he found his father studying him curiously. "Everything's normal, if that's what you mean." His tone was tinged with sarcasm. "We've still got every damned readout flashing red. The displacement spectrometer is starting to give us problems, and God only knows what the computer would be saying if I reconnected the audio."

Max's face was expressionless. "Zeke has the helm?"

A grunt was his answer as Nick took a sip of coffee. "Kendyl's still holding at two and a half hours, and we'll rendezvous with the buoys in about three . . ." He hesitated. "That is, of course, providing this modified space buggy doesn't rattle all her bolts loose before we get there."

Max grinned. "She'll hold. Now, once we hit dirt," he continued, "it will be up to you to call the shots. You're the one who knows the way around.''

''Knows the way around where?'' Clint asked as he entered the galley.

The next three hours flew by as Nick retrieved a crude map he'd sketched earlier. Eventually Marc joined them, and once again they rehashed their plans as Nick went over the layout of the pirate city.

Manmade and more than one kilometer in diameter, Steel originally had started out as a free-floating combination ferry port and refueling station. Nick had never heard exactly how it came to be taken over by pirates.

Like a sequestered island in the sea of space, Steel made a perfect harbor for selling what you didn't need and buying what you did without all the hassle of taxes, duties, and anything else that generally gets in the way of free trade. Rumor had it that Steel was owned by a huge megacorp that used it as a means to launder its own untaxed revenue.

Bracing his weight on his palms, Max leaned over the table. ''I just thought of something,'' he said, a slow smile curving his mouth. ''If what you're saying is true . . . about Laker Metals owning Steel . . .'' Max's grin got broader. ''Laker owes Banner Transport a rather large and so far uncollected barter.''

Nick's head snapped up. ''Yeah?'' His mind spinning with possibilities, a long moment of silence followed as he stared at his father. His respect and admiration rose yet another notch for the man whose image he bore. ''You realize what this means?'' he asked softly.

''It means that while you're tracking down Kendyl, I'll be cashing in the chits to buy our way back out.''

Zeke's voice came over the intercom. ''Buoy coming up. Hang on, gentlemen; we're about to leave hyperspace.''

Zeke was closely monitoring the controls when they entered the helm and slid into their allotted places. *Windstar* had command. Programmed to leave hyperspace on a predesignated coordinate, there was little else for them to do but grab their seats and watch as lights winked out on the console and others came on.

A soft chime sounded. Other than that, the only indication that they were making the jump from hyperspace was the wave of nausea each experienced.

Nick scanned the readings. "Cut the power by fifty percent," he ordered. "We're coming in too fast."

"Brace yourself," Zeke replied, entering the directive. The *Windstar* responded with a sudden jolt, the deceleration jerking them forward. At last the vibration ceased, and the descending whine of overstressed drives resounded throughout the ship like a pain-filled howl.

"We're being probed," Max said, studying the controls.

"It's okay. They're just scanning our memory for language verification."

Steel's shimmering wheel-like image took up half the view screen. Cast against a midnight backdrop, sunlight flickered off its shiny solar panels.

"Message coming through now," Zeke said as the image of Steel wavered on the screen and gave way to a scrolling message.

WARNING! WARNING!
THIS IS A RESTRICTED ZONE. UNAUTHORI-
ZED SHIPS
HAVE FOUR MINUTES TO VACATE BEFORE
BEING FIRED UPON.

Nick rose from his seat, crossing the cockpit and gliding to a halt behind Zeke. Bracing his six-foot-four-inch frame on slightly spread legs, he retrieved his last cigar, bent his head, and lit up. For an instant his mind briefly flickered on a much more pleasant way to spend the final moments of life. One thing for sure, he decided, releasing a stream of smoke into the air; he'd be damned if he'd be cheated out of his last cigar.

"WARNING! WARNING!
THIS IS A RESTRICTED ZONE. UNAUTHORI-
ZED SHIPS
NOW HAVE THREE MINUTES TO VACATE
BEFORE BEING FIRED UPON.

"Now what?" Zeke asked.

"We wait."

The silence lengthened.

The tension stretched.

"Weapons Satellite comin' up in two minutes," Zeke said, his voice much too calm for the occasion.

Nick lifted his sights and scanned the readouts. "Decrease power by twenty percent."

"Power decreased twenty percent," Zeke echoed.

"Steady as she goes."

Intense silence followed as all eyes were riveted on the screen.

"Pulse coming in now!" Max announced. A fraction of a second later the *Windstar* shuddered as an energy pulse slowly slid down the length of her side, setting off a host of Klaxons.

Another drawn-out moment passed with no one so much as taking a breath.

At last a monotoned voice announced the long awaited consent. "Vessel 831.68 *Tango,* cleared for docking."

A sigh filled the room.

"Gentlemen," Nick said softly, "welcome to hell."

Chapter Twenty-nine

Dressed in black leathers, his gun secured low on his thigh, Nick shouldered his way through the crowd. Just as he remembered it, the place was a madhouse of activity. People bustled about. The docking center was teeming with longshoremen loading and unloading cargo bays. Robotic cargo-handling equipment lifted mysterious containers from dark holds onto freight sleds, and marketeers made their way through the rabble, hawking everything from spare parts to quick sex.

But Steel wasn't all weapons, hookers, vendors, and auction arena. Nick knew from past experience that Steel also included several rather pleasant-appearing housing complexes, recreational facilities, and even a large shopping mall for its residents.

Like a private tropical island in the sea of space, Steel was a protected oasis for pirates: a home base for their families; a place where their children could run on playgrounds, where lush plants grew in imported soil, thriving beside artificial waterfalls and tropical trees crested beneath a crystalline-domed ceiling.

Like a gigantic wheel in space, spokelike corridors traversed its center, linking the centralized docking center to any number of destinations within the structure. Taking Corridor Three, Max took off for Laker Metals, while Nick and the others headed for the arena.

"How do you know she's not still onboard his ship?" Marc asked, keeping up with Nick's long strides.

"She's not!" Nick's tone brooked no argument as they headed for a lift-tube that would take them to the arena. Soon they entered an enormous circular hippodrome where a large platform stood in the center and terraced bidding seats encompassed the perimeter.

Slave auctions ran at intervals, four hours apart. A quick glance at an electronic message center told them that Interval Six was about to begin and the crowd was gathering.

"We'd better find our places," Nick said, heading for an empty section of boxed-in bidding chairs. Zeke slid into a seat and stared at the computerized equipment built into the arm. "Okay, pal, the basics I can figure out, but what's the process on bidding with this contraption?"

"It's like this." Leaning closer, Nick briefly explained the process of using the keypad for placing bids. The highly efficient method was not just confidential, it was damn practical. Since there was no way of knowing who you were actually bidding against, the auction was kept reasonably peaceful.

Recalling the time he'd tried to rescue the children from their fate, Nick knew firsthand what happened when things get *unpeaceful*. Those bored-looking security guards with muscles upon their muscles weren't just standing around for decoration.

Glancing up, Nick scanned the crowd. "I'm going to take a quick look around." Turning to Clint, he said, "Would you find out what's happening between Dad and

Laker? We've got no idea what kind of credits we're working with here . . . if anything.''

"And if Tressa's up for bid before you return?" Zeke asked.

"Start without me. I'm not taking any chances. I'm going to pull in a few markers of my own as backup, just in case."

The sign read AUCTION PLATFORM—STAND CLEAR!

Feeling as though her breath had just been cut off, Tressa's legs gave way. Kendyl's arm caught her before she fell.

Terrified didn't even begin to touch it. Bile rose in her throat, and she was about to be sick—again. Swallowing hard, her breath coming in quick, shallow gasps, panic as she'd never known swept through her.

Kendyl nudged her forward. "Move it." Another push emphasized his impatience.

Registration had entailed more than just filling out forms and releases. For Tressa, it meant being stripped, weighed, and measured, and her vital statistics logged with calloused proficiency.

Dazed, eyes brimming with unshed tears, she'd endured it all with rigid dignity while Kendyl busied himself with auction fees and paperwork.

A man passed a small scanner across the front of her lower abdomen. "She's intact," he called out with cool indifference. "Add ten thousand credits onto her base price."

Numbly, Tressa recalled Kendyl glancing up from his work. At first a raised eyebrow was his only expression. Then the corner of his mouth tipped upward, his laser-blue eyes piercing the distance between them.

How could Nick have ever been friends with someone like him, she wondered, much less partners?

"This will come off the minute you're sold, lass." A numbered ID collar was clamped tightly about her neck.

Sensing kindness in the man's tone, Tressa sought his eyes for mercy, but found none. Instead, what she saw was a somewhat bored and scruffy-looking man, old enough to be her father, just doing his job.

"Here, put this on."

She stared numbly at the flimsy one-piece garment that was shoved into her hands,

"And hurry it up. Show's 'bout to begin."

Tressa vaguely recalled stepping into the filmy outfit and pulling it up over her shoulders. Pushing it into place, however, only pulled it out of place somewhere else, exposing more than it concealed.

She gasped as her hands were pulled behind her back and firmly shackled.

"Well, Kendyl, my friend, what y' got here!" someone said off to her right. The man stepped closer. "Bet y' got a fancy price on y' too, don't y', sweetheart?"

"A hell of a lot more than you can afford, McClain," Kendyl said with a chuckle, catching Tressa possessively by the arm.

The back corridors leading to the arena were dark. Dim chem lights, hanging from low ceilings, cast widely spaced circles of light along the darkened passageways. Though she walked with the carriage of royalty, passing through the stockade was a terrifying experience for Tressa, the sights, the sounds, and the stench assaulting her senses.

"Keep moving." A hard shove between her shoulder blades threatened to drop her. Tressa tripped, only to be caught by strong hands and pushed on. They were getting closer. The fanfare of loud music, the uproar of the crowd were all punctuated by shouts from impatient buyers waiting for the auction to begin.

Tressa blinked back tears, refusing to cry. She'd done enough of that already over the last six days. Little good it had done. Kendyl was a man of no compassion.

The only thing she could be thankful for was the fact that, despite his lewd suggestions of rape and revenge in the very beginning, Kendyl had yet to touch her.

The interplanetary bulletin he was clutching when he'd reentered the cabin that first day was the only clue for his sudden change of heart. He'd challenged her and interrogated her ruthlessly about her relationship with Nick. His questions were crude and humiliating. And it was strange how he'd seemed both angry and pleased with her answers, disbelieving and elated all at the same time. Eventually she was moved from his cabin to one of her own, where she spent the remainder of the trip, unmolested.

"Greetings, and welcome to Slave Interval Six." The voice of the auctioneer boomed out over the arena and echoed back into the darkened corridors, rousing Tressa to present reality.

"Need help with that special task?" the voice went on. "We've got just what you're looking for. And if it's pleasure you want, you're going to like what we have coming up. Guaranteed.

"Interval Seven, by the way, will be focusing on mining equipment, everything from power drills to horizontal boring augers, so stick around!

"And now . . . what do you say we get this show rolling?"

The crowd roared and the doors opened briefly to admit the first two people in line.

Nausea swept over Tressa at the sight of the lusty crowd, laser lights flashing wildly back and forth over their heads. Trembling, eyes bleak, she turned to Kendyl.

"No, Tressa. You've already thrown up twice," he said, as though reading her mind. "There's nothing left in you. Now move it!" He nudged her forward, closing the gap in the lineup of human merchandise.

Never had she felt so hopeless. Even if she *could* escape, where would she run? And rescue was out of the question. No one knew where she was. Besides, who would rescue her? Nick certainly wouldn't. He'd made it perfectly clear he wanted her out of his life. In fact, the bastard was probably still celebrating.

Were you expecting more? Hoping that just maybe he'd be filled with undying gratitude for your part in the rescue? For those long hours at his bedside, mopping the sweat from his brow, tending to his wounds, even suffering his agony along with him? You weren't hoping for some sort of . . . commitment, were you? The small voice in her head laughed. *From Nick Banner?*

Stiffening at the memory of his rejection, Tressa vowed she was far from defeated. Her body might be sold, but they'd never have her spirit.

The doors opened, and two more people were ushered out. Again, the auctioneer's voice thundered back through the open doors, announcing the next items up for sale.

Kendyl nudged her forward. Things were moving quickly.

"Look at me." A firm grip on her jaw forced her head around.

Blinking back tears, Tressa stood, frozen in place, as Kendyl's icy gaze moved over her in a critical scrutiny.

Ever so slowly his mouth curved into a chilling smile. "That's right, honey. You just keep that lower lip trembling. It'll drive 'em nuts. Now, when you get out there," he continued, "you do *nothing* but stand there. You hear me?"

Tressa nodded woodenly, and before she knew it the doors opened again. The strobe lights flashed and the auctioneer began his spiel.

"Next, we have the epitome of perfection. Imagine *this* warming your bed at night."

Tressa swallowed a cry of sheer terror as a guard grabbed her by the arm, propelling her through the set of doors and up a flight of stairs.

The crowd's reaction was loud and lusty as brazen comments were shouted back and forth.

Her stomach revolted and once again she choked down

the nausea, shivering as trickles of sweat inched their way down her back and between her breasts.

Pleading words of mercy died in her throat as she was ushered across the stage. There would be no mercy from this crowd, no compassion, no pity, only the vilest of intentions.

"And by the way," the auctioneer continued, "this little package has never been opened. A rare find here at the arena!"

Tressa's knees weakened as once again the crowd was incited, reacting loudly with even more whistles and hungry calls.

"She's a bargain at a base of twenty thousand credits. Now, do I hear an opening bid?"

The bidding began. "I've got twenty-one thousand. Do I hear another?

"Twenty-one, five! Who will give me twenty-two . . . twenty-two . . .

"Twenty-two! Do I hear twenty-two, five . . . five . . . five!

"We have twenty-two, five! . . ."

Finding a sliver of strength, Tressa hung on. Lifting her chin in defiance, she turned her gaze into the crowd, nailing those with whom her eyes came into contact and challenging each one with a glare that blatantly told them that they might buy her, but they'd *never* own her.

"Twenty-four . . . four . . ."

Nick . . .

The noise. The frenzied crowd. The auctioneer's impetuous voice suddenly faded from Tressa's awareness.

Nick . . .

Time seemed to stop as she lifted her sights against the blinding lights and rows of grizzled faces.

He's here! A chill streaked down Tressa's back at the sudden awareness of his presence.

Chapter Thirty

By the time Nick returned the auction was well underway, Tressa was on the block, and the bidding had quickly risen to an exorbitant twenty-three thousand credits.

"My God," he whispered convulsively, his gaze settling on Tressa for the first time. A mixture of raw fury and gut-twisting agony coursed through him at the very sight of her.

"Do I hear twenty-four, five? Twenty-four, five? Who will give me . . ." The auctioneer's practiced patter rang out with systematic cadence over the arena. The crowd was wild, their frenzy further incited as the laser strobes once again were activated.

"It's moving fast, Nick," Zeke said without breaking concentration. "And someone out there wants her *real* bad."

"Like hell." Unable to drag his eyes from Tressa, Nick's jaw tightened as he took his seat. "Thanks, I'll take it from here," he said, calmly belying the primitive mixture of emotions surging through him. The burning need to protect her, to kiss away her tears, to confess his undying . . . *Not love! I don't love . . .*

"We have twenty-five thousand! Do I hear more? Who will give . . ."

The auction continued, sending Nick's denial trailing off as he punched in the next bid.

"We have twenty-five, five!" the auctioneer responded with enthusiasm.

Nick's jaw set, his muscles tensed with each succeeding bid, and the iron fist in the pit of his stomach clenched. It was difficult to make out details from thirty rows back, but who needed details to confirm Tressa's terror?

". . . twenty-seven thousand . . ."

Nick boosted the figure to twenty-eight thousand.

"We have twenty-eight thousand! Who will give me twenty-eight, five hundred . . ."

"Yes! We have . . ."

"Damn, he's just not giving up," Zeke muttered.

Oblivious to everything but Tressa and the fast-paced bidding to claim her, Nick's nerves were at full stretch, his eyes growing cold with determination as he entered the next counter. The auction had become a showdown, a battle between Nick and what he suspected to be one other unrelenting bidder.

"Thirty thousand!" the auctioneer announced with calculated excitement, confirming Nick's bid. The strobes pulsed. "Do I hear thirty, five? Who will give . . ."

"Yes! We have thirty, five . . ."

Nick released a string of muttered curses. "I'm through dancing around with this bastard." Without hesitation he hiked the figure up to thirty-eight thousand.

"We have thirty-eight thousand!" the auctioneer shouted eagerly. "Who will give me thirty-eight thousand, five hundred? Do I hear more?

"No?" With an air of smooth expertise he turned to Tressa and stroked her cheek. "Who will give me thirty-eight, five for this little gem?" His hand lowered, slipping the strap off her shoulder and exposing one glorious breast to the scrutiny of the crowd. Tressa kicked out, narrowly missing the auctioneer's shin, before being jerked back by a guard. The crowd roared with enthusiasm.

But a surge of frenzied rage swept through Nick. "That sonofabitch," he managed to whisper brokenly.

She was his. No one had a right to touch her, to see her.
"That sonofa . . ."

"Easy, Nick. Don't lose it now." It was Zeke's calm voice of reason, and his hard hand pressing down on Nick's shoulder kept him from leaping to his feet and charging to Tressa's rescue. Silently renewing his vow to kill Kendyl, he felt the familiar tug in his left cheek.

"Gentlemen," the auctioneer continued with well-versed timing, his practiced voice becoming a low, husky rasp. "Just think of the ecstasy this little jewel offers. Think of the pleasure you'll find, customizing her untutored body to meet only your needs. Just imagine the thrill of taming her."

Ribald laughter rippled over the arena in response, and the auctioneer stepped back. "I say, don't let this one pass you by.

"Thirty-eight thousand, going once . . .

Nick's gaze narrowed. *Hang in there, honey. If you can sense my thoughts at all . . . then you know I'm here for you.*

"Thirty-eight thousand, going twice . . .

"Thirty-eight thou . . . Yes! We have thirty-nine thousand!"

Nick's guts churned as a wave of desperation swept over him. Without a second thought he jacked the figure to forty-five.

"Forty-five thousand!" the auctioneer screamed. "We have forty-five thousand. Who will give me forty-five, five? Forty-five, five? Do I hear more for this pretty little prize?"

"No?

"Forty-five thousand, going once!

"Forty-five thousand, going twice!

Every muscle in Nick's body tightened. Swallowing hard, he held his breath.

"Sold! To bid number E-2058 for forty-five thousand!"

The laser strobes went crazy.

Mouthing a silent prayer of thanks, Nick slumped back into his seat. "Got'er," he groaned in relief, his possessive gaze following a frightened Tressa every inch of the way as a muscled guard escorted her off the platform and out of sight.

"Now, moving on to our next feature . . ." The auctioneer's voice still held a rasp of excitement.

"Well?" Zeke said. "What are we waiting for? Let's go!"

"Can't. I've got to finalize the sale first," Nick said as a tiny built-in vidscreen snapped to life.

"You want me to go on ahead?" Zeke asked, still standing.

Nick finished entering his bidding code into the minicomp. "I won't know which pay station she's being held at until everything's concluded."

Zeke sat down with a heavy sigh. "Max and Clint had better be tying up all the loose ends with Laker. That's all I can say."

Nick entered another series of figures into the system. "Come on, come on!" he growled, frowning impatiently at the tiny computer.

"Everything *did* go as planned, I hope," Zeke said.

Nick's mouth took on an unpleasant twist. "Not exactly." Waiting for the minicomp to process the information, Nick leaned forward, withdrawing a complimentary pack of slender cigars from a slot in the arm of the chair. "The barter didn't cover the amount we were hoping for . . ." He paused long enough to light up. "I put up the title to the *Victorious* for added insurance," he muttered in a cloud of smoke, choosing not to meet Zeke's look of shock.

"The *Victorious?*" Zeke Slater's normally low voice rose several registers in surprise.

No response.

"Y' hawked the Victorious?"

Finally Nick glanced over at him. "Temporarily. Yes."

"But . . ."

Nick returned his attention to the tiny computer. "We didn't exactly have a selection of options. None of us wanted the *Windstar* caught up in this scheme. She's our ticket out of here. I offered the *Victorious*. It's that simple."

"Sacrificing the *Victorious*? Simple?" Zeke emitted a snort of doubt. "I don't think so, pal."

"The *Victorious,*" he muttered again. Shaking his head in disbelief. Zeke fell silent, as if trying to assimilate something so incredulous.

Nick ignored him. All he cared about was getting Tressa and getting the hell out of there.

"So," Zeke said at last, his mouth still quirking with humor, "how'd you manage to pull it off with the *Victorious* still sitting in home port."

"Let's put it this way. I would have been back here a hell of a lot sooner if it'd been easy."

"Once this transaction is complete," Nick continued without glancing up, "administration will automatically check our account, find us good, and turn Tressa over with a smile. After the arena takes their cut, the records will officially show that the balance went into Kendyl's account."

Nick paused long enough to turn to his friend. "Thanks to the skills of some computer whiz over at Laker, the borrowed funds will remain in Kendyl's account in all of about ten minutes. Then . . . suddenly everything will vaporize back into Laker's holdings without a trace."

"So everyone's smiling except Kendyl," Zeke finished. "You know, of course, that he's not going to take this lying down."

Nick entered a final answer into the computer. "Probably

not, but there's damn little he'll be able to do about it. The records will show both the deposit and his withdrawal.''

Grinning, Zeke merely shook his head. ''I hope you plan to be out of this hellhole by the time it all hits the fan, pal.''

The message SALE CONCLUDED flashed onto the tiny screen.

''She's mine!'' Nick muttered, jumping to his feet. ''Now to find Pay Station C-6.''

Zeke was grinning like a idiot.

''What?'' Nick asked, his tone defensive.

''She's yours, huh? And here all this time I thought *we* were buying her freedom.''

Refusing to take the bait, Nick turned toward the exit. ''I just want to collect 'er and get the hell outta this place!''

''Whew! Forty . . . five . . . thousand!'' Zeke drawled, easily matching Nick's stride as they shouldered their way through the crowd. ''Hell, that's almost as much as you paid for the *Victorious!* And to think you hawked 'er. For a woman, at that! I never thought I'd see the . . .''

That did it! Rounding on Zeke, Nick caught him by his jacket and slammed him hard against the wall. ''If you don't get off my back, Slater, you and I are going to have a serious discussion when this is all over.''

''Good,'' Zeke retorted, still grinning. '' 'Cause whether you know it or not, Banner, you could use a little enlightening.''

The smirk on Zeke's face further incensed Nick. He was already annoyed at the transparency of certain feelings—feelings even he didn't want to see.

With a growl and an abrupt release of Zeke's jacket, Nick turned on his heel and headed for the pay stations.

''Just answer the question,'' the paymaster said, looking up at Nick from his terminal.

''Like I said, if you'd check that computer of yours, you'd find I just went through all this back in the arena.''

344

The man's lips thinned with anger. "Yes . . . or no?"

"Yes!" he snapped through gritted teeth. "Just like it says on the records . . . if you'd look." Nick released a heavy sigh, his irritation and impatience growing. "How much longer do you expect this to take?"

The paymaster returned his concentration to the computer. "You'll have your merchandise just as soon as I'm finished." He hesitated. "But if you continue arguing every time I ask a question, you're going to be here awhile."

Nick was angry, keyed up. Hating the wait, he lifted his sights, scanning the arena. "Where is she, anyway?"

"She's back here. They're calming 'er now."

"They're what?"

"Tranquilizing 'er," the man clarified, once again stopping to glance up at Nick.

Barely leashing his fury, Nick's gaze shot over the man's shoulder. "Where is she?" he bellowed. In one lithe leap he vaulted over the counter, only to be met by two guards. Zeke, still on the other side, was held at bay by a third.

Nerve rods. Of course they'd have nerve rods, Nick realized belatedly, noticing the wandlike implements in their hands. With effects similar to a Ripper, the handheld weapons were just as illegal and just as dangerous.

Instantly assuming a submissive pose, with outstretched arms and splayed hands, Nick smiled pleasantly. "It's okay, fellas. It's all right. I'm under control now. Tell your boys to back off!" he said, casting a glance over his shoulder. "I'm not going to do anything. Okay?"

A nod from the paymaster and the guards reluctantly pulled back. "Now," he said, turning his angry gaze back to Nick, "get back where you belong. And stay there!"

His rage banked but ready to flare, Nick took the long way around rather than over the top again. "I don't want her drugged," he said with forced composure. "No drugs!"

It was obvious the man was taking his time. Nick watched him for all of about ten seconds before slamming his fists on the counter. "Cancel the damn drugs, I said! Now!"

"Okay, okay." The man shrugged. "You want a hysterical bitch on your hands, mister, you got it." With that he hit the intercom. "Cancel the sedative on E-2058." He turned his gaze back to Nick. "Your ID plate."

Searing the man with a look that dared him to call Tressa a bitch again, Nick produced his ID and waited while payment was electronically deposited into Kendyl's account. Then he waited some more for Tressa. He was as tense as a coiled spring and the guards watched him warily while he paced the floor, his eyes never straying far from the set of doors behind the counter.

Why was everyone moving in slow motion? At the rate they were going, he'd still be standing there waiting for Tressa while Kendyl's account was being sucked dry.

At last the doors slid open. Tressa.

"Stay right where you are 'til they bring her to you," the paymaster ordered. The warning in his tone plainly said that next time he wouldn't call off his thugs.

Sheer will and Zeke's steady hand planted firmly on his forearm kept Nick from charging over the top of the counter again. Tressa . . . Their eyes clung in mute appeal as her collar and shackles were removed.

"Dear God," he murmured, rocked to the core by the sight of her. Slowly shrugging out of his leather jacket, Nick took in every trembling inch of her. The tears, the darkened circles beneath her eyes, her quivering lower lip . . . the flimsy costume. But it was her muffled sob that became his undoing.

Unable to contain himself a moment longer, he broke free of Zeke's hold, closing the distance between himself and Tressa in only a few long strides.

"Get your hands off her!" he snarled, shoving one of the men away. And then she was in his arms, clinging to him, sobbing his name over the roaring din of his emotions. His heart wrenched as he drew her into the shelter of his embrace, pulling his jacket around her, covering her half-nakedness as he did so. Dear Lord, his hands were shaking.

"Tressa," he managed to whisper against her temple. "Are you all right?"

"Yes." She buried her face against his chest "I was so afraid."

"I know," he murmured, "I know." Fighting for control, willing himself to be calm, he tucked her head beneath his chin and held her tight. So intense was the force of passion rampaging within him, it threatened to choke off his very breath. She felt so right in his arms, so damn good. The intensity of it shocked him as she fit against the contours of his body like the missing piece of a puzzle.

Nick lowered his voice to speak for her ears only. "Kendyl . . . Did . . . did he hurt you?" he asked, running his hands over her lightly for signs of abuse.

"No. He just scared me. Oh, Nick . . ."

Feeling another shudder course through her, Nick's hold tightened, his face grim as his gaze turned to Zeke. "Let *Windstar* know we're on our way.

"I'm taking you outta here," he said hoarsely, pressing a gentle kiss to her forehead.

Tressa pulled back, muffling a sob as she peered up at him. "I . . . I knew you were here. In the beginning. Then I didn't sense you anymore. I . . . I thought you had gone."

Nick froze, his heart wrenched anew by her words. "And why the devil would I leave?" he asked.

"The cost had risen so high . . ." she paused. "And . . . then I remembered the things you'd said."

"Ah, Tressa . . ." He sighed, tenderly cupping her face between his hands. "I only said those things to convince you to go with Zeke. I wanted you safe."

Drowning in the depths of her eyes, he lowered his head and tenderly kissed her parted lips, his touch like a whisper. "I never meant for you to take off like you did," he murmured against her mouth.

"Nick?" It was Zeke's penetrating voice that brought

Nick's dark head up. "We've gotta go, pal! *Now!*"

Nick nodded in understanding, peeling Tressa's arms from about his neck. "Here, let's get this on," he said gently, guiding her arms into the sleeves of his heavy jacket. It nearly swallowed her up, dropping to below her hips, the tips of her fingers barely peeking out from beneath the sleeves.

"I was so afraid," she chattered on. "I thought someone else had bought me and . . ."

"Never," he said, quickly fastening the front closures.

"But the cost . . ."

"Forget the damn cost. You're safe, Tressa; that's what counts." He reached for her hand. "Come on. We've got to hurry."

"But all that money. Where did you . . . I mean, how could you possibly . . ."

"The *Victorious*," he bit out.

Nick missed the look of incredulity written on Tressa's face as he caught her arm and headed her toward the exit.

Chapter Thirty-one

Nick set a fast pace as he led the way back along the congested corridor. Tressa walked double time trying to keep up. Within minutes they were entering the lift tube that would take them directly to the docking center.

"Now remember," he said, turning to Zeke, "when we enter the hangar you know what to do."

Zeke nodded. "I'll go on ahead as if we're not together."

"And Tressa," Nick said, reaching for her hands, "I hate doing this, but for all practical purposes you must appear as my property." He began wrapping a cord about her hands. "Try to look submissive, drugged. You know . . . hang your head, your eyes downcast. This isn't tight," he added. "If you had to, you could get free."

The lift slowed to a stop. "Ready?"

"As I'll ever be," Zeke muttered.

Nick took a deep breath. "With any luck we'll be long gone by the time Kendyl discovers his loss."

Zeke strode through the door first, as if bent on his own

destination. Nick stepped through next, scanning the hangar as Tressa followed.

Everything seemed as before, with longshoremen busily loading and unloading cargo holds. Tressa was careful to maintain a slave's submissive pose as they moved forward, making their way toward the *Windstar*.

Some of the ships were quite heavily armed, especially the one they were passing. Banner's eyes narrowed. Was that gun turret pointed their way on purpose?

Geez, your nerves are shot, an inner voice taunted.

Hell, yes, his nerves were shot. Drawing his arm about Tressa, he picked up the pace.

Are you taking Tressa back to Loring? You actually think you can go back to the way things were? To the life you led before she entered it?

The devil of it was, whether he admitted it or not, Tressa had become the focal point of his existence, turning his perfectly contented world upside down with just the brilliance of her smile.

It was the jolt of at last holding her quaking body in his arms that had blown his final resolve. In the space of a heartbeat she'd shattered his iron control, the self-discipline he so prided himself on when it came to women.

Ah, yes, he'd sampled his share of feminine charms, even had his favorites, the ones he'd call upon when he'd hit port. But not one of them could make him burn for her. Not one could penetrate his wall of cool detachment.

So what is it about this little slip of a girl that has you all tied up in knots? And why did your hands shake when you held her? God forbid you should fall in love!

Forcing the thought from his mind, Nick's scowl deepened as he recalled the last time he'd fallen in love, and the vow he'd made that no woman would ever again own his heart.

But Tressa's different. She's not like the others . . . not like Linnae.

The inner argument quickly faded as the *Windstar* came

into view. "We're almost there, Tress." The *Windstar* was three bays away now and, from the strobe lights flashing at the tips of her wings, Max was preparing her for lift.

"Tressa!"

They turned to find Burke Sinclair rushing to catch up with them.

Tressa gasped. "Burke! What are you . . ."

"Oh, thank God, you're okay" Sinclair swept her into his arms. "I was so afraid someone else had bought you."

Nick's gaze slid to Tressa, finding her reaction to Sinclair interesting. Odd how she offered him no lover's greeting, no warmth of recognition, not even a smile of relief.

"I was the one bidding against you," Sinclair offered, directing his attention to Nick.

Nick remained guarded, silently assessing Sinclair with impassive coldness. There was something about the guy he didn't like. And how the hell had he managed to clear Steel's security?

"Are you okay? Did they hurt you? Here, let's get these hands untied," Sinclair rambled on.

"I'm fine," Tressa insisted as she attempted to withdraw from his embrace. "Nick saved me," she added.

Sinclair stopped tugging at her bindings long enough to brush a kiss across her lips. "Darling," he murmured, "I was so worried about you."

Tressa drew back sharply. "As you can see, I'm okay."

Nick's eyes narrowed. Impassive coldness flashed to hostile outrage. In fact, if it hadn't been for the roboloader scurrying between them with a train of four cars in tow, Sinclair would have been choking on his teeth.

"I want to thank you for rescuing Tressa," Sinclair offered, leveling his gaze on Nick over the top of the passing cargo.

Nick's emotions were just barely leashed by the time the last car passed. "No problem," he said, his voice low and taut as he closed the distance between them. "Look, Sinclair, we'd just love to stand here and chat with you, but

I'm afraid we're in a bit of a hurry.'' His gaze shifted to Tressa. "Let's go."

Sinclair's hand stopped her. "I'll take her from here, Banner."

Banner's gaze slid to the iron grip Sinclair had on Tressa's arm. "I don't think so." His voice was dangerously soft as his eyes lifted again to meet Sinclair's.

"Tressa will be safer with me than with you." A hint of a smirk crossed Sinclair's mouth. "You're in deep shi . . . trouble, Banner, whether you know it or not. I don't know what you did back there, but some guy's madder than the devil about something. I'm getting Tressa out of here before all hell breaks loose and . . ." Sinclair's words died in his throat as a blue energy beam lashed out of nowhere, narrowly missing Nick and dropping Sinclair instead. Tressa fell with him, and for a frightful instant Nick thought she'd been hit too.

It was hard telling just who the target had been, and Nick wasn't waiting around to find out. In the space of a heartbeat he'd jerked his gun from its holster and, swearing violently, yanked Tressa up and behind a freight sled as another blue lance sliced through the air where they'd been standing. The energy beam struck a power ramp instead, showering the area with sparks and reducing the side of equipment to a mound of molten slag.

The stench of hot metal, ozone, and burned flesh filled the air, along with shouting as people scattered everywhere, dropping everything, leaping off machinery like rats off a sinking ship.

Nick hunkered down by Tressa's side, weapon poised. "Are you all right?"

Tressa nodded woodenly.

"You sure?"

"Yes," she said, tearing her eyes from Sinclair's lifeless body.

It took only a fraction of a second to figure out where the shots had come from. "Stay down," he said as he leveled his sights on a stack of cargo pallets about sixty feet down the corridor and took aim. Squeezing the trigger three times, he felt the weapon buck in his hand as it ripped through the partition of pallets in three evenly spaced points.

Nothing.

Had he missed?

As if in answer, a man suddenly staggered out into the opening, gripping his belly as he collapsed in the middle of the corridor.

Reaching for Tressa's hand, Nick hauled her to her feet. "Move!" he rasped, propelling her forward as they advanced toward the *Windstar*. Again they darted behind cover as another missile of light knifed over their heads, severing the arm of a docking crane directly in front of them. With an eerie groan, the fixture listed, dangling precariously by a single cable.

Nick heard the dull thud of another body hitting the deck somewhere off to his left. In one fluid motion he whirled on the sound, weapon aimed.

"Just thought I'd drop in and help even the odds."

Banner exhaled sharply. "It's about time you showed up," he hollered over the cacophony of shouting and Klaxons.

Zeke crouched down by Nick's side. "I saw Sinclair get it."

"Yeah."

A slug whined passed them, hit an abutment, and screamed down the passageway.

Nick returned the fire. "Stupid bastard's using high-velocity ammo."

Though the likelihood of a slug penetrating the hull of the city was slim, it was always a possibility. The odds doubled, however, with the use of high-velocity ammunition.

Nick's gaze slid to the *Windstar,* eyes narrowing as he gauged the remaining distance. It was at least another twenty yards. "Tressa, come here. Keep your head down!"

My God, he thought, watching her crawl over to him. To think what she'd been through these last six days. Most women he knew, with the exception of a few female pilots, would be blathering lumps of hysteria by now. His esteem for her rose even higher when he threw his arm about her and discovered that beneath that brave exterior she was trembling. "Tressa, you see that stack of crates over there?"

"Yes."

"When I say the word I want you to run as fast as you can and duck in behind them. Okay?"

"I'm not going anywhere without you!"

"We'll be right behind you, Tress. Hey, Slater?" Nick shouted over the uproar. "Remember Fletcher's Haven?"

Zeke merely grinned.

"What do you say we spice up the action?" Nick turned to Tressa. "Ready?"

She nodded hesitantly.

"Remember, keep low and we'll be right behind you. "Okay . . . go!"

Nick turned to Zeke. He punctuated his suggestion by firing a few well-placed potshots at a nearby ship, then bolted behind the crates. But within a matter of seconds a small war had erupted between neighboring pirate ships.

Under the shield of mayhem, Nick, Tressa, and Zeke raced for the *Windstar*, ducking between ships, hiding behind equipment, and dodging energy beams, bullets, and pieces of flying metal.

Within fifty feet of the *Windstar* Nick saw Zeke's body jolt with the force of impact. He'd taken a slug in his shoulder, yet his pace faltered only once.

"Hurry!" Max hollered, grasping Tressa's hand as Nick propelled her through the main hatch first.

"He's been hit," Nick shouted as Zeke stumbled through the entry next.

"I'm okay!" Zeke growled, making his way for the helm as Nick secured the hatch.

Puffing and panting, they followed Max into the control room. Zeke eased into a seat and began tapping a directive into the on-board computer. A shiny trail of blood glistened down the back of his leather jacket.

Max flipped an overhead toggle. "It's going to be rough. Brace yourselves."

"You okay, Tressa?" Marc said, briefly looking up from the controls.

"Glad you're back, sunshine," Clint added.

Nick cleared his throat at Clint's double take at Tressa's half-clad body. "Tressa! Over here!" Calling her to the far end of the command console, he motioned for her to take a seat, then dropped into the seat across from her. "We need you to monitor the acceleration panels."

Clint returned his focus to the monitor, grinning at Nick's posessiveness. The smirk was soon wiped off his face when the *Windstar* reeled under the force of a direct hit, the jolt pitching them against the constraints of their harnesses.

"We just lost our portside shield," Marc snapped. "I hate to rush you or anything, but this would be a perfect time to take off."

Clint glanced up at the view screens, taking in the raging destruction going on outside, the madness, the living inferno that Steel's space port had become in just a matter of minutes. "I see by the war zone out there, Nick, you've managed to once again demonstrate your remarkable command of charm and discretion."

Nick muttered something crude under his breath and feverishly entered the directive that would free *Windstar* from all umbilical connections with Steel.

It was tangible—the sense of urgency that filled the air. Fingers danced across keyboards, chimes proclaimed the completion of procedures, and indicators pulsed their response.

"Docking collars are disengaged," Nick called out at last. "She's free as a bird."

"Affirmative."

"Tressa," Nick said, trying to keep his voice calm, "this panel, here, operates just like the one on the *Victorious*. It's just bigger, that's all." Leaning across the space between them, he pointed to a bank of red-lit indicators. "As soon as these turn green, let us know. You know what to do after that. Any questions?"

"No," she said, studying the panel before her.

Nick adjusted her safety harness. "You'll want this good and tight. It's going to be a rough lift."

"Switching to forward screens," Zeke said.

"Nick . . ." Tressa whispered, her gaze riveted on Zeke. "Look, he's bleeding, bad."

"I know." He knew she wanted to help him, could see it in her eyes. But without another word Tressa turned to the console and the task he'd assigned her.

"Clint," Max shouted, "I need a straight-up reading!"

"We're on line and we reach max in . . . eleven seconds."

"Warning!" a mechanical voice interrupted. "This ship is not designed . . ."

"Somebody shut that damn thing up!"

Seconds seemed like hours as the *Windstar* built thrust, its powerful engines rattling every bolt and rivet in her frame.

"Acceleration panels have been calibrated. All lights are green," Tressa called out, her voice raised against the resounding rumble of straining drives.

Nick silently regarded her no-nonsense ability to follow through with the task he'd given her, even in the face of disaster. Who would have ever thought . . .

"Let's get the hell out of here!" Max hollered, slamming the palm of his hand against a large red knob.

The *Windstar* shuddered violently. With a thunderous roar she lifted under full emergency power, triggering a host of alarms and pulling some heavy Gs—the sort that didn't just mildly pin you to your seat, but drove you down with a crushing weight as it passed a wave of blackness before your eyes.

Fighting to remain conscious, Nick cast his eyes at the overhead monitor. All around them, other ships were also attempting to escape the destruction, some succeeding, others never making it past their docking berths before being annihilated.

After what seemed forever they cleared Steel's boundaries. The ship's thrust decreased sharply, and the tremendous weight lifted off their chests.

"Geeeez."

"Everyone okay?" Max called out. "Zeke? How you doing over there?"

"I'm all right," he muttered.

Nick turned to Tressa. "You okay?"

"I think so."

There was a brief moment of revelry, with everyone breathing a sigh of relief—everyone, that is, except Nick. There was just one problem that still had his attention: Would they pass the security satellite unharmed? As unsettling as the thought was, Nick couldn't help but wonder if the satellites had been programmed to snuff them out the minute their ID was confirmed.

He'd been watching bright flashes of light periodically flaring up on the forward viewscreen. It could even be that the Gate was closed, that those flashes of light were actually ships being destroyed, ships who dared to challenge the system. Nick silently continued monitoring the view screen.

And then it happened: the blinding flash of a nuclear explosion that briefly flared so bright, it lit the entire control room. When it died Nick switched the monitors to high mag, as the core of the explosion continued flickering intermittently.

"What the blazes was that?" Max asked, his eyes riveted to the monitor.

A moment of silence passed as Nick studied the screen. "The weapons satellite." Grinning, he turned to face them. "Looks like some of them combined forces and blew it to hell. The Gate is open, ladies and gentlemen! Let's go home!"

Tressa stood before the mirror, admiring the beautiful emerald nightgown. It was Delta's, and on a crazy whim she'd tried it on, just for the fun of it, before getting dressed. Glancing over her shoulder at her reflection, she admired the open backline, with its tiny crisscross ribbons lacing from her shoulder blades down to the small of her back. Twirling around, she counted ten tiny green bows marching their way down from a dipping neckline to her belly. The revealing gap between each bow was obviously meant for stirring the imagination.

Tressa smiled, wondering if Max had chosen the gown as a gift, or if Delta had simply surprised him in it one night.

The cabin she occupied was their private suite—Max and Delta's. Max had insisted she use the room. Powerless to argue the matter, Tressa hadn't protested when Nick steered her down the corridor.

"I just want a shower," she'd whispered to him.

He'd wrapped a comforting arm around her and whispered back, "I think that can be arranged."

With a heavy sigh, Tressa ran a trembling hand through her still damp hair. Her arms ached from being wrenched to her feet and hauled to safety. Her ears still rang from the intense noise of weapons resounding throughout the docking center and the answering report of Nick's gun at close range.

She'd lived a hellish nightmare over the last six days, one that now left her dizzy in its aftermath.

Just as she'd feared, Zeke's injury was far worse than he'd let on. The charade quickly ended, however, when he tried to get up and passed out cold.

The lack of high-tech equipment made Tressa's first attempt at extracting an embedded slug twice the challenge. Leery of further damaging surrounding muscle, she worked with painstaking diligence, grateful that Zeke remained unconscious during the procedure. Thank God he would be all right.

Tressa's thoughts shifted. Burke Sinclair would never know what hit him, while she, on the other hand, would never forget. With her own scream still echoing in her mind, she vividly recalled Burke's lifeless body dragging her down to the deck.

And then, just like the handsome dark knight out of her favorite Terran fairy tale, Nick was there, weapon in hand as he yanked her to her feet, hauling her to safety in one fluid motion.

Pensively, Tressa's gaze slid to the viewport and the darkness beyond. One hour had lapsed since they'd passed Steel's disabled weapons satellite. One hour since the control room had burst into a madhouse of cheers . . . and Nick had swept her up in his arms and kissed her so soundly, so thoroughly, her head was still spinning. *Nick.* His name lingered on her mind, just as the touch of his kiss lingered upon her lips.

Tressa found herself longing once again for the protectiveness of his arms, for the comforting sound of his heart thudding against her ear.

With a sigh, Tressa's gaze moved to the bed where Nick's leather jacket lay. With it, another private reflection surfaced—one of wearing that jacket. *His* jacket—warm with his body heat, its weight pure bliss.

Tressa moved to the bed and picked up the heavy black garment. Clutching it tightly, her eyes drifted closed as she breathed in its lusty scent. The essence of Nick, a heady mixture of leather, tobacco, cold steel, and something so blatantly masculine, a jolt coiled in the pit of her stomach in response.

"Tressa?" A light knocking sounded at the door. "You awake?"

Nick! With a sharp intake of breath, Tressa dropped the jacket.

Oh, damn . . . oh, damn. Here she was, still in Delta's flimsy nightgown! She should never have tried it on!

"Just a minute," she called out, reaching for the gown's matching robe and quickly slipping it on. Fussing with the clasp at her throat, Tressa took one final look in the mirror. "No need to pinch your cheeks this time, Tress," she muttered, mortified at their telltale glow. She fluffed her hair with shaking fingers, arranging it loosely about her face and shoulders. Then, with a calming breath, she turned for the door.

"Hi," she all but sighed as the panel slid open, her voice sounding far too breathy. And damn if he didn't notice.

Glancing down at her with one eyebrow raised, Nick's mouth curved in that infamous half smile. "Hi, yourself."

Chapter Thirty-two

"Did I wake you?"

It was blatantly obvious that Nick was having difficulty dragging his eyes from the gown. Wanting to die of embarrassment and refusing to show it, Tressa hid behind a radiant smile. "Are you kidding? I couldn't sleep if my life depended upon it."

Nick regarded her thoughtfully. "Mind if I come in?"

"Of course not." Tressa stepped aside as he entered and crossed the cabin to the viewport. His hair swept back like shiny black satin, nearly reaching the top of his shoulders. Her gaze was drawn to the smoothness of his jaw. He'd shaved, shedding his six-day growth along with the roguish look of a pirate. Either way, he was gorgeous.

"For as long as I live," she began, joining him at the portal, "I'll never forget this view. Ever."

"Nor I."

They weren't discussing the same thing. Not at all. Sensing his lazy inspection, Tressa nervously toyed with the clasp at the base of her throat. The tightening coil in the pit of her stomach wasn't helping matters either.

"I've never known a time when I feared for myself," he began, his voice rough with suppressed emotion. "But when I realized you were gone . . . When I couldn't find you I knew fear. And then, when I saw you on the auction platform . . ." His words trailed off.

Time hung suspended for a moment, the only sounds the soft hissing of ventilation and the constant pulse of the drive system.

"Do you know what you've done to me, Irish?" Nick asked in a deep voice laden with sensuality.

Tressa didn't reply. She couldn't.

His hands slipped up her arms, bringing her closer. "You have any idea at all?"

Her heart slammed into her ribs. "No," she whispered.

Nick lowered his head, lightly touching her mouth with his own. "You've managed to bring my perfectly ordered world to a grinding halt," he murmured against her lips. "You've turned everything I've professed and believed in to vapor." His lips recaptured hers, more demanding this time.

Tressa didn't know how long she'd been leaning against him, eyes closed, lips parted and damp, before she realized Nick had stopped kissing her. Slowly she opened her eyes, half afraid of finding him thoroughly amused.

What she found was not amusement, nor laughter, but luminous eyes, hooded and lambent with need. His hand moved to cup her cheek. "Life was so simple before I met you. I knew exactly what I thought, where I was headed, and what I wanted out of life. And now . . ."

Tressa knew she was lost when he began telling her how crazy with worry he'd been. How it had taken Zeke's heavy hand and calm words of reason to keep him seated . . . and then just barely.

"But . . . you would have been killed," she said softly.

"Probably."

At the force of his simple acknowledgment, Tressa swallowed and lightly touched the callused hand that cupped her cheek.

"What is it that draws me so to you?" he asked, searching her face. "Tell me, Irish, have you cast some Creohen spell on me?"

Tressa's senses reeled as his head descended, his lips once again meeting hers. Swallowing a moan, she was vaguely conscious of Nick's hand unfastening the small clasp at the base of her throat. Scarcely aware that in one easy motion the beautiful robe was slipping to the floor, leaving her standing before him in what seemed no more than ten tiny emerald bows.

His gaze, though soft as a caress, was so galvanizing it sent a shudder down her spine. She watched the color of his eyes deepen with feverish desire.

"Do you have any idea how beautiful you are?" Not waiting for a response Nick shifted, one arm sweeping beneath her knees, the other behind her shoulders.

For an instant the dimly lit cabin reeled as Tressa was lifted against his solid chest. Closing her eyes, she wrapped her arms about his neck and clung to him, aware that he was striding toward the wide curtained bed that sat low on a raised dais.

This is Nick, a small voice whispered. Her handsome knight who'd risked his life for her. And now she was safe in his arms.

Nick lowered her to her feet, allowing her to slide down the length of his body, letting her feel the blatant differences in their anatomies. "Emerald. It's a good color on you," he muttered thickly, slipping the gown's flimsy straps off her shoulders. Burying his hands in her mass of curls, he used his hold to gently tip her head back for his kiss, his tongue teasing the corners of her mouth, seeking entrance.

Eyes closed, her mouth flowering under his, Tressa allowed him to possess her with slow, sensuous thrusts of his tongue. She was only vaguely aware of his hands on the tiny closures down the front of her gown. When the first satin bow fell open Nick's lips were right there, searing a sensuous path down her throat to the newly exposed flesh.

A brief instant of panic flashed in Tressa's mind. "Nick," she breathed, "what if someone should come looking for us?"

She felt something suspiciously close to a smile pressed to the base of her throat.

"No one's going to come looking for us, Tressa."

A second bow collapsed and then a third, the gown opening wider with each conquest.

"But Clint . . ." she persisted.

"Isn't stupid. He won't intrude," Nick muttered against her heated flesh.

"But . . ."

"All right, Tressa" came his groan of resignation. "For you." With that, he leaned around and, with a lazy motion, flipped a small control switch on the nightstand. The electronic sound of a locking door echoed through the cabin.

"Now . . . where was I? Ah, yes . . ." Picking up where he left off, Nick continued kissing his way down to the fourth tiny green bow. By the fifth the soft material was slipping to the floor, pooling at her feet, leaving Tressa standing naked to Nick Banner's hungry gaze.

"Dear God," he rasped.

With a flush of heat kissing her cheeks, Tressa stifled a sob, abandoning herself to the whirl of sensation that began as Nick dipped his head to cover and possess her mouth once more. His hand moved to cup one delicate globe, weighing it in his palm, tracing its outline, his thumb teasing a taut peak.

"I want you, Tressa. God in heaven, I want you." The words were wrenched from his throat.

He was trembling, Tressa realized, and for what she suspected to be the first time in Nick Banner's hedonistic life his cool control was slipping fast.

And to think she was the cause. To think . . . A moan

tore from the back of her throat as Nick dipped his head, his hot mouth replacing his hand on her breast. Savoring the erotic sensation, Tressa's eyes drifted closed as he continued his gentle assault.

Then he stopped, leaving the cooling air to chill her kiss-dampened flesh. "Listen to me, Tressa," he grated out, capturing her chin. "If you have any objections to what's about to happen, you'd better speak up now."

This was Nick. And for Tressa the time for speaking up had long passed. There was no hesitation as she melted against him, gently lifting her hand to his face in response. Lightly touching his mouth with quivering fingers, she allowed her heated gaze to communicate for her.

Nick captured her hand, pressing a kiss to her palm. "Very well," he said with gentle finality. And he pulled away.

Heart pounding, knees weakening, Tressa sat down on the edge of the bed, watching as Nick worked the buttons down the front of his shirt, shrugged out of it, and tossed it to the floor. In breathless suspense Tressa's gaze slowly dropped from his magnificent face to the wide expanse of his chest—to the hands that were now moving to his belt. A soft clinking of metal echoed through the silence like thunder as he leisurely unbuckled his belt, allowing the ends to dangle loosely from their loops. The sight of him made her feel fluttery inside. Swallowing, she could only stare when he moved to his pants and began flipping open the metal studs—one by one.

Her stomach clenched. "Stars," she whispered, vividly recalling the last time he'd left her breathless. Tressa lifted her eyes to meet Nick's steady gaze. The memory was there for him too. She saw it in the slight narrowing of his eyes and the sensual twist of his mouth.

Out of nowhere the thought cut across Tressa's mind. *You know nothing about pleasing a man.* With a shiver she looked away, suddenly feeling very naive and unsure of herself. What if . . . she didn't please him?

Nick hesitated, measuring her for a moment, hands poised at the waistband of his open pants. In one stride he was standing before her, drawing her up into his arms and holding her.

"Second thoughts, Irish?" he whispered against her ear.

"No," came her hushed reply.

He flashed her a smile. "Feeling a little afraid?"

"No," she lied, then nodded, spilling a curly lock of hair down over her forehead. ". . . Just a little."

"I won't hurt you," he reassured her, gently lowering her to the bed, the mattress dipping beneath the weight of his knee. He kissed her languorously.

Tressa had braced herself for fierce passion, but instead there was a gentle, slow, arousing glide of his tongue on hers. As if he, too, wanted to savor this moment.

He left her momentarily to finish removing his boots and pants. And though her face flamed with the reality of what was about to follow, Tressa could not look away as he slid his pants down his muscular thighs. She knew his powerful body, recognized the faint bruises he still bore, the scars of previous fights; knew the feel of his heated flesh beneath her touch, his scent.

And then he turned to face her, his face framed by his glorious dark hair, his body awesomely muscled and glistening in the soft light.

Tressa's senses spun as she took in every solid, rock-hard inch of his male strength. "Stars," she whispered, swallowing once. Twice.

He was magnificent, stunning even, as a flash of feminine apprehension crossed her mind. She focused all thought on his face, his sensuous mouth, those magnetic sapphire eyes that were regarding her with a look so intense, it made her breath catch.

And then he was sliding onto the bed beside her, his weight bliss, his scent pure heaven. "I said I'm not going to hurt you. I meant it." His voice was distant, a million

miles away as he brushed the tip of her nose with a feath-
erlike kiss.

Tressa was pleasured by the sensual exploration of his
hands over, around, up and down her trembling body. She
sighed and gasped and squirmed and even giggled as his
hands, lips, and tongue played over her sensitive flesh. Her
giddy laughter turned to a slow moan when his hand
dropped to the apex of her thighs and gently sought entrance.

"You have the damnedest effect on me, little enchant-
ress," she heard him murmur as his skillful fingers began
working a new kind of magic.

Though shocked and embarrassed by what he was doing
to her, the sensations he was creating, Tressa sighed in total
submission to his masterful touch. Turning her face into his
shoulder, she breathed in his scent as her body arched
against his hand.

"Nick . . . please . . ." The words came out in gasps as
she tugged at his arm, trying to pull his hard body closer,
but she was no match against his superior strength.

"No, Tressa. Not yet, sweetheart. Not until you're
ready."

"But I *am* ready."

Languorous laughter filled his tone. "No, darlin'. You're
not. I don't want to hurt you."

"But . . . you're *not* hurting me." She was breathless.

"I know," came his resonant voice. The tempo continued as he nipped at her ear, running his tongue around the
outer shell before blazing a trail of hot, moist kisses down
her arched throat. "Just let it happen," he murmured.

Imprisioning one of her hands above her head, he began
drawing sensuous circles with the pad of his thumb on her
open palm. With the rhythm perfectly matching what he
was doing to her with his other hand, the dual attention
sent currents of molten desire surging through Tressa.

"Come on," he whispered. "Come on."

In her innocence Tressa wasn't sure just what it was he

wanted from her, but suddenly it didn't matter any more when his tongue slipped into her mouth with strong, impelling strokes.

The heat began, and Tressa let her body fly with the new sensations, crying out his name in final surrender, her body racked with spasms as light danced along her every nerve ending.

"Oh, Nick . . ."

Then his body was covering hers, his face harsh with passion. Tressa slid her small hands up his back, over straining, corded muscles. At last she cupped his face, pulling his mouth down to hers, meeting his kiss with unbridled desire.

With thunder still echoing in her ears and the light dance still shimmering along her frayed nerves, she felt Nick's weight shift, his knee parting her thighs to accommodate his body. Moving into position above her, he lifted her hips, murmuring words she wasn't quite catching as his hardness probed against her.

"Oh, my God," he murmured as he slid into her, filling her slowly, pushing past the fragile barrier of her virginity so easily, she hardly noticed the pain through the shimmering luminescence of fulfilled passion.

Hair spilled over his shoulders like shiny black rivulets of water, and Tressa slid her fingers into the heavy mane, glorying in its silken texture. He withdrew slightly, then slowly sank into her again. Tressa gasped, welcoming the hard, swollen length of him as he set a rhythmic motion.

So this was the magic. At last . . . the fantasy she'd only dreamed of. Tressa's gaze lifted to Nick's intense face. He was magnificent. The ecstasy of the building momentum was etched into the straight line of his sensuous mouth and heavy-lidded eyes—eyes, dark with passion as he rocked against her harder and harder, his flesh becoming slick, his breathing ragged.

Gripping his muscled biceps, Tressa held on, instinctively matching his cadence, urging him on with a passion of her own until she felt his body stiffen violently. Until his eyes slid closed, his neck arched, and deep inside she felt him shudder as he gave himself up to the mindless rush of release.

They lay still joined, Tressa clinging to him, cherishing the rapid rise and fall of his chest, the steady thud of his heartbeat. It was a long time before either of them stirred.

When Nick finally rolled to his side he brought Tressa with him, pulling a feathery light cover over them as he cradled her in the circle of his arms. Exhausted, they slept until Nick awoke and roused her with teasing kisses, and they spent the next several hours in passionate loveplay. At times it was slow and tender, as they learned the secrets of each other's bodies. Other times it was hard and fast as they satisfied a driving hunger, shocking in its intensity.

"I never said thank you," Tressa whispered as she lay curled into him, her head on his chest, her arm drawn across his belly.

"Thank you?" he asked. "Is that a generic thank you? Or for something in particular?"

Tressa laughed. "For rescuing me." Inhaling the musky male scent of him, she gazed up lovingly into his eyes. "And for protecting me."

Nick sobered. Cupping her face in his hand, he held her gently. "I'd like to continue protecting you, Tressa." His tone was husky, his gaze intent. "I want to take care of you. I was thinking I'd like you to travel with me for a while. I know of places you couldn't imagine in your wildest dreams."

Tressa hesitated, not sure of just what he was asking. *Go with him for a while? As his wife?*

Nick slid a finger beneath her chin, tipping her face up to his. "Say yes," he murmured, nailing her with his magnetic gaze. He placed a soft kiss on the tip of her nose. "Yes," he coaxed, that easy smile playing at the corners of his mouth.

Tressa swallowed. "I, uh . . . I don't know what to say."

"Say yes." His lips brushed against hers as he spoke. "Look," he continued, drawing back. "It isn't something we have to commit ourselves to. I just thought that since you're so taken with some of the off-planet sights, you'd enjoy seeing a few places I had in mind." He grinned. "I'm not asking you to sail the stars with me forever, lady. I just figured we'd travel around for a little while, then see what happens." He chuckled. "Hell, too long on the *Victorious* and we'd drive each other crazy."

Where were the words of lasting love and commitment?

Realization struck her like a bolt of lightning: He wants a mistress!

So what did you expect, flowers and promises of undying love? The silent voice laughed. *From the notorious Nick Banner? How naive. He's offering you a glorified version of an Accommodation Agreement with no strings attached.*

But what about the love they'd just shared?

From Nick Banner? All physical.

The memory came flooding back of his deep voice whispering rough words of passion against her throat. Shocking things that had her heart pounding as he told her how good she made him feel and how good he was going to make her feel. All physical.

And you walked into this with your eyes open.

It was a blow. Suddenly her dreams of love and the fulfillment of her fantasies were crashing down around her. Tressa pulled away from him, smiling warmly, betraying none of the hurt she was feeling inside. "Really, Nick, I'm going to have to pass on your offer," she began with cool reserve. "I don't think I have what it takes to survive in your intense world."

Nick casually levered himself up on one elbow. "I see."

"In fact," she went on, sitting up, "to be truthful, shipboard life is beginning to bore me. I can hardly wait to get back home again."

"Home," he repeated, holding her with a hard look. Then, as if having come to a decision, he rose languidly from the bed, unconcerned about his nudity as he stalked to the pile of clothes on the floor and retrieved his pants.

"All right, Tressa." There was a note of calm finality to his words as he jerked his pants up over his hips. "I'll take you home. Back to Daddy."

"Back to . . . And just what's that supposed to mean?" she sputtered, bristling with indignation.

"You figure it out." He shrugged into his shirt, not even bothering with the buttons.

Keeping a tight grip on the covers, Tressa rose from the bed. "How dare you insult me with your degrading offer. I'll have you know I've turned down proposals that make this lowly invitation of yours nothing more than a simple Accommodation Agreement."

"Is that right," he replied, hopping on one foot while yanking a boot on the other.

Dragging the covers with her, Tressa crossed the cabin and faced him toe-to-toe. "I'm afraid my goals are just a little higher than free passage onboard a cargo ship!"

Nick's mouth curved into a chilling smile. "Believe me, Irish," he said in a dangerous tone, "it wouldn't have been free. There's a price for everything, and I assure you, you'd have paid dearly."

Tressa slapped him. Hard. Straight across his stubborn jaw. "What woman with a lick of sense would agree to fly around with you onboard that . . . that bucket of rivets you so fondly call the *Victorious?* What woman would even consider traipsing from one stinking space port to the next, while you flirt with every pretty face you come across."

Nick froze, the crimson print of her hand forming on his cheek. Those eyes—oh, those luminous eyes. Glazed with shock and disbelief, his eyes reflected both the pain and the anger her empathic mind was so strongly broadcasting. In a moment of true awareness Tressa knew she had just done something irrevocable.

"And you think *my* world's intense," he said in a low voice. With a short bark of laughter he continued, "Let me tell you something, lady. Since I've known you I've had kidnappers doggin' my trail, tracers onboard my ship, and a whole new set of scars and bruises to show for my efforts in savin' your hide.

"All that, sweetheart . . . *just for the record,* happens to be compliments of *your* world."

He took two strides toward the door, then stopped. Magnetic eyes blazed as he turned, raking her from head to toe. "By the way, thanks for the tumble. Best piece of fluff I've had in months."

Hitting the small plate on the wall with a doubled fist, the door hissed open. Without looking back, Nick Banner stalked from the cabin . . . taking Tressa's broken heart with him.

Chapter Thirty-three

Acacia, Port Imperial

Nick Banner's dark gaze was locked straight ahead as he sat in a secluded corner of the Outbounder. "Tressa." Her name slipped past his lips in a breath of longing. His eyes slid closed and, leaning forward on his elbows, he buried his head in his hands. Too much ale. Too much thinking. Too many damned memories and eight long years of trusting no one but himself.

Problem was, this time the liquor wasn't quite killing the memory. Hell, he couldn't seem to force himself to get drunk enough to quit thinking, let alone forget.

What the devil had happened? He'd been over it a thousand times in his mind. Everything had seemed so right between them . . . so damned good.

After all those years of perfecting his iron control, he'd let his guard down. Damn her for slipping past! Damn her for filling him with hope that there could be a future for them. And damn her to Steel for making him think she was different from the rest. Hell, he'd have given up everything for her.

He poured himself another portion of the harsh brew and swallowed it in one burning gulp, his throat working as it blazed a flaming trail to his belly. The devil of it was, it was no easier now than when he'd first left her.

Needing her was terrifying the hell out of him, and trying to quit needing her was bringing him to his knees.

"I hear that through the combined efforts of several large transporting companies, you'll soon be collecting a sizable reward for your handiwork on Steel."

Silence.

Slowly lifting his weary gaze, Nick's eyes rested upon a familiar face: Shara, her expression one of concerned appraisal. With a heavy sigh she dropped into a nearby chair. "At least for a while that hellhole will be shut down."

No response.

"You ever find out what happened to Kendyl?"

More silence. Then, "Marc saw Kendyl racing for the *Renegade* about five minutes before someone blew it to hell." Nick's voice was edged with steel.

"The *Renegade*? That's Kendyl's ship?"

"Used to be," Nick corrected.

Shara released a heavy sigh. "Thank God somebody got what they deserved."

Once again Nick fell into a brooding silence, but Shara's all-too-cheerful voice continued. "So, what are your plans for the reward? I guess now you'll be able to expand your transporting business as you've been dreaming of doing."

Banner's dark eyebrows drew together as he stared into the empty glass at his fingertips. Again a long moment of contemplation passed before he spoke. "I *was* planning on renovating the *Victorious*, enlarging the living quarters. But now . . ."

"For the love of lasers, Nick, this is the third day now that you've sat back here like this." She eyed the bottle.

"At least you're slowing down on the alcohol. Thank God for that."

"It's not working," came his grave response as he pushed the partially empty bottle aside. "I've tried my damnedest over the last week to get so drunk that I wouldn't even remember my own name, let alone . . ." He left the sentence hanging.

"Could it be you've misjudged her? Zeke seems positive she doesn't even think you love her."

"I don't." A moment passed. "And furthermore, I don't care what she thinks!"

"Sure you don't, darlin', and Saturn doesn't have rings. Talk to me, Nick. I've got all night."

Silence. Banner stared numbly at the stream of smoke trailing up from the cigar he'd left in the ashtray. "All I said was, I wanted to take care of her. What the devil was so wrong with that?"

"And what did she say?"

Silence. Then, "She slapped me." His dark head rose, his gaze meeting hers. "Can you believe that? She slapped me."

Shara leaned back, folding her arms, listening intently as Nick began unraveling an edited version of what had happened.

Lifting the cigar to his mouth, he inhaled slowly. "She said my offer was no better than a damned Accommodation Agreement," he muttered, smoke escaping with his words.

Shara astutely left him to his quiet introspection as he absently rolled ash off the tip of his cigar. Then his eyes narrowed. "Hell with 'er."

"Let me ask you this: Did you ever bother telling her how you feel about her?"

That brought his head up for a long, thought-filled pause. "Well?"

"Maybe not in so many words," he finally answered, his voice husky. "But I sure as hell showed her."

Shara shot him a twisted smile. "In other words, you

375

introduced her to your version of *hyperspaced docking*."

Nick attempted to right his shoulders, fixing her with a hard look. "That's a little crudely put."

"Put it anyway you like, darlin'. If you never bothered to tell her you loved her . . . especially after she gave herself to you, then you offered her nothing more than an Accommodation Agreement."

"I didn't, dammit! I was ready to give up everything for her."

"Did you tell her that? Or did you just assume she could read your mind?"

Frowning, Nick gathered his thoughts, absently fixing his heavy-lidded gaze across the room. "She does," he muttered thickly.

"Does what?"

His eyes slid closed in a lethargic blink. "Read minds," he answered, his gaze returning to Shara. "Damnedest thing . . . She's part Creohen, you know."

Shara's eyebrows rose. "Is she now? Well, Creohens don't read minds, Nick. They sense emotions."

"Emotions . . . minds . . . what the devil's the difference? I was burnin' for her. She knew it."

Shara nailed him with a long, scathing stare. "Y' know, I'm afraid I'd have done more than just slap that handsome face of yours. You'd have been on your knees sucking in drafts of air."

Nick glared at her beneath lowered brows, bewildered by her sudden hostility. "Why?" he asked. "Just what is it I've supposedly done that's so terrible?"

"Men," Shara muttered, shaking her head in utter disbelief. "While you've been sitting here drowning yourself in self-pity, did you ever stop to think that maybe all Tressa had to go on was her ability to sense emotions? You showed her lust, Nick. Certainly not love, not the words she needed to hear. In case you hadn't noticed, there's a big difference between the two. But to a Creohen it could be a bit confusing trying to decipher one from the other."

Shara rose from her chair. "Why don't you spend some time thinking about *that* instead of wallowing in denial?" Snatching the open bottle of ale off the table, she turned for the kitchen. "In the meantime I'm going to get you something to put in that belly of yours besides . . . *this*."

Nick's eyes slid closed as a bitter ache began working its way up from his heart to his throat. Feeling gut-punched all of a sudden, he swallowed convulsively against the searing bands of fire threatening to choke off his breathing.

He of all people should know what it meant to trust your heart to no one. *He*, the biggest cynic of them all, should understand the fear of rejection, the doubt, the hesitation.

Ah, God. Rejection could drive a man insane. It could cause an enamored young fool to bury himself in life-threatening assignments for two years on a harsh planet and not care whether he lived or died. It could cause him to keep an iron control on his emotions, never staying long enough to care for anyone. And it could force a man, so in need of love himself, to withhold the very words from the object of his adoration.

It could also cause a young woman who'd just given her heart and body to feel used and humiliated.

Yes, he understood now. And if he hadn't been so busy constructing his own walls, he'd have understood then, too. Even as he left her with Jonathan on Fletcher's World. Even as he walked away, not looking back until he'd reached the base of the gangplank. And only then turning to hold eye contact for a heart-stopping moment before imparting a cocky salute of dismissal.

Oh, yes, if he hadn't been so preoccupied warring with his own demons, fighting his own battle with distrust, the old fears, the skepticism, he would have understood why she'd refused his offer.

Tressa. The only good thing in his worthless, miserable life, and he'd walked away from her . . . *walked away from her!*

Was it too late? Would she give him a second chance?

Why should she? As she had pointed out, what woman would want to travel around from one stinking space port to the next, cooped up in a tight-quartered cargo ship with the likes of him? Besides, what could he say to excuse the things he'd said to her? That crack alone, about her being the best tumble he'd had in months, was unforgivable.

Still doubting, aren't you? Still listening to the old voice of fear? Afraid she'll reject you again? After all it's been two weeks since you left her. She's had plenty of time to get over you, hasn't she? Besides, even if you left this minute, it's a three-week trip to Terra Four.

Dragging a hand through his hair, Nick rose to his feet and reached for his jacket. If he were to take off right now, and if he pushed the *Victorious* to her limit, he could cut the three-week distance down to a little over two weeks. He'd done it before.

Leaving the Outbounder on a run, Nick climbed into the land craft and turned it for home. Damn, he needed a shower, but he'd worry about that onboard the ship. Right now all he wanted was to collect TiMar and get the hell into space as fast as possible.

TiMar. With luck, the little desert cat would be the key to opening Tressa's heart.

Terra Four, Port Ireland
Two weeks later

With a heavy sigh, Tressa laid the stack of papers aside. It had been over a month since she'd last seen Nick. Over a month of burying herself in long hours of work at LorTech and volunteer service at the Med Center.

Having stopped at Acacia only long enough to drop off his father and brothers, Nick had wasted no time making arrangements with Jonathan to rendezvous at Fletchers World, a halfway point between Acacia and Terra Four.

Despite his wounded shoulder, Zeke had insisted on going with them, using the argument that he could heal just as well onboard ship as he could at home. And with Nick stalking around like a rogue bull *Paka,* his brooding mood becoming darker with each day, Tressa had been thankful for Zeke's company. Besides, while caring for his shoulder, she and Zeke became friends.

During the ten-day voyage Zeke had made several attempts to reason with her, offering excuses for Nick's conduct. No matter how sincere, Zeke's apologies didn't cut it, especially for that remark about being the best lay he'd had in months . . . a comment she suspected Zeke knew nothing about.

"Thank goodness you're still here!"

Jerked from her thoughts, Tressa looked up to see LorTech's night custodian standing in the doorway.

"There's a commercial crate of some sort downstairs with your name on it," he said.

Tressa sat back, frowning. "At the front desk? Wonder why no one brought it to my office?" She glanced back up at him. "Thank you, Patrick."

"I think no one wanted to get near it," he offered hesitantly, "It . . . well, it . . . It growls."

Pinning him with a questioning look, Tressa slowly rose from her chair. "It growls?"

The *Victorious* slid in low and slow into Port Ireland's space port, her distress beacons flashing as Nick banked the ship into a turn, feathering the damaged thrusters.

Actually, he'd made good time, even better than he'd hoped. But pushing the ship beyond her limits had taken its toll. Trouble had begun two days out from Terra Four, when the ship's main drives had failed, stranding him for a full day while he feverishly improvised his own repairs. Unable to leave the command console for more than a few brief moments, and forfeiting sleep as a result, he'd babied the damaged system the rest of the way in.

Precious time had been lost. Time he didn't have. Time he could have been with Tressa.

Sliding a small wooden box from beneath his bunk, Nick

opened it and retrieved a delicate sapphire ring. It was one he'd purchased from a space-port jeweler shortly after Tressa had made such a fuss over his sapphire eyes.

With no strings attached, he'd intended, long ago, to give her the ring but had forgotten it with all the trouble they'd encountered.

Now, grabbing TiMar, he fastened the ring, along with a compelling note, to a makeshift collar hung about the cat's neck. Then skillfully evading TiMar's lethal claws, he stuffed the growling, hissing desert cat into a commercial pet carrier and made arrangements for immediate delivery to Tressa.

Returning to the ship, he quickly showered, shaved, and changed into a clean set of leathers, the only change of clothing he had onboard besides his baggy sweats. Finally making his way back to the space port, he stopped at a flower vendor within the terminal. He was in the midst of a decision between a bouquet of sweet-smelling purple flowers and a dozen red long-stem Terran roses when the marketer explained that the purple ones were imported wildflowers. Instant sale. Nick purchased the bouquet, found a seat, and eased into it.

Would she come? Would she forgive him? Would she even listen? In his note he'd told her he was sorry for everything, for the things he'd said, his lack of respect. But more important, he'd told her he loved her and that his life was nothing without her, and if there was any chance at all, she'd find him waiting at the space port.

If she came, the void in his life would be filled; if she doesn't, then . . . then there would be nothing left to lose. Either way, TiMar was hers to keep. The cat had bonded with her, not him.

Up and pacing the floor for what seemed the hundredth time, Nick glanced down at the old Rolex, and a whisper of terror charged through him.

She's not coming.

Nearly three hours had passed. Three hours of waiting,

of checking the time at five-minute intervals. Three hours of doubt and self-incrimination. Jerk, idiot, fool, were just a few of the names he'd been calling himself.

She's not coming, Banner. Face it, this whole idea of yours was stupid. You blew your only chance at happiness a long time ago, when you stalked out of the cabin after telling her she was the best lay you'd . . . He couldn't even finish the thought.

Tressa had turned to Zeke for friendship. The traitor; he could have helped explain his irrational friend's behavior, could have told Tressa that he'd eventually come to his senses, could have told her anything to help her understand. But instead . . . instead it was Zeke Tressa had kissed good-bye on Fletcher's World.

Panic ripped through him as he fought to keep himself from setting out to find her. He had so many things he wanted to say to her. He wanted so desperately to make her understand, to make her . . . No, Tressa needed to hear him out because she *wanted* to, not because he made her. The answer was to wait, to take his chances.

And if she should come? Look at you! You're not exactly hard to spot, Banner, dressed in leathers and clutching a fist full of wilted flowers. Nick's gaze rested numbly on the once-vibrant bouquet of purple wildflowers. From there his eyes roamed to the condition of his fingernails. Damn, there was still grease under them from messing with that drive system.

The thought broke off as he felt the pull. Like a door opening, a beckoning, an inaudible force compelling him to look up.

She was here.

The space port was teeming with passengers just off a newly arrived luxury liner. Bounding to his feet, Nick's frantic gaze swept the crowd, searching each face. *She was here!*

Then he saw what appeared as a vision, as she made her way through the masses, heading toward him. She was dressed in a soft blue gown that hung to her ankles. Squinting through blurry eyes, Nick recognized the familiar-looking desert cat tucked into the curve of her arm. Tressa.

Unable to breathe, he simply stood there, clutching the flowers tightly in his fist as she came nearer. Someone hurried by, accidentally bumping him. Nick hardly noticed, barely heard the mumbled apology. The noise and the crowd were fading fast as he silently regarded the woman who was now drawing to a halt before him. Tressa. He swallowed hard, rigidly holding tears in check.

High color stained her cheeks. Understanding and forgiveness filled her liquid brown eyes. Dark curls hung carelessly down her back, and she looked, he thought, just as she had the first day she'd set foot onboard the *Victorious*. The day she'd blown his entire world to hell and back by her heart-stopping smile.

"I didn't think you'd come," he managed to get out over the lump in his throat.

"I got your note," was her reply.

A moment of silence followed.

"Tressa, I . . ."

Stopping him midsentence with a single finger placed to his lips, she asked with gentle softness, "What took you so long?"

Nick glanced down at the floor, feeling a spreading warmth begin in the center of his once-frozen heart and radiate outward until it reached and heated every nerve ending in his body.

"Are those for me?" he heard her ask.

The flowers; he was still holding the flowers. "Yes," he said with a shrug, awkwardly thrusting them into her hand. Their stems were crushed, their blossoms wilted, yet as she buried her nose in them, Tressa regarded the limp bouquet with candid delight.

"They're Ayer Lillies!" Closing her eyes, she inhaled the scent slowly.

"Tressa, I need to talk to you. Let's go somewhere quiet."

Glancing up from the flowers, her expression was thoughtful. "How about Crystal Bay?" she suggested. "It's quiet out there and . . ."

Nick shook his head. "Much too far." He took her small hand in his, closing his fingers firmly around it. "Come with me."

"Where are we going?"

"You'll see," was all he said, escorting her through the terminal and out onto the landing field.

The *Victorious* was sitting all by itself at the far end of the L.Z.

"Are we going somewhere in the *Victorious*?" she asked.

"No." Without breaking stride or releasing her hand, Nick withdrew the remote from his pocket, punched in the numbers single-handedly, aimed, and pressed. Immediately the gangplank emerged from a dark, narrow rectangle beneath the main hatch and extended slowly to the ground.

Within seconds they were onboard, the hatch hissing closed behind them. TiMar leapt from her arms and began prowling the ship.

Nick turned to face her. "Tressa, I . . . I'm not very good when it comes to words." He grinned sheepishly. "You probably already guessed that by the now."

"Nick . . ."

He held up his hand. "Let me just say what I have to say." With a heavy sigh, he paused, collecting his thoughts.

"When I was twenty-one," he began, "I thought I knew what love was all about. Like a fool I allowed my misconception to destroy me, and for eight long years love didn't exist in my world. Not until you came along and blew my opinion of love to hell.

"You see," he went on, "after I'd left you on Fletcher's World, I discovered you'd taken something from me. Something I didn't even know I had until it was gone."

Tressa's eyes widened. "I didn't take anything of yours."

"Oh, but you did. Sad thing is, I didn't even know it, until I was sitting in a dark corner, attempting to drown myself in liquor. That's when I realized it."

Tressa was looking at him like he'd lost his mind. "What are you talking about?"

"This." He reached for her hand and placed it against his heart. "You have my heart, Tressa," he said. Then his voice lowered. "My life has been in an upheaval ever since you came into it. You command me as no woman ever has . . ." His voice went lower still. "As no other woman ever will." The words poured forth in a rush of emotion. "What I'm trying to say is that I . . . I can't . . ." He swallowed. "I mean . . . oh hell! *Will* you marry me, Tressa?"

Tressa's eyebrows drew together in a mischievous frown, contemplating his question.

"Tressa . . ." he entreated softly. "I can't go back to my life the way it was before you entered it. I . . . can't go on without you." And then the words he'd never told her burst from his lips. "I love you."

"You do? Well, that throws a different light on things."

Nick hesitated. "It does?" The beginning of a smile tipped the corners of his mouth. "Then does that mean . . ."

Withdrawing a hand from her pocket, Tressa held out her upturned palm. In it lay the ring he'd given her, the ring he had tied to TiMar's collar. "Sapphires?" she asked.

"Yes." He wondered at the sudden flush to her cheeks. She couldn't possibly make the connection to that night onboard ship, when she'd made over his eyes. Not as drugged as she'd been.

"It's beautiful, Nick, but . . ."

Here it comes, he thought. She was about to give the ring back. She was about to turn him down, laughing at his arrogance for even thinking she might accept his proposal.

Breaking into his cynical thoughts, Tressa reached up

and touched his face. "You once told me that love was for fools."

"Yes," he admitted softly, "and I'm guilty of being the biggest fool of them all."

Tressa smiled coyly. "Then if we're to be fools," she said, placing the ring in his hand, "don't you think I should be wearing this?"

"Wha . . . Oh! Y-yes!" Drifting on the edge of euphoria, Nick took the ring and slipped it onto Tressa's finger, marveling at its perfect fit. "Does this mean that . . ."

"Yes," she said, her eyes filling with tears. "I will marry you."

"You will?" Relief flooded through him as he drew Tressa into his embrace. Closing his eyes, he pressed a kiss to her forehead.

"I'm no bargain, Irish," he whispered into her hair. "In fact, most people will say I'm a dangerous risk."

Tressa muffled a soft laugh against his chest. "And just what do you suppose I should tell them in answer?"

The realization of what losing her would mean surged through him with stark reality. Drawing back, he gazed deeply into her eyes. "Tell them . . ." His voice broke. "Tell them," he began again, "that you are my life . . . that I love you. If you don't inhale, Tressa, I can't breathe." The words were wrenched from the depths of his heart.

"Nick." Slipping her arms inside his jacket, Tressa wound them about his back. And for a moment time stood still. It was enough that they were at last in each other's arms.

"I owe you an apology," Tressa finally murmured against his chest.

Nick drew back. "For what?"

"I shouldn't have called the *Victorious* a bucket of rivets," she confessed, peering up at him. "And I lied. I *do* want to travel with you."

Nick's rich laughter floated up from his throat. "Come 'ere, I want to show you something." Guiding her into the galley, he escorted her over to where several large sheets of paper covered the table and several more lay in crumpled wads on the floor. "I've been playing with some ideas. See what you think.

"This is a schematic of the *Victorious*," he said, lifting one print off the bottom of the stack and placing it on top. "You can see the wall that separates the hold from the living quarters and how much space there is in the cargo bay, compared to the actual cabin."

Tressa nodded in answer, studying the drawing before her.

The next drawing he lifted off the stack and placed on top was one of his own illustrations, showing a possible alteration. "Now," he began, "I was thinking . . ."

Tressa bent over the drawings, listening with interest as Nick started describing some of the changes he had in mind.

"And I thought if we were to take out that back wall and literally gut everything from the cockpit back, we could extend the galley at least another ten feet, maybe even more. Then this area here," he said, pointing to the starboard side of the existing cargo bay, "would be the master cabin, and would run down to about here. And see this section?"

Tressa nodded. "Yes."

"Just for you, Irish, we'd extend it clear down to here."

Tressa laughed. "The lav? You'd really make it that big?"

"Certainly. Bigger if you want. And I'll put you in charge of the decorating. You know, deciding on colors, carpet, and . . ." his voice lowered notably, ". . . important things such as whether the bed will sit on a raised dais like the one onboard the *Windstar*. Or whether we want something entirely different," he grinned, "like a Storos anti-gravity bed."

"Storos anti-what?"

In answer, Nick's grin only broadened. "So, what do you think?"

"You're serious about all this, aren't you?"

His amusement faded. "Very."

"But . . . what about your shipping business? How will you be able to haul cargo if you transform the *Victorious* into a pleasure yacht?"

"That's another thing. Zeke and I have been talking about pooling our part of the reward and starting a shipping venture. We figure we could purchase at least two ships to begin with. It's only talk at this point, and before we decide anything, it's something you and I need to discuss." His mouth found hers and he kissed her fervently. "But later . . ." he murmured against her lips. "Much later."

Sweeping her weightlessly into his arms, he made his way to the sleeping quarters, tenderly laying her down on his bunk. And there, within the secluded privacy of the *Victorious*, Nick Banner made slow, passionate, sweet love to the woman he cherished far beyond any treasure imaginable . . . far, far beyond any monetary bonus Jonathan Loring could ever offer, let alone afford.

"Dear God, I love you," he whispered, rolling her beneath him.

Their bodies melding, Tressa sighed in complete submission as once again Nick bore her to the stars, carrying her to the very edge of a galaxy, a galaxy that began and ended in the arms of the man she loved.

Oh, yes, the notorious Nick Banner was at last brought to his knees before the only bonus he could ever accept, the only bonus that could ever complete his life. Tressa.

About the Author

Carole Ann Lee is a native of Oregon, the mother of two children, and married for twenty-one years to her own special hero who shares her crazy sense of humor and love for animals.

When not at her computer Carole can be found working part-time as a secretary, answering the phone for her husband's business, screaming enthusiastically at her daughter's volleyball games, or cheering her son on to first place at the kart races. She is currently working on her next novel, Zeke's story.

You may write her at P.O. Box 56052, Portland, OR 97238-6052.

An Angel's Touch

Where angels go, love is sure to follow.

Don't miss these unforgettable romances that combine the magic of angels and the joy of love.

Daemon's Angel by Sherrilyn Kenyon. Cast to the mortal realm by an evil sorceress, Arina has more than her share of problems. She is trapped in a temptress's body and doomed to lose any man she desires. Yet even as Arina yearns for the safety of the pearly gates, she finds paradise in the arms of a Norman mercenary. But to savor the joys of life with Daemon, she will have to battle demons and risk her very soul for love.

_52026-5 $4.99 US/$5.99 CAN

Forever Angels by Trana Mae Simmons. Thoroughly modern Tess Foster has everything, but when her boyfriend demands she sign a prenuptial agreement Tess thinks she's lost her happiness forever. Then her guardian angel sneezes and sends the woman of the nineties back to the 1890s—and into the arms of an unbelievably handsome cowboy. But before she will surrender to a marriage made in heaven, Tess has to make sure that her guardian angel won't sneeze again—and ruin her second chance at love.

_52021-4 $4.99 US/$5.99 CAN

Dorchester Publishing Co., Inc.
65 Commerce Road
Stamford, CT 06902

Please add $1.75 for shipping and handling for the first book and $.50 for each book thereafter. NY, NYC, PA and CT residents, please add appropriate sales tax. No cash, stamps, or C.O.D.s. All orders shipped within 6 weeks via postal service book rate. Canadian orders require $2.00 extra postage and must be paid in U.S. dollars through a U.S. banking facility.

Name _____

Address _____

City _____ State _____ Zip _____

I have enclosed $_____ in payment for the checked book(s).

Payment <u>must</u> accompany all orders. □ Please send a free catalog.

Futuristic Romance

Love in another time, another place.

Don't miss these tempestuous futuristic romances set on faraway worlds where passion is the lifeblood of every man and woman.

Awakenings by Saranne Dawson. Fearless and bold, Justan rules his domain with an iron hand, but nothing short of magic will bring his warring people peace. He claims he needs Rozlynd for her sorcery alone, yet inside him stirs an unexpected yearning to sample her sweet innocence. And as her silken spell ensnares him, Justan battles to vanquish a power whose like he has never encountered—the power of Rozlynd's love.

_51921-6 $4.99 US/$5.99 CAN

Ascent to the Stars by Christine Michels. For Trace, the assignment is simple. All he has to do is take a helpless female to safety and he'll receive information about his cunning enemies. But no daring mission or reckless rescue has prepared him for the likes of Coventry Pearce. Even as he races across the galaxy to save his doomed world, Trace battles to deny a burning desire that will take him to the heavens and beyond.

_51933-X $4.99 US/$5.99 CAN

Dorchester Publishing Co., Inc.
65 Commerce Road
Stamford, CT 06902

Please add $1.75 for shipping and handling for the first book and $.50 for each book thereafter. NY, NYC, PA and CT residents, please add appropriate sales tax. No cash, stamps, or C.O.D.s All orders shipped within 6 weeks via postal service book rate. Canadian orders require $2.00 extra postage and must be paid in U.S. dollars through a U.S. banking facility.

Name _____

Address _____

City _____ State _____ Zip _____

I have enclosed $_____ in payment for the checked book(s).
Payment <u>must</u> accompany all orders.☐ Please send a free catalog.

Futuristic Romance

Love in another time, another place.

New York Times Bestselling Author
Phoebe Conn writing as Cinnamon Burke!

Lady Rogue. Sent to infiltrate Spider Diamond's pirate operation, Drew Jordan finds himself in an impossible situation. Handpicked by Spider as a suitable ''pet'' for his daughter, Drew has to win Ivory Diamond's love or lose his life. But once he's initiated Ivory into the delights of lovemaking, he knows he can never turn her over to the authorities. For he has found a vulnerable woman's heart within the formidable lady rogue.

___3558-8 $5.99 US/$6.99 CAN

Rapture's Mist. Dedicated to preserving the old ways, Tynan Thorn has led the austere life of a recluse. He has never even laid eyes on a woman until the ravishing Amara sweeps into his bedroom to change his life forever. Daring and uninhibited, Amara sets out to broaden Tynan's viewpoint, but she never expects that the area he will be most interested in exploring is her own sensitive body. As their bodies unite in explosive ecstasy, Tynan and Amara discover a whole new world, where together they can soar among the stars.

___3470-0 $5.99 US/$6.99 CAN

Dorchester Publishing Co., Inc.
65 Commerce Road
Stamford, CT 06902

Please add $1.75 for shipping and handling for the first book and $.50 for each book thereafter. NY, NYC, PA and CT residents, please add appropriate sales tax. No cash, stamps, or C.O.D.s. All orders shipped within 6 weeks via postal service book rate. Canadian orders require $2.00 extra postage and must be paid in U.S. dollars through a U.S. banking facility.

Name_____

Address_____

City _____ State _____ Zip_____

I have enclosed $_____in payment for the checked book(s).
Payment <u>must</u> accompany all orders.☐ Please send a free catalog.

Futuristic Romance

Love in another time, another place.

Don't miss these breathtaking futuristic romances set on faraway worlds where passion is the lifeblood of every man and woman.

Circle of Light by Nancy Cane. When attorney Sarina Bretton is whisked to worlds she never imagined possible, she finds herself wanting to explore new realms of desire with the virile stranger who has abducted her. Besieged by enemies, and bedeviled by her love for Teir Reylock, Sarina vows that before a vapor cannon puts her asunder she will surrender to the seasoned warrior and his promise of throbbing ecstasy.
_51949-6 $4.99 US/$5.99 CAN

Paradise City by Sherrilyn Kenyon. Fleeing her past, Alix signs on as the engineer aboard Devyn Kell's spaceship. Soon they are outrunning the authorities and heading toward Paradise City, where even assassins aren't safe. But Alix doesn't know what real danger is until Devyn's burning kiss awakens her to a forbidden taste of heaven.
_51969-0 $4.99 US/$5.99 CAN

Dorchester Publishing Co., Inc.
65 Commerce Road
Stamford, CT 06902

Please add $1.75 for shipping and handling for the first book and $.50 for each book thereafter. NY, NYC, PA and CT residents, please add appropriate sales tax. No cash, stamps, or C.O.D.s. All orders shipped within 6 weeks via postal service book rate. Canadian orders require $2.00 extra postage and must be paid in U.S. dollars through a U.S. banking facility.

Name_____
Address_____
City _____ State_____ Zip_____
I have enclosed $_____in payment for the checked book(s).
Payment <u>must</u> accompany all orders.☐ Please send a free catalog.

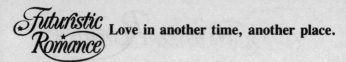

Futuristic Romance

Pyramid of Dreams
Marilyn Campbell

Love in another time, another place.

An outsider in the rainbow-hued crystal city, Aster yearns to lose herself in Romulus's arms. But his fierce ambition makes impossible a formal union with the beautiful pariah—until the fever of mating drives Romulus to teach Aster the exquisite pleasures of his exotic brand of sensuality.

__51993-3 $4.99 US/$5.99 CAN

ENCHANTED CROSSINGS

Three captivating stories of love in another time, another place.

MADELINE BAKER
"Heart of the Hunter"

A Lakota warrior must defy the boundaries of life itself to claim the spirited beauty he has sought through time.

ANNE AVERY
"Dream Seeker"

On faraway planets, a pilot and a dreamer learn that passion can bridge the heavens, no matter how vast the distance from one heart to another.

KATHLEEN MORGAN
"The Last Gatekeeper"

To save her world, a dazzling temptress must use her powers of enchantment to open a stellar portal—and the heart of a virile but reluctant warrior.

___51974-7 *Enchanted Crossings* (three unforgettable love stories in one volume) $4.99 US/
$5.99 CAN

LOVE SPELL

THE MAGIC OF ROMANCE
PAST, PRESENT, AND FUTURE....

Every month, Love Spell will publish one book in each of four categories:

1) *Timeswept Romance*—Modern-day heroines travel to the past to find the men who fulfill their hearts' desires.

2) *Futuristic Romance*—Love on distant worlds where passion is the lifeblood of every man and woman.

3) *Historical Romance*—Full of desire, adventure and intrigue, these stories will thrill readers everywhere.

4) *Contemporary Romance*—With novels by Lori Copeland, Heather Graham, and Jayne Ann Krentz, Love Spell's line of contemporary romance is first-rate.

Exploding with soaring passion and fiery sensuality, Love Spell romances are destined to take you to dazzling new heights of ecstasy.

SEND FOR A FREE CATALOGUE TODAY!

Love Spell
Attn: Order Department
276 5th Avenue, New York, NY 10001